WINTER, WHITE AND WICKED

WINTER WHITE AND WICKED

SHANNON DITTEMORE

AMULET BOOKS • NEW YORK

Cataloging-in-Publication Data has been applied for and may be obtained from the Library of Congress.

ISBN 978-1-4197-4023-7

Text copyright © 2020 Shannon Dittemore
Jacket illustrations copyright © 2020 Ruben Ireland
Map illustration by Yvonne Gilbert
Book design by Hana Anouk Nakamura

Amulet Books are available at special discounts when purchased in quantity for premiums and promotions as well as fundraising or educational use. Special editions can also be created to specification. For details, contact specialsales@abramsbooks.com or the address below.

Amulet Books® is a registered trademark of Harry N. Abrams, Inc.

ABRAMS The Art of Books
195 Broadway, New York, NY 10007
abramsbooks.com

For my Soul Sisters,
because you push out onto the ice and expect a road.

Because you're brave.

And because you keep the drive interesting.

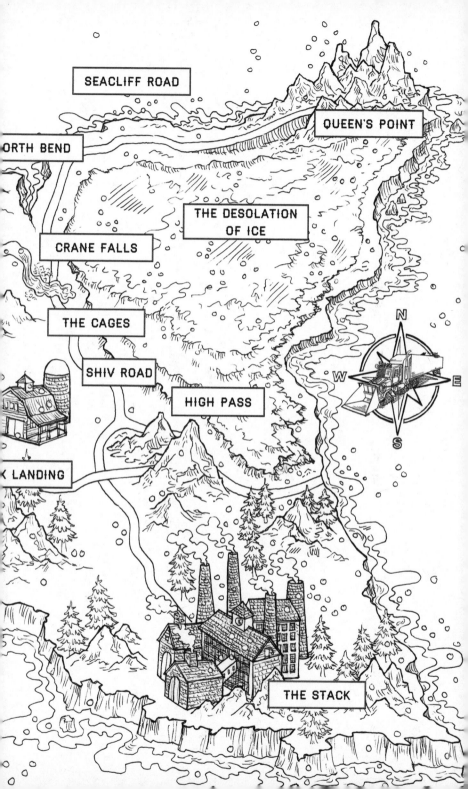

Prologue

WINTER'S ALWAYS TALKING.

Her breath frosts the tavern window, but I can still hear the wind whispering outside. A voice slips through a crack in the pane, tugging curls from my snarled white braids.

COME OUT AND PLAY, she says.

But our tutor would never allow it. Not with the blizzard setting in.

I trace the crystals growing on the glass and let my eyes wander across the ice rigs parked in the lot outside. If I had a rig, I could play in the snow all day long and not risk frostbite. That red truck there isn't so large, and my ten-year-old legs have grown long in the past year.

"Tell us a fairy story, Mystra Dyfan," Lenore calls, suddenly there, tucking a dishrag into the crack, shutting Winter out.

"They're histories," our tutor corrects.

"The Majority doesn't like us learning *histories*."

"We'll tell them they're only fairy stories then." Mystra's left leg drags as she crosses the room. "Come. Bring Sylvi and we'll talk by the fire. The night is growing cold."

"I've boiled chocolate," Lenore says, her fingers closing around my wrist. "Mystra's going to tell us of Sola and Begynd."

"She's told us of them before," I answer, my thumb playing on the latch.

Leni always knows when I'm plotting an escape. We were the same once, both of us wanting to get away. But not anymore. Not since Mystra Dyfan came. Now when I look at my friend, all I see are the differences between us: her auburn hair carefully plaited, her woolen skirt mended, her face scrubbed clean. Without Leni's reminders, I'd forget to change my trousers.

"Please," she says. "I like the stories."

"Can't I listen from here?"

"It's so cold," she says. "Come to the fire."

I let her drag me to the hearth where our tutor has taken up her chair. Leni and I settle in, shoulder to shoulder, passing a mug of steaming chocolate back and forth.

Mystra Dyfan stabs at the fire with the charred end of her cane. She tugs the cape more tightly about her shoulders and shakes her graying hair from the collar. A shard of black marks one of her pale eyes, and just now, it sparkles with magic. When at last she opens her mouth, her voice scratches with a story Leni and I have heard many times before. A story only one of us believes.

"Long ago," Mystra begins, "when the Wethyrd Seas were but a splash of water, there was Sola, a being of great imagination and light. In an act of benevolence, she selected a drop of sea spray and bestowed upon it her character, warmth, and a desire to create. She kissed his face and called him Begynd."

Lenore grins. "She kissed the water."

"It's not real, Leni."

"Quiet now," Mystra Dyfan says, rubbing at her bad leg. "Together, Sola and Begynd stretched the seas. They molded lands from the deep dark beneath the waters and, because it pleased them, they hid great mystery within the rocks. From her own light, Sola crafted folk like you and me, people to fill the islands and to enjoy all that she and her son had made. They were content.

"Creation grew. Men and women became families and families became kingdoms—kingdoms that anointed their own kings and queens. It wasn't long before Sola, High Queen of Creation, and Begynd, her son, were forgotten by all but Paradyia—an island nation devoted to Sola and the works of her hand.

"Desiring a love like that of Sola and Paradyia, Begynd asked for a people of his own—a people he could dwell with, as Sola dwelled with the Paradyians.

"Sola granted Begynd this request, allowing him to select a people from any island in the Wethyrd Seas. Whichever isle he chose would forever be his.

"But as Begynd searched to and fro, he was not satisfied with the forgetful peoples his mother's light had wrought. He preferred the constancy of the mountains and trees. He remembered then a cropping of jeweled rock he had long ago lifted from the waters."

"Layce," I say.

"But they didn't call the island Layce back then," Leni corrects. "That's a Majority name, isn't it, Mystra?"

3

"Yes. Now, hush. The island was flinty, sharp as a shiv, and void of life. A winter spirit was its only inhabitant and she wore the land ragged with a perpetual snowy gale. From somewhere deep within the rock, a black mineral spilled into the surrounding sea. A mineral that rode the waves and addled the mind, keeping the forgetful peoples at bay. This, *Shiv Island*, would be his."

"See," Lenore says. "Shiv Island. Not Layce."

I shrug, my eyes wandering to the window.

"From the rock," Mystra continues, "Begynd carved a people and, as Sola had done for him, he gave to his children his character, loyalty, and devotion. Desiring to be near those he loved, he poured himself into the depths of the island's deepest valley, emptying all that he was until Begynd was a vast pool the color of starlight, rich with the power of creation.

"Winter fled the warmth of Begynd's waters, confined now to the mountaintops high above. But Begynd's people—the Shiv—lived and breathed on the shores of the great pool, providing for their families, watering their crops, birthing their young—their sustenance drawn from the waters of the one who had chiseled them from stone.

"Begynd knew them there. And they knew him. They brought him their joy and he rejoiced. They waded into the pool with their tears and he healed their wounds.

"And the island, which had once appealed only to Winter, grew fertile and ripe. Settled in the heavens, Sola smiled down on her son's great triumph, the Pool of Begynd sparkling like a gem set deep in the flinty rock. Beyond the isle, the sea churned black, rich with dangerous magic. *Kol*, the Shiv called it.

"Begynd's presence on the island changed everything. Like the many wild spirits scattered across the seas, Winter had never before thought to care where she was sent or what she destroyed, but now she *felt* for the first time. And what she felt was loneliness. From her seat on the highest peak, she attempted to climb down into the valley, attempted to mingle with Begynd and his people, but the heat of the great pool turned her away time and again. Winter could not exist where Begynd reigned."

A gust of wind strikes the window and Leni jumps, nearly spilling the chocolate. The latch rattles, sounding like mischief, and I hide a smile.

Mystra frowns at me and continues. "Locked away with naught but her wolves and the kol to keep her company, Winter's despair turned to anger. For a millennium she raged while far below, on the land that was once dazzled by her charms, the Shiv prospered."

"And then a shipwreck!" Leni exclaims.

"Yes," Mystra says, her voice suddenly full of adventure. "A shipwreck. Black waves delivered to the island a shattered vessel and an exiled queen. Once the sovereign of a thriving people, Maree Vale arrived with so little. There was the prince in her arms, the promise of another fluttering inside, and, holding her together, a burning desire to see her kingdom reborn.

"Only a small remnant of her royal entourage had made it to the ship before the invaders arrived. Fewer than that outlasted the storm. Forced to abandon their home on the neighboring island of Kerce, the queen and her subjects had drifted into unsafe waters. Those who washed up on the rocks would have died had it not been for the Shiv. But they were a resilient people. They'd survived the monsters that crawled out of the sea, and the kol that slipped into their minds and brought madness."

Mystra pauses, her lined face careful. Talk of madness always silences Lenore, wrinkles her brow with questions that have no kind answer.

I steal the chocolate from her hands, sloshing it onto my chin as I gulp down the dregs. "Let's make more," I say.

Leni swallows hard and shakes her head. "We'll spoil our supper." Her voice is quiet and sad, and I hate Mystra for making her cry.

Our tutor leans forward in her chair, cups Leni's chin and brushes a tear from her cheek. "Shall we move on to languages then?"

Leni forces a grin and shakes her head. "Finish the story, Mystra. Please."

"Very well," she says, straightening as best she can. "The shipwreck, I believe?"

With a huff, I push away from the hearth, my face hot from the flames. "The Kerce survivors had just washed up on the island," I say. I hate this part of the story. Where everything becomes Winter's fault.

"Ah. Yes," Mystra Dyfan says. "And though it was the Shiv who came to their aid, it was in this broken people that Winter saw her chance."

A chill breath of air stirs the hairs curling on my neck, and I turn toward the window. Leni's dishrag has fallen to the floor. I wander closer, Mystra's voice following me as I go.

"Like the Kerce queen," she says, "Winter knew what it was to have her home stolen from beneath her throne. And so she waited. And she planned. And when the time was right, Winter struck a bargain that buried Shiv Island in snow."

I'VE SOMETHING TO SHOW YOU, Winter whispers, her voice skating inside.

In the window's reflection, I see Leni and Mystra tucked in comfortably, the fire wrapping them in warmth.

Will they notice if I slip away?

NOT IF YOU'RE FAST, Winter says. QUICK! QUICK!

A giggle grows in my belly and I flip the latch, flinging myself out the window. The snow is knee deep and I have to fight my way toward the corner of the tavern. I chance a peek over my shoulder just as Lenore's braids swing into view above the sill.

"Sylvi!" she calls. "You promised Grandfather you wouldn't!"

But Old Man Drypp isn't much for discipline. I flatten myself against the wall and Winter laughs, a rumble that sets the icicles ringing overhead.

"Foolish child," Mystra grumbles.

"She'll be back," Leni tells her. "She always comes back."

"My dear girl," Mystra says, the window squealing on its hinges. "I'm not entirely sure she was ever here."

CHAPTER 1

Seven Years Later

WINTER DOESN'T LIKE THE SMUGGLER who's come to Whistletop. She doesn't trust him, doesn't want me to take this job.

HE'S A LIAR, she says.

"Then you should have stopped him. Should have kept him away from Lenore," I mutter.

But she's not listening to me just now. She's too busy blustering.

I swipe a gloved hand over my face, wiping away the sleet. Across the lot sits Drypp's tavern, alive with light and noise. It's a two-level structure, part waste rock, part timber, snow piled high on the roof, wood smoke rising from the chimney. There's a diverse assortment of rigs parked outside tonight. Big trucks and small ones. Some with studded snow tires. Some with chains. A few have trailers still hitched, but most have dumped their hauls and are settling in for a hibernation of sorts that will take them clean through the wet season.

Our rooms are above the kitchen, Lenore's and mine. Her windows are bright, a flame flickering somewhere inside. A curtain shifts and, for a moment, I swear she's there behind the glass.

But they're frauds, those windows. Lenore's gone. And if I can't get her back quickly, we'll lose everything we have.

We're not sisters, but we well could be. Raised, both of us, by Lenore's grandfather, Old Man Drypp. The tavern was his and the garage behind me too. He'd kept up his taxable relations with the Majority, so when he died two Rymes back, they allowed the property to pass to us. A small victory for mountain folk. But there are rules. And we have to be here. One of us has to be here.

The storm bucks and, like that, the village vanishes in a swirl of snow and ice. I tuck my white braid into my stocking cap and sink deeper into my hood.

Whistletop is a depot of sorts—a last-chance stop for a hot meal and an engine check before the trucking turns hazardous. Winter's only given us the two seasons here: the freezing months of Ryme, and the miserable wet months of Blys. Rig driving in the Kol Mountains is difficult in either season, but we're entering the Flux, the melting weeks where the ice and snow give way to rain. The frozen roads that have formed across lakes and rivers will thaw. Snow slips from its rocky ledges in great wide sheets, blanketing towns and roads, making trade—and trucking, in particular—a hazardous way to earn coin until Ryme returns and our island freezes solid once again.

I wouldn't take this job unless I had to.

Winter knows I wouldn't. And still she rages.

Her words are everywhere. Above me, below me, seeping into

the soles of my boots and climbing up my calves. She's cold on my skin and blistering as a stove fire in my chest. That's how it always is when Winter speaks to me.

HE'S COMING, she says. **CAREFUL NOW.**

Mars Dresden's early. It's not yet midnight when he emerges from the tavern and crosses toward the garage. Several feet of snow have fallen in the last day and a half, but beneath his boots, the ground is dry; the storm that blows the rest of us sideways is nothing but a soft breeze on his uncovered head.

No wonder Winter hates him.

Beyond him, swamped in snow and wind, I see the outline of two or three others. I could wait out here for them, but I don't. I retreat into the garage, hollering at the guys finishing up repairs, and take my place in front of my rig.

When Mars sweeps through the garage doors, there's not a flake of snow on him, and his black leather coat has its zipper undone. Around his neck hangs a small medicine bag—dark leather ribbon and a beaded pouch that rests against his sternum. My childhood tutor had one that looked similar. I never did find out what she carried inside it.

The smuggler's flanked by a short, stocky man and a woman who stands taller than both of them. Hyla, she calls herself. She's unmistakably Paradyian, with golden skin and eyes, and a thick mane of hair that hangs in long curls over the shoulders of her red jacket. She lifts the goggles from her nose and perches them atop her head, her eyes narrowed. She doesn't like me much, not after I turned down the job she offered, but my fight is with her boss—a man I know only by reputation.

Mars Dresden's black eyes are legendary in the Kol Mountains. A village boy said he paid a Shiv warlock to cut them out and replace them with kol from the rock beneath our feet, but whoever started that rumor hasn't seen him from as close a distance as this. It's not stone buried in his face. The black orbs—no white to speak of and not a hint of color—are clearly natural. He was born this way. He's Kerce through and through.

"Miss Quine," he says. "I've heard so much about you."

I've heard plenty about him too. Mars had a reputation long before he arrived in Whistletop, but I hear he's been spending a fair share of his time hanging around the tavern while I've been out on runs.

"Sniffing around that friend of yours, the pretty barmaid," Cringle Kerr told me. "You'd best watch out for her."

"I'm not her ma, Cringle," I'd said. "I can't be here and out on the road at the same time. I've my work and she has hers. Lenore knows her own mind."

Words that turn my stomach now. Lenore's mind! I can't fathom what she was thinking throwing her hand in with the rebels. I should have stayed closer to town. Should have taken shorter runs. Should have sought out this smuggler the minute I heard he was in Whistletop and plowed him over with my rig.

Mars Dresden's name has been on every villager's tongue for months now and I've done well to time my trips to avoid his stays. He has a big job, they say. Is looking for help.

But people only come to Whistletop looking for a particular brand of *help*. He's looking for a rig and a driver. While I have very few scruples about which jobs I'll take, I steer clear of rebels. They have the kind of convictions that could get a girl blacklisted by the Majority.

He steps closer, dips his head so his eyes are flush with mine. He doesn't have to stoop far. Mars isn't a large man, just a few inches taller than me, but there's power there. I feel it. Winter feels it. She's a whining squall inside my head.

"Mars Dresden. They weren't lying," I tell him. "Your eyes are spectacular."

"Yours aren't the standard issue either, Miss Quine."

I know what he's seeing, of course. Bright gray irises—sylver, Mistress Quine called them—with pinpricks of black dust across the whites. The kol in my eyes has taken a more subtle approach than his.

He smiles now. A smile that serves as a terrible warning. The insides of his lips are lined with blisters—streaks of black kol and flecks of ice frozen to the sores.

"There are ways around that," I say.

He pulls a square of white cloth from his pocket and dabs at a sore in the seam of his grin. "Keeping my mouth shut, you mean. Not my style."

"You could give a little care who you order around at least."

He folds the cloth and tucks it away. "I'm nothing if not careful."

I'm dead on my feet, but I find the energy to lift the monster wrench in my hand and jab it at Mars's chest.

"You and one of your people. That's all I can take."

"The Sylver Dragon," he croons, stepping around me, his pale fingers playing lightly over the tank tread beneath the rig's bumper.

It's the tank tread that makes the Dragon so popular. Caterpillar tread, tank track, articulated bands—they're called many things, but in place of rubber tires, my rig has six individually mounted track systems. Technology that's not available here on Layce.

"What changed your mind, Miss Quine? Hyla told me your refusal was absolute."

"There is a rebel camp in the mountains," Hyla whispered, leaning across the tavern table, her Paradyian inflection turning the flat common tongue to music. It was the first time I'd spoken to anyone from the golden isle. "Do you know it?"

"I know very little about the rebels," I said, wishing I'd taken supper in my room. "And that's far more than I ever wanted to know."

"It's no matter. Mars Dresden knows where the camp is. And he needs you. The rebels need you."

"Not interested." I stabbed a carrot with my fork.

"Sylvi," Lenore said, pulling the fork from my hand, pushing my plate away. "Listen to her, please. This isn't just another job. Mars is asking you to help with something that actually matters."

Leave it to Lenore to assume the jobs that paid well didn't actually matter. But even if I'd been interested in helping the rebels, I was already heading out with a haul and it was my last run of the season. The melting weeks had arrived and it was foolish to tempt Winter. There wasn't a job Mars Dresden could offer that would be worth losing my rig.

Until now.

"I'll make you a deal," I say. "I'll truck your haul to this mysterious rebel camp, and in exchange—"

"You're chasing your friend," Mars says. "You're chasing Miss Trestman."

"Lenore never would have gone if I'd been here."

"You think so little of your friend's convictions?" Hyla asks. "She believes in what the rebels are doing."

I snort, the memory of our fight still sharp.

"You never, ever do anything unless there's coin in it," Lenore yelled.

"It's coin that keeps this place open," I said. *"Coin that keeps a roof over our heads."*

"We could sell them, Sylvi. The garage and the tavern both. Leave it all behind and do something that really matters. Please."

"Is that what he's told you? Mars Dresden? 'Sell all your possessions and follow me?' You're not that stupid, Leni. That black-eyed snake will say anything to flip your skirt."

I shouldn't have said that. It was cruel. Lenore has no love for the Majority, I know that, but that's not why she left. She left because Mars told her that her life didn't matter. And she believed him.

When I climbed into the Dragon to deliver that final haul, she was raging. So it's my fault too. I should have stayed. It just never crossed my mind that she'd pack her anger alongside her belongings and climb into Bristol Mapes's rig.

"In exchange for my services," I tell Mars, "you'll convince Lenore that she's misguided. That the rebels do not need her in their camp. You'll do whatever it takes to get her into my rig and away from Bristol Mapes."

Mars slides his hands into his pockets. "What's your problem with Bristol, Miss Quine? He's always seemed affable to me."

"Then you've not seen him drunk."

His brows lift and I realize he hasn't. "What else can you tell me about the plow driver?"

I know more than anyone could ever want to know about

that bastard. And I should have told Lenore what kind of man he was. But I didn't. And now she's tucked in next to him for the next who-knows-how-long, heading to a camp very few can find. If I don't get her back here soon, we'll lose everything Drypp worked so hard to give us.

"You want the Dragon or not?" I ask. "There isn't another rig that can truck any distance this time of year. And you can be sure there isn't another driver who'll haul a trailer this close to the Flux. I'm guessing that's why you're still sniffing around Whistletop."

Hyla moves to speak, but Mars holds up that pale, white hand.

"She doesn't breathe fire, does she?" He tips his face to the shimmering dragon painted across the cab. "That could prove hazardous on the river crossing."

"Which river?" I ask.

He clicks his tongue. "Not so fast, Miss Quine."

"Look. If I need her to breathe fire, she will. The Dragon does whatever I ask her to do. That's why you'll talk with Lenore and you'll pay me double what your woman offered."

"I offered you nothing," Hyla says.

"But you will," I say. "If you want me to get your precious cargo to the rebel camp, you'll pay."

Hyla's eyes flash. "Do you not want to see your people free of Majority rule? Will you not help those who do?"

She's all virtue and ideals, light and fire. She knows nothing of existing on the dark cold of Layce.

"My cargo is of the utmost importance," Mars says. "I'll pay whatever it costs to get it there."

"You and one of your people then. Choose."

"You seem to think you're in charge, Miss Quine."

"It's my rig."

"Yes, but it's my haul. And it needs protecting. The Shiv Road is dangerous."

"The Shiv Road," I repeat, Winter's chill climbing my neck.

"Yes, Miss Quine. That's our path."

Then the camp will be somewhere in the northeast wing, somewhere near the Desolation of Ice. A curse skates across my teeth, but Mars is still talking.

"You and Filde are small," he says, clapping a hand on the shoulder of the man scowling next to him. "Together you count as one."

"Your Paradyian is massive," I say, pointing the wrench at Hyla. "How should we count her? Look, I need my guy"—I gesture to the cab where one of my mechanics gawks down at us from an open window—"to drive us to your trailer and oversee the pickup. Where is your trailer, by the way? I assume it's ready to go."

"Buttoned up and awaiting a driver, Miss Quine. It's parked in Hex Landing."

"Hex Landing it is. I'll take the wheel from there, but I've been awake for more than a day. If I don't get some sleep, the trip across the Shiv Road will be nothing but a funeral procession. That leaves two seats for you to divvy up as you please."

The sheen coating his eyes shifts—the only hint I have that he's moving his gaze from one of my eyes to the other. I resist the urge to look away. This isn't negotiable. The cab isn't large and there must be room for Lenore.

"Filde," Mars says, "you'll stay behind."

The short hairy man spits a wad of something green onto the floor, but I don't miss the relief on his face as he turns to go. No one wants to be out on the road during the Flux.

"Good," I say. "Thank you."

Mars lifts his right hand, blue veins tracing over his knuckles. "Kyndel," he calls.

The garage door swings open and another goon steps inside, a rifle resting against his shoulder and snow caught in his black curls. The lookout, I presume. I'd heard Mars had a Shiv youth traveling with him and he doesn't disappoint.

Kyndel's younger than Mars and a hand's width taller. Built like a man, but with a wide-eyed cockiness found in boys just brave enough to steal a bottle of ale when the barkeep's got his back turned. Lenore used to chase pups like him from the tavern every night of the week.

Most of the Shiv pulling through Whistletop keep their stone flesh covered. Leni hired a waitress a while back with some Shiv in her. The marbled blue stone across her pale forehead was all the invitation necessary for some riggers. They abused and ridiculed her for the violent actions of her kin, and she took to wearing a scarf to stave off their ignorance.

But Kyndel here's not interested in covering up. Despite the cold, his missing shirtsleeves show off shoulders and biceps made of stone, the same red-brown as his eyes and a shade warmer than his dark skin. Another line of red rock curves along his right cheekbone, stopping only when it reaches his temple.

He leans in, letting Mars speak something into his ear. Whatever it is, it isn't the dismissal I'd assumed was coming. The Shiv passes his gun to Mars and climbs up into the cab.

"Hey!" I yell, leaping onto the running board. "What are you doing? Get out of there."

My mechanic sits in the passenger seat pulling metal glue from his thumb. He's a nightmare with that stuff, he's gotten it on everything. The door, the wheel. Even now, with his mouth gaping stupidly at Kyndel, he drags his sticky fingers through the mop on his head.

"It's a beautiful machine," Kyndel says, his hands moving over the gear shift and the instrument panel, the toggles that adjust the outside mirrors and the loader bucket.

"Can you drive it?" Mars asks.

"Through the forest to Hex Landing? Not a problem. But the Shiv Road?"

"The Shiv Road will be her problem," Mars says.

I drop to the ground, chucking aside the wrench. "Absolutely not. The kid's what? Twelve?"

"Seventeen Rymes," Mars says. "Same as you, I believe."

"The Dragon's not like the other rigs on the island."

"Kyn's a capable driver, Miss Quine. Far more capable than your . . . guy. He knows how to handle a gun, a necessary skill when you're hauling contraband. And he speaks Shiv. If we run into trouble out on the road, we'll need him."

"I don't think *your guy's* up for it anyway," Kyn says, jumping down, taking the gun from Mars. "He just glued his eyelid shut. You're the ice witch, yeah? Sylver Quine?" He extends his hand.

Loath though I am to share my driver's seat with anyone, Kyn here looks far more competent than my mechanic.

"Stop scowling, Miss Quine, and shake the boy's hand. He's the only reason you'll get any sleep tonight."

I don't shake, but Kyn doesn't seem bothered. He bumps my chin with his knuckle instead. "You rest up, little ice witch. I'll get us to the trailer."

He's a cocky pup, but there's a steadiness to his hands. The kind of steadiness I look for in any trucker.

"If your man is so capable," I ask Mars, rubbing absently at my chin, "why are you still looking for a driver?"

"I don't have a dragon," Kyn says, running his hand over the hood.

"You could have left ages ago and the Flux wouldn't have been nearly the problem it is now."

"Kyndel's abilities have their limits, Miss Quine."

The insinuation being that mine do not. "I don't throw around magic like you do."

"Thus far, you haven't had to. That might change."

"Fine. Kyn goes. But why the Paradyian? She's hardly built for the cold."

Mars almost smiles. "Hyla spent six years as a mechanic in the Paradyian army. I'd wager she has more experience with tank tread than you do."

And that's when I run out of arguments.

A Kerce smuggler, a Paradyian mechanic, and a Shiv driver. All in my rig. And I'm not great at sharing.

"I need to sleep," I say.

Mars smiles. "Let's get going."

Before we load up, I plunder the cab of an ancient pickup collecting snow in the lot. It's the rearview mirror I need. The Dragon doesn't have one. Most days, there's no need; the sleeper compartment blocks any view to the rear. But mirrors are handy for keeping an eye on the guy sitting behind you, and with my rig suddenly full of people, the addition feels necessary.

The mirror is spotted and cracked, but once it's mounted, I hand Kyn-the-Shiv my keys and climb in, over the driver's seat and the bench behind, into the sleeper compartment. It's nothing fancy, just one big mattress and a box of dried food stashed in the corner.

Lying on my stomach with my face pressed through the velvet curtain, I watch as the others load up. Hyla's next, settling onto the bench, her thigh blocking much of my view. Mars follows, a gust of wind lifting him into the passenger seat. Winter rankles at the command and I roll my eyes at his petty, unnecessary use of magic.

Kyn can't decide what to do with his gun. He eyes the rack over Hyla's head, but Drypp's old shotgun is mounted there. I offer to stow his in the sleeper, but he slides it under Mars's seat so it's close at hand. How he plans to shoot and drive is beyond me, but I don't care. We need to go.

"It's a blind turn out of the lot," I say. "Ease off the brake slowly or you'll—"

"Skid? Slide? Tumble down the mountainside?" Kyn's eyes sparkle in the mirror and he flashes me a grin. "Yeah, snowflake. I know. I grew up in these mountains same as you."

That smile. If I was the kind of girl who took to melting, he'd be dangerous.

"Just be careful with her, all right?"

"Sleep, Miss Quine. When you wake, your rig will be hitched to a trailer full of things you'd rather not know about, and you'll need all your wits to get us to the rebel camp."

Mars knows a lot about me for a man who's only been hanging around Whistletop a few months, but he's right. As a policy, I don't ask my clients what they need hauled. I learned the hard way that knowing doesn't bring peace of mind, and it certainly doesn't help me get where I'm going.

"Sleep," he commands.

I flick my cheek at him—a crass gesture common in the Kol Mountains—but he just smiles and reaches past Hyla.

"One day I'll tell you what that means," he says, yanking the curtain shut.

My eyes close against the whipping drape and though I'd like to take Mars's head off, that hot burn in my stomach says Winter's close.

REST, she tells me. I'LL KEEP WATCH.

So instead of arguing with the snake-eyed smuggler, I curl into a nest of blankets, say a quick prayer asking Winter to wake me if Kyn-the-Shiv takes his eyes off the road, and I sleep.

CHAPTER 2

ON THE INSIDE OF MY EYELIDS, I SEE OLD MAN Drypp. Ratted gray beard, bright eyes, red nose and cheeks, lanky arms and legs covered with mismatched scraps of material. He swings his pickaxe over and over, breaking apart the thick ice that's encased his ale barrels.

Every strike of the axe sets my body trembling, pain leaking from my elbows and knees down toward my hands, my feet. My fists ball, my toes curl, but the dream never changes. Just slap-happy Drypp swinging that axe, my joints splitting like the ice, feeling Winter's pain, wishing with everything in me that he'd stop.

When at last, I think I won't survive another strike of it, I wake.

And I flail.

There's a hand over my mouth. The fingers firm, the knuckles stone.

Kyn.

His other arm comes down on my shins, pressing hard. "Stay still," he says.

He's too close, something that might have me biting off his fingers in another scenario, but Winter's wrapping me tight as well—I recognize her frigid hold on my arms, the burning singe of her against my breastbone—and I understand danger is near.

Gunshots ring out and my eyes widen to match Kyn's. I nod, more intention than movement, and he releases the grip he has on my face.

"Who's shooting?" I whisper.

"I don't know," he says. "I was back here with you. Grabbing a sleep."

"You slept back here? With me?"

"*Next* to you, little ice witch. Just while they finished hitching up the trailer."

"But it's a one-man sleeper."

His lips quirk and a dimple appears. "There was only one man back here, I promise."

Heat climbs my face and this time, it's not Winter.

"All right in there, Kyndel?" Hyla calls from somewhere outside.

"We're good," he calls back. "You?"

"We're not good," I hiss, panic rising at his proximity. I've got to get off my back. It's a posture that gives me nightmares.

"Nothing to concern yourself with," Hyla yells. "Mars is taking care of it."

"Get off," I tell Kyn, bringing up my knee, fast and sharp.

"Whoa, whoa!" he says, dodging. "Relax." He releases my legs and backs out of the sleeper. "You cried out when the shooting started. I was just trying to keep us hidden."

"I'm sure," I say, sitting up, the knives at my waist a reminder that even when I'm on my own, I'm not helpless. I place my palm flat against their hilts, my heart banging around in my chest.

I've both my knife and Lenore's—identical except for the names etched into the bone handles. They were gifts from Drypp and it bothers me that she left hers behind.

"Hand me the gun, yeah?"

I swipe a shaking hand over my face and yank the half-open drape to the side. Outside the windshield, morning glare fights its way through the thick, ever-present cloud cover and I blink back at it. We're at a familiar truck stop in Hex Landing, a solid seven-hour drive from the garage in Whistletop. The lot's only half full, but it's early.

"Gunshots," I say, pulling Drypp's shotgun from the rack and passing it to Kyn. "Is that common when you collect a haul?"

"Nah. Most people are smarter than that. Not this guy though." Kyn presses his eye to the sight. "You know him?"

Just this side of the refueling station, I see Mars. He's facing off with a man nearly twice his size, beer belly pushing at the zipper on his parka, spit flying as he issues demands.

"It's Jymy Leff," I say, suddenly understanding Winter's concern. My last experience with him is not one either of us would like to relive.

"A Ranger, yeah?"

"Yeah."

White trousers, white parkas, white guns. But dirty as kol,

every single one of them. The Rangers are the closest thing we have to law in the Kol Mountains. They report to the Majority, and while it's true their information has, at times, made it down into the valley, the bribes they take to look the other way never do.

"Jymy's captain of the squad here in the Landing," I say. "His greatest talent is showing up at the worst possible moment."

Jymy's pickup is parked just beyond the two men, tailpipe still pumping exhaust, driver's door wide open. The front bumper has seen better days, but it's a sturdy truck. Squat with thick snow tires and a harpoon gun mounted to the roof. A gray wolf stands at attention in the bed.

"Pretty ballsy, waving that gun in Mars's face," Kyn says.

And then he isn't. Hyla strides into our line of sight and yanks the weapon from Jymy's hand. She releases the mag and drops it to the ground. Then she ejects the loaded round and chucks the gun to the edge of the lot.

It happens so fast, Jymy's hands are left grasping for air. His face turns red and he takes a step toward Mars, points at Hyla. He waves his arms, pounds his fist, demanding things Mars looks very reluctant to give. We're too far away to hear anything from here, but it's not uncommon for a Ranger to stop a rig out on a run. It's expected.

"Mars is going to pay him, right?" Because that's what we do. We pay them off. All of us. Rangers are duty-bound to check our loads for contraband and our permits for errors, but a bag of coin and it's like we were never there. It's how rig drivers survive up here. How we carve out a life in the unforgiving wilderness.

"Just having a little fun first, looks like," Kyn says. "I like this gun. What's it loaded with?"

"Buckshot."

"Large game then?" He moves the gun left and right, scanning the tree line.

"It's not for hunting. Not buck anyway."

"You're small, quiet. Winter favors you. You could be an excellent hunter if you wanted."

"I prefer fishing," I say. "And if Winter favors me it's because I don't order her around."

"But you could," Kyn says. "You're Kerce and that means you could."

I ignore him, my eyes on Mars. His lips are moving now, saying things we can't hear, things most people could never understand. Words that have Winter angry and blowing hard.

A gust of wind strikes Jymy in the chest and his boots slide backward on the ice. His arms flail and he cries out, but it's his wolf that goes ballistic. Snarling and snapping, his mouth frothing.

Mars speaks a final word and Jymy's lifted off his feet and thrown into the side of his own truck. Ice and snow rain down on him as he crumbles to the ground. The metal sign on the refueling station swings wildly.

"Fluxing smuggler," I say, pulling on my gloves and kicking the driver's door open.

"Sylvi—" Kyn's fingers snag my stocking cap, but I'm gone. I'm not going to let this go to hell. Not when I have more than enough coin to pay for safe passage.

"Back inside, Miss Quine," Mars says, heading toward me.

"Just pay the man so he doesn't chase us down with that harpoon gun and drag away your precious haul."

And then Jymy's on his feet again. He pulls a knife from his boot and flings it at Mars's back.

"Watch out!" I cry.

And though I thought Hyla was fast, it's nothing to Winter's magic working through Mars. Kerce words spill from his lips and his body spins out of the way. At his command, Winter catches the blade and flips it.

Jymy's knife hovers in the air for a moment. Then, with another twitch of the smuggler's lips, it shoots like an arrow back toward the Ranger and sinks into his chest with a wet thud, the force throwing him into a tower of snow tires. The tires scatter and Jymy falls, grasping at the hilt, trying to pull it free.

My knees buckle, but Hyla is there to hold me upright.

"He just . . . you just . . ." I can hear Jymy gasping from here, pulling at the knife, his chest gurgling.

Mars stares at him for a long second before making his way back to the Ranger. But instead of kneeling to help, he turns his attention to the wolf in the bed of the pickup. The beast snaps and snarls, yellow eyes flashing, heat rising off his coat.

Mars is facing away from us, so we can't hear, we can't see. But, after a moment, the wolf's yapping falls away. The air rings with silence as the animal settles back onto his haunches and allows Mars to scratch his head.

"I'll be damned," Kyn says, his arm brushing mine.

I shake my head, slow, confused, my eyes moving from the Ranger to his wolf and back again. I've heard stories about

Winter's wolves, heard tales of her speaking to them, teaching them her language. I didn't realize that made the animals subject to Kerce magic. Would never have thought—

"My apologies for the delay, Miss Quine," Mars says, suddenly there, pulling the square of cloth from his pocket, and dabbing at the new sores on his lips. "Business to attend. Terms to negotiate."

"You don't negotiate with the Rangers," I say, my voice shaking. "You give them a bag of coin and they wave you on your way."

"I'm afraid Leff wanted more than that this time."

"If the load is important enough to risk losing it to the Flux, surely you'll pay whatever Jymy's asking."

Mars tucks the cloth away and chuckles, a low, quiet sound. "I'm done here. We can go."

He leaves me there staring at the Ranger's body, whose blood is spreading like oil, melting the snow. Rig drivers watch from their open windows, their mouths gaping, their eyes popping.

Kyn tugs the sleeve of my coat. "Let's go, snowflake. Please."

"All he had to do was give Jymy some coin," I say. "All he had to do . . ."

It's not that I liked Jymy. It's just, I knew him. He was a greedy, self-serving lawman who cared little about the law. But he was a survivor. Like the rest of us. There was no reason to take that from him.

"I would have paid. For Lenore, I would have paid anything. We didn't— He didn't have to kill—"

And then Mars is there again, in front of me. Black eyes and blistered lips, and something like pity on his pale face.

I spit at him, watch it freeze on his cheek. "I would have paid."

"He didn't want coin."

"That's all Jymy's ever wanted."

Mars pulls the cloth from his pocket again, wipes the spit from his face.

"His brother is indentured," I say. "Working in the Stack. The money Jymy stole went to pay off his debt."

"Feel sorry for the brother if you must. But do not spare a tear for Jymy Leff."

"Who are you to decide—" The air freezes in my lungs. I can't breathe. I can't talk. And for the briefest moment I can't decide if Winter's turned on me or if it's the shock of what's happened. And then I realize, it's neither.

It's Mars.

I'M SORRY, Winter tells me. **SO SORRY.** She's obeying the smuggler. I taste his breath mingled with the magic sitting on my tongue, keeping me silent.

"That's enough, Mars," Kyn says.

"Hear me, Miss Quine. If our passage across the Shiv Road could have been secured with any number of coins, I would have paid."

Air leaks into my lungs and I find strength enough to swing my fist at his face. Mars catches my wrist easily.

"Choose your foes with care," he says, his voice dangerous. "Jymy Leff wanted *you*."

His hold on my lungs is gone now, but he's left some of his magic behind. It rattles in my chest and I have to hack and spit to rid myself of it.

"Imagine my surprise when he told me all he required as

payment was that I turn you over to him." He leans close, flecks of kol shimmering between his teeth. "He told me what happened at High Pass. I don't know him all that well, so you'll have to tell me—was he prone to exaggeration or did you stop a rig from plowing over a girl?"

He's talking about Jymy in the past tense. Because Jymy Leff is dead. Because just moments ago he killed a lawman who wanted to trade safe passage for me.

"Why?" I ask. "Why would Jymy Leff want me?"

"You said it yourself. Coin is all he's ever wanted."

"Spit it out, Mars," Kyn says. "What do the Rangers want with Sylvi?"

Mars slides his hands into the pockets of his black jacket, rolls back on his heels. "It seems word of your encounter at High Pass made it all the way to the Port of Glas. Jymy made a full report himself and now the Majority would like a word. They have great use for a rig driver who can bend Winter to her will."

"I can't—"

"The kol in your eyes says you can. I think it's time you told us what happened at High Pass, Miss Quine."

CHAPTER 3

MARS DRESDEN, KERCE SMUGGLER AND murderer of lawmen, wants to know what happened at High Pass. He wants to know what happened with the girl.

Winter showed up. That's what happened. And the girl's lucky she did. The kid shouldn't have been out in that weather. She shouldn't have been anywhere near the road.

But I shouldn't have been out there either. It was a reckless decision, taking the route through High Pass on my way home from Kasebyrg. The highway through Hex Landing was safer, but I'd spent the first five years of my life in that rattrap and that was more than enough to scar me. It was careless, but I'd already dropped my haul, and after my fight with Lenore, I was ready for a little challenge.

And Winter delivered. The storm was raging when I reached the summit of the Kol Mountains. It was all noise and bluster and the terrifying kind of beautiful only Winter can be. It took all my skill to keep the Dragon on the road.

The girl was just a slip of a thing—all legs and arms, little more than a dishrag draped around her body. I was caught up in the sights and sounds of the season and it's a miracle I even saw her astride the snowmobile.

For a terror-stricken moment, I didn't know if I could stop the rig. If it was any other truck . . . but it was the Dragon, and so, with my foot pushing hard on the brake, I slipped and skidded to a choppy halt just feet from disaster.

Every muscle in my body was pulled taut—horror at what could have happened and anger at this stupid, stupid girl for underestimating Winter.

I kicked the door open and dropped to the snow. It was only then that I caught a clear look at her pale face. Half of it was made of stone, a crescent of amber rock bending from her left temple to her chin. After a quick glance around, I realized I was closer to the turnout than I'd thought. Her home was likely up on the rise. I craned my neck to the mountains above me. The Shiv are fiercely protective of High Pass and, outside the Dragon, I had no protection.

I backed toward my rig, but the mountaintops were absent any movement, the cave openings empty except for the flickering of firelight deep inside. She really was out here alone, and my anger dimmed. She was in shock, frozen where she sat, one hand on the handlebars, the other halfway to her mouth.

I thought perhaps I should ask her if she was OK, but I never got the chance.

Headlamps flashed over the rise, two beams on the snow

beyond the girl. And then a pickup thundered into view, bouncing around the corner, metal barrels in the bed slamming around, the harpoon gun on the roof of the cab threatening.

I never did find out what Jymy Leff was doing out there.

The girl's hair flew wide as she turned to face the oncoming danger, his headlamps capturing her, turning her to silhouette.

Jymy's brakes squealed but he was going too fast. He was going to hit her. There was no way to stop in time. Even if he cranked the wheel . . . there was just no way . . .

I ran toward the girl, screams tearing at my throat.

A gust of wind slammed through the pass then, so fierce it sent me sprawling. Before I could pull myself upright, a wall of snow shot up from the ground between Jymy's truck and the girl. She turned toward me again, her stone face freckled with powder. I blinked at her and she blinked back.

And Jymy's pickup slammed into the wall with a crunch I can still feel at the base of my skull.

For a moment all was quiet. And then the girl jumped off the snowmobile and ran on tiptoes across the road, sliding down the bank and disappearing from sight.

I didn't see the Shiv man until later. Not until after I confirmed Jymy was well enough to start his pickup. I didn't see him until I'd climbed into the cab of the Dragon and navigated around the debacle in the middle of the road.

He was standing on the shoulder, not far from the turnout that led down to the ancient Kerce Memorial. One wizened hand held a walking stick and the other rested lightly on the girl's head. She waved up at me and it was all I could do not to pull the Dragon over, climb out, and slap her.

CHAPTER 4

MARS WANTS TO KNOW WHAT HAPPENED with the girl, but there's too much there. Too much I don't understand. And the Kerce collect stories to use as weapons.

"Jymy's a liar," I say, "but you'll have to make do with his version. A detailed history of my comings and goings was not part of our deal."

His nose flares. "Very well, Miss Quine. But the past always demands a reckoning. Denying what happened will not save you from the aftermath."

"Duly noted," I say, but my voice cracks and I can't help wondering what Jymy told him. What Jymy saw that night.

Mars turns on his heel, but Hyla steps in front of him, blocks his path.

"We can't leave the Ranger like this," she says. "He was a keeper of the law. Ignoble, but appointed by a higher authority. He deserves better."

"We don't have time for a funeral, Hy," Kyn says.

"They'll find him soon enough." I jam my hands in my pockets, fight to keep my eyes off Jymy. "There were plenty of witnesses."

Out on the road traffic is already starting to back up, the drivers gawking and craning to see what's going on in the lot. Hex Landing is a busy thoroughfare, even during the Flux. The south fork leads toward the Stack where raw kol is taken and processed, while the north fork climbs higher into the mountains, leading to a string of twyl farms in constant need of supplies. Past the farms, the highway dead-ends at the Shiv Road. The farther north we go, the fewer rigs we'll see. But this knot of traffic is going to have to be navigated first.

"I don't like leaving him out here any more than you do," I tell Hyla, "but we have to go. Jymy's squad isn't going to be happy when they see what's happened. We need to be long past Hex Landing when they find out."

"What does it say about us if we show this man no honor? Mars?"

For a long moment, they stare at each other, their eyes speaking a language I've not been taught. And then Mars nods, a simple dip of his chin. "It'll be faster if I do it," he says.

"Mars, really. We can't afford—"

"Go, Miss Quine. Take Kyn and the Dragon and get in that line of rigs out there. We'll meet you at the fork."

I curse and turn away, and that's when I get my first look at Mars's trailer, hitched to the Dragon while I slept. Despite the tangle of emotions twisting my gut, I stand impressed. It has a storm-gray body with studded snow tires and a modern design that won't look nearly so sleek after it's trucked the Shiv Road.

And on top—

"Is that a turret gun?" I ask, climbing into the driver's seat.

"It's Hyla's," Kyn says. "She has access to all sorts of Paradyian gadgetry."

Of course it's Paradyian. Hyla hails from the only nation in the Wethyrd Seas that has the ability to fashion such vicious machinery. The Majority tries, but despite the technology they've collected in their parasitic quest to conquer the world, they just can't compete.

"She can't fire that up here," I say. "She knows that, right? This isn't Paradyia. On Layce, that thing's an avalanche maker."

"She won't do anything without Mars's say-so. Rest easy, yeah?"

We inch out onto the road and I release the latch on my window, dropping it down. The rig driver pinned in next to us has his window down as well. He's puffing on a cigar, marking the frigid sky with smoke rings.

"Sylver Quine, is it?" His gaze lingers on the Dragon's tank tread. "You just pull in?"

"This morning."

I don't know this rigger, but he's driving a truck owned by one of the larger firms in these mountains.

"You've crap timing then," he says.

"What's happened?"

"Rebels blew the road to bits yesterday, took half that mountain with it." He juts his chin toward the horizon. "Shut down the highway north of Hex Landing."

My heart shrivels. "Shut down the highway?"

"Avalanche," he says. "Don't worry, doll. South fork's open. It's just going to take a mighty long time to get to it."

"So there's no getting out onto the Shiv Road then?" Kyn asks.

"No one's stupid enough to truck the Shiv Road this time of year, kid." He flicks his cigar, sending ash to the road. "But there's no getting anywhere by that road. Not until after the Flux. Get on in here," he says, signaling us ahead of him into the line. "I want a closer look at that trailer."

I wave a thank you and pull the Dragon onto the road, flexing the cold from my fingers and scanning the lot for Mars and Hyla. But they're gone. Jymy and the wolf too.

"If we can't take the highway . . ." Kyn says.

"We'll have to take the pass." I yank off my stocking cap and rub my forehead. "I thought you guys were *with* the rebels."

"I'm just a driver, snowflake. Mars is the one with principles."

"He just killed a Ranger. That's not going to go away. At some point we'll all answer for that."

"Mars will take care of it. He always does."

"You know there are about a thousand different outfits you could truck for out here," I say, pulling my cap back into place. "Some of them are even legal."

"Yeah," he says, a smile tugging at the corner of his mouth, "but Mars is the only one who lets me sample Paradyian wares."

Mars's connection to Paradyia isn't news to me. The criminal element in the Kol Mountains is smaller than you'd think, and someone's been importing Paradyian goods for years. The Dragon's tank tread arrived that way. And Hyla's turret gun, I'm sure. Drypp had an old music box that was made on the golden isle. All of it's illegal. We're not allowed to trade with Paradyia, but I don't imagine Mars cares much about Majority laws.

He trades in kol as well. Most of the smugglers do, but Mars is particularly good at it from what I hear. And now that I've seen him face to face, I understand why. The amount of kol in his blood would make him entirely immune to the effects suffered by the rest of us—the hallucinations, the madness.

"Be honest," I say. "Why Mars?"

Kyn shrugs, his smile falling away. "I've known him all my life. He's not easy, Sylvi, but he's been good to us. To my ma. She's not well, but Mars found a medicine that helps. Can't get it on Layce, but Mars makes sure she never runs out. Couple years back he told me if I learned to drive, I'd never want for work. And he's made good on that."

Everyone has twisted loyalties, I guess. Why should Kyn-the-Shiv be any different? "You're from Dris Mora then."

"You know Dris Mora?"

"I know it's a Shiv town." I've asked around but no one can tell me why Mars makes his home with the Shiv. "I know it's on the north shores of the Serpentine. Far from here. Far enough that you can't possibly know how dangerous the pass is going to be. The Desolation Shiv hate people like you."

"Nobody hates me," he says, offended. "I'm not that kind of a criminal. Drive faster, snowflake. Something's going on."

A splash of color in the road. Movement against the white backdrop. He's right. There's a commotion up ahead.

"It's not the criminal they'll object to," I say, accelerating. "The Desolation Shiv aren't keen on deserters."

A muscle ticks in his cheek, but he keeps his eyes on the road. "My people moved away from the Desolation a long time ago. I was born in Dris Mora, but that doesn't make me any less Shiv than those living in High Pass or out along the Desolation stretch. We're the same."

"You're nothing like they are. Trust me."

"'Cause they're ugly and mean and can't find their way around a toothbrush?"

"Because they'll kill you for choosing freedom over duty." I say it baldly and let it sit there between us. Trucking the Shiv Road is dangerous, especially for him, and he seems to think a pretty smile will get him waved through. "When was the last time you were out on the Shiv Road?"

"Never," he says. "I've heard stories—the Pool of Begynd and all that—but my people were never believers. Not in my lifetime anyway. Is it true there are Shiv frozen beneath the ice?"

"There's no knowing what's true, but they believe it. Venturing out onto the Desolation earns you a death sentence. They believe it froze solid with supplicants still swimming in its waters. And what *they believe* is the only thing that matters on the Shiv Road."

"So the gun," he says, his hands resting on Drypp's shotgun.

"The gun."

Kyn leans closer to the windshield. "The old rigger's right. Look."

Up ahead, the turnout onto the north fork is nothing but a wall of rubble. Lumpy, churned-up snow and rock—the pile so high I can't see the top.

"The Dragon's an impressive rig, but—

"There's no way we're getting through that."

"Mars could melt the snow, maybe?"

"It wouldn't matter. They've destroyed the road. The Dragon could navigate it, but not with a trailer hitched." I scan the wreckage. "Where are Mars and Hyla? They should be here by now."

"They'll find us," Kyn says. "Keep moving."

I have little choice. There's nowhere to pull off and the line of trucks behind us has started blowing their horns.

"What about High Pass, Sylvi? Is it even possible this time of year?"

That's the question, isn't it? Because if the only way to get to Lenore is via the Shiv Road, I can't see another way. Not one that won't cost us days. This time of year, we don't have days to work with. We have hours, minutes.

"Sylvi?"

"I've trucked the pass," I tell him. "But not this close to the Flux, and never with a trailer."

"The snow, yeah?"

I nod. "It's magicked somehow, the snow in the pass. It does something to rubber tires, eats through them. I'm sincerely hoping Hyla has a Paradyian answer to that problem."

The cab goes quiet as we turn south, both of us lost in our thoughts. As slow as the traffic is, Hex Landing isn't large and it's not long before we're skirting the trees and turning onto the main stretch.

I DON'T LIKE IT HERE, Winter groans. IT REMINDS ME OF YOUR MOTHER.

She's not spoken much to me today, not directly, and I nearly jump at her voice. I cut my eyes at Kyn, wondering if he's heard her too, but a moment later I feel the hot burn of her in my chest, and I know her words were for me alone.

Sometimes it's hard to tell if she's talking solely to me or if she's allowed others in on the conversation. Unless they speak Kerce, they wouldn't understand what she's saying, but Winter's more than words and wind. She's a chill that clings to everything. She's power. And, like all great powers, she likes her companionship recognized. If she's talking to you, you'll know.

I can't answer her aloud, not with Kyn in the cab, but she's not the only one who hates Hex Landing. For me, it's the worst kind of nostalgic being back here. It always is. The view is far too similar to the one I had as a child, hiding under the wood stove, peering out at the town center from between the slats of Mistress Quine's cabin. Her place sat a little deeper in the woods, the hustle and bustle farther away, and yet bigger to my child eyes. Louder somehow.

Every log, every nail of that cabin is gone now—Winter saw to that—but beyond the windshield, little has changed in the twelve years since I moved away.

The storefronts are perhaps more weathered, and the townsfolk too. Miners trudge up and down the wooden walkway in tired groupings. Shift workers punched out after a long night of digging, looking for a drink or a bite to eat before they catch a few hours' sleep and start again. There's no shortage of kol miners here, but it's rig drivers who make up the bulk of the clientele splashing down coin in the town center.

They loiter in front of the petrol station, chatting up the pleasure girls still made up from last night, spilling out of taverns up and down Rigger's Row. Out of habit, I scan the town for Bristol's ugly yellow plow, but it's not here. If he and Lenore passed through, they're long gone now.

Just past Rigger's Row, the road turns again and up from the barren landscape shoots a string of bunkhouses. The mine yard sits to the west, halted mining equipment collecting snow out front. Tin-roofed structures laden with white powder stretch all the way to the mine entrances.

But where is everyone?

It's too quiet. Too still to be the site of the Majority's flagship mining operation.

And then we see them.

Kol miners lining the road to our left and right. Unlike those wandering the town center, looking for food and drink, these laborers clearly don't have any standing with the Majority. They're underfed and underclothed, likely indentured servants or lesser citizens who couldn't find work elsewhere. Their coveralls are smeared head to toe in kol, black dust shimmering in Winter's light. It's not just the standard dusting that comes with the job either. This is intentional. Excessive. And dangerous.

"What in Begynd's name?" Kyn whispers. "They've killed them."

My stomach rises to my throat, the taste of bile sharp on my tongue. "Probably," I say, swallowing it down. "One way or another."

The effects of raw kol range from mild hallucinations to full-on madness, depending on the length and intensity of the exposure. But kol dust is also addictive. It was the cravings that killed Lenore's ma and it's what keeps her father chained to the refinery at the Stack.

I switch off the heater. Best keep the kol outside.

Despite its hazardous nature, it's our most valuable commodity. Kol is a mineral that amplifies things, makes them more than what they are. It's used in all sorts of goods: cosmetics, medicine, petrol. But of all the islands on the Wethyrd Seas, it can be found solely in the mountains of Layce and, as such, only the Majority is allowed to mine it. They tell us it's so the council can ensure the proceeds benefit all the islands under their control, not just a small smattering of mountain folk. Not just the ones digging it from the rock.

You can imagine how Layce feels about the Majority stealing the land from under their feet.

And still we truck and still we work, and, excepting the rebels, we keep our mouths shut because as long as the kol deliveries arrive on time, the ruling class mostly leaves us alone; they keep to the lowlands where Winter's not quite so frigid. They want our kol, yes, but our Winter? That they could do without.

Rangers move up and down the road, hollering, pointing guns at the workers, though most of them are standing as compliantly as they're able. Their arms wave in the cold air and they whimper, eyes seeing monsters that aren't there, bodies twitching.

This isn't punishment. These workers aren't responsible for the raids. They were just unfortunate enough to be on shift when the Majority ran out of patience. This is a warning. To the rebels. To every sympathizer passing by.

You attack us, we attack them.

The rebels went too far this time—and the Majority isn't leaving us alone any longer.

The traffic grinds to a standstill, but we've finally caught sight of the reason for the backup. There's a fire in the road. Crates stacked high, hissing and popping as flames bite through cheap wood.

"It's twyl chewing gum," I say, recognizing the packaging. "They're torching it."

The gum is used to combat the negative effects of kol. Miners and those working in the Stack are given daily allotments of it, but the quantity is rarely adequate. Whenever we visited Lenore's father, we'd take extra coin so he could buy his own supply, but the Majority allows their merchants to charge exorbitant prices for their recipe. Prices very few laborers can afford, which keeps them dependent on the Majority. I unlatch my window and let it fall. The unmistakable honeyed stench of twyl rides the wind, mixed with smoke and kol dust. Kyn pulls his shirt up over his nose and mouth.

"There's gum in the glove compartment," I say. With this much kol in the air, we need to protect ourselves.

He tears himself a piece and passes me one as well. I tuck it in my cheek, but I haven't got enough for all these workers and I don't imagine the Rangers would treat them kindly if I offered.

"My ma burns twyl blossoms indoors when the winds are high," Kyn says. "Says it keeps her head clear of the kol."

"Lenore does the same thing. But torching the gum isn't going to do any good."

We're approaching a broad-shouldered man clad in Majority red and black, the word SUPERINTENDENT stitched onto his lapel. He's standing in the center of the road, waving rigs around the fire.

"What's all this?" I ask, leaning out my window, catching his attention.

"Week's supply of twyl," he says, ambling over. "A shame isn't it? These poor souls are going to have to be about their business for the next seven days without a stick of gum to share."

"The rebels did this?"

"Oh no, ma'am. We did it." He taps the Majority patch on his shirt sleeve. "Every action has a consequence, I'm afraid."

"But your workers didn't blow that road," Kyn says, leaning past me. "They aren't rebels."

"Most of 'em aren't, you're right about that. Best keep your fingers crossed these poor mucks make it through the week. Have to scrounge up some more workers if their brains turn to mush, and who knows where we'll come knocking. You know all about that though, don't you, Shiv?"

Kyn's fingers tighten around the windowsill. "Know all about what?"

"Oh nothing," the superintendent says, scratching his beard. "Just making sure you'll pass the message along. Not everybody will have the pleasure of seeing what you're seeing today. Off you go, now."

Kyn grabs my window and yanks it back into place, scraping his cheek at the superintendent. We should go, but I can't stop staring at the haunted line of laborers. Not far from where the Dragon idles, a woman chews her fingers, bloodying them trying to get at the kol. It's how Lenore's ma looked before she passed. Before we buried her in the cemetery outside the Stack.

"Sylvi?" Kyn says.

I tear my eyes away and shift the rig into gear. But my hands are cold and clumsy and behind us, horns blast.

"Fluxing Majority," Kyn says, as I get the Dragon rolling. "They lose more of their workers to kol madness than anything else, but they don't give a flux about the people cutting it from the rock. The bastards deserve every fight the rebels bring their way."

I take a deep, shuddering breath, and work to erase every desperate face we just rolled past. "And you said it was Mars who had the principles."

Kyn's not wrong. The Majority's asking for a fight and there are plenty of people who will bring it to them. But the superintendent does have a point: Every action has a consequence.

At the very least, we've lost half a day. But with a trip through High Pass suddenly on the horizon, I fear we'll lose more than that by the time we reach the end of this road.

And it's the rebels who have left us no choice.

CHAPTER 5

MARS AND HYLA ARE STANDING ON THE SIDE of the road when we make the turn south. I stop just long enough for them to load in. We endure the blast of a single horn, but the road opens up here and traffic starts to even out.

Kyn moves to the bench seat next to Hyla, giving Mars the passenger seat.

"There's a shop rag in the glove compartment," I tell him, nodding at his hands. Blood creases his knuckles, turning his nails black and crusted.

"Thank you," he says, digging out the rag, wiping at the stains.

"It won't be long before they realize Jymy's gone," I say.

He tucks the rag away with a flourish. "I'm not afraid, Miss Quine. Are you?"

"Of all the things I'm afraid of in this moment, the Rangers concern me least."

"High Pass then?"

"High Pass. But first, we need to talk about the tires on your trailer."

"I know all about the problems with the snow at High Pass, Miss Quine."

"And your tires?"

"They're Paradyian-made, Sessa," Hyla says, leaning forward between the seats, perching her goggles atop her head. "Like your Dragon's tank tread, like the trailer's turret. Fear not."

My gaze moves from Hyla to Mars. "You've tested them in the pass then? Because there's something seriously wrong with the snow there. No one trucks the summit anymore."

"Miss Quine, this haul is of the utmost importance to me. I would not risk losing it to anything so maddening as snow."

He says "snow" the way the riggers say "flux." Like it's a dirty word and he's happy to pull it out and slap you with it. But I decide he has a point about his haul. He's gone to a lot of trouble to make this trip happen.

"Mars tells me there are monsters on Layce, Sessa. Do they live in this pass? Is that why you do not want to go there?"

"Why do you call me Sessa?" I ask, pulling my eyes from the road, catching her fractured gaze in the mirror. "What does that mean? Is it Paradyian?"

"It is. A title bestowed on women of great honor."

She's so serious, I can't help but grin. "And do Paradyians show such deference for all their truck drivers?"

Hyla blushes, her face flustered.

"It's a formal moniker," Mars explains. "An indicator of respect. Hyla was being polite."

Kyn snorts. "You're going to have to watch that, Hy. No one fears a polite soldier."

"I'm always polite," Hyla says. "Kindness does not make me weak. It allows others to be strong as well."

"An army of polite Paradyians," Kyn ponders. "Something I'd like to see before I die."

"I shall show you then. Soldiers with manners and high-powered rifles. They are not as contrary as you believe." Her tone is so severe Kyn howls with laughter.

Hyla shoves him into the corner of the cab, spreading her knees and pinning him there. Kyn's laughing too hard now to fight back and Hyla has to lean forward to be heard.

"Are there monsters, then, Sessa?"

Mars could answer this question, I'm sure, but he watches me instead. I have to wonder what Lenore's told him. If he knows what happened to Old Man Drypp.

"Not in the pass," I tell her. "No."

But like all the magical places of the world, there are monsters on Layce.

"Why come here?" I ask Hyla, eager to change the subject.

Paradyia is known for its artists and musicians. Its warm, blue waters and sunlit skies. It's known for its refusal to engage in the politics that govern the Majority's islands, and indeed, they're the only kingdom in the Wethyrd Seas that has consistently been able to defend themselves from Majority invasions over the centuries. The Paradyian army is massive, their king respected—begrudgingly by the Majority ruling class—but respected nonetheless.

They are a kingdom untouched by the magic that has cursed Layce and they've worked hard to keep it such.

"A debt," Hyla says. "A debt I am happy to pay."

"You owe me nothing," Mars says, adjusting the mirror and meeting Hyla's gaze in the reflection. "You've only ever been a faithful friend."

"But the saving of a life is something a Paradyian is bound to repay."

"Have you not saved mine a dozen times since we left Paradyia?"

"I've done only what you've allowed me to do. Your life cannot be threatened as mine can," she says, settling back in the seat. "Until I am sure, until I know in my heart that I have paid life for life, I cannot return home."

It's so noble I have to remind myself this woman nearly shattered my arm last week.

"As it happens, returning to Paradyia isn't something that can be done without extensive planning," Mars says.

"But you will return?" I ask Hyla.

She runs her finger over the gun strapped to her thigh, her words slow and deliberate. "The children of Layce are told not to dwell on the past, yes?"

"History is not taught in our schools," Mars says.

"In contrast, we Paradyians are told not to promise the future. I cannot say where I will be tomorrow, Sessa. I wish I could. I've a husband across the sea who fought and slept alongside me for nearly ten years. Even now, I feel him in here." She presses a hand to her chest. "We have become one person—he and I—and he has the great privilege of taking care of our two girls while I am away.

I do not know what this road will bring, but Paradyia is home. My family is home, and I long to see them again."

She smiles and I find myself returning it. I know what it means to have a home. It's how I feel about the Dragon. How I feel about Lenore.

"You said Mars's life can't be threatened the way yours can. What did you mean by that?"

"Mars is strong in ways I've never seen," she says. "How do you kill a man who could encase himself in ice with the snap of his fingers?"

"Finger snaps do nothing," Mars says, his face turned away, distanced somehow from a conversation that revolves around him. "It's words, Hyla. The power is in the words."

"How did he save your life?" I ask, thinking of Lenore. I understand what it is to owe a debt.

"It was not my life he saved—"

"If you're ready to hear a story, there are a few I would gladly tell you," Mars says. "But not this one. Not now."

Hyla claps Mars on the shoulder and settles back. "Another time then, Sessa. Another time."

I grind my teeth at the mindless obedience. "We're coming up on High Pass. There isn't time for stories anyway."

The road has emptied now. We're alone out here, save Winter. And as we approach the pass, I feel her hot and restless in my belly.

Snow has fallen steadily since the moment we left Hex Landing. Now though, the wind picks up, battering the rig from all sides and sending snowflakes into a flurry. Winter's never suffered visitors to the pass lightly, but there's no forgetting my last trip here. I suck at the phantom blister inside my lower lip and focus on pushing through the snow. The blister's gone now, but one Kerce word was all it took.

We're high now, thousands of feet above sea level. Higher even than the village at Whistletop, and the mountains here are loud in ways that still surprise me.

YOU SHOULD NOT HAVE COME, Winter snarls.

I chance a peek at Mars, but despite Winter's rage, he's relaxed. Visibly so. His pale face has some color, his black eyes shimmer, and in the light bouncing off the mountains, I see something in them I hadn't noticed before: There's an iris visible beneath the kol.

"What?" Mars says, turning his face to mine.

"Nothing."

"You're staring."

"I'm driving."

He chuckles—soft and light. It's almost endearing and I hate him for it. I don't want to like this man.

Up ahead is a narrow fork. To the left, the road climbs down, a byway cut into the mountain that swings out and around, heading back toward Whistletop. But there's no turning for home now. Not if Lenore's at the end of this road.

The mountain looms large in the windshield, the incline steep. Kyn's leaning so far forward his face is inches from my own. In the rearview, I see Hyla, her brow wide and flat, her golden eyes round and hungry, devouring the road before us.

My eyebrow hitches. "First time through High Pass, then? You all picked quite the season."

The engine groans as the Sylver Dragon climbs higher

up the mountain. I shift gears and press my foot to the floor, flooding the rig with enough power to get us to the top. The tank tread spins, digging into the snow crust. Even with the steady, faithful push of the tread, it's a slow climb. The lower fork drops behind us as we press forward toward High Pass, the long narrow passageway that marks the summit of the Kol Mountains.

"What's that?" Kyn asks, pointing to the ridge high above the roadway.

"Shiv caves," I say. "Shouldn't you know that? You're the Shiv *expert*, remember?"

"They live in caves?" he asks, gaping.

I bite back a retort. His lack of knowledge scares me. Kyn might speak Shiv, but he's a liability up here if we're forced into an encounter. "There's a series of dwellings on both sides of the pass," I say, my tone measured. "But the view from here is deceptive."

"Why?" Kyn leans farther forward, craning his neck left and right. His ear brushes mine and I have to shove him back into his seat. "Sorry," he mumbles. "Are their numbers fewer than they appear?"

"Far more," I say. "The cave openings you can see from the road are nothing compared to the network beyond."

We're still too far away to see individuals, but it's clear there's movement.

"They've seen us," Mars says.

In the mirror, Kyn is a mess of awkward elbows as he attempts to remove Drypp's shotgun from the mount behind Hyla.

"You can't shoot that up here," I say, catching his gaze in the mirror.

"We can't just let them attack the rig."

"Look at the ice, Kyn. It's barely clinging to the north peak. You fire that in the pass, the mountain might come down on us."

IT MIGHT COME DOWN ANYWAY, Winter whispers.

Mars hears her, grins.

Kyn takes aim. "That's what you and Mars are here for."

"You *can't*," I say, focusing now on Mars, panic rising in my chest. "You can't use magic. Not up here. Winter makes her home in the pass."

"Your point, Miss Quine?"

"She may suffer you fairly if you let her be, but what would *you* do if a crew of smugglers rolled into your home and started rearranging things?"

Mars sits taller. "I'd offer them a bottle of my favorite red and ask for the latest news."

"Mars—"

"We need to make a stop," he says.

"Bad time to have to take a leak, boss." Kyn's grip is still tight on the gun.

"It's up there, isn't it?" Mars asks, a thin white finger jutting toward the south peak.

I know where he wants to go, but I won't. I'm not stopping here. Not after what happened last time.

"I understand the draw, Mars. I do," I say, trying to keep my voice calm. "But the best way to get your haul safely across the Shiv Road is to first, make it through High Pass alive. Stopping to pay homage—"

"Make the turn, Miss Quine."

"I'm telling you—"

"I can make you take it," he says, his voice deadly.

"And risk losing your haul?"

"Make the turn."

"For some stupid Kerce sentiment?"

Mars clears his throat and turns his black eyes to the road. I follow suit, proud to have stood my ground. It's insanity to make this stop. To take the turnout. He's never been told no. Never been refused. He's held that power over everyone's head until they've handed over their own free will.

But I won't. Not for a pile of stones.

The ground shakes and, from somewhere high above, a boulder slams into our path. Hyla lets out a string of Paradyian curses, and behind me, Kyn's hands tighten hard around the seat. My braid catches in his grip and hair is yanked from my head. I fight every flight instinct I have, refusing to crank the wheel hard to the left—a jackknifed trailer will be impossible to right. I slam my foot to the brake and the tank tread skids, the steering wheel useless in my fisted hands.

The trailer slips left and right, but before it can really get swinging, we stop. It's the incline that saves us, the climb working alongside the brakes to slow our deceleration. If we'd been any heavier . . .

I kick my door open and jump onto the highway, my boots slipping on the ice.

Two of my thumbs! That's all there is between the massive, frosted boulder and the Sylver Dragon's grill. Two of my skinny little thumbs.

THE SMUGGLER WANTS A FIGHT, Winter hisses. **SHALL I GIVE IT TO HIM?**

My legs shake and I have to brace myself against the boulder. Our path is blocked. The highway, impassable. Our only option is to take the byway to the right. The broken road that leads to the Kerce Memorial.

Kyn's next to me now, a high whistle gliding across his tongue. "Mars said you were good, but—"

"Mars did this," I say, stomping around the truck, pulling myself back into the driver's seat.

"You're wasting time," Mars says, his fingers drumming hard on his knees. "Make the turn."

"You could have killed us," I say.

"You could have stopped me. You could have stopped the boulder."

"You could have KILLED US!"

"*You* could have killed us."

"You're crazy."

"I am a force of nature. Like Winter. Like the Shiv who were carved from these mountains. Treating my commands as suggestions, as if the danger I present is negligible, will certainly result in someone's death."

"I could make the same threat," I say.

"I wish you would. Now, make the turn."

"Should we wait for your man or leave him to the Shiv?" I ask.

By way of answer, Mars turns his face to the window and watches as Kyn nudges the boulder with his boot and then his shoulder. It stays put. He whacks it with the butt of Drypp's gun, then strides back to the rig, a dark smudge against the churning onslaught of snow.

"It's coming down hard now," he says, climbing back inside, his head and arms iced white.

"I keep a spare coat in the back," I say.

"You know you're small, yeah?"

"It's an old one of Drypp's."

"I'm fine," he says, "but it looks like the storm's driven the Shiv inside."

"Would it drive *you* inside?" I ask, genuinely curious despite my irritation. Winter's different for the Shiv. Not so cold, not so damaging to their flesh. It's the stone maybe—though Mystra Dyfan says it's the heat of Begynd working from within. They're so impervious, a gift I've envied more than once.

"Ah, yeah. I hate being cold."

"You get cold then?"

"Not as fast as you do, sure. But up there it's the driving wind that'll have them running for cover. Hell on the eyes and what's the point if you can't see?"

I was wondering the same thing.

PLEASE, Winter begs. **IT'S NOT SAFE.**

But snow is blustering about the cliffs, stealing visibility and there is no point sitting here stewing. I crank the wheel to the right and ease off the brake slowly. Despite Winter's warning burning hot in my bones, we take the road toward the Kerce Memorial.

CHAPTER 6

THE MONUMENT IS TALL AND PRECARIOUS—
stone stacked upon stone—large rocks perched on
smaller ones, balancing, almost tipping, but holding firm.
It makes no sense, really, how they stand, how they face Winter so
valiantly. Some three hundred years ago, the Kerce fashioned this
tower. After all this time it should be nothing but a pile of frozen rubble. But for reasons that are all her own, Winter's left the
memorial untouched. The shine has worn away but the stones are
still brightly colored like the mountain buried beneath its Ryme
coat. Green and blue and red and orange, various shapes and sizes,
all with ribbons of kol marbled through them.

Some say it's Kerce magic that keeps the monument upright,
the kol asserting its dominance over Winter and gravity alike.
Others say it's nothing more than ingenious engineering.

I don't have any idea how the tower has remained standing
for so long. I didn't pay near enough attention to Mystra Dyfan
to have the details of Kerce mythology memorized.

What I do remember is that long ago, on this very spot, Winter made a deal with the Kerce Queen. Here, at High Pass, Winter taught a dying sovereign to speak her own tongue so they could strike an accord—words that would eventually come to be known as the Kerce language. The people's original dialect was lost to antiquity and replaced with the whispers of a bartering power.

Sad, but likely a fairy story. And I've heard plenty of those. Sometimes they flatter the Shiv, sometimes they flatter the Kerce. But they're always whispered. You wouldn't want the Majority to hear you speaking of the past.

I won't deny there's something *different* about High Pass. But did Winter really take advantage of a dying queen here? It feels desperate, the Kerce and Shiv doing their best to explain things they weren't meant to understand. Some days I see the wisdom in the Majority's laws.

There is no yesterday, they say, *only a thousand tomorrows.*

It's a maxim they teach every child, a message they scrawl on their buildings.

And while I'm no fan of the Majority, I know this: We have to keep moving forward. Sifting through myth and legend looking for actual history requires too much stationary contemplation. In these mountains, only an impervious monument could afford such a thing. We'd freeze to death if we stood still long enough to figure out where we've been.

Mars stands beneath the monument now, a thin shadow against the whiteness. His head is bowed low, his hands stitched together behind his back. Despite Winter's flailing winds, not a hair on his head moves. Snowflakes hover in the small circle around the rock tower. They don't fall; they don't bluster.

It would be easy to attribute the stillness around him to the kol racing through his veins, to the words sitting so lightly on his tongue, but I've been here before.

High Pass is just different.

Hyla and Kyn stand some distance away, giving Mars a bit of privacy, but they've forfeited their comfort in doing so. Hyla flips up the hood on her red parka, holds it in place with both hands, her goggles frosting over. Holstered to each thigh is a handgun, flashing gold in the dimming light.

Kyn stands next to her, his legs shoulder-width apart, fighting to keep himself upright. The wind is ferocious, tugging at the strap of the shotgun draped around his neck. He's wearing a coat now—his own, not the one I offered—pulled from an oversize duffle they've stowed beneath the bench seat.

Kyn's coat is a dark green utilitarian thing, lots of pockets, very little down. The hood is lined with brown fur—maybe mink—and it billows in the wind. Snow collects in his tight curls as he squints at the storm.

Watching him and Hyla struggle against Winter thaws a smile on my face, but it's a fleeting pleasure. Winter's ready for us to move on.

THERE ARE SECRETS HERE! MY SECRETS!

Her words ramble about on the wind, gusting up and down.

THEY CLIMB THROUGH MY HOME, she screams, **DESECRATE MY THRONE. PULL IT APART WITH THEIR STONE HANDS AND HIDE LIKE THIEVES.**

She howls about trickery and lairs. About mysteries and invaders. It's hard to follow her logic, but one thing is clear: She doesn't like sharing this place. Not with us. And not with the Shiv who've burrowed into her walls.

There's a cave cut into the cliff face about twenty feet above Kyn and Hyla. It catches at my peripheral, but the shadows within are still.

Mars hasn't moved in ages except to drag his finger over the kol marbled into the stones. I'm tempted to lay on the horn, but before I can lift a hand, Hyla moves toward Mars. With a quick twitch, she shoves him to the ground. Kyn lifts a gun, sighting something high on the cliff behind the trailer.

Behind me.

And then a jolt as something lands atop the cab. The distinct shuffle of bare feet overhead and I know: It's not a *thing* on the Dragon's back, it's a person. A Shiv. Has to be.

Despite my caution about not using guns in the pass, instinct has me reaching for the gun rack. It's empty. *Flux.* Kyn took Drypp's shotgun.

I scrabble into the passenger seat, reaching beneath it for his rifle, praying I won't have to fire it here. My fingers find the strap and I yank until it's in my hands. Peering over the dash, I fight to swallow down my hammering heart. It tastes like blood and bile and it tastes like the magic I refuse to use. If Mars dies, if the Shiv kill him, I'll never find Lenore.

Then Mars is on his feet again, white powder on his knees, his hands extended, frostbitten lips moving. He presses his wrists together, fingers curling around an invisible ball as he strides forward, Hyla in his wake, two golden guns taking aim.

It takes me a minute to find Kyn, who is hidden by the angle of the Dragon's hood. He's in front of Mars, a step or two closer to the rig. I can make out only his raised hands. He yells something in Shiv, and the scraping feet atop the cab still. A man's voice responds.

Kyn repeats himself but I have no idea what he's saying. Much to Mystra Dyfan's chagrin, I never learned the Shiv tongue. Too much studying, too much confusion. Kyn's tone is placating, peacemaking. Almost pleading.

I understand, then, something about Kyn. The pitch of his voice, the open posture of his hands. He could have blown this Shiv man away with one pull of the trigger, but he didn't. He knows Mars will kill these people with little thought if they attempt to block our passage. And despite the risk to himself, he's doing what he can to prevent that.

Kyn's desperation crawls up my own back, circles my chest, constricts.

I find myself begging the wretched Kerce smuggler to breathe, to drop his hands. The Shiv here in the pass are not the friendly, laughing comrades he's found in Dris Mora. They are devout about the Desolation and they would rather die than let anyone desecrate it.

The feet overhead shift, metal creaking under the weight of them, and despite my own reservations, I tighten my grip on the rifle, watching the ceiling bow and curve.

The Shiv man is speaking. His voice is low, the words pulled from somewhere dark. His feet are heavier now. More determined as they move left and then right—I follow them with my gun.

And then the window next to my head shatters.

Splinters of glass fly and I throw myself to the left, smacking my head on the steering wheel. My ear buzzes but I whip around, the rifle pointed at a long pale hand clenched tight around a slick knife.

Not a knife. A stone, sharpened to a point—a triangle of rough serrated edges.

A shiv.

The fist pulls back, glass shards slicing as it slams the window once again.

He's trying to get inside.

I clamber upright and aim Kyn's rifle. But before I can pull the trigger, the hand is yanked backward, out through the broken window. The hand has a body now. A long, rangy body, wearing only a pair of trousers dripping with sleet. A fiery orange stone covers his bare chest and abdomen, clashing with the yellow beard hanging from his face, snow clinging to its bristles.

Mars has control of him now and the Shiv is not at all pleased. He's hovering over the hood of the rig, snow and ice whipping around him. I watch as slivers cut into his face and arms. They chip away at the stone on his chest.

Mars tilts his hands, pushing the Shiv higher into the sky. I lean forward against the windshield, trying to see. With a twist of Mars's wrists, the man starts to spin. He's fighting hard to hang on to the knife in his hands, his face strained with the effort of it. Just when I think he'll keep his hold, he pulls his hand away like the weapon's stung him. He's a good ten feet above the hood of the rig and the blade is falling hard and fast. Too fast.

I throw myself back into the seat as the weapon crashes into the glass, sending spider cracks across the windshield. I catch only a glimpse of the makeshift knife before it slides to the ground, frozen solid in a block of ice.

Mingled relief and horror race through my veins. Through the shattered glass, I see Mars drop his hands, satisfaction somewhere amongst the rage. And then the Shiv is falling.

"The window!" I yell. "The window!"

But it's no use. The Shiv tumbles from the sky, his knees crunching into the hood, his face smacking the splintered glass with a thud that has his arms flopping forward and the air audibly squeezed from his lungs. He's hurting, clearly, but he catches himself before he can slip to the ground.

In one swift move, his feet are underneath him again, and in two leaps he's back on top of the hood, warm handprints fogging the broken windshield. His blue eyes narrow at me and he punches at the glass separating us. I whip the rifle around, but he's done nothing more than bloody his hand.

Mars flings his right arm wide and the Shiv skids across the hood, flying into the air again. This time, he collides with the mountainside and crumples to the snow.

For a moment, all is still.

I watch each of the crew in turn. They scan the cliffs above us, Kyn with Drypp's gun locked and loaded, Hyla with both her handguns raised, and Mars—looking far more dangerous than either of his comrades—his feet spread wide, armed with only the disgust painted on his face.

I climb back into the driver's seat and kick open the door.

"Stay in the rig," Kyn yells.

"Because it's safer?" I drop off the running board and whip around, the rifle aimed at the rocks beyond the trailer. We could blow these caves to smithereens with Hyla's turret gun, but we'd bring the entire mountain down on us too. "He won't be alone."

"Get back in the rig, Miss Quine."

I can hear the sneer on Mars's face, but I'm backing toward him now. "There's a string of dwellings on the other side of the ridge," I say. "And more behind the monument, deep in the mountains. They're accessible through the cave there."

Hyla spins around, her handguns aimed at the cave.

"Kyn," Mars says, almost bored, "get her back in the rig."

"Why don't we all get back in the rig?" Kyn asks.

"Do it," Mars says.

Kyn sighs and drops the gun to his side. "Let's go, Sylvi."

I wheel on him, raise my gun. "Don't even think about it."

He takes another step toward me. And another. My hand shakes, but I jab his own rifle into his chest. "Don't touch me."

"You want to shoot me?" he asks, something sharp in his eyes. Eyes that were quick to smile just moments ago. The encounter with the Shiv has shaken him, a wound festering so near the surface I find myself wanting to pick at it, to see what oozes from beneath. "Do it. I dare you."

I'm trying to understand just what he's daring me to do when I see a rock sail toward us. Kyn grabs the barrel of the rifle and pulls me out of its path, but when I whirl around, Mars has caught the rock with a gust of wind. It bobs midair and then, with a whispered word, Mars sends it flying toward an outcropping of trees hanging out over the mountainside.

A thud as the rock connects and a Shiv woman falls from her cover.

"You're becoming a liability, Miss Quine."

Another rock whizzes toward us—toward Mars—and another. A flurry of stones now, pocking the cold air, cutting through it.

"I told you," I growl, dropping to the ground. "They don't fight alone."

Hyla and Kyn drop to the ground as well, but Mars stands his ground. He speaks into the cold air and every one of the stones freezes in midflight. With a dismissive gesture and a growled command, the colored rocks explode—shrapnel spreading away from our huddled forms.

Shrieks and grunts fill the pass as the shards find their marks. Kyn and I follow the sounds with our guns.

"Mars," Hyla warns. "You have to keep moving."

I turn and, despite the gravity of the situation, I almost laugh. Mars has stepped out of the safety circling the Kerce Memorial and beneath his feet, snow has begun to gather. Winter is taking advantage of his divided attention.

"Something funny, Miss Quine?"

"She doesn't like being commanded," I say. "I did tell you."

Winter has hold of him now—his left boot is encased in ice. He curses and drops down to examine it. Kerce words slide off his tongue, melting the ice.

"Mars!" Kyn yells, as another rock sails toward him.

But there's nothing to be done, and no time to do it. Mars can only speak one word at a time, can only give one command. The rock connects with his temple and he drops to the ground, awkward, his knee bent, his foot still frozen in place.

And then an arrow wings toward me. I flinch but it passes overhead, disappearing into the cave, a rope fluttering behind.

The rope bobs and then snaps taut. It's been anchored. Which could only happen if—

The shadows inside the cave move and a whistle slices, echoing off the stones, bouncing from rock face to rock face.

"We have to go," Kyn says, "we have to run." He's standing now, pulling me, half carrying me. I'd fight, but all my energy is focused on the entrance to the cave, suspended halfway between the ground and the road above. Shiv fighters emerge and slide down the rope, their hands wrapped in thick cloth.

"Hyla!" I scream. "Run! Run!"

But Hyla does nothing of the sort. She pulls herself upright and stands over Mars, her golden guns aimed at the Shiv fighters descending on us.

Men and women appear, clad in thin, snow-soaked clothes, their bare skin a mixture of color and stone. One by one, they drop to the ice. Surrounding us, separating Kyn and me from Hyla and Mars—still fallen, thoroughly unaware of the danger he's placed us all in.

The Shiv are close. So close I can see their heat lifting into the cold air, smell the sweat freezing on their skin. Kyn releases me and we both raise our guns. I don't want to fire this gun up here, I don't want to shoot anyone, but Winter is worming her way up my chest, spreading out along my arms, tightening my finger on the trigger.

DANGER, she says.

She's just trying to keep me safe, but my hands are shaking with nerves and cold and again the girl's face flashes clear and bright in my mind. I shouldn't be here. I'm afraid I'll do something I can't undo. I work to pull my finger away, sliding it slowly out of the trigger guard.

"We're not here to cause trouble," I say to the Shiv man who's not four feet from the end of the rifle. He's not as dark as Kyn, but his skin is brown, the stone like milk spilled across his face, patches of white rock on his elbows and knees. A triangular gold medallion hangs against his thin chest, but despite his brittle frame, he spins the walking stick in his hand and jabs it deep into the snow.

"Why have you returned?" he asks me, his words clear if menacing. He's speaking in the common tongue. The language of the Majority.

"You know him?" Kyn asks.

I shake my head.

"I did not think you were stupid enough to venture this way again."

My throat is tight, sweat breaks out along my spine. "I mean no harm."

"We're just passing through," Kyn answers.

The old man blinks at him and turns back to me. "You cannot leave."

"The gun says I can."

And then it's not in my hand any longer and my fingers are stinging. A rock flung from somewhere nearby.

"You cannot leave," he says, leaning onto his stick.

In the strange stillness of the sacred memorial, I hear Hyla cock her weapons. Two Shiv children have emerged from the brush.

"Back up," she growls.

The children carry their weight on their fingertips and toes as they creep toward Mars. A girl and a boy. The boy is a younger version of the man with the staff, the white stone running along his spine and across his forehead.

I try not to look too hard at the girl. But I see her nonetheless. I see her everywhere.

Hyla steps toward the children, but they continue forward. She fires a warning shot that sends snow flying inches from their fingers.

"Don't," I say, panic rising in my chest. "Hyla, let them be."

"They will not approach Mars, Sessa. Not while he is like this."

"We're leaving," I say to the Shiv, my voice remarkably steady. "We're just passing through."

He twists the walking stick in his hands. "You stay and we will grant your companions safe passage."

I feel the confusion on my face. It's unlike the Shiv to be so accommodating. "Why would you let them pass?"

But I don't get an answer. His mouth moves but only squeaking gasps of air cross his lips. He turns his face to Hyla—no, to Mars. And though his chest is heaving, his eyes bulging, he manages a quick nod of his head. Stones fly from the hands of his companions once again.

But Mars is on his feet, Winter pulling him upright. Blood blackens his face but there's magic on his tongue. It sounds like the chip of a hammer on solid ice.

The ground shakes, icicles ringing as they fall from the frozen trees. Two Shiv fall from their hidden perches. Then three. Hyla fires into the cold and blood marks the snow. I reach out, try to grab the guns from her hands.

We just need to go.

A stone hits me in the gut and I double over, only to take another to my shoulder. But Kyn grabs my belt and lifts me back to my feet.

"Get to the rig!" he yells in my face. "Go!"

I grab his sleeve and reach out for Mars and Hyla. I'm leaving this place and I'm taking them all with me. But we're too far away and Kyn is pulling my hand. We manage two steps before the mountain skitters and I lose my footing. A plate of ice shifts somewhere high above and my gut clenches tight, my head spinning.

Last Ryme, a bar fight broke out at Drypp's. Roughnecks with too much beer and not enough road to truck. A man was thrown into the wine rack and the mess was unbelievable. It took Lenore and me all night to get the tavern back in order after that brawl. All that spilled wine, all that shattered glass.

That's what I'm thinking as I watch the mountain come down. Someone's yelling my name but I can't breathe, I can't move. All I can think is that after this fight there will be no one left standing to clean up the mess.

CHAPTER 7

THE SCENE IS SO CLEAR.

Drypp's swinging his pickaxe again. It's the one Lenore and I bought for his eighty-second Ryme. The wood handle is wrapped in leather cord and we'd paid the local smithy a child's fortune to work the axe head to perfection. Leni and I must've scrubbed hundreds of windshields to pay for it, treating them with weather repellent for a bit of extra coin.

And now Drypp swings the axe, breaking up the frozen earth, churning the ground behind the tavern for the vegetable garden ten-year-old Lenore insists on trying. She stands there with her hands full of seeds, though I know that's not how it was. Lenore would never be so careless with her seeds.

But this isn't a memory. This is a dream. And in the dream Lenore's hands are full, seeds squeezing through the cracks between her fingers and her face desperate for a place to plant them. She bounces on the balls of her feet, waiting, waiting for Drypp to clear away the snow and ice. And though I've only ever wanted Drypp's granddaughter to like me, to love me like her own sister, I hate the glee on her face when Drypp breaks through to soil. I hate the victory in the set of Drypp's shoulders when he's done it.

Lenore dumps the seeds into my hands. "Plant them, Sylvi," she says. "Plant them!"

But in my hands they're no longer seeds. They're words. Kerce words chalked in Mystra's hasty scrawl. They inch up my arms, these words I never want to speak. I fling them as far as I can.

The disappointment on Lenore's face is painful but it's short-lived. The words fall on hard ice and before Lenore can gather them back up, they eat through the sludge, spitting as they fight their way into the soil below. The ice melts and the mud sprouts grasses and reeds and flowers all green and yellow and bright.

"You did it!" Lenore says. "Now the flowers can grow."

Tears prick my eyes. "I thought you wanted vegetables," I say.

Or maybe I just think I say it because there's a pain growing in my chest and I can't imagine speaking anything ever again. Agony spreads, pushes. I fight for air but with every breath, the pain expands and my ribs threaten to crack.

"Breathe small, Sessa," a quiet voice says. "Breathe small or the stone will win."

The dream fades and my eyes open. Hanging over me is the girl. The girl Winter saved.

"No, don't move," she says. "Shyne had a stone placed on your chest. To keep you still."

I try to lift my arms, but they're pinned as well, rocks weighing my palms. And my legs, I think. I can't see past the remarkably dense stone sitting on my chest.

"Shyne's very good with stones," the girl says. "With their weight. He chooses the rocks carefully. This one, yes. That one, no." She leans closer. "If you lay still, they will not break your bones."

Half the girl's face is cast in shadow, flames flickering across the other half, the stone half. They're burning twyl nearby—I can smell it, the flames warming my right side, turning the rock weighing down my chest luminous. Still, my fingers are numb. Winter's touch or lack of circulation, I can't tell—probably both.

I wriggle my fingers, my knuckles scraping against the cave floor. That's where I am, certainly. One of the Shiv caves. The ceiling is dark, firelight climbing the walls, jagged outcroppings everywhere, stones of all colors piled by size. Water trickles, splats, and echoes off the frozen walls. A stack of metal barrels catches my attention and I understand something I didn't before.

I'd like to crack one open, look inside. But every shift, every breath feels like it could be my last. The ground beneath my hand is giving way, yielding as I grind my knuckles harder into the thawing mud. The girl squats, her knobby knees bare, her amber eyes almost liquid as she watches me work.

"You shouldn't," she says. "Shyne will be back soon."

"I'm not afraid of Shyne," I lie. But the words cost me and my lungs burn as the rock sinks deeper into my chest.

The girl presses her face even closer to my arm. "You should be," she says. "He was not happy to see you with a Shiv traitor."

My thoughts whirl before they land on her meaning.

"Where's Kyn?" I regret the question as soon as it's crossed my lips. Words are expensive—every one costs me a breath.

"The traitor? Just there," she says, jerking her head to somewhere beyond the flame. "Let's not wake him. Small breaths are easier when you're sleeping. He's strong. It took seven men to hold him down. In the end, Shyne had to knock him out to place the stones."

I arch my palm, grind my thumb. "Where are the others?"

"Winter swallowed the Kerce smuggler and his strongwoman. We let her have them."

There's no use worrying about Mars. He can handle himself where Winter is concerned, but I have to get out of here. If I can't get back to Mars—if we can't get back to the Sylver Dragon—there's no knowing what will happen to Lenore.

"Most Kerce are not welcome here. Only you, Sessa."

"Why—" My throat catches and I start again. "Why do you call me that?"

Her eyes widen. "It's what your friend called you. The tall woman with the guns. Is that not your name?" She rolls back on her heels. "Maybe it's not. Shyne calls me Little Fox and that is not my name. You've made him very angry."

"You're not speaking Shiv." The words are nothing but a whisper.

"Shyne teaches me lots of things. Mostly I like to learn about the stones."

Dark spots fill the corners of my vision. I try to blink them away but they simply shift and transform, a thousand walking sticks bumping into one another.

"Shyne?" I ask, my voice scratching, my skin tearing as I rub my hand against the ground. My lungs are on fire, the stone heavier with every word, with every breath.

"He'll be here soon." The girl is little more than a dark outline now and I can't tell if the fire is dimming or if it's the lack of oxygen reaching my brain. Her shadow reaches out and removes something rigid cutting at my wrist.

"I told you to stay still," she says. "Now you're bleeding."

But the space the rock left behind is a gift. I can almost tilt my palm. I'd thank her, but there's no air left for that.

There doesn't seem to be any air left in the world.

And I'm tumbling into darkness.

I yank my hand hard and fast. Pain shoots down my shoulder and explodes across my chest as the massive rock presses me deeper into the mud. I can't breathe, but my hand is free.

And then it's not. Spot by spot, my vision starts to surface. Everything's still gray and shadowed and I have to blink the tears away before I realize the girl is standing over me now, her bare foot pinning my forearm.

"You have to talk to Shyne first," she says, her words strange and meaningless when all I want is air. I think to pull my arm away—she can't weigh sixty pounds—but there's only enough strength to gasp, an action I lament. The last crumbs of breath are forced out of my lungs in a raspy choke and though I can feel the damp air licking my lips, there is no room for it inside my chest.

A blink and the girl's shadow lifts a spindly arm. There's something there—in her hand.

"Don't be mad, Sessa. You'll breathe easier this way."

She shifts and in the flickering light I see it's a stone. Amber like her eyes, like the shimmering crescent moon covering half her face.

There's a protest on the tip of my tongue, but the girl's shadow swoops down before it's fully formed and, with a crack that must split my skull wide, the world goes dark.

*

I wake to the sound of wheezing. My chest burns so fiercely I think the sound is mine—but as the cave swims into focus, I realize I'm not alone.

New shadows shift throughout the cave, long and lean. The stretched forms of men dance across the walls and floor. I try to count them, but my head aches and I cannot keep hold of the images for long.

Frigid mud splashes onto my cheek as someone moves close. A walking stick pierces the ground before my eyes.

Shyne.

"Crysel has been here, I see," he says. "She thinks herself clever, but she never clears away her footprints. She's as bad as the little foxes who rob our fish houses."

The girl has a name now. Crysel. It's a beautiful name for such a miserable child.

"She leaves half prints, see? All toes, no heels. It's how I found her that day. But I was slow, my legs aren't what they used to be. The rig almost devoured her."

The rig did almost devour her, but it was her own fault. She should not have been in the road. I don't dare speak though, the pain still fresh in my mind.

More wheezing from somewhere beyond the fire, but my attention is settled irrevocably on Shyne's knotted fingers. They tap slowly, one after the other, on the rock pressing on my chest. Every tap is a hammer chiseling fear into my rib cage.

"I would like to have this stone removed," he says. "So we can talk. But you must promise me something."

He raises his brows and suddenly he reminds me of Drypp, wanting a confession for the missing bottle of rum. But I can say nothing—confess to nothing—pinned this way.

I attempt to raise my own brows. To what success, I cannot say. My eyes are watering, stinging, closing.

"You must not use the Kerce language here in our home," he says. "You must not use your magic."

I don't even have the energy to move my head. To nod or decline. A tear leaks from the corner of my eye and races down my temple and into my ear.

"You must not."

Two men flank him now, their silhouettes blurred and hazy. My eyes flutter and I drift. Something changes then, relief and pain flooding my lungs in equal measure.

I breathe deep but it hurts—the air like gravel as it scrapes its way home. It sets me coughing.

"Slowly, slowly," Shyne says. "Give your lungs time to remember what it's like to be full."

I gasp and spit and wheeze, my chest burning, blood on my tongue, a cold sweat breaking out across my neck.

"You will not call for Winter. Not here."

He's waiting. Waiting for an answer that will steal the little air in my lungs. I'm reluctant to give it, to let him win, but he seems content to wait forever.

"I won't . . . I don't call her."

A sound, deep and primal, curdles in his chest. "But Winter calls to you." He crouches at my head and lifts the stones from my hands. "I'm going to have my men leave the ones on your legs. Just for now. I don't want you moving too much."

I want to sit up, I want to kick out, but I'm so grateful to have air again, I do nothing to jeopardize the small relief I've been given. My hands tremble and a chill clenches my stomach tight. My parka lays open but I've no strength to wrap my arms around myself.

The wheezing is heavy now, desperate. Shyne pulls his walking stick from the dirt and strides over to a body on the opposite side of the fire. The shadows shift and I see Kyn, eyes bulging, veins taut in his neck.

"Sylvi," he gasps.

The rock on his chest is much larger than the one I had on mine and, atop it, perched like a finch too stupid to seek warmer skies, sits Crysel.

"Get off him," I say.

"He just needs to sleep." The stubborn tilt of her chin is familiar. It's me at that age. Not mean, but brash. It's terrifying on her sweet face.

Shyne kicks the bottom of his walking stick, hard, and it connects with Kyn's temple. His eyes shut and his head lolls and the wheezing falls to silence.

Crysel leans forward, peering into Kyn's face. "He breathes, Sessa. He will be all right."

But every breath is a fight. They rattle and hiss as his lungs work to survive.

"Get off," I gasp, pleading with the girl. "Get off. Please."

"His rocks are for more than confinement," Shyne says, but Crysel slinks off the stone and disappears into the shadows.

Shyne backs slowly toward the cave wall, settling onto an outcropping of stone. The fire plays off his face, shadows falling into the age lines cut there, deepening them until he looks so like the rock behind him, it's only the sheen of his eyes that tells me he's man and not stone.

"Do you know why the Ranger was here that day? The man they call Leff?"

"I think so." The words send me into a coughing fit that burns my throat and jabs at my insides. My ribs are cracked, I'm sure of it, but there's nothing resembling remorse on Shyne's face.

He picks at his fingers while I recover. I take my time, my mind spinning again with the revelation. "The barrels," I say, choking on the words. "Jymy had the same barrels in his pickup. It's acid, isn't it? What's it—" But I'm coughing again, blood on my tongue.

"What's it called? I couldn't say. But the Ranger brings it to us in bulk when he can. Mixed with kol, the effect is remarkable."

Jymy won't be bringing them anything ever again, but I know better than to tell him that.

"It eats through the tires," I say, finally able to breathe and speak at the same time. I take another breath. This one as deep as I can manage. "Then Jymy and his boys show up and collect a hefty fee for rescuing the poor stupid riggers."

Shyne's eyes sparkle and I know I'm right. "They used to, yes. But the trick worked so well, it's been some time since any real effort was made to cross the pass. Only you. And your tires are not the same."

I close my eyes, walk my fingers down each of my ribs, wincing with every touch. "What do you get out of it? The Shiv."

"Peace," he says. "And the assurance that our slopes will not be plundered for twyl."

My ribs are broken, I'm sure of it. At least two. Panic rises in my chest at the thought of how desperately the injury will slow us. I push back the tears and clear my throat. "The Rangers keep the farmers away?"

"Winter, the Rangers, rumors of dark magic and crazed savages. Oh yes. We know what is said about us." A one-shouldered shrug. "We will be what we have to be to ensure Begynd's Pool is not desecrated and the Shiv people survive to see his rebirth."

Rebirth? I sit up, though this too is a fight. The fire is roaring now, popping and snapping, the stench of twyl spiraling up and through a chimney hole high above. Winter's white light is visible just beyond. It strengthens me to see her again, gives me hope.

"Do you want to know why I let you pass time and again?"

Aside from whatever chemical they're using on the tires, I've never known them to wield anything but bows and rock pulled from the mountain. It would take much more than either to stop the Dragon's tank tread.

"Could you have stopped me?"

He doesn't answer and I realize that perhaps he could have. With the help of the Rangers. Their pickups are armed, the men too. If he had wanted to, perhaps he could have found a way to stop the largest, most powerful rig in the Kol Mountains. It hardly matters.

"I only care that you let me pass now." I can't tear my eyes away from Kyn. The firelight playing across his face, the smears of dirt and agony.

"I cannot let you go," he says.

"I have no desire to take your twyl. And I won't tell a soul about your arrangement with the Rangers. If you ask it of me, I'll stay clear of the pass from this day forward. I will do anything you want, but if you kill me—"

"I will not kill you."

Relief pricks my eyes and nose. I sniff it away. "Because of Crysel?"

He rolls his walking stick back and forth between his palms. "Others would not have been able to do what you did."

"Perhaps the girl has a friend in Winter."

"Winter has long hated the Shiv. My daughter is no exception. It was your magic that built that wall. Your magic that stopped the Ranger's rig."

A groan echoes off the walls and I twist my neck to see Kyn. He fights to lift his head, but it's no use. His eyes flutter open and then closed. His chest rattles and the rock sinks lower into his rib cage.

"I'm begging you to let us pass. Another girl's life is in danger."

His brow lifts. "If you insist on saving Shiv Island one soul at a time, it will take far too long. We don't have that kind of time."

"Please."

"There are other things that need your doing."

"I don't know what that means."

"When you do, I will let you pass."

"And my friend?" Is Kyn my friend? Hours ago I would have said no. But now, locked away with the Shiv, he's the closest thing to a friend I have.

"His sins are many. Not so many as the Kerce smuggler's but more than enough."

"What sins?"

Shyne grunts, clamps his mouth shut. The silence grows until finally I can take it no longer. I peer past Kyn's sleeping form, deep into the cave, looking for some way to escape and wishing I could see through the darkness like Winter's wolves. She's not far off. Just up that chimney. If I called, she would come. But I wonder if I could even form the word. The only Kerce words I can remember speaking were accidental, desperate compulsions.

The wall of snow. The dice. The squall at Mistress Quine's.

"I will show you the sins of Mars Dresden," Shyne says, his gaze following mine. "You should not love Winter the way you do. She has an evil heart."

"Would it surprise you to know that you and Mars agree on something?"

"Does it surprise you?"

It does, actually, but I let silence be my answer.

"It shouldn't. We are victims of the same curse."

He nods at the men hovering by the fire. They stand and, each of them hefting one side of the flat rock, they lift it from my thighs. My legs have no feeling and I have to be helped to stand. Hands under my arms and around my waist, lifting, tugging. It's more than I've let any man do and even in my wretched state, I'm tempted to fight them off.

"Take it," Shyne says, offering me his walking stick. "Take it."

He nods at the men and they release me. I grab for the stick, nothing but my own stubbornness keeping me upright.

Shyne stalks toward the shadows in the far corner of the cave, but I don't follow. Instead, I limp to Kyn's side, and though my thighs scream with the effort, I crouch near his shoulder.

"He comes too," I say.

"*He* is a traitor."

"I need him," I lie. "I can't save my friend without him."

"We've discussed your needs," Shyne says. "There are other things to be said now."

I pull myself upright, look him in the eye. "Move these rocks and you can tell me of Mars's sins. And Kyn's. You can tell me of Winter's. Whatever it is you have to say, I will listen. But only if you let him up."

My legs tremble but I stand firm.

"I will hold you to your promise," Shyne says, the words a threat.

I clear my throat, nod.

His eyes slide away and he jerks his head, a curt movement that brings two men hovering near the fire closer. They crouch next to Kyn and lift the stone from his chest. An action that sends Kyn into a coughing fit. I move back to give him space while the other stones are removed.

"Sylvi?" he rasps.

Shyne's men reach down to help him up, but Kyn's having none of it. He kicks out a leg, knocking the first man into the wall. The second has a shiv pulled before Kyn can swing his body around, but I'm impressed. I can barely walk, much less fight. A coughing fit swallows Kyn whole and he drops to his knees. Shyne clicks his tongue and the men back away.

"It's OK, Kyn. We're off to a history lesson." There's a plea in my voice, a tremor I wish I could steady. "You like history?" I offer him the bottom of Shyne's walking stick and for a moment I'm not sure he'll take it. He's disoriented and fighting for every breath. But he's going to have to get it together. I need him to get it together.

He blinks up at me, muddy tears streaming down his face, and with a brute sort of effort, he reaches out and wraps his hands around the walking stick. I hold it as steady as I can while he pulls himself upright, great, shuddering breaths keeping him off-kilter.

"You OK?" he asks me, watching Shyne from beneath hooded eyes.

"Never better."

Shyne turns his back on us and trudges toward a corner of the cave the firelight has left in shadow.

"Thank you," he whispers. "They meant to kill me, I think."

"They still mean to. We have to get out of here."

Shyne scoops up a stone and knocks it against the cave wall. Rocks shift and a massive archway appears. Winter floods through the gap. She wraps my calves and my thighs, her touch waking me, dulling the pain. I stand taller.

"Stay close," I say, as we follow Shyne out into the snow.

But Kyn's eyes are on the valley floor below. On the sprawling lake of ice known as the Desolation.

"Begynd's Fount," he says. "It flows."

Somewhere deep beneath the ice, near its center, a ribbon of molten sylver spreads.

"How long has it been, Traitor, since you've paid your respects?" Shyne asks.

"I've only ever heard stories," Kyn says.

How curious it is that the Majority's desperation to wash away history correlates so completely with the Shiv and Kerce need to pass theirs down. Threats of punishment have not stopped the telling.

"But the fount was stoppered hundreds of years ago, I thought. Frozen solid."

"What stories have you heard?" Shyne asks.

"Rumors," Kyn says. "Nonsense. Magic and ice and a prince bent on revenge."

"None of it is nonsense," Shyne says, turning, starting up a rough-cut trail on the mountainside. He moves slowly without his walking stick.

"A queen," I whisper to Kyn.

"What?"

"It was the queen who wanted revenge."

Kyn shakes his head slowly, the reflection off the snow brightening his dark eyes.

"Half of the stories can't be true," he says, "but there's enough evidence on Layce to prove the island wasn't always covered in ice. Something happened. Something stoppered Begynd."

A smile creeps into my voice. "You believe in Begynd?"

"You don't?"

"The creator of the Shiv? The great god who cut a people from the rock and took up his throne in the valley?"

"I know it sounds . . ." Kyn stops, looks me in the eye. "I'm not a zealot, but I can read the mountain as well as anyone. Winter came after centuries of light and heat. If it wasn't Begynd . . . what do you think happened?"

"It doesn't matter," I say, taking another step, pulling him with me. "We survived. We move forward."

"Not everyone survived." Shyne whips around, his voice

calling down to us. "Shiv families are buried beneath that ice. Because they tried to help the Kerce. All of them, buried because of the selfish ambitions of a queen."

"I told you it was the queen," I mutter.

"History matters. What happened here matters. It mattered then," Shyne continues, his hand clutching the gold medallion hanging around his neck. "It matters now."

"Why?" I shout, my voice ringing off the ice. "All the past does is keep your people hiding in the mountain, staring at a mass grave."

"We hide because our gifts are exploited by those who took our land. We stare at the grave to remember. We remember because those buried beneath the ice belong to us."

Shyne turns and continues up the incline, rage still fogging the air where his words seared the cold. He doesn't stop until he reaches the cave opening above.

It takes considerable effort for Kyn and me to make the climb. Shyne lingers, staring out over the Desolation, exhaustion in the slope of his shoulders, the sway of his back. *This* is what's killing the Shiv. Their refusal to let the past be the past. With their knowledge of the mountains and their resistance to Winter's chill, they have considerable advantage over the Majority. They'll never wield it though—not while they dedicate their lives to watching the dead.

"Look," Shyne says.

"Why?" I ask, his exhaustion the catching kind.

"Because it happened. Because looking the past in the eye is the respectful thing to do."

"Look at it, Sylvi," Kyn says, his voice all awe and childish fealty. "How can you not believe in Begynd?"

Despite the pain he's in, the sight of the Desolation smooths the creases in his brow, brightens the shadows under his eyes. Shaking the tension from my own shoulders, I turn and look, half wishing I could see what he sees.

There's no denying the power of the Desolation. I've driven past it dozens of times, but from up here, there's a sad sort of gloom that lingers over the site.

"How could I not believe in a creator powerful enough to carve a people out of stone?" I ask. "Perhaps I'm not the one who needs to look. The Desolation itself proves Begynd is not who you claim he is. *If* he exists, he's frozen solid. Defeated by Winter. How many gods would allow a winter spirit to best them?"

I turn to meet Kyn's gaze, but he's looking over my head to Shyne. "How long has the fount flowed beneath the ice?" he whispers.

Shyne and I answer at the same time.

"Always," I say.

"Seventeen Rymes," Shyne says, his voice stronger than mine. "What is it they teach the Shiv traitors in Dris Mora?"

"They don't know about the fount," Kyn answers, and then with conviction: "I didn't know it was flowing again."

"Strange, don't you think? Considering the company you keep."

"Why do you say that?"

"The smuggler has known about the flow for some time."

Kyn swallows.

"And you," Shyne asks, tilting that furious chin toward me. "What does the kol smuggler want from you?"

"I'm just the driver," I say, trying to order my thoughts.

"Mars Dresden is a smuggler," Shyne says. "He trades one good for another. He wants something from you."

I shrug. "My rig is unique. Without it, he can't get where he's going."

The corners of Shyne's lips pull down so far they hang like fangs over his chin. "No," he says. "That's not what he wants." He grabs the top of the staff and gives it a tug. "Come."

Kyn and I stumble after him, but not into the warmth of the cave. We're climbing higher.

"Kyn?" I ask, our feet shuffling like a strange four-legged creature, our hands alternating on the pole—his, mine, his, mine. There's an etching in the stone on one of his knuckles. I hadn't noticed it before. "Do you trust Mars to do the right thing?"

His hands tighten on the walking stick and his pace quickens. I stumble in my effort to keep up.

"Mars is my best friend. I've known him for ten years and in a little more than ten words, a half-naked man has destroyed everything I thought I knew about him."

My heart falters. "But Lenore? He'll help me get her back, won't he?"

Kyn's eyes close. He's tired. Hurting.

"Kyn?"

"Mars won't leave us behind, Sylvi. He needs you."

"He needs my rig."

He stops and turns his face to mine, his russet eyes catching the light, the stone on his cheekbone lifting as he narrows them.

"No," he says. "He needs you."

CHAPTER 8

I'VE NEVER SEEN SO MUCH TWYL. LENORE would faint dead away. She's been trying to perfect a twyl gum recipe that lasts longer than the Majority's, but there's a lot of trying and failing involved and she burns through the flowers quickly. Her meager planters could never produce a crop equal to this.

Here, the blue blossoms push willfully through the snow, a long band of thick clumps that run the length of the mountainside next to my ear. The ledge is so thin, the cliffside so steep, my face and shoulder press deep into the sticky leaves as we trudge forward. Sap smears my face and grabs at my hair, but the very real threat of a drop keeps me wading through them.

Kyn insisted I take the walking stick when the trail shriveled and we were forced into a single row. My legs are feeling better now, probably better than his, given Winter's help. She's wrapping my legs and waist tight, straightening my back, her cold fingers keeping me alert.

A quick glance behind me and I see Kyn's deep in the twyl as well, grasping at the deeply rooted plants, pulling himself along. His curls are damp and pressed to his forehead, his hands shaking. Air whistles through his teeth; his jaw is clenched so tight the joints bulge beneath his ears. Another step and he stumbles. His fingers catch my shoulder as he grabs at the twyl. I throw myself back against the wall, my heart pounding.

"Take the stick," I say.

He sucks air through his clenched teeth and rests his head against the stone wall. "I'm all right."

"You look like hell. Take the stick."

"My ribs are broken, little ice witch. Not my legs. I can walk."

"I'll just leave it here then." I prop the stick against the cliff face and continue forward. It's a minute before I hear his feet dragging behind me, the dull thud of the stick leading the way.

"Your ribs aren't broken," he says. "Why is that, you think?"

"They are," I say, almost offended, the pain I felt in the cave flashing a dark memory. But my hand slides up, moves slowly over my rib cage and I know they're not. Nothing about my body is broken. Sore, yes. Tired, certainly. But Winter's done something for me she hasn't done for Kyn.

"Believing her lies is one thing, snowflake. Lying to yourself is something else altogether."

I flick my cheek at him and push forward, leaving him dragging behind. I'm not through walking, not through putting distance between Kyn and myself, but Shyne's stopped in the middle of the trail, his hunched body blocking my way.

"Here," he grunts, ducking into a hole set so deep behind the twyl I would have missed it entirely if I'd been here on my own.

I follow, ignoring Winter's cautions. She's grown loud as my feet have sped along the cliff-high trail.

NO, she says. **NOT HERE.**

No good has ever come from ignoring Winter's pleas, but Kyn's behind me now, gently nudging me forward with the rod. I kick at it and duck inside after Shyne.

Winter is forgotten entirely when I see what's before me.

The cave is full of Shiv, their mingled stone and flesh bodies a mosaic unlike anything I've seen outside the paintings in Mystra Dyfan's rooms. Men, women, children—hundreds of souls, pressed tightly together. Their hands are clasped, their faces drawn, their collective gaze directed at the center of the large space. I've never seen such unity and, as an outsider, I take no comfort in it. It's suffocating.

It's what I imagine a fox might feel submerged beneath the thawing mountain streams of Blys. Bluefin herring and striped cod swimming, breathing, thriving—drawing life from a realm made just for them.

Life teems, but all the fox can do is drown.

I take a great, shuddering breath just to prove I can.

All the energy in the room is directed at a man infinitely older than Shyne. White light drops through another opening high above, turning his grim form vaporous. He's more stone than flesh, his rock gray and cobbled like the streets down in the Stack. It covers most of his torso and arms, pebbles spread like age spots across his face. He's lying on a bed of animal pelts. One on top of the other, so tall Shyne does not have to bend as he approaches.

A fire, low and smoldering, sits not far from the bed. Burning twyl fills the air, making the space feel smaller than it is. A cooking stone has been placed over the flames, water gurgling from a vessel on top. Three women tend to the old man. Crysel sits next to him on the pelt bed, his hand held tightly in hers.

"He won't change his mind," she says to Shyne as he approaches.

The man flinches and barks a few short words. His voice is stronger than I expect; the words fly from cave wall to cave wall like the wool-feathered bats of the north. The room shifts collectively and Crysel bows her head low, murmuring words too soft for me to hear.

"I'd learn Shiv if that's all it took to shut the girl up," I whisper.

"He doesn't like them speaking the common tongue," Kyn says.

Gah, he's close. I didn't realize. But we're pinned in now, the crowd closing around us, pressing nearer to the elder.

Shyne speaks, but it's in Shiv. Low, respectful tones that tell me he holds the prostrate man in great regard. The elder's reply is not nearly as civil.

"What's he saying?" I ask.

"He wants Shyne to honor his promise," Kyn says.

"What promise?"

"Shyne's asking him to reconsider. Something about the water being tainted." Kyn leans forward and I shift so he can move closer. "Oh."

"What is it?" I ask, following his gaze, trying to understand.

"They've dug up some of the Desolation ice. See it there?" The vessel atop the flame—water hissing and spitting over the rim and onto the cooking stone. "The old man thinks it will bring him some kind of cure. He wants to drink it."

"The waters of Begynd," I say, curious.

"But Shyne says it's been cursed by Winter's magic. *It cannot offer life,* he's saying, *not until Winter is sent away can the fount flow freely.* Shyne's angry because he says the old man is the one who taught him this. Says he should know better than to look for answers in a desolate place."

The elder's eyes have yet to really open, his face balled tight as a fist.

"He says Shyne promised. He insists Shyne honor his vow."

Shyne leans in now, and I find myself doing the same. But his words are for the elder alone. There's no hope of us hearing from here.

The elder's reply is loud. No deference. No respect for the man speaking to him.

I turn to Kyn. "What—"

"He says he's not afraid of pain. Says he's the last of the Begynd Shiv. He says that if he dies, the past dies too."

Shyne chokes now, great tears spilling onto his cheeks as he appeals to the elder.

"*Father!*" Kyn translates. "*You tear at my heart with this sadness. Can you not trust us to carry the past into the future? We will not forget.*"

All around us, voices echo Shyne's words.

Like the fall of rain, their promise—a staggered chorus powerful in its simplicity.

The elder's eyes snap open, and the sight steals my breath.

"What is it?" Kyn says, as Shyne continues to argue with the old man.

"His eyes," I say. "They're sylver like . . ."

"Like yours," Kyn says.

"But without the kol."

Shyne turns toward me now, his emotions raw, unveiled. He's desperately sad, his expression so like Lenore's when I first came to Drypp's. She missed her parents in wild, brutal ways when she was young, grieved more than I ever did for Mistress Quine. Whenever her eyes took on that sadness, I knew I'd wake to find her bags gone and Drypp wandering the highway looking for her.

Escape. That's what I saw in Lenore's eyes. And it's what I see now in Shyne's.

He's looking for a way out.

I try to step back, to disappear into the crowd, but my knees buckle.

"Sylvi?" Kyn takes my hand and wraps it around the walking stick. "You OK?"

I find my legs but by the time I've pulled myself upright, Shyne has turned back to the elder. "I may have another way, Great Father."

He's speaking in the common tongue now. The Majority tongue. The room doesn't like it, but I can't tell if it's because the Shiv understand what he's saying or if it's because they don't.

"And if I have?" Shyne is asking. "If I found a way to send Winter from the island forever, would you set aside this foolish endeavor? Would you meet Begynd with joy on your face?"

A hacking cough erupts from the elder—he's laughing.

"What's he saying now?" I ask Kyn.

"It seems Shyne has been threatening to send Winter away since he was a boy. Shaking a stick at the falling snow and the ice hanging like knives from the rocks. The elder says not even the Kerce wield that kind of power."

"The Kerce," Shyne spits, again in the common tongue. It feels like rebellion, his choice of language. Like when I ran off with Mystra Dyfan's cane simply because there was no way she could catch me. "Their power is watered down. Diluted through the generations. Whatever authority they retain, they use only for gain."

More Shiv words from the elder. More anger. I can't stop staring at his eyes. I've never seen another pair that glowed like mine. Not once in seventeen Rymes.

Shyne explodes. "You've done *nothing* but think these three hundred years. White winter after white winter. Each one more terrible than the last. The answer cannot be found here in our caves or with our kin along the river. Sit him up," Shyne demands.

Crysel jerks in surprise. "Father?"

"Do it. Sit him up."

The women tending to the elder rush forward and together, with the girl, they pull him upright, adjusting the pelts, rolling furs and stacking them behind him. He protests, but all his power is in his voice. He's weak, frail. Eventually, he's propped into place, his head lolling on emaciated neck muscles.

The crowd is restless now, divided. Even in the circle of flesh and stone pressing against me, I hear divided loyalties whispered and I don't need to understand their language to understand their debate.

Is the elder to be heeded? Or is it Shyne?

"Hear me," Shyne says, spinning, facing his kin. "All of you, hear me. Remember the stories your mother told you at the evening meal, the histories your father made you recite as you sharpened your shivs. Remember, please, the devastation wrought by the Kerce when our people rushed to their aid. When we pulled their kol-addled bodies from the sea and led them to the healing waters of Begynd. Remember, please, that their queen had two children. The Prince and another child—"

"Buried," the elder growls. He's switched to the common tongue now. To force Shyne to hear him, maybe. Whatever his reason, he's shocked the cave into silence. "I saw the babe go under myself, in the arms of a Shiv woman—a compassionate heart who'd forsaken her own safety to tend the laboring queen. Dead because of kindness. Dead because of compassion. Dead because she ministered to a queen poisoned by Winter."

LIES! I NEVER KNEW THEIR QUEEN! Winter's voice is loud. So loud I look around to see if the Shiv nearby hear her protest. But they're held captive by the scene playing out before them. Even Kyn, his brow furrowed, his mouth slightly open.

"The babe did go under, yes!" Shyne argues. "Like so many of our own. But just hours before, the child had been born in the waters of Begynd. Like you, Great Father. That alone would give her length of days."

"She's buried," the elder snarls. "The least of all the living souls beneath the ice."

Shyne's dark eyes flash. "What if she's not? What if the Desolation gave her up?"

The elder falls silent as the crowd begins to murmur.

"What if she's here?" Shyne continues, his body opening up, turning toward me. "What if she could send Winter away?"

"Sessa?" Crysel says, her mouth dropping into a small round circle. She climbs off the bed and scampers across the cave toward me.

I try to step back, but I meet only elbows and knees. And then she's there, her hand in mine. The little brat's pulling me. I grip the walking stick fiercely with one hand and fight to tug the other from hers. I could do it, I realize. Her child fingers are strong, but I'm stronger. I could free myself and make a run for it. I wonder how far I could get before—

Crysel yanks my wrist and I jerk forward, taking Kyn and the walking stick with me. Kyn cries out in pain and crashes against my back. I curse and help him stand, pressing the stick into his hands.

"You got it?" I ask. "You got it?"

He nods, his eyes pinched shut. And then the crowd closes over him and Crysel's dragging me toward Shyne, something like fear building in my chest.

We're just steps from the pelt bed now, Winter falling slowly through the crevice overhead. I breathe her in, let her cold wake my aching body.

"Seventeen white winters have passed," Shyne says, "since the Desolation shook. Do you remember, Great Father?"

"Three hundred and twenty-five white winters I've survived, young Shyne. I forget nothing."

"The mountain skittered. It was the first time you'd known it to do such a thing. Remember how shaken you were. How shaken we all were." The cave buzzes. They know the story. "Our own stone remembrances toppled. We had to rebuild. So you sent me, Great Father. You sent me to the Desolation. You sent me to investigate. A flow of light had broken free, deep beneath the surface. Dove foxes, a pair of them, were huddled on the ice. As curious about the change as we were. Or so I thought."

He sees me now, the elder. "Who are you?"

I look to Shyne.

"Answer him."

"My name is Sylvi."

"She is called Sylver Quine," Shyne says, my answer somehow lacking.

The elder's face puckers. "Quine? The whore of Hex Landing had a daughter?"

"It happens," I say.

"Come closer."

I'm reluctant, but Crysel's behind me now, pushing on my back—little rodent—and I'm shoved up to the bed. The elder's wrinkled hand closes around my wrist, papery and cold.

"Your eyes," he says, squinting at me. "How?"

"How did you get yours?" I ask.

His head sways and then steadies, his gaze never leaving mine. "I was born into the waters of Begynd, Sylver Quine. It is *his* light you see."

A chill races my scalp, my spine. Asking about the past is dangerous, a knife to your most vulnerable parts, and I knew better.

HE'S MAD, Winter whispers. HIS MIND GONE WITH HIS YOUTH.

"You were born in the Desolation?" I ask the old man. "And is that what you think of me?"

He glares from beneath stone brows. "I do not know what to think of you."

Shyne turns to the crowd with a flourish, lifting his arms and raising his voice. "The Kerce queen had two children," he says. There's something of victory in his tone now and it scares me. "The youngest was born here, on Shiv Island after the Kerce ship was lost at sea. In the healing waters of Begynd the queen labored and gave birth. But she had already struck a bargain with Winter and when she plunged the island into a deep freeze, the babe and her Shiv nurse were among those swallowed by the ice. It's the story we all know. The story we tell our children. The young prince had a sister."

"You're a fool, Shyne," the elder says, shaking his head. "Beneath the ice, the child is dead, like all the others."

"Begynd's magic is strong. It was his magic that cut our people from the mountain. His magic that filled a desolate valley with life. His magic that still stirs our blood hot and vibrant within us. It is how we know he will one day shake off the bondage of the ice and dwell with his people once again." He's breathless, gasping. "Begynd's magic is the magic of new beginnings. If the souls buried beneath the ice are living souls—as you've taught us these many, many years—it is not impossible to think Begynd would answer our prayers by shaking the ice and giving us a savior from among them. And if that savior were Kerce, would that not be very like Begynd? That such a salvation would repay the goodwill we once offered their queen and her people."

He looks at me now and I almost laugh. Is this what Mars believes too? That I am the long-dead child of the Kerce queen? That it's Begynd's magic shining from behind my eyes?

"Living souls are not the same as living bodies, Shyne. You blaspheme by claiming such." The elder's eyes find me again, rest on my face with a question I've no problem answering.

"I'm with you, sir," I say, still fighting the hilarity building in my chest. "I'm no one's savior."

"You saved me," Crysel chimes.

"I could have killed you," I say over my shoulder. "Want me to try again?"

"Where *did you* come from?" the elder asks, his grip tightening on my wrist.

I fight every urge I have to be free of him. Of all the lunatics I've met in the past two days, this one might be on my side. And I could use someone on my side. "The outpost at Whistletop. I live over the tavern there."

"The tavern?"

"I'm a rig driver. That's all."

"No," he says, his lips soured. "You come from somewhere else. Somewhere across the sea. I smell the Paradyian sun on your skin." It's an accusation, something that does not please him.

"I've never been off the island."

"Mistress Quine died years ago," he says. I don't ask him how he knows this—the story made its way through the surrounding mountain settlements. The bloodied body. The shattered windows. The missing child. Though I am surprised the tale made it as far as High Pass. "Who raised you?"

"A widower named Cornelius Drypp—he owned a tavern in Whistletop." Thoughts of the tavern, warm and bright, thoughts of Drypp wrapping Lenore and me in heated blankets after a day of skating on the ice, assault me, make me desperate. "His granddaughter, Lenore, was my closest friend—is my closest friend. She's like my sister and she's been . . . taken." It's true, isn't it? Lenore never would have gone on her own. "I need safe passage across the Shiv Road so I can find her. Please."

His face is shriveled now, his eyes sharp and narrowed. He presses his thumb to my eyebrow and lifts.

"Don't," I say, attempting to pull away. But there are too many hands pushing and shoving, too many bodies holding me still. My chest rises and falls, and my eye waters as I fight to close it against his grip.

"Kol and light," he says.

"You can be certain she inherited neither from Mistress Quine," Shyne says.

After another long moment, the elder releases my brow and his hand cups my chin softly. His gentle touch is worse than his grip, but this time he lets me pull away.

"Foxes are not interested in light," the elder says. "In the depths of white winter, when rodents are scarce, foxes are interested in only one thing: a ready meal."

"They licked at her wounds," Shyne says. "Nothing more. They scattered at my approach and left behind, I found—"

"The newborn daughter of the Kerce queen," the elder says, falling back on the pelts, a sickening strain of revelation in his voice.

Now I do laugh. It's ridiculous. Three hundred and twenty-five Rymes, he said. It's not possible.

"Winter serves her," Shyne says. "I've seen it myself."

"I had a Kerce tutor," I say. "That's all you've seen. Shyne, please, you're misinterpreting what you saw the other day in the pass. I do not speak the language of Winter. Winter saved the girl of her own accord—she's not the evil power you make her out to be, and I do not order her to do my bidding. I am not some ice-resurrected daughter of a dead queen."

"And what if you are?" Shyne says. "What if it is your duty to command Winter?"

I laugh, but he scowls. He genuinely expects me to answer.

"That's ridiculous . . ."

"What if it is your duty?" he demands.

"Winter has always been good to me. I could never send her away."

The cave is silent, so silent I wonder if they can all hear Winter purring in my chest.

"And why do you think that is?" Shyne asks, my own desperation radiating from his eyes.

I can't have this conversation. Not here. Not when these people think I'm something I'm not.

I look to the old man for help. It's not clear who's in charge—who the cave full of Shiv will side with—but he's the best chance I have to get free.

"How old are you really?" I ask him.

He clears his throat—or attempts to. The rattle tells me he's been trying to clear it for years. "I do not know."

"Did your mother not tell you the date of your birth?"

"We lived differently in the days of Begynd, on the shores of the great pool. I had many mothers. Many fathers. Begynd provided for us all."

"What say you, Great Father?" Shyne says. "Will you give me time with this reluctant royal? If she can send Winter fleeing from Shiv Island, the fount will flow freely again, ridding itself of the kol and magic that have long tainted Begynd's Pool. A little patience and you can bathe in its healing waters. A little patience and the living souls buried beneath it can sit at your feet and hear you tell of all that's happened while they slept."

The elder's eyes haven't left my face. He's searching it, searching me, for something. Something I know he will not find.

"She doesn't believe," the elder says.

Shyne clicks his tongue at me. "She will."

"I won't. It's ridiculous. Your stories are myths. Legends. Every people has them."

The snapping teeth around me, the looks on their faces. I've offended them. Something I cannot afford to do.

"They are *histories*," the elder says.

My hands fly up in defense. "You've lived a long time. There's no arguing that. You're wise, I am sure of it. But you weren't born in the Pool of Begynd hundreds and hundreds of years ago. And neither was I. I won't believe such an impossible thing."

A gasp ripples around the cave.

"Then we've something in common," the elder says. "I look at you and I hear Shyne's story and it is I who does not believe. You will not save our people. You cannot. Even if you are everything Shyne believes, you do not hate what Winter has done. You do not hate her." He reaches out and grabs at my open coat, his brittle nails scraping my skin. "And you should."

I'm so tired of being told what I should and should not do. Who and what I should hate.

"It is not Winter's fault your histories cast her as the villain. If you think I'd ever banish a spirit that's only ever watched out for me, you're wrong." I point at Shyne. "He's wrong."

"He's been wrong before." The elder lets his head fall back onto the pelts. "Bring it to me, Shyne. The water of Begynd. I will not wait on this one."

"Great Father, I beg of you. Winter has worked hard to befriend her. If I had some time—"

"It is I who need time! The life in my blood is freezing solid. I cannot wait any longer." He reaches a shaking hand up and cups Crysel's cheek. "Once again you'll have to do for me what your father will not. Bring me the water, child. Quickly."

She avoids Shyne's gaze and pushes toward the fire where the vessel bubbles fiercely. She grabs a scrap of fur from the end of the bed and wraps both her hands before lifting the bowl and removing it from the heating stone.

Another bowl is brought, this one larger and full of snow. Crysel sets her vessel into the snow and then takes both bowls in her tiny hands. The cave has gone quiet, quieter than should be possible for so many people. I feel their eyes on me, wandering my back, and I realize how out of place I am here.

Whatever this moment is, I should not be part of it. I am an intruder. An imposter. Though it was not by choice, I find my own presence a shameful thing and I back into the crowd. They let me go. No one is watching me now. I don't realize I'm shaking until Kyn takes my hand and wraps it around the walking stick.

"He's insane," I whisper, mostly to say it out loud. "To believe I'm the child of some ancient queen."

I expect a mocking reply from Kyn. A joke. A laugh. Something. I turn to see if he's still there, if he's heard me, and find I'm surprised at how well he blends in to those around him. Not just the stone on his skin, but the look on his face as he watches the scene unfold before us. The irritation my own presence seems to cause him.

"He's insane," I repeat again, louder, needing him to see me.

"Maybe," Kyn says. But he shifts to look past me, and I decide it's not so big a thing to let him down. To let any of them down. They are nothing to me. Shyne and Crysel. Kyn and Hyla and Mars. Kidnappers and criminals, all of them.

Crysel withdraws the smaller bowl from the snow now, dips a thin finger into the liquid. Satisfied, she turns back toward the old man. But Shyne is in her way.

"Excuse me, Father," she says.

It's painful for Shyne to move, to give the child room to pass—I can see it in the lines of his face, in the rigid set of his bones, in the burden he carries on his aging shoulders. But he steps aside and allows her to slide between him and the bed of furs.

Crysel lifts the vessel and closes her eyes. She begins to speak—a prayer maybe. The other Shiv join in—their words jagged and rough and entirely Shiv—their supplication bouncing off the walls, pummeling my ears. Thank Winter, it's short. The voices fall away and Crysel offers the vessel to the man they call Great Father.

He drinks.

And he changes.

CHAPTER 9

THE COLLECTIVE GASP IS SO LOUD THE CAVE shudders; rock shards break free from the walls and tumble to the ground. The old man is sitting up, his gray face brightening, his sylver eyes—so like mine—shining with emotion.

"Begynd," he says, his deep voice lower still. "He heals."

Crysel drops the bowl of snow and scampers up onto the bed, wrapping her arms around the old man, around shoulders that grow thicker and stronger by the moment. My teeth rattle as I shake my head back and forth, unbelieving. Always unbelieving. What am I seeing? The melted ice of the Desolation healing a dying man? No. Surely not.

And yet.

The elder drops the empty cup and wraps his own arms around the girl, strokes her hair with steady hands. "Thank you," he says. "For the drink that may save us all."

Shyne has gone gray. His mouth gaping, his eyes wet. "I am sorry, Great Father. Sorry I didn't believe."

"But you will now," the elder says, gently pushing the girl away. "You will believe, all of you, that Begynd lives beneath the ice. That the only lasting healing in this wretched world comes from his waters. And that we, the Shiv, must see it restored."

"We have always believed that, Great Father," Shyne says. "Always."

Assent echoes all around—shock and relief and something else mingled with it.

The elder throws off his coverings and swings his legs to the floor. He's clothed in a simple shift that hangs from his waist to his knees. He stretches his limbs, muscles rippling where, moments ago, there had been only soft, weak flesh. The stone on his body shimmers like polished gems and his sylver eyes shine bright.

"Winter's magic is nothing to the power of the pool."

"Forgive me," Shyne says, bowing, stepping back, making room. "I thought Winter's magic and kol together would be too much for—"

"For Begynd? Never."

"Forgive me."

"Forgiveness is easy, and I offer it to you freely." He spreads his strengthened arms wide. "But what comes next will require—" His words are silenced by a gag that shakes his entire body.

He staggers.

"Great Father?"

His arms fold in, hands wrapping around his own throat. His mouth moves, forming words but voicing nothing.

Winter laughs. A tremor that ripples through the walls of the cave.

Shyne and Crysel, the women nearest the bed—all of them rush forward, reaching, asking, offering help in their own tongue.

The elder's face drains of color—even in the firelight it's ashen. He stumbles backward into the bed, his long fingers scratching at his chest, his throat.

"He can't breathe!" the girl cries.

"Lay him back," Shyne says, taking control, finding his own voice. "Let me—" But the elder lurches forward, stumbling, scrabbling until he's directly in front of me. I want to run from this place. To climb into my rig and disappear into the folds of Winter. The wall of people at my back keeps me where I am.

The elder's hand wraps around my arm and he pulls himself upright, stiff and tall. I try to yank my hand away, cursing and fighting against him, but the strength in his hands is merciless. Desperate.

Kyn lifts the walking stick and swings it at the old man—it strikes him once on the stone of his chest before Shyne is there, his arm raised, staying the attack.

"Don't!" he cries, grappling with Kyn for the stick.

The elder's chin, which had been resting on his chest, tips up, and as his mouth continues to search for air, his eyes change. The transformation renders me completely still. All around, the gasps turn to whispers, to cries.

"The kol," Shyne says, fighting to pry the elder's hands off me. "Begynd on High."

The elder's eyes are black now. Solid black. But for a moment there, as the kol emerged, they were so like mine I wanted to dig my eyes from their sockets and fling them into the sea.

"I tried to tell him," Shyne weeps. "I tried."

"Get him off her!" Kyn cries, raising the staff over Shyne's head. "Do it! Or I will!"

Flakes of ice appear on the elder. First his neck, and then his face and chest—the ice spreading like a rash up and down his body. His legs stiffen. His knees pop.

The crowd backs away, clenching at one another. Sobs and shouts sound all around.

"Sylvi!" Kyn yells. "Your arm!"

I curse, yank my arm harder now, feel the flesh tear and the bone bruise as the elder grips more fiercely. But I have to get my arm away—the ice is spreading, flaky flowers climbing onto my skin, up my arm.

The elder—and he does look old again, wrinkled and gray, diseased even with the blue chill blossoming all over his flesh—is turning to ice.

Kyn pushes Crysel aside. When she'd gotten so close, I can't say. Everything is happening too fast. I'm aware of Shyne reaching up, trying to stop the blow from crashing down. Aware of the crowd around us, backing away from the swing of the staff. Aware acutely of Crysel's piercing scream.

And then the stick comes down on the elder's arm.

The damn thing splinters.

The elder's black eyes shimmer at me and then fade—fast, fast. One minute they're dark as kol and the next, they're as sylver as the ribbon of liquid slipping beneath the ice of the Desolation.

Kyn cracks the walking stick against the ground; the splintered end shatters and breaks off.

"Back up," he says, forceful, commanding. "All of you!"

Only Shyne refuses, stepping between Kyn and the elder. "You mustn't."

Ice spreads past my elbow—I feel it trying to claw its way inside my skin. "Kyn!"

Kyn jabs the walking stick at its owner, striking Shyne in the mouth. Bloodied, he stumbles back and Kyn swings the stick in a gigantic arc, putting the full weight of his stone biceps and back into the effort. It connects.

The elder's hand shatters, ice freckling my cheeks, slicing my lip. My arm is broken, I'm sure. With my other hand I reach for my knives, but they're gone. I cradle my wrist and scrabble behind Kyn.

He jabs the staff at those nearest, but no one's interested in us anymore. Every eye is on their Great Father, now a statue of solid ice. From crown to toe, the elder's body is a frigid blue, all except his eyes; they've turned to sylver once again. His piercing gaze grabs hold of me and won't let go.

Accusing?

No, that's not it.

Angry?

Maybe.

It doesn't matter—what matters is that now the cave is shaking.

I curse.

Kyn curses.

Shyne and even little Crysel.

We all curse as the mountain skitters. Rocks dislodge from the cave walls, falling, tumbling to the ground. The Shiv dive for cover as the mountain implodes. Shifting stones separate one end of the cave from the other. Families reach and scream for their loved ones as the world tilts and bucks.

And then it stops.

Everything stops.

The hole in the roof of the cave has widened and snow falls freely through the gaping mouth. Cool, fresh air pushes inside and wraps my legs, forces them upright.

GO. NOW.

"We have to get out of here," I say, grabbing Kyn's arm. "Winter's not done yet."

I don't wait for him to argue. I pull him behind me, begging Winter to wrap him tight as well. To heal his ribs so we can move faster. It might be the first real thing I've ever asked of her. But no. There was the other thing. The thing with the dice. And then Crysel and the pickup.

Maybe I am needy. Maybe I do ask a lot of Winter.

We push past the Shiv.

"Get up!" I yell to the huddled groupings. "You have to get out of here."

Kyn joins me, pleading with the Shiv to move, but they've lived through skitters before, taking shelter in these caves. They're content to hunker down behind the very rocks that just killed their kin. I don't understand it.

I leap and duck, the rabble between us and the cave opening a gauntlet that is no easy passage. Kyn's hand tears free of mine and I turn back only to have him run into me. He groans, but lifts me to my feet and pushes me forward.

"Go, go!" he says.

We're just feet from the mouth of the cave when the mountain skitters again. Rocks fall from above, blocking my path and clipping my shoulder. Kyn cries out behind me, and I turn once more. But he's not injured. He's turned back, limping, wincing as he goes—he's going back for the girl.

Crysel stands in the light of Winter, her arms wrapped fiercely around the frozen elder. "Great Father," she cries. "Great Father!"

She's small but Kyn won't be able to heft her. Not with his ribs broken. Not for any distance.

I could flee. I could leave this cave and probably make it back to the road before anyone here could recover enough to come after me.

And then a voice in my ears. A hand on my arm. "You could stop this."

Shyne, muddy, kol-streaked tears smearing the milk-white stone on his face.

"You could tell Winter to leave. You. Daughter of the Kerce queen."

"You're insane."

I shake him off and step toward the mouth of the cave—step toward freedom—rocks falling all around me.

"Little Fox, you must run!"

The agony in Shyne's voice turns me around. His face is tipped to the crumbling ceiling over the heads of Crysel and the treasured elder. And I'm running at Kyn. Running at Crysel as the roof hanging over her head sags and trembles. A rock breaks free and falls. It hits the frozen man and his already shattered arm is sheared off at the shoulder.

Crysel is hit too. *Grazed*, I think as I pick up my pace. *She's just been grazed.* She falls back, hard, on her backside, her arm cradled, her cries echoing.

Kyn reaches her first, wraps her in his arms. He lifts her kicking, screaming form into his chest.

"Give her to me," I say. "My ribs aren't broken."

Kyn glares down at me. "I was cut from stone, yeah? I can carry the girl."

For a moment we're locked that way, in a battle I don't quite understand. And then another rock falls, slamming between us.

"GO!" Kyn yells. "GO!"

I do. I sprint toward the rapidly shrinking opening, yelling for others to do the same. Very few heed my cry, but some stand and brave the falling stones, fighting their way outside.

I burst onto the thin trail with such speed, I tumble over the edge. Fumbling, spinning, I reach for something, anything. My fingers find purchase in a tangle of twyl branches. The roots hold and my body slams hard against the stone wall. Shiv bodies tumble past me. They reach for salvation but find only air, their screams swallowed by more of the same. I don't know how to help. I don't know how—

PULL, Winter tells me. PULL.

My strength is waning, but I obey, pulling myself hand over hand toward the ledge above me. My fingers find the edge and I swing my legs up and onto the trail, the snow muddied and crowded with Shiv. I press myself between their scrambling legs up against the wall and I try to catch my breath.

Kyn is there too, the girl thrashing in his arms. "You're OK," he says, touching the toe of his boot to mine. "Holy Begynd, you're OK. I thought . . ."

"We need to go," I say, pushing to a stand.

"I'll put you down," he tells Crysel. "But not here. The mountain is coming down."

Her cries are hoarse now, her body trembling. Around us, pressed up against the twyl are twelve, maybe thirteen Shiv. They cling to the climbers along the cliff face as more of their kin emerge from the cave.

"We can't stay here," I say. "If the mountain skitters again—"

And then it does. The path to the right of the cave opening lifts and cracks and falls away in heaps of colored rock and snow. The Shiv standing there are thrust into the air, kicking, flailing.

I reach, but it's just a reflex. They're far beyond my help now, sliding down the mountain, the avalanche growing as it nears the Desolation far below.

"This way," Kyn calls over the roaring wind. "Sylvi. This way!"

I follow, a cluster of Shiv in my wake, but it's not easy passage. The climb is steep and narrow and the mountain far from steady. Behind me, misery is loud. Fatigue and desperation. Grief. How many died in that cave? How many of their mothers and fathers, children? How many?

NOT NEARLY ENOUGH, Winter says.

She's vulgar and blustering and I keep my face ducked against her. I look up only to see how Kyn fares. If the Sylver Dragon has taken any damage in the storm and skitter, in the skirmish with the Shiv earlier, I'll need him to help me get her up and running so we can find Mars and Hyla. I can't do the work alone. It's what

I tell myself when I squint into the flurry, checking on him again and again.

The trail flattens out ahead, storm-ravaged trees jutting their spindly branches into the gray sky just over the rise.

And there stands Shyne, as bent and wind-battered as the evergreens, but still standing. At his back are a ragged group of fighters. I can't tell if they're armed, but when your choice of weapon is a rock, there's never one out of reach here in the mountains.

It matters little. When at last we claw ourselves up the mountain, it isn't the same Shyne waiting for us. He's defeated, his dark eyes dead as Kyn places a quiet Crysel into his arms.

"She'll be all right," Kyn tells him. "It's shock only. Exhaustion."

Shyne stares long and hard at Kyn. So long, I twist my hand into the sleeve of his jacket and start to pull him away. We can leave. No one will stop us. Not now. Shyne certainly doesn't have the strength, the presence of mind. But that won't last. He has designs on my days and I won't stay here and let him press another stone to my chest until I agree.

"You're selfish like she was," he says. "You could have saved everyone."

But Kyn and I are already pushing through the trees and Winter's here and she's concerned the Shiv have spoken lies about her. Concerned she's been blasphemed.

I tell her I'll never believe what they said.

AND WHAT OF THE THINGS YOU'VE SEEN?

I won't believe that either, I promise.

A blast of icy air cuts a trail through the swaying branches, picks me up off my feet and throws me backward. Kyn too. We land in a heap of tangled arms and legs and frozen branches, hail raining down, wet snow soaking through our already damp clothes.

"It's Kyndel! Stop!" Hyla says, her musical voice ringing loud. "And Sessa! You're safe!"

Beneath us, the snow melts clean away, leaving Kyn and me on a patch of wet dirt. We're huffing, fighting to peel the soggy branches from our faces, to find our feet, catch our breath.

"Took you long enough," Kyn says.

Mars steps into the clearing, his black eyes so alive in his pale face it's hard to reconcile how dead the kol made the Shiv elder look.

"How was it?" he asks. "I've never shaken an entire mountain before."

Kyn throws a branch at Mars. "You almost killed us."

Mars catches the branch, twirls it. "Stay close to Miss Quine, Kyn, and your safety is assured. Even at my command, Winter will protect her favorite toy."

"You killed a lot of people," I say. "Shiv. Not Majority scum. Women and children. You killed them while they . . . while they mourned a loss."

I'm not sure I want Mars to know Shyne's motives for taking me captive. There's no knowing how he'd use that information.

"Would you rather we spend this day mourning you?"

"I'm a means to an end," I say. "What's there to mourn?"

His face darkens. "I cannot get my haul to the rebel camp without you, Miss Quine. If you fell, I assure you, I would mourn."

I stand and reach a hand down for Kyn. He takes it and pulls himself upright, wincing and nearly pulling me over in the process.

"You're a bastard, Mars," he says.

"Aren't we all?" A permafrost grin slips up his face and he slaps Kyn on the back. "Come. The rig doesn't look nearly as broken as the two of you, but she's making a sound that is far from pleasant."

I stalk toward him. "You started the engine?"

"For the heater only," Mars says. "Hyla was cold."

"He speaks true. I stayed with your Sylver Dragon while Mars searched the caves. I promise you, Sessa, I did not drive it." Hyla's very serious. Despite my angst concerning the Shiv and my exasperation with Mars, I almost laugh.

"I . . . believe you," I say.

"It took some time to find the cave they'd moved you to after the avalanche," Mars says. "I do apologize. Winter is not a willing helpmate."

But she seemed more than willing to destroy a cave full of Shiv. The idea spins inside my head, but he doesn't wait for a reply, instead turning and striding down the path he's cut through the snow.

Anxious to see the Dragon, I follow, unaware I've chosen Mars's path over Winter's until she bites a warning at my heels. I climb up and into the snowbank, fighting my way forward, while next to me Kyn shakes his head and offers me his hand when my leg sinks so far into the fresh powder I can't tug it out on my own.

"Thank you," I say. "Your ribs . . ."

"I'll survive. The cold air feels nice."

"Thank Winter," I say.

He bristles. "I'll thank you instead."

"Is it stubbornness or your Shiv forebears that won't let you thank a spirit that offered you comfort when you were hurt?"

He's quiet for a moment. And then: "Shyne is crazy."

"Thank you, yes. He's out of his mind."

"Maybe. Probably."

My leg free, I push forward and Kyn catches my wrist. "Your arm should be in two pieces."

I look down, remember the painful strike of the walking stick, the shattered ice of the elder's hand.

"I don't have an answer, Kyn. I don't know why your ribs broke and mine didn't. I don't know why my arm is still in one piece. Why she offered you relief. Winter's good to me. I've never asked it of her."

It's more than I've ever admitted about Winter and guilt seeps in. Why does it feel like I've broken a confidence?

"Shyne is crazy, but I don't think he's wrong about Winter. And I don't think he's wrong about you."

"You're serious? You believe I'm the Begynd-born princess of a Kerce queen who lived so long ago no one remembers her name?"

"Her name was Maree Vale," Kyn says. "And it's not Shyne I believe. It's the evidence of my own eyes."

"What is it you've seen me do that gives any credence—"

"Listen," he says, stepping closer and dropping his voice. "You asked me if I trusted Mars to do the right thing, yeah?"

That pulls me up, makes me stop. "Do you?"

He drags a hand over his face and leans in, turning so his back is to Mars and Hyla, even though they are so far up the road they couldn't hear us if we yelled. "I always have. But after

Shyne . . . I'm just thinking, it might be best if you knew what we're hauling."

A white-hot flash of irritation shoots through me. "How in Begynd's name is that going to help?"

"If you knew—I'm not saying you'll like it—but if you knew, you'd understand what the rebels had in mind—"

"I couldn't be less interested in what the rebels are doing! Have I not made that clear? Now, if you want to share the location of their hidden camp, that's a scrap of information I could do something with."

His eager face goes cold. "You'd leave us behind?"

I clear my throat, lift my chin.

"You're a bit mercenary, you know that?" He shakes his head. "But you made a deal, little ice witch. If you want to do this blind, who am I to stop you?"

With that, he flips his hood up against the cold and, as it turns out, I'm the one who's left behind.

CHAPTER 10

THE SNOW AROUND THE RIG HAS BEEN entirely melted away, leaving nothing but frigid mud beneath the tank tread. Sludge splashes onto my boots and soft brown trousers. Something I might complain about if I wasn't exhausted.

"What's that mess?" Kyn asks, pointing his chin at a slapdash covering secured over the shattered passenger window. It seems years since the Shiv attacked the Dragon. But it was, what? Twelve hours ago? Fifteen?

"My tool bag," I say. It's been sliced open and flattened out, the edges affixed to the door frame. Smart, actually. We won't survive long with Winter pressing herself inside the rig. But I was fond of that bag.

"It was all I could find, Sessa," Hyla says. And there's almost an apology there.

"It's fine," I say, scooping up the half-empty container of fast drying, waterproof glue she'd discarded. "That glue's serious stuff. It'll hold."

I shove the container into the tool compartment and pull out a tub of weather repellent, passing it to Kyn. I'm hoping the sticky concoction will fill in the spiderweb of cracks on the windshield and keep Winter's chill outside the cab. It won't last long, especially if snow turns to rain, but it's all I can think to do.

Out of habit, I climb into the cab to check the fuel gauges, but we're fine. I pay good coin for long lasting kol-petrol. If we do find ourselves stranded and desperate, there are fuel stores hidden all over these mountains. Old Man Drypp made me memorize their locations before he handed me the keys to the Dragon.

"We need to hurry," I call, dropping my window down.

Kyn's buffing protectant into the windshield, avoiding my gaze even though his face is only inches from mine. Hyla's beneath the rig somewhere, fiddling with the tank tread. In my side mirror, I catch a glimpse of Mars's arm as he disappears around the back of the rig. After a moment, the trailer's roll-up door rattles on its track.

Checking the haul then.

It's a good call. Especially if we're hauling what I think we're hauling.

I'm not stupid. The weight of the load, the shift of the trailer on the slick highway. It's not so hard to guess what they've got locked away back there. But if this run goes bad, I need the privilege of claiming ignorance. It's my only out with the Majority. And if there's any possibility Leni and I get to keep the tavern and the garage after all this, I'm going to need an out.

Overhead the clouds shift, throwing light onto the Kerce Memorial, setting its colors aglow, and hijacking my thoughts. The storms of Ryme rage, the mountain shakes, and plates of snow crash down on top of it, but year after year, this impossible stack of rocks takes a beating and looks no worse for the wear. It's like the entire Kerce people are scraping their cheeks at Winter.

The stories say she gave up some of her power to them and I don't understand why.

Curse Mystra Dyfan for not being better at keeping me indoors. But she wasn't the first who'd failed. When the teacher at the little mountain school had washed her hands of me, Drypp yielded to the old Kerce navigator who'd wandered into Whistletop one day and found, in me, the likeliest candidate for her tutelage.

Mystra Dyfan had approached Drypp many times before, but teaching children history was not allowed on Layce. We were to look to the future, to the prosperity of the Majority. But the idea of private tutoring appealed to his granddaughter, so Drypp agreed to let Mystra teach me the language and history of the Kerce on the condition that Lenore could take lessons as well.

As tedious as Mystra Dyfan was, escaping her rooms at the tavern was much easier than escaping the schoolhouse, and Leni was happier than she'd been in a long time. I kept my complaining to a minimum.

Mars opens the door and I realize I could ask him to finish the story Shyne began in the caves. I could ask him why Winter bargained away her power to the Kerce. I could ask him about the elder and his sylver eyes.

"I was born into the waters of Begynd, Sylver Quine. It is his light you see."

That's what he'd said. Almost like he believed Shyne's theory that I too was born in the great pool. Like he expected me to see the truth of my birth reflected in his eyes. Instead, his answer fills me with questions I'll never voice. Asking them feels too much like believing, and I promised Winter I wouldn't do that.

"You all right, Miss Quine?"

"Yeah. Of course. Your haul?" I ask, cutting my eyes at Kyn.

He and Hyla are climbing past me now, jostling for room on the bench seat. Mars is next.

"A little shaken up," he says, sliding the trailer key into the medicine bag around his neck and slamming the door, "but no permanent damage."

"Like the rest of us then." I twist the key in the ignition and the Dragon roars to life. The incline is slick and I ease her slowly toward the highway. I press my hand to the dash; the thrum of the engine churns beneath my fingers. She's all right. There's a rattle under the hood—a belt that will need replacing, but the repair can wait until we're on safer ground.

I lift my hand to the windshield and press a sliver of glass back into place. The repellent grabs it and I smooth it flat, sealing out a tendril of icy air biting at my fingers. It's going to cost me a fortune to replace the windshield—but it should hold for now. So long as Mars and Winter can play nice.

The smuggler is far too proud of himself after mimicking the mountain skitter so perfectly—puffed chest, chin high, almost relaxed here in the cab. I don't know what I expected, but anger seems most appropriate. At the Shiv for attacking him, for damaging the rig, for slowing us down. But for all the animosity between the Shiv and the Kerce, he's strangely silent as Kyn tells him most of what happened in the caves.

Kyn avoids my gaze as he talks. He doesn't ask me to fill in parts of the story he's forgotten, and I don't offer. He simply, easily tells Mars and Hyla about Shyne and the stones of torture, though he downplays the severity of it all. He tells them about the old man who wanted healing from the ice of the Desolation, but he says nothing about Shyne's expectations of me. Nothing about Shyne's theories. And though I'm certain Kyn has his own reasons for keeping those things to himself, I'm grateful.

"I'm not surprised they took you. Not at all surprised that they hurt you. What does surprise me is that you survived." Mars fiddles with the mirror. It's dangling from the broken window, swinging lightly as the rig jostles along. He tilts it so Kyn's face fills the glass, a faux reprimand in his scowl. "The Shiv do not take abandonment of duty lightly."

"Maybe we did abandon them," Kyn says, fingering his ribs, wincing at the tender spots. "The Shiv in Dris Mora. I had no idea what it was like out here. Mars, you should have seen them. Rags and mud. And the children." He shakes his head. "It's no way to live."

"You didn't abandon anyone," Mars says. "Least of all your kin. You were born in Dris Mora to a Shiv mother who needed you. Where would she be if you left her behind to tend to these people—people who would likely reject your assistance?"

"Especially after today." I don't know why I'm helping, why I care what Kyn feels for the Shiv at High Pass, but it's insanity to think they'd accept anything from him after Mars's little trick with the mountain. Winter isn't happy about it either. The more Mars talks, the more she whines. She's noisy in my head and hot in my gut. For the first time, her presence is uncomfortable.

And still he talks. "The Desolation Shiv have always thought themselves superior to those who made their homes elsewhere. They consider it a betrayal of duty, of calling. The Shiv people exist to guard Begynd—any other life is shameful. That they're experimenting with the ice is an interesting development. I would not have thought them capable of such . . . desecration."

To that, I say nothing. Kyn too remains silent, reaching instead for Drypp's shotgun settled once again on the rack. It drips sleet and black mud onto the seat.

"How'd you get it back?" I ask Mars. "The shotgun. Beneath all that snow—"

"Snow isn't a problem for me, Miss Quine. But it was Hyla who dug the weapons out. Winter and I had business to attend to."

"Your knives, Sessa," Hyla says, passing me the blades.

"Thank you," I tell her. "I didn't expect to see them again."

I let the knives rest on my lap; *Lenore* and *Sylver* glint dully in the fading light.

It's work to keep my eyes on the road—they keep finding Kyn in the rearview. He digs a rag out from under the seat and busies himself, wiping down the gun, checking the action for moisture. He pulls a box of cartridges from the sleeper and reloads it.

He has beautiful hands, Kyn does. Long, deft fingers, patches of red-brick stone sitting like rings just above his knuckles. My gaze is drawn to the carving on his index finger, the one I noticed back in the cave.

I want to ask about it, but he's ignoring me and there's something sacred about ignoring someone you can't quite escape. It's a task you have to commit to wholeheartedly, so I leave him to it.

"Things are decidedly colder in the cab than they were before," Mars says.

"If you're cold," I say, "leave Winter alone. The broken windshield is on you."

"It's not Winter's chill I'm referring to, Miss Quine. I think you and Kyn have had a disagreement."

"Yeah, Mars," Kyn says. "We fought about who we'd eat first if the Shiv refused to feed us."

"Do the Shiv eat their own?" Hyla asks, her nose wrinkling.

Mars smiles. "No, friend. They do not. Kyn is avoiding the question."

"We didn't fight," Kyn says, jamming a shell into the shotgun.

Mars turns to face me, amusement on his lips.

"We didn't fight," I confirm. "For a Shiv zealot and a reluctant ice witch, Kyn and I get along impressively."

Now Kyn does meet my gaze. He stares me in the eye and flicks his beautiful fingers across his cheek. I return the favor.

"Decidedly colder," Mars says, but he's amused and I imagine that's why he lets it be. There's little to entertain us just now. But the calm won't last. Once we clear the pass, we'll turn north and the Shiv Road will be waiting.

"What is that?" I ask Hyla, feeling kindly toward her after she scrounged up my knives. "The song you're humming?"

"It's the anthem of the Paradyian king," she says. "Do you like it?"

"I do."

"Don't encourage her, Miss Quine."

"There's so little music here," I say, enjoying Mars's discomfort.

"Miss Quine, she will try to teach you."

"I *could* teach you," Hyla says, clearly thrilled at the suggestion. "Would you like that, Sessa?"

Mars rolls his head sideways, scowls.

"Another time, maybe," I say, chewing my lip. "Did you sing at court? In Paradyia."

"Not often. My other talents were of greater use."

"Other talents?"

She flexes, nearly knocking Kyn in the face with her elbow.

I laugh. "I see."

"We all see," Kyn says, jabbing Hyla in the ribs with the stock of the shotgun. "Put that thing down. It smells bad enough in here."

He's right. With all the damp clothing—leathers and fur and woven fabric—the sweat cooled to our skin, and the heat pumping away just to keep the cab above freezing, the stench inside the cab is unpleasant and worsening by the mile.

Hyla gives her underarm a sniff and shrugs. "Sweat is honorable. A gift from Sola."

I find her face in the mirror. "The Paradyian goddess gives what we can earn ourselves then?"

I meant it as a joke, something lighthearted. But Hyla's face turns serious again.

"Can you?" she asks. "Without strength to do the work, can you earn a good day's sweat? Nothing is accomplished without the strength of Sola."

"Nothing?"

"Nothing."

The thought eats at me, salt on snow, and I find I have all sorts of problems with the idea.

"So, it was Sola's strength that brought you all to Whistletop? Helped Mars coerce Lenore into joining his little rebel band? That's good to know."

"You've a curious view of your friend, Miss Quine. I wonder if you know her at all."

"I'm not talking to you," I say. "I'm talking to Hyla."

"By all means," he says, waving his hand.

I find Hyla's golden eyes in the swinging mirror. "Was it Sola's strength that brought down the mountain on hundreds of Shiv? Sola's strength that loaded this trailer with whatever illegal wares we're delivering? Does she empower criminal deeds as well?"

"Unpleasant though it may be to hear," Hyla says, "yes, Sylvi of Whistletop. She has given us strength for this task and she will give us strength enough to keep you safe."

My laugh is rough, angry. "And what of Bristol Mapes?"

"What *of* Bristol Mapes?" Mars asks.

"It doesn't matter," I say, rolling my head on tired neck muscles. "Forget it."

"Miss Quine, Bristol has been useful to me since I arrived in Whistletop but I confess I have not known him long. Miss Trestman wanted to join the rebels and I wasn't in a position to offer her a seat—I had my haul to think of and a rig to hire. Had you agreed to this job a week ago, your friend would likely be sitting next to you now."

My face burns and I twist the steering wheel in my hands.

"As it is, the rebels are not in the habit of turning down help. Bristol had run afoul of the Majority and he needed to leave at once. When he offered Lenore a seat in his plow, I had no reason to dissuade her. If there is something about the man I should know—"

But I won't be baited. It's a story I should have told Lenore; Mars has no right to it.

"And the Majority?" I ask, turning the conversation back to Hyla.

"I do not understand your question," she says.

"If nothing can be accomplished without the strength of Sola, are we to blame her for the actions of the Majority? Any god who empowers—"

"I did not say—"

"—the persecution of others is not a god worth serving."

"You misunderstand me, my lady."

"It's a line of logic that cannot be framed in any way that makes it palatable," I say, thinking of the kol miners lined up on the road at Hex Landing. "Not to those who suffer."

"Is there no good that can come from suffering?" Hyla asks, her voice gentle.

It's a question I have no answer to, so I do what I always did when Mystra Dyfan left me confounded. I raise my chin and avert my eyes.

"Good answer, Miss Quine. Good answer. It's a point upon which Hyla and I can find no peace."

"The Paradyians have never been conquered," Kyn says. "Have never been forced off their own land. Suffering is not something they understand."

Hyla colors, temper purpling her face, but it's Mars who speaks, turning to face Kyn as he does so. "Are you suddenly so sympathetic to the plight of your kinsmen? It's almost worth the cost of losing a day to see you so impassioned."

"It's almost hard to believe you had nothing to do with it," Kyn says, his knee pushing into my back as he fights to get comfortable.

"What is it you're accusing me of, friend? Enlisting the Shiv to abduct one of their own? They hardly need incentive."

"But *I* do, don't I? I need motivation. You've always said so. And now that I've seen their suffering—"

"You've had a long night," Mars says, turning around. "Rest."

Kyn grabs the shoulder of Mars's coat, pulling him half out of his seat.

"Stop!" I yell, reaching out with my right arm, trying to get between them. "Kyn, stop! Stop!"

But Hyla has things under control. She pulls Kyn away, slamming him hard into the back of the cab, pinning him there with Drypp's shotgun.

Kyn's laugh is a brittle, jagged thing. "You looking for a fight, warrior woman?"

"I am not," Hyla says. "But I believe you are. I suggest saving it for the challenges ahead. A fight with Mars is not one you can win."

"Who says I want to win?"

But the fight's gone out of him and Hyla sees it too. She releases him and relinquishes the shotgun.

Mars shrugs his coat back into place, pulls the square of cloth from his pocket, and dabs at a scrape on his neck. "Sleep, Kyn. The Shiv at High Pass aren't the last who'll need saving."

For a minute I think Kyn's going to argue—his eyes hot, his chin fisted with all the words he wants to say—but then he's shoving Hyla out of the way and climbing into the sleeper. He jerks the curtain shut behind him.

The tension is thick, but the cab's gone quiet.

"We're going to start descending soon," I say. "With the rocks rising above us, it's as good a place as any for the Shiv to mount another attack. We could use a lookout as we make the turn onto the Desolation stretch."

Mars reaches up and flips the bolt on the roof hatch.

"I'll go," Hyla says. "I would like to check the turret for damage."

She's standing, already shoving at the hatch, but I grab her arm.

"You absolutely cannot use that turret gun, Hy. Not in the pass. Winter will bury us alive."

"I have my handguns," she says, flipping up her hood, zipping her coat.

"And where's Kyn's rifle?" I ask. "You may as well—"

"Taken," Mars says. "The Shiv brats are probably passing it around, wondering what that little trigger does."

My stomach drops as I consider Crysel with a rifle.

Hyla opens the hatch and Winter trades places with her as she climbs up and onto the cab.

"She's intense," I say, while Hyla's boots clatter overhead. A moment later she drops into the turret.

"Wait till you meet her husband," Mars says.

But I've no desire to step foot on the shores of the golden kingdom. Lenore's always been fascinated. She pored over Mystra Dyfan's maps as a child, copied them in her own hand.

"Of all the islands in the Wethyrd Seas," she'd said, "Paradyia is the brightest."

I'd look at her newly inked map and disagree. I preferred the clean, pure shine of Layce's snow-white wings. But Lenore would hear none of it. She dreamed aloud of boarding a ship and sailing away from Layce to a land where the skies were always blue and the unveiled sun turned faces warm and brown.

I wonder, now, what she'd say to Hyla. To the Paradyian idea that some good can come from her suffering. I try to picture the conversation, how Hyla would respond, the arguments Lenore would make about her own dead mother. I've had my share of fights with Lenore, but I can't imagine how this one would play out. And I wonder if Mars is right.

I wonder if I know my friend at all.

CHAPTER 11

IT'S BEEN HOURS AND KYN HASN'T EMERGED from the sleeper.

Despite the awkwardness, I wish he would. Open hostility is highly preferable to the speech Mars launches into. With great passion, he enumerates all the reasons one should hate Winter. He's methodic in his reasoning, single-minded as he lists the merits of other winter spirits throughout the Wethyrd Seas.

"They visit their own islands once in a year," he says, "and for only half so long as Ryme visits us here. Did you know that, Miss Quine? Those winters understand their purpose. To water the dead earth and to court it to another year of growth and prosperity. The winter spirit that enthroned herself here is vindictive, addled by the kol—"

"The same kol that runs through your veins?" I ask.

"She has been made more than she ever ought to have been. She is dark and ugly."

Winter roars, and, from the mountain to our right, a giant spruce flares into movement, ice-slicked limbs growing and stretching across the road. They're not thin spindly things either, but robust beneath the ice, heavy beams that will slice the rig in two if we strike them at our current speed.

"Shut up, Mars." I fight the urge to slam on the brakes, pressing my foot down slowly, steadily.

The branches of the spruce split and grow, twisting and knotting until they've formed a wall before us.

Next to me Mars laughs. "Sensitive, this spirit, isn't she?"

"You were baiting her," I bark, my foot pressed so hard to the brake, I'm standing. I can't stop the rig. This isn't fresh powder beneath the tread. This is the Flux. "Hold on to something."

I brace myself for the collision, but Mars cries out in Kerce and the limbs shatter into splinters of wood, the ice melting as we connect. I take a face full of water as a crack in the windshield opens.

The curtain flies sideways and Kyn emerges, the shotgun tight in his hands.

"Fluxing Blys, Mars!" I'm easing off the brake, letting the Dragon push forward. "What were you thinking? Winter could blow us off the road if she wanted to."

"Oh no, Miss Quine. She could do much. But she could not do that." A new layer of blisters has erupted on Mars's lips, but he's so pleased with himself, he doesn't even notice.

"And your haul? What of your precious haul? If I turn the trailer on its side and your merchandise goes sprawling across the road, what will you do?"

"You'd never let that happen," he says, his smile slipping. "You care about Miss Trestman too fiercely for such a mistake."

I duck as a loud pop sounds. And then another. And now I do slam on the brakes.

Nerves, frustration, exhaustion.

Mars.

Everything conspiring to keep me stupid on the ice.

The tail fishes around, but we're traveling slower now and the Sylver Dragon slides to a stop. I kill the engine and turn to glare at the smuggler.

"What did you just do?"

His features are disheveled: eyes wide, brows cocked at weird angles, blistered lips curved low. One hand grips the door, the other tight on Kyn's shoulder. "I genuinely do not know."

Outside, Hyla's curses are loud and indecipherable, but at least she's able to speak. It means I didn't throw her from the turret.

"Those were tires blowing," Kyn says.

"The trailer." I kick the door open and drop to the road. Kyn's half on top of me as he follows. His boots land hard on the ice and he groans, closes his eyes, leans against the rig.

"Your ribs?"

"They're OK," he says. "Come on."

We turn toward the trailer and I gasp.

Winter's built herself a castle.

A low whistle skates across Kyn's lips. "Begynd almighty, she's fast."

On the strip of highway we've just trucked, she's constructed towers of frosted orbs and spires of soft white powder. So tall, they disappear into the heavy cloud cover above. Panes of ice connect one pillar to another, curtains of hardened sleet hanging majestic over passages crafted out of sculpted snowdrifts. Icicles, clear as glass, grow like the twyl in Lenore's planter boxes—up from the ground, mingled with triangles of hardpack—penitent snow, we call it, because it bows before Winter. From somewhere deep inside her masterpiece, a frigid wind begins to blow.

"She's taken out the tires," Kyn says, awe fading to irritation. "Barbs of ice shot straight through the rubber . . ."

"Paradyian rubber too," I say.

We have to hurry. I know we do. But I need a closer look. I've seen Winter do some miraculous things, but I've never seen her show off so stunningly. So pointedly.

The ground is slick, so I reach down and flip the lever on both boots—the one that extends the crampons—and then I'm moving forward, into the ice castle she's built. I run my glove along a wall lined with hoarfrost and wander deep into the belly of her creation. It's like a maze, shorter walls mixed with larger ones. Staircases of ice and archways of crusted snow hover threateningly over my head like stalactites.

It's so quiet. So still I can hear the others' boots echoing as they examine Winter's handiwork. Kyn finds me first. He wanders to the center of the vast room I've stumbled into and runs his bare hand over the crystalline banister of a massive staircase. It climbs on and on, vanishing into the haze overhead.

"She could do so much, yeah? And yet she chooses destruction. Do you ever wonder why she is the way she is?"

"She's cold and ice and power. A force of nature," I say, remembering how Mars referred to himself in the same way. "Her actions do not surprise me."

"The look on your face says otherwise, Miss Quine." Mars

and Hyla enter the room, one scowling at Winter's artistry, the other gawking.

"You called her ugly," I say. "Dark. Said she'd been addled by the—"

A gust of wind swoops down the massive staircase and knocks Kyn sideways. It slaps my face and pushes the words back into my mouth. I curl forward coughing.

Hyla brandishes another of her Paradyian curse words and offers Kyn a hand. Mars waits until I'm recovered before he speaks.

"I apologize, Miss Quine. She's not vindictive. Not in the slightest."

He turns away then, leaving me gaping at the staircase. Hyla follows, guns in each hand.

I pull myself upright, strange emotions bumping like an ice floe behind my rib cage.

I've only ever defended her. To be slapped like a petulant child . . .

Hot tears prick my eyes. I blink them away and look to Kyn. "How many tires did we lose?"

"Two," he says. "Sylvi, are you all right?"

"There are spares bolted to the outside wall of the Dragon," I say. "They're not Paradyian, so you'd best hope Mars keeps his opinions about Winter to himself from here on out. She's not playing anymore."

The need to be anywhere but inside Winter's castle is suddenly a living thing slithering in my gut. I turn away, weaving in and out of the bowing snow until, at last, I'm at the Dragon's side once again. My ears are buzzing with cold and it takes a minute to shut out the noisy silence and focus on the conversation Hyla and Mars are having.

"Can you not melt the ice on the roadway?" Hyla asks. She kicks out at one of the flattened tires. "Remove Winter's ammunition?"

"The roads are not paved beneath the ice," I say, moving toward the tool compartment. "This isn't Paradyia. The ice *is* the road. Beneath it lies shifting, unpredictable mountain rock and kol. That's it."

"*You* could navigate it," Mars says.

"Flattery won't save the tires on your trailer. Without the ice, we're guaranteed to find every pothole on the Shiv Road. You realize we're still a half mile from the Desolation stretch and you, our reckless leader, have become the biggest obstacle. Not Winter. You."

Mars picks kol from a blister on his lip. "Change the tires and let's be on our way."

But Kyn's already on it. He's positioned the jack, cranking, cursing.

Mars grins. "I'm not familiar with this side of my friend, Miss Quine. Angry, moody. What did you do to him in that cave?"

I slam the tool compartment shut, a pair of wrenches in my hands. I use one of them to shove Mars out of the way.

"No, no," he calls after me. "Don't say a word. Some things should remain intimate."

I flip my hood up, shutting out the world as I set to work on one of the shredded tires. I'm struggling with a lug nut when Hyla's voice rings out.

"It is best to hurry," she calls from the top of the trailer. "There are Rangers heading this way."

"Of course there are," I say, kicking the tire.

"What do you see?" Kyn calls.

"A pickup full of men and wolves. They are moving cautiously toward Winter's"—she waves a gun at the castle—"ice house. But it won't be long before they're here."

"Flux," I hiss, searching the pass for Mars.

He emerges from Winter's palace, his nostrils flaring.

"This is your mess," I say. "I told you they wouldn't forget what you did to Jymy."

"You're wasting time, Miss Quine. Best get those tires off." And then a gust of wind lifts him into the sky.

I'd never require Winter to carry me around, but for the first time I wonder at the thrill it would be.

The wind is raging now and, in the ice-cold tendrils that chap my face, I feel Winter's despair. This isn't a storm of her making. Mars is pulling the strings, using her to slow the Rangers. I want to be angry. Want to hate him for using her as a weapon, but my face still stings from the thrashing she gave me, and I find myself wanting to know if she too can feel a cold shoulder.

CHAPTER 12

THE WRENCH IS STUCK. I KICK IT UNTIL THE lug nut twists and falls to the snow, and then I jam the wrench onto the next one. Hail falls now, pelting my back and shoulders.

"Stupid Kerce smuggler," I say. "He could at least keep the storm off us while we work."

"He'd keep it off us if he could," Kyn says. "All he can do sometimes is keep us alive. Winter fights him every step of the way."

"She fights *him*?"

"It's always been like this between them. Everything's a battle. Every step he takes in her ice-white world, every breath of her air in his lungs. Everything. All of it. A fight. Could you imagine living like that?"

"He could stop using her as a weapon. Make peace."

Kyn grunts and rolls his tire to the side of the road. "After the scene at the Shiv settlement, you still think she wants peace?

You have any idea what she whispers to him? The things she puts inside his head. She cares nothing for peace."

My hands are clumsy. I've never had to do this and argue at the same time. Kyn moves me out of the way and sets to work on my tire.

"Ask yourself the difficult questions, little ice witch. Why does Winter try so hard to keep you happy? Why are you different than the rest of the Kerce?"

He rolls the final tire onto the shoulder and pushes his way toward the back of the cab where the spares are bolted.

"You saw her slap me, right?"

When he returns, we work in silence, mounting the spares and lowering the jack until the tires touch the road. Kyn gathers the tools and retreats to the tool compartment.

"Hey, Sylvi," he yells, holding up a hinged rod. "What's this?"

"It's for the rock saws," I call. It's not. It's the stem of Drypp's old ice bike, but I've reasons for keeping that to myself.

He turns the device in his hands, eventually sliding it away.

"I trust you're done, Miss Quine." Mars drops lightly from the top of the cab to the hood of the truck, and finally onto the ground. "The wolves won't have any trouble navigating Winter's little fort there, but it will keep the Ranger's pickup from getting through. Remind me to thank her."

A crack and a splash and Winter's design folds in on itself. The spires crumble, the icicles stream water—water that rushes toward the Dragon.

I back toward the rig. "Mars—"

He moves fast; a muttered Kerce word and a gust of wind

lifts me off the ground. My stomach lurches and suddenly I'm on top of the Dragon, watching as he advances on the melting citadel, his hands outstretched, Kerce words spilling from his tongue.

I drop to my knees to catch my breath and watch as Mars strides fearlessly toward the most fantastic thaw I've ever witnessed. Kyn scales the trailer and joins Hyla in the turret, the two of them watching just as I am. Kyn's arms lift and come to rest on top of his slowly shaking head. Hyla's guns are drawn but to what advantage, I can't say. She's just frozen there, I think. A spectator. The sight, breathtaking.

I jump the gap and run the length of the trailer, dropping into the lookout between the two of them, watching as Mars fights the castle's disintegration. He's able to slow the collapse, to steady a few of the melting walls, but he cannot stop the thaw entirely.

When at last Mars's hands drop to his sides, water rushes beneath the trailer and around the tank tread, but Winter's left the road frozen and intact. I whisper my thanks, but my gratitude is limited. Winter's thawed a thoroughfare through the center of her palace. A chilly haze rises from the ice-white ruins and, as it clears, a pickup comes into view on the other side, harpoon gun mounted on top.

Even from this distance, I can see men clad in white standing in the bed, loading it on approach.

"Weapons!" Hyla calls, swinging out of the turret.

I reach for her arm. "Hy—"

"Yes, my lady, I know. I won't fire the turret gun here."

Kyn and I climb up onto the trailer and sprint toward the cab. I jump the gap first and fling open the roof hatch to drop inside.

I kick open the driver's side door and climb out onto the highway, Kyn just behind me. When he emerges, he has Drypp's shotgun in his hands.

I slam my fist into the tool compartment and it springs open—a coil of rope and a box of bolts tumbles to the snow. I wrench Drypp's old pickaxe from its mount and I'm running now, toward the back of the truck, Winter securing my footing, holding my ankles steady.

Thank you, I tell her. *Thank you.*

"You want the gun?" Kyn asks.

No, I don't want the gun—I'm still not sure we should be shooting anything up here—but I don't have time to answer. The Rangers fire their harpoon and a shock trembles through the pass. The projectile whistles as it cuts toward us. I drop to the snow and the rig shudders as the harpoon embeds itself in the door of the trailer.

The angle of the rig is such that—even from here, with my face flat in the muddy snow—I see the line snap taut. Despite the Dragon's heft, she shimmies backward an inch or so.

"Hold your ground, girl," Kyn tells her as he jumps up and sprints forward.

Mars launches himself into the air, the wind violent and angry as he flies toward the slumping castle.

I'm on my feet when the harpoon's reel grinds to life, the crank fighting against the Dragon's weight and winning—the rig slipping backward. I'd heard about the harpoon gun. Seen it even. But I've never been there when the Rangers used it to steal a haul. I can't work out their endgame—they'll never drag the trailer back to town this way—but the harpoon is impressive, the power of it, and I have to wonder if it's also Paradyian. If their reel holds, they could yank the door clean off the trailer. Perhaps that's been their intention all along.

Hyla's boots pound the top of the trailer, running, then stopping. She fires her handguns. Kyn too, is firing. At what, I can't say, but the ferocity of the noise is loud, bouncing from mountain to mountain. I'm terrified Winter will shed her coat, terrified of another avalanche. I push harder, running, raising the axe over my head.

"Kyn!" I yell.

He turns and his eyes widen. He drops the shotgun and links his fingers together, bracing his back against the trailer. My boot strikes his cupped hands and he launches me into the sky. I swipe at the harpoon cable and the axe slices through, the cable snapping back on itself, twisting like a sea snake into the snow. The harpoon shaft juts from the trailer door, but it's harmless, no longer attached to their crank.

I land in a crouch, my eyes on the road. They'll load another harpoon, surely, but we've bought ourselves a good two-minute head start if we get moving.

"You'd be terrifying even if you weren't Winter's plaything," Kyn says, offering me a hand. But I'm halfway to my feet and don't need any help. Disappointment flashes in his eyes, but there's no time.

"We have to hurry," I say.

"Right, yeah. Stay behind me." He hefts Drypp's shotgun and turns, jogging toward the Rangers and their pickup.

"Hey, *hey!*" I call. "We'll be safe in the Dragon."

Kyn pulls up. Turns to face me.

"We just have to get out of the harpoon gun's reach," I say.

"You always run from a fight?"

"Everybody back in the rig!" I yell. "Now!"

"Mars hasn't returned," Hyla hollers, the toes of her boots hanging off the end of the trailer.

"What do you mean he hasn't returned?"

"The harpoon machine—he thought to freeze it."

Stupid, idiotic—

"The Rangers aren't Shiv," I yell. "They're armed with more than rocks and arrows."

"There!" Kyn says, pointing at the sky.

Mars flies toward us, the storm following, smacking us hard, numbing my face.

He's bleeding.

Flux.

Blood drips from his boot, a steady trickle freezing and falling to the snow. Both hands are pressed to his side, the wind keeping him afloat, though barely. He's only three or four feet off the ground. Hyla steps off the side of the trailer and drops to the road.

"How bad?" Kyn says, swinging his gun around, crouching as Mars lands. Mars lets him examine the wound while he rests against the trailer.

"Flesh wound," Mars says. His pale face is gray and he fights to keep his black eyes open. "But the harpoon gun is a block of ice. They'll have to kill us if they want the haul."

"They have wolves and more guns than we do. With you down, I can't imagine that being difficult. At least stay awake," I tell him. "Keep him awake, Hyla. And get that blood flow stopped." The Paradyian crouches in the snow now, pulling the scarf from around her neck and using it to bind Mars's waist.

"Keep him off the ground," I tell Hyla. "The wolves like Kerce blood." It's how Mystra lost her foot. A bite that got infected.

Hyla grabs her boss under the arms, but Mars stays her hand. "Don't bother."

A twitch of his lips and he's in the air; Winter deposits him on top of the trailer. Hyla climbs up next to him and Kyn and I turn to face the footsteps pounding the ice.

Cramponed boots stomp closer. But it's the padded footsteps I don't hear that make the axe tremble in my hand. Kyn hefts the gun and I tighten my grip.

We don't stand a chance.

"Three men," Hyla yells. "Five gray wolves. All approaching."

"What of Mars?" Kyn yells.

"He'll live," Hyla says.

"Keep him awake!" I yell, shaking a tremor from my foot.

"He is my boss, Sessa. I do not tell him when to sleep and when to wake."

"If he loses too much blood—"

"That would be very unlike Mars," Kyn says. "And what do you care if he dies?"

"Can *you* find the rebel camp? Can you convince Lenore to climb into my rig?"

A moment of silence and then, "No. I don't think I can."

"Then Hyla better keep him alive."

There's something sharp in Kyn's gaze, and I realize he likes a fight. But there's no time to give him one. The Rangers and their Grays are coming, and, like a punch to the gut, I feel Winter's loyalty dim. She may like me. She may prefer me to others living on her island, offer me some semblance of protection against the harshest parts of her own personality, but she loves her wolves. And as a confrontation is now inevitable, the conflict rages fierce in the ice beneath our feet and in the chill of her breath.

A massive wolf crests the rise, but it's not the size of the Gray that makes this one dangerous. It's the thick wreath of twyl tied around his neck. I've never seen the wreaths used on wolves, but the farmers near the coast use them on their animals when the winds off the Kol Sea are high. Animals aren't nearly as susceptible as we are, and the freshly cut twyl is enough to dampen the brain-addling effects of kol. The impact is short-lived, but knowing what I know now, I imagine that wreath will be enough to fend off Kerce magic as well.

Relief stirs in my chest. I don't want to order these wolves into submission. It's a dirty way to fight.

The alpha is followed by four wolves, slightly smaller, all of them with wreaths of twyl around their necks. The Rangers hang back—one in the pickup, two on the ground. They're trusting the wolves to do the grunt work.

We'll have to be smart. Have to show restraint. There are only three of us, a shotgun, two handguns, an axe, and the sylver knives at my waist. The five wolves have claws and teeth and animal instinct.

And they have Winter.

YOU SHOULDN'T HAVE COME, she says. **I WARNED YOU.**

Kyn fires Drypp's gun, a blast that has no hope of reaching the pack. Buckshot peppers the snow and still the wolves press forward.

"What are you doing?"

But Kyn's not the only idiot along for the ride. Overhead, Kerce words fly from Mars's mouth.

"Fluxing Blys, I thought he was unconscious," I mumble. "They're wearing twyl!" I yell over the sound of the shotgun. "You can't command them."

But the pack has taken offense—like Winter, they don't like being ordered around. Their footfalls quicken until the salivating beasts are in full sprint.

Kyn fires again. The spray is too wide—if the wolves take any of it, it doesn't slow them. They're powered by something other than bloodlust. They've Winter in their veins. And still Kyn keeps firing.

"You're wasting shot!" I yell, and then I hear the action on the shotgun lock open. That's it. Kyn's out of shells.

He curses and the alpha launches himself into the air. Kyn backs up, reaching for my arm. I dodge his grasp and step toward the beast, Drypp's axe lifted over my head.

I can't stop the memories flooding in. Drypp cracking away at the ice, splintering it, hurting it. Hurting *her*. I don't want to kill this wolf.

I'm sorry, I tell Winter. *So sorry.*

And then I swing the axe.

My momentum spins me around—I've missed.

How did I miss?

The blood in my head rushes, dulls the sound of a projectile flying by my ear. It sinks into the beast with a wet thud and the alpha falls to the ground, skidding toward us, taking my feet out from under me.

He's dead, but not by my hand.

A long, narrow icicle protrudes from his eye socket, the splash of blood like hysolberry wine on linen tablecloths.

A sob rips from my chest and I crank my head to the wretched Kerce smuggler standing on the edge of the trailer, twelve feet above. He's barely upright, faltering in the wind, but he's fighting. Using Winter against herself. Dozens of icicles hover in the air around him.

"On your feet, Miss Quine. There are others."

I spring to my feet, my heart racing, and aching, and hating Mars with each frantic beat. I can't explain the rage. I would have killed the beast. I lifted the axe. I tried. But I wouldn't have used Winter to do it.

The four remaining wolves have slowed. Their eyes are still trained on us, but they mewl and moan. I feel their conflict, feel it as I feel Winter's moods. They don't know who their leader is now.

Kyn reaches deep in his pocket for more shells. He's still loading when the pack chooses their new alpha.

This one has two different-colored eyes: one the color of boiled chocolate and the other a cool blue. She moves to the front of the pack and then they're racing toward us.

"Hurry up," I tell Kyn.

I turn the axe in my hands, whispering unintelligible things to Winter. Things about Lenore. About Drypp. About the day she blew out the windows at Mistress Quine's. I whisper promises I have no way of keeping.

It doesn't matter. She's not listening to me anymore.

From overhead, an icicle flies and then another. A gust of

wind carries them off course, but one of Hyla's guns has aimed true. It strikes the wolf behind the alpha. He stumbles and goes down, his cries horrible. It wasn't a kill shot.

The pack picks up speed, their fallen brother screaming behind them. My stomach churns, flips. I refuse to be sick.

Icicles fly left and right but none of them finds their target.

Kyn curses, drops a shell. Crouches to retrieve it.

And then the wolves are on top of us. Hyla drops from the trailer, a gun in each hand. She lands directly in front of the wolf bringing up the rear.

Kyn's abandoned his efforts to reload the shotgun. He swings the butt of it around, cracking a wolf across the jaw. It snaps and snarls and shakes his head. Kyn flips the gun in his hands, presses the barrel to the wolf's chest and fires.

"That's it," Kyn yells. "My last shot."

I'm swinging my axe, fear trumping angst as I stare down the wolf in front of me, his jaws snapping, frothing.

"Knives at my waist," I say.

Kyn kicks out at the wolf in front of me and slides closer, grabbing both daggers from my belt.

Hyla dispatches the wolf in front of her, then turns and scales the trailer once again, taking aim at the Rangers gunslinging this way. I catch it all in my peripheral vision. I don't dare take my eyes off the circling beast before me.

The wolf orbits me and Kyn orbits the wolf. There's only this one left. This one and the poor beast howling and bleeding and not dying fast enough.

Kyn strikes out with one bone-handled dagger, jabs the wolf

in his rear flank. The wolf flips around, backs toward me, his snapping jaws turned on Kyn.

I lift the axe and swing. It sinks into the wolf's back and he howls, falls. Kyn drives a dagger through his rib cage. It takes far too long, but eventually the wolf goes silent. He strides to the mewling, flopping beast next. The wolf who can't quite die.

"Hyla," he calls. "Help this guy out, will you?"

From the top of the trailer, she fires. A headshot that silences the suffering animal.

The wind picks up, gusting so strong it's hard to stand. I tip my head and high above, Mars hovers; he's nothing but a gray splotch against the ever-present cloud cover. Torrents of wind and hail spin from his body, pummeling the pass. Blood mingles with all of it.

"He's going to kill himself," I say.

Kyn grabs my hand and presses one of my daggers into it. "I'm going to get more slugs."

And then he's gone and I'm surrounded by dead wolves, nothing but the Sylver Dragon at my back. I drag the flat of the knife's blade across my pant leg before sliding it into its sheath. I should reclaim the other one from the wolf at my feet, but hefting his body is a task I can't quite fathom. My legs shake—Winter's absence dark and lonely inside me.

I'm sorry, I tell her again, refusing to look at the creatures at my feet. *So sorry.*

The Ranger's pickup grows large in the distance, Winter's breath rising from the moldering towers of ice on the truck's left and right. I see the Ranger's harpoon gun mounted on top, frozen solid. I see two of the men walking toward us almost lazily, their guns hanging loosely around their necks, their laughter high on the wind.

"Come hither, Sylver Quine!" one calls. "The Majority wants a word with you!"

Don't they know this fight is over? That what comes next is just a waste of life? Is it wise or foolish to laugh in the face of such a thing?

Mars drops to the road, the storm thrust in front of him, but still whipping at us—pelting us with hail and biting flakes of snow.

"There are more," he says, tightening the scarf wrapped around his waist.

"More what?" I ask.

"Wolves. Seven more. Following the pickup. Frost Whites."

My stomach heaves.

There are stories. These ones told in the tavern after dark, myths not so different from the one Shyne wanted us to believe. Tales of Winter's passion for the first wolf to take refuge in her mountains, a Frost White with eyes like goldstone. He was her one great love but her affection froze him solid. She was more careful after that, mourning him, favoring his kin, admiring their beauty from a distance, and allowing them the freedom to roam the mountains as they liked.

I had no idea a pack had taken up with the Rangers. While a Gray is nothing to be careless with, I'm downright terrified of the Whites.

"We can't win this, Mars. Not with Winter on their side."

"She has to obey. She has no choice."

"It's cruel, what you're doing. Using her to destroy her own."

"It's survival. And you'd best choose the right side here, Miss Quine. The rebels are the ones who will suffer if you don't. Miss Trestman will suffer. They need what we're hauling."

He's still leaking blood. It's pushed through the scarf Hyla tied around his waist.

I think of what Drypp once told me about those forced to work at the Stack. Those going slowly mad with all the exposure to the raw kol.

"Even slaves fight back," I say.

"What?" Mars asks.

"Like the workers in the Stack obeying their overseers, Winter will do exactly what you ask of her and no more. She'll look for ways to fight you, ways to rebel. She'll help the wolves however she can without violating the magic that binds her to the kol in your blood."

"That's why I need you."

The wolves are in sight now, coming up alongside the pickup. They're beautiful, the wolves. One and a half times the size of the average Gray, their eyes like gems. It's easy to see why Winter loves them as she does.

"I won't. I won't order her to massacre her favorites."

He shakes his head, his grin mocking. "I thought you didn't believe in fairy stories, Miss Quine."

"I won't do it. Not when we can climb into the cab right now and drive away. They will not pursue us out onto the Desolation stretch."

"And if they do?"

"They won't get far. Their pickup can't navigate the Cages. We can outrun them."

Kyn joins us, his eye pressed to the gun sight. "Hyla's taken out one of the Rangers, but there's still the driver in the truck and another on the ground. Seven wolves. A pickup with a disabled harpoon gun and several frozen projectiles. Not much there to improvise with. The wolves are between us and them now. We either run while we can," he says, clearly disgusted by that option, "or we take on the wolves and then the men."

"We run," I say.

"And if the Majority is paying them good coin to track us," Mars says, "do you think they will just stop pursuing you? If we leave them alive, you'll never be able to go home again."

From somewhere deep inside my chest a roar shakes its way into the air. "I'd be of no use to the Majority. It's you they should hunt down. You enjoy barking at Winter, killing her pets."

"Do you think they haven't? There's been a price on my head for years."

My jaw clenches. Right now, they're not the only ones who want him dead.

A smile slithers up his face. "You need me to get to Miss Trestman. Never forget."

"Come on, little ice witch," Kyn says, leaning in, pressing his mouth to my ear. "We can end this." Winter bellows loudly now, like a bear about to attack. Mars stands some distance from us—I don't know if he can hear Kyn's words, but I'm suddenly aware that despite the tension festering between us, there are things Kyn feels comfortable whispering in my ear.

I turn my face to his. "If we leave, no one else has to die."

"And what of the Shiv?" Mars asks.

"What of them?"

"You forget I've heard Leff's version of that night at High Pass. I can guarantee these Rangers have heard it too. You think they'll simply let Shyne and the girl go free? You think they won't gather them up to face questioning in Glas? What do you think will happen to the girl, Miss Quine, once she's told the Majority all she knows about you?"

She'll end up in the Stack. That's what'll happen.

Crysel and Shyne—they wouldn't be the first Shiv rounded up and put to work. But they would be the first enslaved because of me. I stare into the anguish on Kyn's face and I swallow back the bile that burns my throat.

From overhead, Hyla drops to the snow. "I've plenty of bullets left," she says, "Shall we continue?"

"Yes," Mars says. "I think so. We end this here." He steps closer, wraps a hand around Kyn's bicep, the other around mine. "We can't be plagued by the wolves or their Rangers for the duration of the journey. It's foolhardy to leave them salivating in our wake. And when this is all over, Miss Quine, and you're able to sleep in your own bed at night, you can thank me."

He releases our arms and strides away, as if that's settled it.

And I suppose it has.

The Frost Whites have closed the distance and are spreading out, widening their circle. Like an unwilling dance partner, we counter, moving toward one another, the mountain suddenly at our back. They're hemming us in.

I can't tell who the alpha is—which is unsettling. You can usually tell with wolves. The alpha's out front, head high, snapping jaws, larger than all the others. These seven look nearly identical.

"It's her," Mars tells me.

"Which one?" I say, desperate, scanning the bloodthirsty eyes raking over us. Ruby and sapphire and emerald and amber. Violet and rose and crystalline.

"Winter," he says. "Can't you hear her whispers? She's their alpha. She's taken control."

I can't hear her whispers. She's shut me out. But the wolves step closer, snarling, their teeth glistening. My mind tosses and turns, but I don't know how to do this. I don't know how to fight Winter.

"I tried to leave," I remind her. "You heard me. I tried."

But she's silent. She's nothing. She's cold and wet and miserable. And the silence pisses me off.

I flip the axe in my hand.

"Mars," I call. "I have an idea—"

Before I can voice my plan, a wolf lunges at Hyla, its amber eyes flashing. Kyn turns, finger on the trigger of the shotgun, but he never gets to squeeze it. A wolf takes advantage of his divided attention and leaps at his chest, knocking him on his back. The gun goes off and I drop as spray peppers the wall behind us.

I inhale a mouthful of powder as I gasp. The beast opens its massive jaws and clamps onto Kyn's shoulder, his neck. I scream and throw my axe.

It skids harmlessly across the wolf's back, but there's no time to think. Another wolf is on top of Kyn. Hyla fires her guns again and again. Around me, wolves and men alike are tripping and falling. They howl and bleed, but the two beasts inching toward me with their chests rumbling have secured my undivided attention. The closest has eyes of ruby red, and just behind her, a gaze of emerald green. Twyl garlands swinging, they are terrible in their splendor.

Somewhere in the distance, I hear Mars screaming words in Kerce, but it's futile. They won't obey him—not with the twyl around their necks.

And then I know: We've only the one option.

I stop swinging my dagger, let my hand fall slightly. Ruby pounces. I drop to the snow, belly up, and let her land on me, my fist tight around the bone handle of my blade.

"Mars!" I scream, slicing a straight line with my dagger. "Now!"

The wreath falls from the wolf's neck. Her teeth close on my arm and I gasp. But she doesn't clamp down. I see her confusion. Feel it in my chest.

I kick out at her and yank my arm from her jaws, but she's already crawling off me. I scrabble away, toward Kyn. I can hear him struggling with the sapphire-eyed wolf, but I don't dare take my eyes off Ruby. She ducks her head, eyes on either side of that white snout, roiling and hot as a chimney. Her lip curls and I think I've miscalculated.

And then she whimpers. Her face turns toward Mars. I follow suit and I see his Kerce lips moving, see the kol crusting in the corners of his mouth.

He's whispering, speaking softly into the wind. I have no idea what he's saying, but it bothers Winter. Her displeasure is like hot coals in my gut. Uncomfortable and inescapable.

Hyla is covered in scrapes and gashes, but she steps in front of Mars, brandishing her handguns, firing them when the wolves get too close. She's keeping the beasts off him while he works his magic.

Mars sends words skimming across the air into the pricked ears of one of her favorites. He's speaking to Ruby. No, that's not it. He's forcing Winter to speak to her. The hairs on the wolf's back bristle and then she tips her snout to the sky and howls.

The remaining wolves stop, crank their heads toward her. Their eyes are wrong. Unfocused. A glossy patina covers the jewels there like hoarfrost. She's the alpha now. And Mars has her ear.

A simple command and Ruby leaps onto her own brother, onto the wolf straddling Kyn. They tumble into a snowdrift, a mass of fur and claws and gemstone eyes. But they've left behind a splotch of red snow.

I scrabble toward Kyn, my heart thudding.

There's a lot of blood.

More than—

He's not going to make it.

No one could survive this much blood loss.

Some of it is mine, I realize. I'm bleeding from somewhere. My arm, maybe. The skin stings, up my biceps, down to my wrist. I'm not weak though—my muscles are strong. I sheath my knife, vaguely aware that its twin is buried somewhere beneath the wolves and the storm. There's no time to fetch it though, no time to waste. I wrap my arms around Kyn's chest and pull him backward toward the Sylver Dragon.

The rig is a ways off now. The battle's pulled us from her, but I can make it. I can get Kyn to the rig. To the kol Mars certainly has in the trailer. Because that's what it has to be. Refined kol.

No one had to say a thing—it was the weight that gave it away. Light as air once it's been processed and useful for all sorts of nefarious rebel activities. If it were a trailer full of Paradyian wares we were hauling, it's unlikely I would have been able to keep the Dragon from jackknifing earlier.

I can mix the processed kol with the snow. Dilute it. Press it into Kyn's wounds, and it should help some. It's what Lenore did to treat Drypp's injuries. The kol made him loopy, but it quieted his cries, dulled the pain. And Kyn's in a lot of pain. Every movement I make sends his mouth gasping for air and his fingers fighting for purchase on my arms.

He does it once. Grabs on. Flips me to the snow. I can't tell where his blood ends and mine begins anymore. But the energy it took to tackle me was all he had left and his head falls back, his eyes shut, his breathing negligible. I right myself and wrap him up again, pulling, pulling until I have no strength left.

I vaguely hear Mars in the distance. Winter's gusts are less powerful here, less deafening, and the Kerce words Mars directs toward the wolves find their way back to me somehow.

He's telling them to attack, turning the wolves back on their masters.

I don't hate him for it. I can't. Not while looking down at Kyn's neck and chest, shredded and gaping. There's a murmur in the back of my mind that insists we could have avoided this if we'd left when I suggested it. When I begged. When I was overruled.

But it's such a small feeling compared to the terror of Kyn's certain death that I can't even make myself revel in it.

Mars is at fault. Yes. Of course. Everything is his fault. But the Rangers also hold blame here. They unleashed Winter's dogs. They did it in a way that left us little recourse but to kill. They made the glorious Frost Whites expendable. They tore this beautiful, conflicted boy to pieces.

Rage rattles in my throat, spills over my lashes.

We're at the trailer. I drag Kyn to the far side, position him between the mountain and the truck where we're protected from the wind.

He's not breathing well, but he is wailing. The sound climbs my spine, my neck, the chill worse than anything Winter can unleash.

I sprint to the back of the trailer, slipping despite the crampons jutting from my boots. It's only when I reach the roll-up door that I realize I don't have the key. Mars has it. It's in the medicine bag around his neck.

I turn, yell: "Mars!"

The storm has turned the sky white and Mars is nothing but a gray speck in the distance. I can't see Hyla at all. I step away from the trailer, cup my hands, and yell again.

But there's nothing. Not even an echo.

Just the sound of Kyn's misery.

I turn back to the trailer, desperate. I'm not going to lose him. He may be the only one of my companions with a conscience. A confused, myth-believing conscience, but one that could come in handy when Mars gets tired of me.

The harpoon jutting from the top left corner of the trailer catches my attention. It's not a large hole, but I'm not a large girl. If I can work the harpoon into the trailer, work the clamps free, I can probably wriggle in after it.

I have nothing but a single dagger now—Lenore's dagger. Where its twin and the pickaxe are, I can't recall.

In the tool compartment, there's a massive wrench and a rubber mallet. I grab the tool belt and jam the things I'll need into it. And then I waste a solid minute scrounging the cab for my gloves. Something's been in here. Foxes or coons. A scavenger raided the food stores while we were fighting. The seats are slashed to pieces, the contents of our bags scattered. My gloves are nowhere to be found.

Giving them up for lost, I prop my foot in the windowsill and swing up onto the cab. From there I launch myself across the small divide and onto the trailer, the tools smacking my thighs, bruising my hips as I go.

When I reach the end of the trailer, I drop to my stomach and inch to the edge, so I can get a good look at the harpoon.

Fluxing Blys.

The clamps have pierced the door inside and out. Four sharpened points twisted into the metal. It would be easier if I had metal cutters, but that might also do irreparable damage to the door. And I can't afford to lose this haul. Not if I expect Mars to help me with Lenore.

I go to work with the pliers, prying at the metal points, my hands blistering without the gloves. I'm making very little headway.

I ask Winter for help.

She ignores me.

I curse her because none of this is my fault.

Kyn's face fills my mind, his bloodied, broken face.

I curse her again.

"Please," I beg. "Please."

But there's something strange in the breeze that smacks me flat in the face. Something gleeful in the chill that works its way down my spine.

How does she do that? How does she make me feel her emotions? And why?

I twist hard at the metal pinched inside my pliers. Finally, a prong gives.

I cry out—exhaustion and frustration mixed with a small triumph—and then I set to work on the others.

The wind has died away now. Everything is still. Flakes of snow float on the air and settle on my chapped face. I brush them away and grin as I work another prong free. The sense of victory is overwhelming and it takes me a minute to realize the only one I'm fighting here is Winter. She wants this to be hard. She wants Kyn dead.

AND WHY SHOULDN'T HE DIE? she screams, suddenly there, suddenly everywhere. **SOMEONE SHOULD PAY FOR MY WOLVES.**

"But not him!" My teeth grind and my hand twists on the tool.

Kyn wakes. I hear his cries. Words now, not just unintelligible groans. I'm not brave enough to ask Winter if it was her doing. Instead, I work harder.

Three prongs free, and then four!

But I'm too tired to rejoice. I drop the pliers to the ground and yank the mallet from my belt.

I have to pull myself upright in order to reach the back of the harpoon. Have to sit on the edge of the trailer. I lean out as far as

I can and whack the end of the projectile with the mallet. Again and again.

The projectile shifts forward with each strike and still I swing harder.

I pull it back one last time and the mallet flies from my hand. I wheel around and find myself looking up at Hyla standing behind me on the trailer.

"Mars is asking for you," she says, my mallet held aloft.

"Kyn needs kol," I say. "Can't you hear him?"

And then I realize there's nothing to hear. The sky has gone quiet. Kyn's wails are gone and there's nothing but a deadly silence glistening on the snow.

CHAPTER 13

"HE'S NOT DEAD, MISS QUINE."

He's not. Kyn's not dead. He's been ghosted up and into the trailer, into the sleeper cab. The mess has been shoved to the far corner and, despite the cross-hatching of red slashes across his chest and neck, Kyn looks almost peaceful against the mismatched blankets and pillows that make up my bed.

"He looks . . . better," I say. The blood has been dabbed away and something shimmers on Kyn's wounds, something wet.

I'm sitting next to him on the bed, my hands clasped, not quite resting in my lap, not quite reaching for his softly curled fingers. My heart bangs about in my rib cage, its edges sharp, its corners jagged. Every beat stabs and slices and I know my insides will never be the same again.

I've never felt what I'm feeling right now.

"You had kol," I say, surprised by my own surprise. Mars has it running through his veins. Should I be shocked that he carries some on his person? "What did you mix it with? Snow?"

"We don't mix kol with her magic. It's blasphemous."

I knew that. Somewhere in the back of my mind I did. I'd been taught the Kerce beliefs about Winter's magic and kol.

"You need to stay with him," Mars says. There's something in his voice. It sounds a lot like guilt.

I turn to face him. "We need to go."

"We will," Mars says.

"We can't linger here. Not in the pass. There shouldn't be another squad of Rangers nearby, but there's no knowing what Winter will conjure next. She's strongest here. We need to go."

"We will. But not before we've gathered what twyl we can."

"Twyl?"

"Dove foxes ravaged our store. Adorable little lovers, aren't they?" He closes his eyes, rubs a heavy hand over his neck muscles.

We really need to go.

"How much twyl do you think we need?"

"We've still got the Seacliff Road ahead of us, Miss Quine. I know from my experience on the Kol Sea that we can't navigate that without a decent store of it."

I go still, fighting to keep my face clear. Maybe he trusts me now. Maybe it isn't just fatigue that has him spilling his secrets, but he's given me a lot of information in very few words and my mind spins, looking for answers. Looking for the rebel camp.

The Seacliff Road.

That means we're taking the Shiv Road all the way to the mines at North Bend.

From there, you can't turn west along the northern coast, not in a rig. The road turns east on a roughly cut stretch of rock called the Seacliff Road.

But that road was abandoned years ago—the waters in the surrounding seas have the highest concentration of kol anywhere on or near Layce, and it is prime hunting grounds for the Abaki.

"Abaki" loosely translates to *abomination* in the common tongue. Few on the island have ever seen one and lived to share much about the encounter. Everything I know about that stretch of road says there's no safe place for a camp. Which really only leaves one option for a legitimately hidden location.

Queen's Point, the tip of Layce's northeast wing. A mountainous peninsula that could combat some of the kol blowing in off the sea. Anything beyond that and we would have turned south after High Pass, approached the eastern shore from the other direction.

And Kyn. Kyn's never taken the Shiv Road—he said as much—but he has been to the camp. And if Mars has spent time on the Kol Sea, that means there has to be a hidden port somewhere along the northern coast.

Of course there is! It's how he gets his Paradyian wares onto Layce. And given the bounty on his head and his reputation as a smuggler, he'd never be allowed to dock alongside the Majority vessels in Glas. It'd have to be as far from there as possible. In a location the Majority would never risk investigating.

With the Kol Sea pushing violently against the cliffs, and those rife with its monsters—real and perceived—the rebels would have no fear of a surprise visit by a Majority vessel. If you had enough twyl and a way to keep the Abaki out, it might just be the perfect location for a hidden camp.

Suddenly the twyl loss isn't just an inconvenience; it's a desperate thing. If we're going to truck the Seacliff Road, we need twyl. And a lot of it.

"We've passed the bulk of the Shiv crop," Mars is saying, "but there's a small patch beyond the tree line. I saw it from above. Hyla's headed there now."

Shyne wouldn't like us helping ourselves to the twyl at High Pass, but as our relationship is already strained . . .

"I can go," I say, dragging my eyes from Kyn's face.

"Stay," Mars says. "We'll be back shortly."

And then he's gone and I'm left with the first bloodied boy Winter's ever laid at my feet.

She's killed before. Of course she has. She's a force of nature. I've never blamed her for that. We're on her island, not the other way around. When I stare at her mountains and her crystal trees, when I look into the vicious eye of a storm or stare into the gaze of a Frost White, it's like looking into the spotted mirror dangling from the windshield of the Dragon.

I see myself in her. We disappoint people, hurt them sometimes. But we're only being what we were created to be and there's beauty in that. For the first time, I wonder if the beauty is there to shield the other.

The rage.

Kyn's hand twitches, clenches. A word dribbles from his lips.

"It's OK," I say, reaching out, taking his hand in mine. "You're OK."

He grips my hand and his body stills, but as we sit here perched in the throne room of Winter's glory, I know it's a lie. And when Winter slinks into the cab, when she climbs up my calves and settles in my lap, when she whispers her apologies and coos about misunderstandings, my lip trembles.

How is it I've made friends with such a monster?

How have I garnered her affection?

What have I done?

"Leave," I tell her. "Leave me alone."

It's not really a command is it? Not so much. Not one Mystra Dyfan ever heeded anyway. She never let me be when I just wanted to think.

No, it's not a command, but I feel Winter's absence nonetheless. And though I'm tired of her duplicity, I'm afraid of what happens if I truly offend her. If she leaves me for good. I can't lose both her and Lenore.

I blink back a set of warm tears. Swipe them on the shoulders of my parka. My vision is still wet, but through the moisture I see the etching on Kyn's index finger. On the stone flesh covering his knuckle. I can look at it properly now, without an audience. I lift his hand and run my own finger over the carving. It's a Shiv symbol—a letter maybe—two half-moons facing each other, staggered, a line bisecting them. I don't know what it means.

But I've lost track of the minutes since Mars left to track down twyl, and that tells me it's been too long. I release Kyn's hand again, intending to back out of the sleeper cab, when my thoughts snag on the three lines of crusty brown scab that have formed on his cheek.

Not scab. Surely not. It's too soon for that. Even with the kol.

Winter's white light is all I have in the sleeper—the windows in the cab let it in. It pushes weakly past the open curtain, long stretches of shadow painting the small alcove. I'm half off the bed, but I climb back up, kneel on the soft mattress, and lean over Kyn's face.

I've never watched a man sleep before. Not unless you count Old Man Drypp. And I didn't need to watch him to know he was good and tired. Snores rattled from his throat, filling his rooms and bullying their way into ours. But not Kyn. Kyn is quiet. If it weren't for his warm breath on my lips, I'd be forced to search for a pulse.

But he's breathing.

He's alive.

And the deep gashes on his face are closed. I run a soft finger over their rippled surface. The kol never acted this quickly on Drypp.

It was Winter who did this. Winter who closed Kyn's wounds.

I asked and she answered.

And then I sent her away.

"Your hands are cold," Kyn says.

I start, pull my hand back. He catches it, pressing my palm to his fevered skin.

"Stay," he says, his voice tired and scratching.

But I roll back on my heels, putting some distance between our faces. "We have to go," I say. "I'll get you some snow for this."

"Always taking off when things get interesting," he says, but my fingers slide easily from his and I back out of the sleeper cab, my face as hot as his.

The running board on the passenger side has been mangled beyond use. I drop from the seat to the road. But instead of crunching into fresh powder or even the slippery ice pack, I splash into a puddle.

Ah, flux.

"Mars!" I scream, taking off, running. "Stop! You have to stop!"

Water splashes onto the road around me, the mountains on my right and left melting like Lenore's famous icy creams.

I follow a trail of melted snow into the trees edging the highway, yelling for Mars. For Hyla. Under the pine cover, it's darker and I nearly smack into them as they emerge from behind a massive tree.

"If you're going to bark orders at anyone, Miss Quine, bark them at Winter."

He's limping, in pain, but the look on his face is sheer anger. He's holding Hyla up, his arm around the woman's waist, hefting her as best he can. Blood pours from her shoulder.

I move to help, but Mars raises his hand, Drypp's pick axe in his grip. "You were hurt before. Bleeding."

"I'm fine. It's stopped." I bat his hand away and slide under Hyla's other arm, doing what I can to help, but I barely reach her chest.

"What happened?" I ask.

"Winter threw a tantrum while we were gathering the twyl."

"It was an icicle, Sessa."

"Mars is the only one I've seen flinging icicles."

"It was not Mars who did this. It was her. Your lady, Winter."

Habit begs me to argue, but the tree overhead is melting away, snow turning to water, dripping from its branches, slipping down my collar.

"You have to stop, Mars. If you melt away the road—"

"We've covered this, Miss Quine. And you were quite convincing. This is not my handiwork."

We find the highway, but it's slick. The ice hard in some places and wet in others. It's impossible to know where to step.

"Winter wouldn't do this to herself. She wouldn't destroy . . . Even in full Blys, even when the avalanche risk is at its highest, the road here stays frozen. This isn't something she would do of her own accord."

"Her game is bigger than this moment," Mars says. "Like all warriors, she's not above a strategic loss. Not if it convinces you I'm to blame."

"She's not a warrior. She's . . ." *A friend?* "She's a season."

"Not *a* season," Mars says. "She's the *only* season on Shiv Island. Her power cannot be allowed to go unchecked."

I haven't the energy to heft Hyla and argue, so I focus on my feet and the uncertain terrain under them. We skid and slip our way to the Sylver Dragon, but there's no hope of us hoisting her up into the cab.

"Stand back," Mars says, reaching out, pushing me aside.

I stumble away and watch as Mars whispers something in Kerce. Winter kicks up a gust of wind. It fights with Hyla's weight and Mars has to repeat himself, louder, more insistent. Hyla's boots leave the ground and Mars lays her gently in the passenger seat.

"Would you prefer I take the lookout, Miss Quine?"

"What?"

"Are you still concerned about a Shiv attack? If so, I could take the lookout," Mars says, tugging the bloodied scarf away from his side and dropping it to the ground. "It's fine," he says, catching my stare. "Like you, I'm a quick healer. The lookout then?"

"No," I say, the idea of breaking up our little party a discomfort not worth analyzing just now. "You'd best stay inside with us, keep an eye on Kyn."

The water at our feet is rushing now, coming at us from all sides, splashing against the tank tread, spilling over the top of our boots. It steals the muddied scarf and drags it over the shoulder and into a swift-moving current rushing downhill. "I could make her refreeze it?" Mars ponders aloud. "The highway."

"No, don't. Let's just get out of the pass."

I follow Mars around the front of the rig, gripping the Dragon's grill, fighting to keep my feet underneath me. Hefting Hyla took what little energy I had left. "You couldn't have asked Winter to carry Hyla back here from the forest?"

"Look at you, Miss Quine, encouraging me to use magic."

I flick my cheek at his back as he climbs up and into the cab.

A thin crack splits the air and I watch as a slab shifts high on the mountain. Racers of powder slide down the rock face. Every bit of displaced snow, Mars's fault. I feel it in my bones. Bones that are wrapped tightly in Winter's hold. She's angry I sent her away, but she hasn't left me. She hasn't—

"We were in a hurry last I checked, Miss Quine."

In two steps, I'm up and into the driver's seat. I turn the key and the engine jumps to life. Forcing my jittery legs to calm, I ease my foot onto the gas. The tread catches immediately and the Sylver Dragon rolls forward.

"There are things about Winter—"

"You say nothing," I say, shifting until I find a comfortable gear. "Not now. Not until I get us out of the pass. The ice is gone. The highway's a rutted mess. I've never had to navigate this stretch in these conditions. Five minutes, Mars. Can you keep your mouth shut for five minutes?"

If he's seething next to me, I can't tell and don't care. There's very little room to work with here. The mountains press in on both sides, scraggly trees jutting here and there from the rocky wall. They brush the sides of the truck, scraping at windows that are barely hanging on. I eye the branches as we push through, beg and plead with Winter to let us be. Her hatred of Mars is a palpable thing. But she's exhausted. The fight in the pass, the death of her wolves—it's taken something out of her.

I push the gas pedal closer to the floor and the Dragon barrels over the summit, breaking free of the dark trees and imposing mountain walls, out into the white light of day.

The road drops immediately as we start our descent. I pull my foot off the gas, letting the weight of the Dragon do all the work. The front end bobs and sparks fly as the bucket strikes the road—it's to be expected with the exposed potholes and the lack of ice, but it throws us around the cab, making our teeth rattle and Kyn cry out in the sleeper.

For a solid minute we'll have an unfettered view of the Desolation. I take it in. The vast spread of ice. So cold, smoke rises off it, hanging thicker in some places than others. Despite the thawing pass, the Desolation far below is frozen thick, but if there is life beneath it, there are no signs from here. Still, that strange, sylver ribbon remains. From somewhere deep, just north of the pool's center, it twists westward.

"What is it?" Hyla asks.

"Begynd," Mars says, his voice quiet. "The fount."

An irrational rage bubbles inside my chest and I wonder if

it's me—truly me—who's angry. Or is it Winter? Has she crawled inside my ribs, built her home near my heart?

The road forks here—a wide left toward the Seacliff Road or a sharp right to the southern tip of the isle. With the rebel camp shimmering bright in my mind, nestled on the northeastern wing, I take the turn north.

"It's almost like you know where we're heading, Miss Quine."

I twist the wheel in my hands, checking the mirror for his expression. But he's draped elegantly in the corner, his face turned toward the Desolation. It's better if he doesn't know I've sorted out the location of the camp. Not until I've decided what to do with the knowledge. But he's right. I'm driving with the confidence of a rigger who knows her way. And that's something I haven't felt since we left Hex Landing.

"You did mention the Seacliff Road," I say.

He takes a deep breath and lets it go, his exhale fogging the window. "Did I?"

He's so rarely quiet, I leave it there, the Dragon filling the silence kindly. She rattles and drones, her pieces and parts chattering constantly. But even over the constant hum, even over Hyla's moans of discomfort, a rumble cracks its way into the cab and shakes what's left of our windows.

"Avalanche," Mars says, without bothering to check the mirrors.

I've no such restraint. In my side mirror, I see a plume of snow. It fills the pass and blots out the sky beyond it.

"She hated you before," I say. "She'll try to kill you now."

"This is not the first battle between Winter and myself, Miss Quine. We've bloodied each other plenty."

The road curves for another mile and then straightens out. We've reached the Shiv Road, a stretch of highway that has a very different feel. There are kol mines and twyl farms beyond the mountains to our left and the Desolation constantly on our right. We catch glimpses of it between gaps in the line of snow-plastered evergreens trimming the road.

"I wonder what it was like for the Shiv, swimming in the pool, taking their leisure in waters that heal." With her window covered by canvas, Hyla watches the Desolation through the windshield. "Do you ever wonder such things?" She doesn't look at me, doesn't address the question to me, but she's speaking so softly no else could be expected to hear.

"No," I say.

"Truly?" she asks, wincing as she turns to face me. "You truck this road all the time, do you not?"

"Not all the time."

She stares back at me, her goggles tangled in her hair and warmth bleeding from her eyes. She's like Drypp, I think. Warm. Kind. Out of place in this frozen world. Why did she ever leave Paradyia?

"It would insult Winter," I say, forcing my eyes back to the road. "To imagine her any other way. I wouldn't do that."

Beneath the tank tread the ice is solid again. I adjust myself in the seat and loosen my grip on the wheel.

It's not long before Hyla's asleep.

"How long have you been friendly with the Rangers?" Mars asks.

"I don't know what you think you saw back there, but we're not friendly."

"But you pay them for safe passage?"

"Clients won't trust your abilities if you have a reputation for losing your haul to Rangers. I learned early on that a few coins are the best way to get them to leave you alone."

"If the Majority found out—"

"You're a smuggler, Mars. Flouting Majority law with every shipload of goods," I say, testing.

"But outlawing the private mining of kol, keeping it only for their own profit, enslaving two peoples who lived here long before they did—those are laws I cannot support. Laws I happily bend."

"Bend?"

"Break. Shatter. One day I hope to use their own laws against them."

"And how do you plan to do that?"

"There are ways."

It's easier to talk to him like this. With him behind me, with his sneers and piercing gaze impossible to see so long as I avoid the mirror.

"I hate kol," I say.

"Do you?" He's amused.

"It has its uses. I know that. But there are other ways—there have to be—ways that don't have us playing with a mineral that causes so much harm."

"Shiv Island *is* kol. The black veins are at its very heart, buried beneath the snow and the colored rock. You speak of dishonoring Winter by imagining her differently. What does it say that you would imagine your home another way? The island that cradles you."

"It's not the same."

"The kol has taken no pains to befriend you," Mars says, a smile in his voice.

"That's not it."

"Kol knows its place, Miss Quine."

"What does that mean?"

"It means that Winter does not. She oversteps."

"Is that why you hate her so much?"

"I hate her for what she did to my family. What she still does to them."

"The Kerce?"

"They should have been left in peace on their own island. To live and thrive as they had for generations. Instead, the Majority invaded and the Kerce people fled here—in desperation, needing help—"

"From the Shiv."

"—but they were too different."

"Is that real feeling I hear in your voice? I'm surprised."

"That the heartless smuggler has convictions? I have my own law, but I would never condemn the Shiv to live as they have done. In caves, exposed to Winter's hate, yearning for—"

"Begynd?"

"Your doubt feels desperate, Miss Quine."

I don't reply.

"I suppose they've done all they could while they waited." His last words trickle away, swallowed by the Dragon and her rumblings.

"What was that?"

"The Kerce have meandered and peddled their gifts—"

"No not that. You were speaking of the Shiv."

He finds my gaze in the mirror. "I was saying that the Shiv did better than the Kerce. They did the best they could while they waited."

"While they waited for Begynd to climb up out of the Desolation and save them?"

"They did the best they could while they waited . . . for you."

My eyes snap to his, and suddenly he looks like Shyne. The set of his jaw, the wide-open dare in his eyes. *Ask me*, it says. *Let me tell you who you are.* But before I can say a thing, the rig takes on a pothole and the mirror swings wildly, breaking our eye contact.

"No more talking," I say. "We're coming up on the Cages."

CHAPTER 14

WINTER ISN'T THE ONLY ONE WHO NEVER shuts up.

"Miss Quine," Mars says.

"We're not talking, remember?"

"Why would a mapmaker call this section of the road the Dark Depths?" He stretches a crumpled road map on his knees, flattening the edges.

"Where'd you find that?"

"Dove foxes must have dug it up. Found this as well." He lifts one of my old stocking caps from the seat, a faded blue-and-gray-striped thing I couldn't be happier to see. My favorite cap is buried somewhere beneath the melting snow of High Pass with Kyn's rifle.

The bench seat squeals beneath Mars and his fingers catch in my hair as he moves forward. My braid's a knotted mess, but there's no time to fix it now. Instead, I take the cap from his hand and wedge it on my head. We're not far from the first drop.

"Strange thing," I say. "There isn't a single rebel camp on that map. Something you could remedy if you wanted to."

"I bet I could," Mars says, his voice quiet.

"Still don't trust me?" I ask. "I told you, I need your help with Lenore. She's not going to climb into the Dragon on her own. Not after the fight we had."

"I imagine you can be quite convincing when you want to be. And it didn't sound like much of a fight at all, Miss Quine. Not from Miss Trestman's account."

"What did she say?" I ask, irritated he knows things about Lenore that I don't.

"She was angry that you wouldn't listen, frustrated that you wouldn't help. She was ready to fight for what she wanted, but you? You slammed the door in her face and took to the road."

I can hear Lenore's voice. The waspish tone she used when she told him that.

My answer was one I've given her time and time again. Now I spit it at Mars. "I had a job to do."

"Then you understand my dilemma, Miss Quine. I too have a job, and it requires we reach the camp together in one piece. Now," he says, "tell me why this old map refers to your cages as the Dark Depths."

I roll my neck, blow the tension out through my nose.

"Miss Quine—"

"It depends on who you ask," I say. "To the kol miners who first called this stretch of road the Cages, the steepness of the grade reminded them of the large metal enclosures that dropped them deep into the island. Combine the sharp incline with the grabbing knot of trees we'll encounter on the way down, and it's impossible not to feel caged in."

"And the Dark Depths?"

I shrug. "I've heard a few rig drivers use that name. Mostly though, riggers avoid this stretch of road. The darkness here is a problem, especially in the night hours."

"Your Dragon has headlamps, does it not?"

"It does, but they work against us down there. Fog settles in the low places and bounces the light around, blinding more than helping. If we can manage it at all, we need to clear the Cages before the sun goes down. Which means . . ."

"No talking."

"And sit back. I can't do this with you breathing down my neck."

"Whatever you say, Miss Quine."

I press my foot hard to the brake and the Dragon screams to a stop, the trailer fishing around. Mars is thrown backward— something I hear rather than see. Hyla gropes for a handhold, but it's reflex only. Her eyes never open.

"Miss Quine—"

I turn my face to his, my braid flying. "Can I hold you to that?"

"To what?" He's rubbing at his head, checking his fingers for blood.

"To doing whatever I say? Until we get through the last of the Cages, can I trust that you will do whatever I need you to do?"

"I assure you, Miss Quine—"

"Yes or no, Dresden? Can I trust you?"

His face is unreadable, his crusted lips a thin line, his gaze holding mine. I look for a challenge there, a fight. But all he says is, "You can."

"Good." I flip forward once more and my hair snags again in his knuckles. I yank my gnarled braid away and tuck it up and into my stocking cap. "Now, back!"

He settles against the wall of the cab and the air is suddenly lighter around me. I slide the Dragon into gear and push her forward. Ahead, the highway drops. It'll drop and climb three separate times, the grades steeper with each incline. The first will take us close to sea level, forcing us through a knot of grandfather oaks that grow humped and knotted in a tangle over the road. Unlike the highway west of High Pass, the Shiv Road is not maintained—the Rangers don't patrol it with any regularity and the trees are left to do their worst.

I can tell Bristol's been here. He must have taken the road through Hex Landing and made the turn onto the Desolation stretch near Kasebyrg. Snow has fallen since he's passed, but it's minimal, and the tracks from his rig are still visible. Small mounds of snow line both sides of the roadway where his plow has made a way forward.

With the first of the cages dead ahead, the road disappears, and nothing but a wide expanse of sky fills the shattered windshield. The cloud cover is purpling, the sun far beyond it slipping toward the horizon. I do the math and curse.

"We won't make it before sundown. It'll be two solid hours before we clear the last cage."

"If we wait out the night, we're complicating matters," Mars says.

"I know," I say, shifting gears as the drop approaches. "We can't wait. Layce is already melting."

"You can do this, Miss Quine? You've done it before."

"A little late to worry about that now, isn't it?"

The Dragon trundles forward and over the top of the first drop. My stomach plummets as we rock forward; the bucket smacks the ice, shaving it as we plunge headfirst into airy wisps of fog. I cringe but keep my foot on the gas. Another two smacks of the bucket and the rig settles in.

"Shouldn't we slow down?" Mars asks, his hands wrapped around the edges of my seat.

"Not if we want to make it up the next incline," I say. "We'll need every bit of the momentum we can generate on the downside of this thing. The trick is not to lose control."

"I thought you said the darkness is our greatest problem?"

"A nightmare," I say. "But not until we get to the bottom. Now, sit back." I drag my stocking cap down over my ears, muffling the noise.

The fog thickens, pressing against the glass in great white swirls. I don't need the headlamps just yet, so I leave them switched off. Our visibility is already scant.

The trees aren't an issue until we're about a quarter of the way down. And then they leap in with a ferocious hunger, their knobby branches present and sudden and groping through the fog.

Ice coats each limb, but it's thawing. Water drips in a thin, steady trickle, turning the white ground to mud—a visual we only get in spurts and stops. The trees slap the cracked windshield and scratch at the trailer. They snap off left and right, the frozen appendages popping and bending.

We're moving fast, dropping deeper and deeper into the cage, and I have to work my jaw to clear my ears. After fifteen or twenty ticks I notice more proof of Bristol's passing. Recent breakage and dangling limbs. Markings where his rock saw cut away stubborn branches.

"I was hoping to save the motors," I murmur.

"Louder, Miss Quine."

"I'm going to need your help," I say, raising my voice and turning my face but not my eyes.

"Yes?"

"Beneath the passenger seat is a lever. Normally I can reach it, but Hyla's—"

"—in the way." Mars moves so that he's between the front two seats. He leans forward and pushes Hyla's legs aside. She moans and shifts, but she doesn't wake.

"Can you reach it?" I say, glancing back and forth between Mars's twisted body and the hazy road.

"Yes, Miss Quine. I can reach it. What does it do?"

"The rock saws will engage. The motors will wear quickly in this thick growth, but the trees . . . I was hoping to make it as far as the second cage before we had to use them."

Another barrage of limbs. The Dragon is much taller than Bristol's rig and we're taking a beating from the higher branches. The windshield groans and snaps, bits of glass flake away. The canvas on Hyla's hastily patched window tears, the sound lost in the chaos. The limbs will be inside soon if we don't do something.

"Would you like me to pull the lever, Miss Quine?"

"Yes," I say, and then, with conviction: "Do it."

Mars flips the lever and though I'm tempted, I don't ask Winter for assistance. I don't ask for her help. I'd rather she keep her distance just now. I'm not sure I've forgiven her for what happened to Kyn at High Pass and though I'm glad she hasn't left me for good, I can't handle another confrontation between her and Mars.

The mechanism engages and the blades whir to life. My right hand finds the control panel—two dowels, one for the right arm and one for the left. With my little finger on one and my thumb on the other, I work the arms into place—branches shear off as I go. When both arms are extended out to the left and right, their saw blades spinning, I lock them into position with a flick of my thumb, my foot still pressed hard to the floor.

"You use these often?" Mars asks, lingering between my seat and Hyla's, watching the blades spin.

I shake my head. "No. But before she was mine, the Dragon was used for rock trenching. The blades are not ideal for half-frozen trees, but there wasn't time to retrofit them. You can see Bristol had the same idea, though his saws are better suited for this kind of growth."

The Dragon's blades are large, five feet across. They pivot on their hefty arms, rotating as they spin, hacking away at the branches, their motors making it impossible to hear anything quieter than a holler.

"What's that glinting from the blades?" Mars asks.

"Diamond," I say.

He snorts.

"You disapprove?"

"Not at all. Though it would stagger the Paradyians to see diamond put to such a use. It's a difficult rock to come by there and highly sought after. The women wear it around their necks and in their ears."

"Is that true?"

"Yes. But only for the very wealthy."

"It's waste rock here. In the mines they have to battle it to get to the kol. It's impossible to cut through but it makes a wicked tough blade."

"Supply and demand, Miss Quine. It's what makes me rich."

"Are you rich?" I ask, yelling over the sound of the saws.

"Not nearly rich enough."

The fog is dense now, my visibility gone. I can't see past the bucket but I don't dare slow.

"I've never cared much for coin," I yell.

"That's not at all what I hear." There's a challenge in his voice, a question.

"People say what they want. Doesn't make it true."

He strokes his chin, narrows his eyes. "But if you were rich—let's say you're as rich as the King of Paradyia. What would you buy?"

The rig plunges deeper and deeper and I do the same, searching my heart for anything I need that I don't already have. "There is nothing," I say, honestly.

"Liar."

It's loud and my voice is tired from yelling, but there's something about the steady racket, the contentious banter—it's so alive.

"I have everything I need in the Sylver Dragon. I'd have her repaired, I suppose. Give her the royal treatment. But as long as I have the rig, I have freedom. That's all I've ever really wanted."

"And the tavern?"

"It's Lenore's home, her livelihood, so of course I'd want that. But for her. Not for myself."

"And what of Miss Trestman?"

The resentment I'd been ignoring splits wide at the question, pricks my nose with hurt. I'd done everything I could to see that Leni had all the coin she needed and yet . . .

"If I could buy her safety," I say, "I would. But that can't be done here."

"You make a fair point," he says, thoughtful. "Some things cannot be secured with coin. And still, I do not believe you have everything you need."

Another face breaks into my thoughts. A dark face with a stone cheekbone and eyes like spiced wine. A mouth that smiles easily.

I don't need Kyn—I barely know him. But the stirring in my chest reminds me that there are other things in this life I didn't know I wanted. Things I might come to need.

I sit taller in my seat when another desire surfaces. "I'd buy freedom for the workers in the Stack."

"How noble of you," Mars says. The saws drag, the motors struggling, and I'm too distracted to read his tone. Can't tell if he's serious or mocking.

"What about you?" I ask. "What would you buy?"

"If I had all the riches of the Paradyian King? Simple," Mars yells. "I'd buy an army."

I laugh. "And would you lead it?"

"Perhaps. Why? Do you not think me capable?"

"I think it unnecessary. What is it you want that you cannot take with your magic? Why indebt others to violence when you can carry the burden alone?"

"You forget, Miss Quine, that if Winter leaves Shiv Island, much of my magic goes with her."

"What do you mean?"

"The kol in my blood gives me a measure of authority over Winter. That's all it does. Were she to be banished from Shiv Island—"

"You'd be just a man."

"A devilishly handsome, charismatic, swashbuckling man. But yes. I would be less than I am."

"And still you want her gone from this place?"

"More than life itself."

The road bottoms out, the blades now slogging their way through wet foliage. As we begin to climb, the trees thin, and then the fog, the momentum of our swift drop propelling us up the mountainside.

"We should save the motors," I say, reaching out.

"I'll do it," Mars says, batting my hand away and leaning forward.

The motors grind to a halt and the arms fold in on themselves, elbow and wrist tucked close, until the saws are resting against the Dragon.

"So quiet," Mars says, more to himself than anything. It is quieter without the saw blades spinning, but we're still fighting branches here and there, still taking swats at the windows and the bucket. It's nothing the Dragon can't handle and I press my foot down hard on the gas as the incline steepens.

"You've a strange look on your face, Miss Quine."

"A strange look you wouldn't be able to see if you were sitting back in your seat."

"Ah, but if I were sitting back in my seat, I would be no help with the lever."

"We've a good half hour before we'll need the saws again." Still Mars doesn't move. "Why don't you check on Kyn?"

He meets my gaze in the mirror. "I'm not quite sure you understand the caliber of people I employ."

"Is he your employee or your friend? You seem confused by the distinction."

Another long stare before Mars grunts and withdraws. A small victory, I think.

He disappears into the sleeper cab, the curtain snapping shut behind him, and it's almost like being alone for a moment. Hyla's here, but she's settled down again and is snoring, her golden curls resting against her cheek, turning the bloodied soldier innocent.

Useless, the lot of them.

CHAPTER 15

VOICES PUSH THEIR WAY THROUGH THE sleeper's velvet curtain and another knot of something unwinds inside me. Kyn's awake.

Why his injuries bother me more than the outright murder of Jymy Leff, I can't say, but it's not a feeling I enjoy. Kyn's a hired gun, a smuggler, and going by the company he keeps, a rebel sympathizer. Are his crimes less than Jymy's? I don't know. Neither concerned me much before recent events. I just wish I knew what it was about Kyn that makes me . . . worry. I've only ever worried about Lenore.

A grain ball drops into my lap. "You're not sleeping are you, Miss Quine?"

"I'm tempted," I say through my teeth as I use them to untie the twine.

"Well, don't. Kyndel's doing much better, but I doubt we could depend on him to negotiate these cages."

"How is he?" I ask, fighting to keep my voice even.

"Awake. Testing your store of rations. It seems the foxes were more interested in the twyl chewing gum." Behind me, Mars is unwrapping something himself.

"Did the kol help?" I ask.

"I wouldn't use kol on Kyn," Mars says. "The Shiv are especially sensitive. It's why the Desolation Shiv don't like their twyl stores threatened, why they burn it day and night in their caves."

"But Kyn's wounds? How—"

"Do you believe in anything, Miss Quine? Anything at all?" My heart is thundering and I can't understand why. I'm considering the question but he doesn't seem to need an answer. "A brief stop would do us all good, I think."

I raise my brows at him in the rearview.

"You want me to stop?"

"Even smugglers need to relieve themselves, Miss Quine. And if we won't make it through before nightfall, we might as well be comfortable."

A quick respite wouldn't be the worst thing, I realize, shifting in my seat. "It'll have to wait until we clear this cage."

"Fair enough."

We're hardly climbing now, the engine growling with the effort of dragging us up and over. The last quarter of a mile is painful, my calf cramping as I fight to keep the pedal to the floor. It's a strange thing, climbing and climbing and never feeling any closer to the clouds overhead. They're more gray than purple now, the night brutish in its constancy.

"I see now what you meant about momentum," Mars says.

"We'll make it. If your haul was any heavier, though . . ."

I try to find his eyes in the rearview, but his gaze is on the dried meat in his hands. He takes a bite, his face betraying nothing.

The rig shudders and spits a plume of exhaust out the smoke stack and we finally crest the top of the hill. The air is still and clear, the fog far below us now. The clouds are still in the darkening sky and I pull to the side of the road, more out of habit than necessity. There's no one out here.

"We should wake Hyla and Kyn," I say. "It'll be hours before we reach North Bend."

"I'm awake," Kyn says. His voice is groggy but strong.

"Think you can walk?" I ask.

"He can walk," Mars says, a satisfied grin on his face as he takes in his old friend. "Lead the way, Miss Quine."

"And Hyla?" I say. She's still snoring.

"One invalid at a time."

I drop to the snow and turn to offer Kyn some help. But he's landing next to me already.

"You *are* better," I say.

"Much." He's changed his shirt and the jagged cuts on his face are nothing but pink memories. Hardly raised. Hardly visible. A familiar chill climbs my back and I know there's only one explanation for it.

"I think Winter has another favorite."

"Is that what you think?" Kyn says, a sad smile on his face. He steps past me, making for the trees. They're of the evergreen sort up here. Tall and full and iced like the sugared cakes we haven't had since the day we put Drypp in the ground.

Mars follows him, dabbing at his lip. "Not too far, my friend.

We should stay close enough to hear Sylvi's screams if Winter forsakes her."

Kyn slaps Mars on the back and it seems bygones are truly that with these two. I can almost feel Kyn choose to let it all go. To see the friend he has in Mars instead of the secrets and deceit. The realization does strange, swooping things to my stomach as I pad into the trees on the opposite side of the rig. I'm still lacing up my trousers when they return.

"Hustle, hustle, Miss Quine."

"Some of us can't just whip it out," I call, but I lace faster.

I hear their voices as they unload Hyla, hear her discomfort as they guide her away and into the trees. I wonder if it should be me offering to help, but they're out of sight by the time I work up the courage to ask.

This isn't something that would be foreign to her though. Hyla works in a world of men, much like I do. To survive, she would've learned to handle these moments long ago. But when they return, it's clear she's worse off than I realized. The wound on her shoulder has started bleeding again, her face gray and slick with exertion.

"Isn't there any kol?" I ask, racing forward, but with little purpose. Kyn and Mars are entirely capable. As they clear the trees, they kneel, lay Hyla in the snow. She's fevered and delirious.

Mars pulls on the leather ribbon that's hidden beneath his shirt and tugs a pouch from his collar—the Kerce medicine bag. He withdraws a phial, removes the stopper, and runs his fingers over the top of it. They come away wet with oil and he presses them to Hyla's shoulder, working it in small circles.

Twyl liniment.

It's the burnt-honey smell that gives it away. The tincture is made from equal parts twyl oil and horn leaf—an herb that won't grow on Layce. Lenore has a small stone vessel of it in her chest of drawers at home. Expensive, if you can find a vendor willing to part with it, but it's a good pain reliever and works on all sorts of minor wounds: bruising, abrasions, burns. Ingested, it can be used as a sleep aid. When we ran out of kol, Lenore mixed the liniment with wine and spoon-fed it to Drypp. It was the only thing that kept him comfortable.

Mars replaces the phial and withdraws another, this one kol. He pulls the stopper free and dust peppers the sky.

"She's going to be all sorts of fun after this," Kyn says, stepping away.

Mars spreads a thin layer on Hyla's wound and restoppers the phial. "She'll sleep through the worst, I th— Back up, Miss Quine."

Embarrassed, I roll back on my heels.

"We're desperately short on twyl and you'll need your mind clear if we're to traverse the final two cages in short order."

I didn't realize I'd gotten so close. It's not that I've never seen kol before, but it's expensive, even on the black market, and it's a cost I've only ever paid once—just after Drypp's attack. The kol we bought then wasn't raw, but refined, the side-effects tempered by the processing it goes through at the Stack.

I see now the appeal of the raw mineral. The magic in its appearance. And I wonder, for the first time, what it would be like to rub it on my gums, on my teeth. I wonder what it would be like to simply not care for a while. To not need food or drink. To need nothing but the kol.

"Miss Quine—"

I roll back again. I can't remember inching forward, but clearly—

"Come on," Kyn whispers. He's behind me now, turning me toward the rig. "Let's give the Dragon a quick look."

"The Dragon is fine," I say, a statement far from true.

He steers me around the rig and I listen to his observations about the damage the wolves and their masters have wrought. The hurt inflicted by the trees. I offer a few words, but mostly I'm fighting to see through the black haze that has clouded my vision. It's alive, the fog: kol-dusted rabbits bouncing through it; foxes digging through the crust for fish hiding below; monsters stomping toward me, their heads in their hands.

I bat them away.

"Sylvi," Kyn says. My eyes focus on his. Slowly, like binoculars when they're being twisted into position. "You in there?"

I nod. "I'm here."

His hands are on either side of my face. I'm not sure when that happened, but they're warm. Hot, even, against my chilled skin. "I'm here," I say, nestling into his palm.

He looks from one of my eyes to the other, and I fight the urge to lean into him, to let him hold me up. Sleep sounds so lovely. Singing sounds so lovely. Before I know it, a tune pushes its way through my lips, vibrating on my tongue, making me laugh.

"No, you're not," he says. "Here." He reaches into his pocket and pulls out a mangled twyl blossom. I see it all through a sheet of glittering black—Kyn twisting the blossom so that the stem falls away and then pulling a flint striker from the pocket of his coat. He strikes a spark onto the blue flower. It lights and in one puff of fire, the blue is an orange flame. Kyn opens his fingers and the blossom falls, spinning to the snow where it hisses into ash. He stoops and picks up the melted innards of the flower. A wad of warm, soft sap.

He offers it to me, the white gum harsh against his dark fingers. *Velvet*, I think, reaching out. He makes to hand me the gum, but I reach past the pale wad and stroke his hand. Yes, velvet. Like the drapes Drypp pulled tight around the bed Lenore and I slept in when tallying the tavern's coin kept the lamp burning late into the night. Velvet like the curtain separating the sleeper from the cab.

"The twyl, Sylvi." I hear a reprimand in his voice. Faint but disconcerting, like Mystra Dyfan's constant disappointment. I shake my head trying to make sense of it. What have I done now?

"What does it mean?" I ask, running my fingernail through the thin lines of the etched stone on his index finger. "The carving."

And then the twyl is in my mouth, pressed against my teeth. It's sweet and smoky. He forces my mouth open and pushes it onto my tongue.

"There," he says. "Chew."

I do, the warm gum hardening with every bite. There's very little magic in a single blossom, and even less when it isn't prepared properly, but it's strong. The twyl eats away at the black haze that's swallowed me whole, the gum leaving pocks in the veil until, at last, my vision is entirely restored and I'm left with nothing but the shame of my kol-induced actions.

Heat climbs my neck and face.

"I did tell you to back up," Mars says, swaggering over. He makes no attempt to hide his amusement while he leans lazily against the trailer, arms crossed.

"I thought the Kerce had some measure of protection against the kol," Kyn says, tipping my chin up, checking my eyes. My face is aflame.

"They do," Mars says. "Miss Quine should be quite immune, but she's let Winter in."

"Flux," Kyn says, the word thin and low.

"The kol is dormant in your veins," Mars says, ducking his head, finding my gaze. "Frozen, I'd guess. I can only imagine what it's doing to your insides."

"OK, Mars. That's enough." Kyn takes my elbow and starts back for the cab.

I tug my arm free. "What do you mean?" I ask. "*What it's doing to my insides*—what does that mean?"

He pulls that square of cloth from his pocket again. It's no longer clean and white. It's ratted, smeared with crusted blood and kol. He folds it in half and dabs the corner to his lips.

"These scabs are proof that I've wielded my power over Winter. Kol magic has consequences—it does, you're right. The words open a conversation between her and I and she takes every opportunity to bite at me. The kol mixes with her magic and tears my lips to pieces, but using the magic I've been given keeps the kol running fast and potent through my veins." He flattens his pale hand against his chest. "It keeps her out."

"I don't—"

"Not wielding your power has consequences as well. Winter is not warm, Miss Quine. She is not comfortable. If her words burn inside your belly, consider that it's likely a cold burn. The kind that kills. You can remain silent—that is always your prerogative—but just because we cannot see the consequences of your inaction doesn't mean you will escape unscathed."

LIAR, Winter whispers. She's listening. Of course she is. HE LIES.

"I'm not lying, Miss Quine." He steps closer, his boots knocking mine. "The authority over Winter is a birthright you cannot escape. It sits dormant in your veins and if you do not use it, if you invite Winter in, there's no knowing what all she'll freeze."

"You think Winter's—"

"I have no idea what she's doing to your heart, Miss Quine. There is no one like you. Not one soul with your unique relation to both the kol and Winter. But there is a reason the Kerce do not mix kol with her freezing magic."

"It's blasphemous," I say, remembering.

"Yes, Miss Quine. It is blasphemous. It's how she makes her monsters."

CHAPTER 16

THE DRIVER'S SIDE WINDOW WON'T LATCH properly anymore. Two finger-widths sit between the glass and the top of the sill. I pull the twyl gum from my mouth and pinch it out the window. The wind catches it and pulls it from my fingers as we rumble into the second cage.

It's bright enough up here, with the Desolation and the ever-present cloud cover bouncing moonlight back and forth, but we're descending now. The atmosphere grows blacker with each rotation of the tank tread, tendrils of fog fingering their way into my line of sight. I'll have to make a decision about the headlamps soon.

Everyone in the cab is awake—the first time since High Pass. Hyla's wound has been bound, and, after chewing our only surviving stick of twyl chewing gum, her eyes are clear. Mars and Hyla were able to collect a few blossoms before her injury, but they're unlikely to be very potent by the time we reach North Bend. Once we clear the Cages, we'll have to keep an eye out.

If my reaction to the spray off the Kol Sea is anything remotely similar to what I just experienced, we'll be in serious trouble if we don't have a stash of twyl before we reach the Seacliff Road.

Kyn is settled into his seat now, crunching on my store of honeycomb and passing around a canteen that's partially iced over. He taps it against my shoulder and I take a swig, not quite meeting his eyes.

I stroked his hands, didn't I? Rubbed them.

I don't know how to process what happened before. Where to tuck Mars's words so that they don't jab at my spine, at my ribs. He's made me uncomfortable and that's the thing I work hardest to avoid.

The water is cool and bright as it washes away the taste of twyl, but I allow myself only one small sip.

"Put it away now," I say. "I'm not stopping again until we reach the mines at North Bend."

"They're luckier in that way than you and me, Sessa," Hyla says, adjusting her arm. "They don't need a safe place to squat."

"Just an empty container," Mars says, taking a sip.

"The road's melting, Dresden. I don't imagine a pothole would be a pleasant obstacle while you're making use of a tin can."

Kyn snorts. He dumps a sip of water into Hyla's mouth and then caps the canteen, tossing it over his shoulder and into the sleeper cab. He's in a remarkably good mood for a man who was mauled by wolves.

Hyla swallows and uses her good arm to swipe at the water dripping off her chin. "Have I missed the Abaki, Sessa? You and Mars were talking about Winter's monsters, were you not? Did you see one?"

Mars catches my gaze in the mirror and I look away.

"My lady?"

"No, Hy," Kyn says, kindly. "You haven't missed the monsters."

"Good," she says. "That would be most disappointing."

In the hours since Mars mentioned the coastal stretch, there have been plenty of things to focus on, plenty of things to keep my mind from drifting too near that memory. But with talk of the Abaki so near and the kol softening my resolve, images from that day barrel in.

Drypp and I fishing a kidney-shaped pond the Blys before he died. My calves burning from the hike. The snow hadn't fully melted and it took us time to find a suitable fishing hole. White bricks bobbed in the shallow pool, but we could see life flitting below the surface of the black water. We'd settled in, both of us using our fishing buckets as stools, our lines nothing but sylver threads disappearing into the chill darkness.

Lenore hadn't wanted to come. She ventures out more in Blys than she does in Ryme, mostly for the sake of her garden and her hens, but when the outdoor chores are done, she keeps to the tavern.

Back then, she was taking on more of Drypp's workload. His mind had started to slow, hands shaking with age, eyes squinting at the barrels as he struggled to distinguish ale from lager.

The Kerce lessons had been abandoned the Ryme before when Drypp no longer had the energy to force me to go, and I'd already added my name to the Dragon and started taking her for short runs around town.

On this particular day, we were all precisely where we wanted to be. I needed nothing more than to be sitting on my bucket, listening to Drypp tell stilted tales about his childhood, about stealing skates when the smithy had his back turned and busting his lip taking his first go on the ice. I loved when he talked about his eight brothers and the snow caves they built, the month-long trapping excursions they took through the tightly knit trees of the northern woods.

I was just about to ask Drypp where his brothers had gone off to when a lone Abaki crawled over the rise.

My grip on the wheel tightens. "Unless we are extremely lucky, Hy, you'll see more than your share of monsters before this trip is over."

"I would like that very much," she says. "My father had a Kerce advisor who wrote out the Shiv and Kerce accounts for us. So we could shelve them next to the Paradyian histories in our library. So we could share them with our children."

"Why would Paradyian children care about our old myths and legends?"

"We collect them, Sessa. Paradyians value history. My father especially. Begynd, creator of the Shiv, was Sola's son, was he not? Together they created the islands scattered across the Wethyrd Seas. Begynd's work is Sola's work then. And we honor Sola above all."

"So you believe the stories?" I ask. "The accounts of Begynd and the Shiv. The Kerce exiles and Winter's vengeance."

Hyla shrugs, the action sending a shiver of pain through her body. "I do not know what I believe, Sessa. Your own people do not seem convinced. Mars tells me that the monsters are real, but the Majority—"

"You can't trust the Majority, Hy," Kyn says. "Not about the Shiv. Not about the Kerce."

Hyla groans and nods, sweat glistening on her lip as she rotates her injured shoulder.

"They're real," I say, the memory a flurry of snow and kol

climbing, spinning, moving toward Drypp and me. "Whatever else they are, the Abaki are real and they're dangerous."

"Like the rest of Winter's atrocities," Mars says.

"Maybe," I counter, keeping my eyes firmly on the road. My mind has cleared and I find I do have something to say about the monsters. "Maybe not."

"Even *you*, Winter's great defender, would not deny the destruction the Abaki have wrought."

"No," I say, blinking at the headless monster climbing through the years. "I wouldn't."

I've seen an Abaki. Felt his dead hands bloated with damp, fought them as they closed around my neck. And yet—

"Winter can be blamed for many disasters . . ."

"But?"

"I'm not sure it's fair to hold her responsible for the Abaki."

"Explain yourself, Miss Quine."

I attempt to press my back into the seat as the road tips us forward. It's dark now—like driving into the black sea. I flick the headlamps on and find we're still some distance from the fog.

"It's been argued that the Abaki are a consequence of the raw kol mingling with the ice and snow."

"Oh yes," Mars says, his eyebrow hitching. "I've heard that as well."

"Mars—" Kyn says.

"The kol makes the snow more than what it is," I say. "Gives it the . . . visage of life."

Visage. It's the word Drypp used to explain the encounter.

"Lazy reasoning, Miss Quine. The kol is ubiquitous. If every flake of snow it touched sprouted into a monster, the island would be overrun. But it's not. The Abaki crawl out of the sea and never venture south of the Serpentine."

"Not never," I say.

I can hear his eyes widening in the tone of his voice. "You've seen one then? Where?"

"Three miles north of Lake Road." I fight to keep my voice even. "Give or take."

"Halfway between Hex Landing and Whistletop, then? A rare sighting. Did your rig take much damage?"

"My rig?"

"When you hit it? I imagine you—"

"We didn't have the rig." Though that could have made all the difference. Drypp and I had snowshoed in.

"What did you have?" Kyn asks.

"Fishing poles," I say, mustering a smile. I try to continue, but my throat is closing up. Knotted hard. And this time it's not Mars's doing. It's recollection and sentiment; it's the past.

There is no yesterday . . .

But there is. And it hurts.

"Miss Quine—"

"We made it out," I manage. "Just."

Kyn places a hand on my shoulder, squeezes. "Winter does favor you, little ice witch."

"I don't know," I say, shaking my head, "but if it is true, if she favors me as you say, why would she have set her monsters on us? On Drypp and me." It's a question I've avoided thinking about. The likely answers take me down roads I've never wanted to travel. But in light of Mars's claims about kol and snow mingling, in light of his accusations, I can't help the question forming on my lips. "Why?"

"Miss Quine—"

"I'm not asking. Not really. I'm just trying to show you how flawed your logic is. If Winter controls the monsters, if she favors me, I would never have been attacked. And we were. Drypp was."

Kyn squeezes my shoulder again. "I'm sorry, Sylvi. Is that how you lost the old man?"

I clear my throat, blink away images of Drypp. "He hung on for a while. Better some days and then bad again. He never fully recovered."

Fog now, creeping into the beams of the headlamps. The road tips harshly and the bucket strikes the mud just as a tree swipes hard at my door. Curses fill the cab, but the moment passes. Mars waits a total of two seconds before he starts in again.

"Did you know, Miss Quine, that the Abaki were Winter's first attempts at companionship?"

Kyn groans. "Mars—"

But the conversation is cut short by a battering of trees. The limbs here are spindly, snapping off as we strike them, some of them bending to give way. I'm not inclined to engage the saws. Not if I don't have to.

We're near the bottom of the second cage when the fog thickens. I hate giving up the light, but finally, when the windshield is nothing but a vast white blur, I switch off the headlamps and we're swallowed by darkness.

"How the—" Kyn says. "Can you even see?"

I can see the road if I lean forward and place my chin on top of the wheel, but I can't watch for trees and highway at the same time. It's like wearing a blindfold and sprinting through a field of children swinging butterfly nets. I know I'll take one to the face eventually—I just have no idea which direction it'll come from.

I'm on the verge of asking Hyla to engage the saw blades when the road bottoms out and we start the climb up and out of the second cage. I twist my boot, ensuring the gas pedal is touching the floor. The Dragon complains and creaks, but she pushes hard, taking a beating as she fights her way through the fog and out of the forest.

It's only when we clear the trees and I flip the headlamps back on that the breath searing my lungs fights its way free. It shudders through my teeth, and I settle back in my seat.

I've been so consumed with the cage that I didn't fully appreciate the conversation unfurling like a satchel of forgotten game meat behind me.

"There are things she must know, Kyn. Errant thinking cannot be allowed. Not for her."

"'Cannot be allowed'?" Kyn asks. "She's not a child. Your hatred for Winter seeps into every story you tell. She won't listen if you can't—"

"Then she is selfish."

"*I'm* selfish?"

"Welcome back, Miss Quine."

"Selfish is coercing a defenseless girl into joining a ratted group of rebels," I say.

"Miss Trestman was hardly defenseless."

Our words are angry, bouncing off the cab, growing louder.

"May I?" Hyla asks, speaking above the din. "Mars, Kyn? If you will allow me . . ." But no one stops. No one listens. She jams her gun out a hole in the canvas and fires a shot. It startles me and I almost pull my foot from the gas. The cab falls silent.

"Sessa," Hyla says, setting the gun calmly on her lap. "I would like to tell you this story as it was told on Paradyia. Will you allow me?"

"I had a tutor," I say, still fuming. "I've heard many versions of the story."

"But you have not heard mine. You have not heard the Paradyian version of your history. Does that not interest you?"

"It's the best offer you're going to get," Kyn says. "Take it, Sylvi. Before Mars starts talking again. For Begynd's sake."

Finally I nod, exhausted by the sheer volume of words spoken in the last few days. I'm not used to it. Not in my cab.

"I'll start at the beginning, shall I?"

"Give it to us, Hy," Kyn says. "Tell us about the monsters."

Hyla begins with a dip of her chin. "When Begynd, son of Sola, cut his people from the rock of Shiv Island and poured himself like water into the great valley, his presence stirred something in the land and in the winter spirit that had enthroned herself in the mountaintops. Suddenly aware of herself and the world she inhabited, Winter craved another spirit to share her existence with. She craved friendship. And she sought it first in the Shiv people. But they belonged to Begynd and Begynd alone, the warmth of his kindness toward them keeping Winter's touch at bay."

I sigh. "So she created monsters?"

"Listen, Miss Quine." Mars dabs at his lips, but his words prickle. He approves of the Paradyian account. Wants me to hear it. It's enough to poison the tale entirely.

Hyla clears her throat and continues. "Winter looked to the black mineral buried beneath the rock. The kol had a power—that she could not deny—but time would teach her that it did not have a will. The kol was not spirit like she was and made for a poor companion. Frustrated, she built men out of snow, imitating the work of Begynd. But try as she may, she could not breathe into them life."

"It was then that she gave the kol its first command," I say, bitter, annoyed. Already the story is turning Winter into an unfeeling dictator. I can't reconcile all that she is, but it seems too simple, unfair, to brand her so carelessly.

"Very good, Miss Quine," Mars says, watching me from beneath hooded eyes.

"I told you. I've heard this story before."

"Hearing and listening are not the same thing."

"Listening and believing are not the same thing either."

"Shall I continue?" Hyla asks.

"Just yell over them," Kyn says. "When they're all grown up, they'll realize they don't have to have the last word."

Mars snorts and I force my gaze back to the road.

"Sorry, Hyla," I say. "Yes, please. Go ahead."

"Winter's first request of the kol was modest," she says, her words painting a picture. "She could not venture from the safety of her mountaintops, but the kol permeated every part of the island, all four wings and beyond. Surely, the kol knew where she could find what she so desired. 'Find me a people to love,' she told the kol. 'Flesh and bone. Find them. Bring them to me.'

"The kol knew precisely where to look, for it had long ago

searched out the mysteries of the sea. *Flesh and bone*, Winter wanted. And it was flesh and bone she would receive."

Despite my frustration, I shiver at the thought. We're rounding the top of the road, leaving the second cage and entering the third. I adjust, nearly standing in an effort to keep my foot on the gas. This incline is by far the steepest and it won't take us long to reach bottom.

"The kol brought arms and legs of wayward sailors," Hyla says. "Bodies that had been torn apart by crashing waves and shiv-sharp rock."

It's a learned behavior, then. The dismemberment. I haven't thought much on the tragic circumstances that provided the Abaki with their limbs. After what happened to Drypp, it's uncomfortable to think those hands had once belonged to someone who'd lived just as fiercely and clumsily as us. Uncomfortable to think they were torn from their own bodies and bent to Winter's will.

"The kol could not breathe life into the dead souls, but it could make them more than they were. From the mountains above, Winter watched as her kol monsters crawled from the sea. And they were monstrous. It was Winter herself who first called them abominations, for they were nothing compared to the beautiful men and women cut from the rock of her own mountains."

"Beautiful," Kyn says, waggling his brows and running a finger along his stone cheekbone. "I like this version."

"They had no thoughts of their own," Hyla continues. "No songs. No worship to give. They could not bring her the love she so desired. But her will had crafted them. Like snow and storm, rain and sleet, hoarfrost and hail, blizzards and squalls and flurries, the kol monsters were now hers to care for. They were hers to command."

"And so she cursed them," I say.

A curt nod from Hyla. "From that day until this, they climb in and out of the black sea, searching for arms and legs, for their souls—which had been stolen by death—so that they can one day be the very companions Winter craves."

The Dragon falls quiet and my anger seeps away. Her account was not so different from Mystra's. But there's something in it that catches at my breastbone. And it isn't Mars's threat that something monstrous is growing inside me.

It's Winter's loneliness. I've heard enough of her whispers to know it's true.

"Have you seen them?" I ask Kyn.

His chin is on the corner of my seat. When he answers, his breath moves the hair on the back on my neck. "Ah, yeah. We post a lookout at Dris Mora. It's the ones with the heads you have to watch out for."

I swallow down the knot that won't relinquish its hold on my tongue and I nod. "I remember."

The forest is closing in now, the relighted headlamps casting duplicitous shadows, turning one branch into three, three branches into nine. A tree reaches out and scrapes the length of the trailer—the sound is like a screw dragging against my spine. Another branch joins in, snaps free. And then there are far too many to count, grabbing at the Dragon. Clawing and scraping away.

"Hyla," I say, "beneath your seat is a lever. I need you to pull it."

She leans forward and with her good arm, she reaches for the lever. Her face pales as she yanks the metal bar and engages the saws. The diamond blades whirl into view, their motors loud and laboring. These saws were made to grind away at rock with the rig rolling at a much slower clip. Our manic pace alone is enough to strain the motors, but the diamond blades aren't ideal for iced wood, damp with impending Blys.

The branches are firm enough to damage the rig but far too pliable for the blades. At this speed, they shred instead of slicing cleanly through. And this cage is by far the woodiest. If either of the saws survive, we'll be luckier than we ought to be.

"When we clear this last cage," I yell over the din, "we'll be just a few miles from the Serpentine River crossing—"

"Will we make it?" Kyn asks.

"Before the ice turns to slush?" I ask.

A noisy silence mingles while I turn it over in my mind.

Come Blys, the Serpentine is the fastest flowing river in the Kol Mountains. It never fully freezes, but throughout Ryme, the ice is several inches thick. That's deep enough for a rig and trailer to truck it, but beneath the ice, the river rushes, crossing the Shiv Road and tumbling out over the cliffs at Crane Falls. The falling water freezes as it goes over, the ice building into glorious cascades and looking so much like the wing of a Wethyrd crane, you could imagine the entire mountain range detaching from our white world and flying away.

But the wings aren't nearly so light. In Ryme, the ice builds as the river continues to send water over the cliff. Eventually the weight of the ice tears the wing free and it drops in immense sheets, disappearing into a crevice cut by the raging waters of Blys.

"We'll make it," I say.

"Holy Begynd, you're a bad liar," Kyn says.

Mars tugs his sleeves over his wrists. "It won't matter. Winter will do as she's told."

I bristle, but it's what I've had to depend on when thoughts of cracking through the ice shake my nerve. We have to get across. There's nothing for it. Lenore is on the other side of the Serpentine and if Mars is going to anger Winter, it might as well be in a noble pursuit.

The windshield takes an elbow from a brittle limb. Flecks of glass scatter, and Hyla and I flinch, trying to cover our faces. But the limb is sheared off and the windshield holds.

"I do not like these cages," Hyla says, pulling her goggles into place.

"No," I say. "There's not much to like here. But after the river crossing, it's a straight shot to the mines at North Bend. We'll stop there for repairs. The opening is wide and we can pull the Dragon in out of the cold to work."

It'll buy me some time too. Some time to consider my options. I'd have to be sure though, that the rebel camp really is where I think it is. I'd have to know—

A jab to the shoulder pulls me from my thoughts. I snatch the finger needling my arm. It's Kyn's. And his face is far too close.

"We've lost a motor," he says, using the offending finger to point at the round blade hanging lifeless on Hyla's side of the rig. The dangling blade catches a branch and the arm groans and bends before we're past it.

"Kill the motor, Hy."

But she's slow to move; Kyn crawls forward and does it for her. The saws grind to a halt, but only the left one retracts.

"Both motors are tied to a single lever," I say. "I can detach it from the right blade, but I'll have to stop. And if we stop, we'll lose all momentum for the climb."

"You drive. Kyn can take care of the repair," Mars says. "Tell him what to do."

"The cable needs to be cut on the arm itself. It's outside."

"We can't stop, Miss Quine. You said it yourself. We'll never make it up the incline if we lose momentum."

Our options are limited, but if we're going to do this, there's really only one way.

"Here," I say, flipping a glance at Kyn. "Take the wheel. I'm smaller. I can climb past Hyla and cut the cables."

"Yeah?"

"Yes. Seat's coming back." Using my left heel, I kick the seat release and shove back, keeping the gas pedal down.

Another massive branch to the shattered windshield and glass rains down on the dash.

"Flux," I hiss. "We've got to get the left saw moving again or we're going to lose the windshield."

Kyn's already behind me in the seat. His long legs are under mine, and his hands take the wheel. I'm pulling my own foot off the gas pedal when the rig strikes a rut and I fall back onto Kyn's chest.

"Sorry, sorry!"

"It's fine," he says, one hand steadying me, the other on the wheel.

"Your ribs," I say, pulling up and climbing off his lap.

"They're fine. Really. Good as new."

His reassuring grin tells me it's true, but it's unlike Winter to be so generous. A thick, knotted limb strikes the window next to his head, and I realize there are more important things to focus on just now.

"Go, go," he says as the window splinters.

I shift so that I'm perched between the seats, one foot on Hyla's leg, one on Kyn's. Kyn's hand is around my shin now, still steadying me.

"Lean back, Hyla," I say. "It's about to get really cold in here."

With my weight on my left leg, I lift my right boot and kick, once, twice, three times at the canvas window covering. The adhesive gives and the old bag detaches, tangling in the icy limbs before it's snatched away.

Now, to get outside without the trees snatching me away as well. I shift again, redistributing my weight.

"I need my foot now," I tell Kyn.

He squeezes my boot and then the warmth of his hand falls away.

I flip up my hood and pull the string so it closes tight around my face, leaving me only a few inches to see out of. I lunge over Hyla and push my way onto the windowsill. One boot secure and now two.

"Take hold of my belt," I tell Hyla. "Don't let go."

Her face is pale, the blood still fresh and bright on her shirt, but she does what I say. She wraps her fist around my belt and the set of her jaw tells me she'd lose an arm before she'd let me fall.

My hands grip the top of the sill, but the ice is wet and they slip. My fist tightens and I find purchase. The wind is sharp and cold—it fills my mouth and burns my lungs—but it's nothing to the trees that slap at my face and stab at my ribs.

And then the Dragon's engine lets up. I wheel on Kyn, glaring at him through the open window. "Do. Not. Slow. Down."

His eyes are daggers, but he pushes his foot to the floor—I hear it in the kick of the engine. I give him a curt nod before I turn.

Now, I lean away from the rig and with one hand I grab hold of the saw's arm. With the other I pull the dagger from my belt, flip it in my hand. Limbs continue to pelt me, but my parka keeps the worst of it off my face. I take a skinny branch to my lip, which makes blood pool in my mouth and my eyes water.

The cables are housed inside the arm, but they're exposed where they connect to the useless blade. Cut that line and this arm will fold in on itself. I'll be able to re-engage the left arm without burning out the motor. Though, the hinged joint is farther out than I can reach from here.

"Don't let go," I yell to Hyla, the wind shoving the words back into my mouth. I shimmy as far down the sill as I'm able, then I push to a stand, stretching my legs and reaching for the cables.

Hyla's hand is still wrapped around my belt but I'll dislocate her shoulder if I fall now. I chance a quick look at the tank tread churning far below. Kicking up dirt and ice, grinding the slush beneath it, noisy and menacing.

I'm having trouble seeing, the rabbit fur lining my parka tickling my face and blocking my view. My hands are full, so instead of loosening the string tightening my hood, I slice it through with the dagger. The hood falls away and a branch slaps me in the face.

My cheek stinging, my nose running, I rise on my toes and reach as far as I can.

And there!

A single swift flick of the dagger and the cables are cut through. The arm drops down, folding back into position.

It's done.

I feel the relief in Hyla's hold and turn to grin at her.

Her shining smile is the last thing I see.

A tree grabs my hood and I'm yanked sideways. The zipper cuts into my throat and I'm pulled from the windowsill. It's so sudden, there's no time to react.

And then my hood tears free and I swing violently toward the rig. Hyla's half outside, her face stricken with pain and determination.

I hit the door beneath the window, hard. Then I'm bouncing away and back again. I'm sprayed with slush and mud, but it's Hyla's grip that has my heart missing beats. Will it hold or will I be ground beneath the Dragon's tread?

There's something darkly poetic about dying that way. With someone else driving my rig and the only freedom I've ever known crushing me whole.

I slam against the Dragon as my thoughts fly to Winter. To the slush on the ground, to the melting snow peppering me as I flounder. To the things Winter can do, the things she has done for me. She could save me if she wanted to. But I handed her wolves over to Mars. I sent her away.

It's all so fast. The stupid thoughts colliding inside my head, regret and angst roiling. And then I'm lifted up and with another pummeling of branches, Hyla pulls me into the rig.

"I've got you, Sessa, I've got you." But my arms and legs are unwieldy and her strength is spent. Half my body flops across the seat and onto Kyn's lap.

His hand finds my forehead, shoves my matted hair up and away from my eyes. I've lost my second stocking cap.

"You're crazy, you know that?" His eyes move from my face to the road and back again. Vigilant on all counts.

I move to speak, but my mouth is dry. I swallow down a scratchy gasp.

His fingers tighten in my hair. "Are you OK? What is it?"

Finally my lips cooperate.

"Don't slow down."

CHAPTER 17

RESTING THE TOP OF THE LAST CAGE IS rough—the Dragon sputters and protests, but she never stalls. Winter tries to take the credit.

SEE, she says, **SEE**.

But this one's on Vaxton, the rigger who built the Dragon. He was a pompous old codger, but there's no denying he was a top-level wrenchman.

Kyn stops in the dead center of the road and the two of us climb out. Most of the repairs can wait until we reach North Bend, but with the canvas covering Hyla's window gone, we're going to have to improvise.

"A blanket maybe?" Kyn's staring up at the gaping hole, his hands in his pockets. "You've got an itchy wool one back there that's not good for much else."

"I'm sorry," I say. "I didn't realize your skin was so sensitive."

"And beautiful. Don't forget beautiful."

I snort. "The blanket will be soaked through in no time, but I'm out of ideas. Let's give it a go."

While he digs out the waterproof glue and the blanket, I crawl up on the hood and apply another layer of weather repellent to the windshield. It's hardly worth the effort, the glass crumbling, chunks missing.

"We're going to have to bundle up," I say, sliding to the ground. It's gusting now, Winter blowing straight in our faces. "Even with the heater, the Dragon's going to be an icebox."

"We could snuggle," Kyn says.

"I'll let Mars know you're available."

We're about a quarter of a mile from the river crossing, but the road bends just ahead and we can see Crane Falls from here: blue streaks of snow and ice, frozen as they fell, glistening wet in the light of the Desolation. My legs tremble with the temperature, but it's warmer than it should be. Warmer than we can afford.

Overhead, the clouds shift and the moon presses her advantage. A starving slip of a thing begging to be seen.

"I can't remember when I last saw the stars," Kyn says, his boots settling next to mine.

"Me neither."

And then with a great, frigid exhale, the heavenly lights are gone, hidden again beneath Winter's gray gloom.

"Not one for sharing attention, is she?"

No, she isn't.

"We should go," I say. "There's a Shiv settlement in the mountains above Crane Falls. I don't know if they'll have heard what happened in the pass, but—"

"We'll keep an eye out," Kyn says, and then, after a moment: "You're a good driver, Sylvi. What you did back there—"

"The Dragon's a good rig."

"She's better with you behind the wheel. I'm a fine driver, yeah? I know I am. I get the job done every time. But I wouldn't have braved the Cages. Not even with the Dragon. I understand why you didn't want to take this job."

There are things I could say. About how Lenore left me no choice. Arguments to be had about all the decisions that led to this one. The people who suffered so we could get here. But it's all much more complicated than it was when we started. And not just for me.

"I want you to know—"

"We need to go," I say, not wanting him to voice that injured thing thrashing around inside his chest. I've been ignoring it since High Pass. At first I didn't understand how I could feel the catch of his breath, the rapid beat of his heart, but as one feeling layered over another, as they knotted and tangled, I was reminded of Hyla's words about her husband. And now I wonder if there's any truth to what she said. If, over time, two people really can become one. It's a dangerous thought, and if Kyn's tempted to speak any hint of it, I'd rather he didn't.

But his eyes are on mine, his jacket open and blowing in the wind. Winter's light turns his cheekbones sharp and it's not hard at all to imagine a craftsman chipping him from the mountain rock with exacting precision. His mouth opens but then his brow furrows.

"You hear that?" he asks.

But I'm already turning, already looking to the road. "I hear it." Up ahead, the ice is cracking—a sobering, ominous sound. "Blys is coming. Faster than is natural."

"Almost like Winter wanted it that way."

When I turn back to him, his eyes are climbing my chin, the bridge of my nose, the curve of my forehead—his gaze piercing, like crampons looking for purchase in the snow. I feel it as surely as I feel Winter warming my gut, both of them wanting my good opinion, both of them needing me to see the world as they see it.

I back away, retreating to the only safe place I know—the driver's seat of the Sylver Dragon.

"Take the lookout," I say, tossing Drypp's gun out the door. I don't need him following me. I don't need him close right now. "Keep an eye out for the Shiv settlement. It'll be high on the rise, just before the river."

"Sylvi—"

"Two shots and I'll stop the rig. But don't screw around. If you fire that gun, I'm going to assume there's danger."

And like that, his gaze is flint. Good. That's what I need right now. I don't need convictions weakening his spine and revelations stirring up sentiments like silt. I need Kyn-the-Shiv hard as stone.

"No games," he says, swinging the gun onto his back. I slam my door so he can scale it. Another crack splits the ice and Kyn moves quickly, past my window and onto the roof of the cab. I crank the ignition and listen as Kyn's boots make their way down the trailer. When they've fallen from hearing, I wait another fifteen seconds—time enough for him to settle into the turret, and then I shift the Dragon into gear.

The road leans left and I lean with it, taking the Dragon

around the bend and out onto the straightaway that leads to the river crossing. Another half mile and the Shiv caves should be in view.

"How's your shoulder, Hy?"

"Good, Sessa."

She's lying. There's no way it's good after the fiasco with the rock saw, but that's not the point. She's willing to bury the discomfort and push forward and that's what I need to know.

But when the river comes into view, Kyn's gun remains silent. Hyla and I lean forward, pressing our faces to the ruined glass and trying to catch a glimpse of the camp high above. At first I think there's nothing there, but then I see it. A string of rounded shadows, dark against the white mountain.

"Abandoned," Mars says, suddenly pressed between Hyla and me. "Interesting."

It's possible we're too far away to see, possible our perspective will eventually make fools of us, but I'm thinking the same thing. There's no smoke rising into the night sky, no firelight flickering in the openings, no movement at all.

They're gone. The settlement is empty.

"That's good for us," Hyla says. "Is it not?"

"Very good." Mars settles back in his seat, stretches out.

I'm not nearly as comfortable with their apparent absence as he is, but I'm grateful to avoid a skirmish. Especially here where the road is so treacherous.

I slow the rig to a crawl as we approach the Serpentine. The toggle for the bucket is beneath the wheel. I feel around until the knob is under my thumb and I inch it up. The bucket lifts—not much, just enough to keep it from smacking the ice. The road dips as the highway gives way to the frozen river and we take the transition as slowly and carefully as possible.

I flip the latch on my shattered window and drop it down. The cracking ice is ominous, the sound bounding from river to rock. I keep the Dragon rolling slowly and lean out the window, surveying the frozen water below. The ice looks OK. Slick but solid.

I don't see a single crack, but I know from experience that the ice is always thinnest at the drop-off.

I pull the Dragon tight to the cliff on our left, so close I can drag my finger through the loose snow clinging to the cliff face. I drop the slush onto my tongue, relishing the chill as it slides down my throat and hating what it means.

Two shots crack the air and my heart fires to match.

"Kyn." I lean forward over the wheel, searching the cliffs for Shiv. But I see nothing. Just the ice. Just the shadows of clouds dancing on the mountaintops.

"You see anything?" I ask.

"Nothing," Hyla says, tying back her hair.

"Mars?"

"Not from here." He stands and slides open the roof hatch. One foot on the back of my chair, and then he's on top of the rig.

"What do you see?" I call up.

"We have to get off the ice."

"I can't exactly floor it."

Mars drops onto the hood and then to the frozen river. He strides out in front of the Dragon with his black-clad legs, his gait strong, his arms wide open, fingers splayed. The ice frosts over beneath his feet. Thick, hard. He stumbles and then catches himself.

Winter laughs, low and deep.

I LIKE WATCHING HIM FALL, she says.

I curse.

"What is it, my lady?"

I shake my head, my eyes on Mars. His shoulders stiffen and he shoots into the air, up and forward, the path beneath him freezing hard and smoky white as he crosses to the other side.

We're still rolling at a safe clip, the ice cracking somewhere in the distance, the danger still hidden to my eyes. "What is it, Hy? What do they see?"

And then footfalls and a crash as Kyn leaps from the trailer to the cab.

"Go, Sylvi, go!" His boot catches my braid as he drops into the Dragon and throws himself onto the bench seat.

Slowly, steadily, I give the Dragon more gas. "What is it?"

"A rig," he says.

"Coming this way?" The tread spins on the ice, catches, and spins again. Now we're moving forward at a slightly faster clip.

"Like a Shiv demon," Kyn says, reaching forward and slamming his fist into the knob that engages the beacons on top of the rig. Flashing lights to warn oncoming traffic that we're here. "It's a small rig, but he's rounding the bend at breakneck speed. If he hits the ice going that fast—"

I push the gas to the floor. "We'll all go under."

Hyla shifts, squints at the rig in the distance. "Is it the Rangers? One of their trucks?"

But there isn't a squad on Layce that's stupid enough to be out here just now. Maybe a Majority mining rig? Maybe . . .

And then the telltale yellow of a familiar snow plow comes into view.

"It's Bristol," I say, punching the dash.

He and Lenore should have arrived at the rebel camp by now. I know they made it as far as the Cages—I saw evidence of his plow there. But the breakage and tracks were days old. Even if the rebel camp is on the farthest point of the isle, his ugly rig could have made it. At the very least, he should be long past this crossing.

"What is he doing? Why are they here?" I get no answer to my question and it infuriates me.

"Kyn!" I yell.

"I don't know, Sylvi. I don't . . ." He leans even farther forward and places his hand on the dash. "Do you see them? Can you see Lenore?"

But the rig is too far away and all I see is a yellow machine growing larger and larger in my windshield.

"Perhaps he left the girl at the camp and is returning to Whistletop," Hyla offers.

"Not possible," I say. "He couldn't make it there and back . . ." But I'm thinking, my mind racing, trying to calculate, to count the hours, the days. "It's too fast," I say, but it sounds so much more like a question than I mean it to.

I look to Kyn.

"I've never approached the camp by this road," he says, an apology in his voice.

My hands twist on the wheel as the Dragon trundles toward the far shores of the Serpentine. Bristol's rig grows large in the distance, large by measures that seem unwise, even for an idiot like Mapes.

"He's going too fast," I say. "If he doesn't slow down . . ."

But he doesn't slow and my breath hitches.

Bristol's rig careens off the shore and onto the Serpentine. The weight of the rig and the slight dip force his plow down hard. It smacks the ice. The plow blade catches and the rig pitches around—the tires and brakes both useless as it spins toward the center of the crossing. Toward us.

I curse and push my foot to the brake. Slowly, slowly. I can't afford to lose control here, but where is the wretched thing going to stop?

And then Bristol's plow blade catches on the ice and his momentum is slowed. Another two rotations and the rig stops in the dead center of the river crossing. We all push toward the glass as the Dragon rolls closer. The yellow plow's taken a beating. The hood is dented and the front quarter panel is missing entirely. Bristol's windshield is worse off than ours, dark flakes shimmering in every crack.

"Flux," Kyn says. "That's a lot of kol."

"The wind off the sea," I say. "They've been out on the Seacliff Road."

I lean left and right, but I can't see past the cracks and the kol, can't find Lenore. And then beneath Bristol's plow the ice splits. Wide and sudden.

The tires go under and then the blade.

Kyn and Hyla cry out, "Go, go, go!"

But I'm frozen where I sit. Twelve Rymes have passed since that terrible day, but the things I never told my best friend slam hard into my chest.

Lenore, who never liked the cold, who did everything she could to avoid it, will die, clutched in the freezing arms of Winter.

Sitting next to Bristol Mapes.

CHAPTER 18

I WAS UNDER THE STOVE WHEN HE ARRIVED. IT was my favorite place to hide when Mistress Quine kept me indoors. And that day, she'd insisted. There was a hole in the wall behind the cooker where critters had gotten after it, and if I pressed my face to the floor of the cabin and tilted it just so, I could see past the tree line to the general store in Hex Landing.

It was a busy place, Hex Landing. Especially in the nighttime hours. Each evening, when the cloud cover turned dark, a bell would echo through the small town signaling the end of the work day. For the next few hours, kol-streaked miners would drift across the main stretch, mingling with the rig drivers who'd pulled in for the night. Tucked in my hidey hole, I sucked on pine needles and watched their boots stomp up and down the wooden walkways, leaving prints in the soft white snow.

It was the snow I liked most of all. It bit at my cheeks and stung my eyes, but the stove kept me warm and I passed hours like that. When the noises in Mistress Quine's bedroom grew too loud, I jammed my fingers into my ears, shutting out everything but the beating of my own heart.

That's how I first heard Winter. Her words fell lightly into my head as I lay there, soft and enchanting like the snow gathering just outside on the ground. The names she gave each flake, the songs hidden in the storms she spun across the isle.

My thumbs were in my ears, and it's why I didn't hear him knock. Why I didn't hear him enter the cabin. Two hands wrapped around my stockinged ankles and I was tugged from beneath the stove, a threadbare quilt saving my belly from splinters. I flipped onto my back and looked up at him. His dirty boots, his large hands.

I still think about those hands.

"You're a pretty thing, aren't you?" His suspenders drooped like heavy branches from his waistband, snow dripping from his clothes and hair, pinging off my knees. "No wonder she keeps you hidden."

I remember thinking he had it backward. I mostly kept myself hidden.

"I don't blame her in the slightest," he said.

Candlelight caught his face, scruffy and pink from the cold. I knew him; he was the driver of the yellow plow. The rig that kept the roads clear when the snow piled high during Ryme. I'd seen him in town but never here. He wasn't one of Mistress Quine's regulars.

I didn't know to be afraid.

"Where is she? Your ma?"

My eyes drifted to the only other room in the small cabin. The room where Mistress Quine made her bed and took her men.

"Ah," he said, his gaze following mine. "I see." He crouched down then, his face just inches from mine, his breath like the stink that Mistress kept bottled in her cupboard. The stink was my first warning. Mistress was wicked mean when she took to carrying her liquid stench around the house.

He took my chin in his hand, but his grip was rough and I inched backward. My shoulder touched the stove and the heat blistered through my shirt. I cried out.

He moved fast then, covering my mouth with his hand and pressing me to the floor.

"Let's not disturb your ma," he said.

His whiskers brushed my face, and then his hands replaced them. They were everywhere—that's what I remember most. Grease caked beneath his fingernails, calloused palms scraping my skin. One roamed my face, and the other hand wandered my body. Pushing aside the quilt and sliding beneath my shirt. When he grabbed my wrist and pressed my fingers to his belt buckle, I kicked out and he howled.

His hand loosened on my face and I bit him. First the fat part of his palm and then his cheek. The taste of copper filled my mouth and when he reached for me again, I spit blood in his face.

"You little wretch."

And then Mistress Quine was there, standing in the doorway of her room, her blouse open, her skirt askew. She was tired, as tired as I'd ever seen her.

I've replayed that moment more times than I can count. Shifting it, changing what really happened. In the happier versions, Mistress Quine grabs the kitchen broom and beats Bristol Mapes off me and out into the cold. I'd seen her do it before, with the men who got too rough with her.

But that's not what happened.

Not that day.

Instead, she set to work on her buttons. Slowly doing them up, her lips set in a hard line.

Bristol was still half on top of me. My teeth marks were red on his face and when he spoke, a harsh laugh edged the words.

"Your girl's got some pluck in her," he said.

With her eyes staring into nothing at all, Mistress agreed. "That she does. And it'll cost you double. Leave your coin on the table when you go."

She retreated into her room, her eyes never once finding mine. The bedroom door slammed and a vase of withered snowblooms tumbled off the hutch and smashed against the floor.

Bristol's face slid into a ghoulish smile and he pressed closer, said things I'll never recall. Things I never could hear.

I was flailing hard by then, trying to get off my back. I screamed words into his face. Words with meanings I couldn't fathom, sounds I'd only ever heard when my ears were plugged and I'd shut out everything but Winter.

Mistress Quine's door opened again. I remember that—her mouth moving, the ferocious set of her chin.

And then Winter.

Swooping down the chimney, snuffing out the fire and slamming Mistress's door. The cabin's four windows shattered. Glass flew like snow spray as Winter exploded through the cabin. Kitchen chairs toppled and the table skid across the room. It barreled over me and pinned Bristol to the wall.

He was bleeding. Not just from the bite I gave him, but from the window shards and stoneware from the open cabinets. From the hail cutting in from outside. All of it finding its way to his pinioned form up against the timbers.

The wind was deafening, so I curled into a ball, my hands over my ears. Winter took the roof next, rusted nails pulling free of the weather-warped boards. The front door swung madly on its hinges and then, like the hand-stitched curtains, she pulled it clean away.

Winter was violent but brief and when she was done with Bristol Mapes, when she was done with the cabin that had held my first five Rymes, the world was quieter than I'd ever known it.

YOU'RE SAFE, Winter cooed. EVERYTHING WILL BE DIFFERENT NOW.

She climbed into the hollow between my ribs, and, like the stove that had always been my comfort, she warmed me through.

It was an eternity before Mistress Quine stumbled out of her room, her face streaked with tears and grime. She wobbled through her fractured doorway, blood trickling from her temple, eyes roving around her destroyed home. For a long time she stared at the spot against the wall where I'd seen Bristol wedged and bleeding. I couldn't imagine him being anything other than dead, but I didn't want to look. I'd seen enough of him already.

When she spoke, her voice was low and dangerous. "Get. Out."

A chill raced down my arms, my spine, but I didn't move. I couldn't. I had no idea what she wanted. Where would I go?

She found her legs then, faster than I found mine. She grabbed my hair and yanked me to my feet, but before she could give me another command, she paused and tipped my face to hers.

"Stupid girl. You've ruined your lips," she said. "Now there'll be no hiding what you are."

It wasn't until much later that I understood what she meant. Not until days had passed and Lenore found me in the woods. Not until she'd cleaned me up and placed Drypp's looking glass in front of me so she could braid my hair.

I saw then what Mistress Quine had seen. It explained the crusty feel of my mouth, the stinging bite whenever the air touched my face.

It was frostbite.

And it was bad.

I'm not entirely sure when Winter swooped in and finished off Mistress Quine. I heard about it much like the rest of Whistletop. A freak storm. A destroyed cabin just outside of Hex Landing. A missing child.

Bristol's name was never mentioned, but it wasn't until my twelfth Ryme that I realized he'd survived. Lenore and I were shoveling the walkway outside the tavern when his yellow rig pulled into the lot. He'd been hired to service the roads around town, and though it was days before I was able to keep down a meal, I never told Drypp or Lenore what happened that day at Mistress

Quine's. It was a shameful thing—him putting his hands on me, forcing me to put my hands on him—and I wasn't shameful, not like Mistress.

No one had to know.

Plus, I had my knife and Lenore had hers, and it was easy enough to avoid the man and his yellow rig.

Winter knew what he'd done and that was enough. And though she never said as much, it was clear that as long as she was around, I'd never again find myself alone with Bristol Mapes.

CHAPTER 19

I STOMP THE PARKING BRAKE AND REACH FOR the door handle.

"Sylvi," Kyn yells, "you can't. Look at the ice."

A vibration quivers up from the Serpentine, trembling through the Dragon. A clap like gunfire, deep and ominous.

"Sessa—" Hyla doesn't finish, but she doesn't have to. I see it. A fissure spreading from beneath Bristol's plow—slow at first and then racing straight toward us.

"Drive, Sylvi," Kyn says. "Drive!"

I release the parking brake and jerk the rig into gear. My foot's pressed to the gas, but we're not moving. The ice hisses and spits as the crack widens.

"Go!" I tell the Dragon. "Come on, girl!"

And then Mars is there, hovering unsteadily over the fissure, his words drowned out by the splintering river. I can't see any obvious effect, but Mars brought down an entire mountain. Surely he can stitch a seam in the ice.

"Sylvi—"

"I'm trying!" I downshift, letting the clutch out slowly, hoping for any forward momentum at all. "Come on," I plead, "come on."

And then, movement! The Dragon inches forward, the tank tread spinning stupidly as I give it more gas. Our progress is slow. Too slow. Kyn and Hyla are cursing while I beg the Dragon for a miracle. At last we find traction and we're moving. Past Mars, Bristol's rig just up on our right side.

I crane my neck to look around Hyla, but the Dragon's too tall and as we roll past, I see only the roof of the smaller truck. We're nearly parallel with it when Mars crumples to the ice and the river splits wide. Bristol's rig bobs and threatens to go under.

"Mars!" Hyla yells, struggling to open the door. "We must help him!"

My chest heaves and tears race down my face, but I don't stop. If I do, we're all dead. Instead, I give the rig more gas.

We're past Mars now and approaching the far shore at break-neck speed. I'm still not sure it's fast enough. The splitting ice is loud, the Dragon rocking as she goes.

I don't know what to do. Mars would tell me to demand Winter do something, but I don't know what to ask of her. I just know that if I don't get the Dragon onto land, she's going to go under. And if she goes under, there will be no helping Lenore.

I don't bother braking as we smack onto the shore. The three of us ricochet around the cab, Hyla slamming her face on the dash, my head bumping Kyn's. I don't waste time asking why he's half in my seat again.

As soon as the trailer's wheels are clear of the Serpentine, I kill the engine and I'm out the door, Kyn behind me. I hear him demanding that Hyla stay where she is, but I don't stop to see if his commands are obeyed. There isn't time. Lenore is out there.

The river is cracking with impatient glee, dark water spilling unhindered onto the ice. Bristol's back tires are still above the surface but they won't be for much longer.

I step out onto the river, slower than I want to go, testing— my heart a sharpened awl chipping away at my ribs.

"Miss Quine," Mars warns, his voice frail in the distance. "Stay there."

But I'm done taking orders.

The creaking, crunching ice is not at all stable and I curse Winter for bringing Blys on so rapidly. She could stop this. She could. She could save Lenore. She could at least make it easier for me to save her.

"Miss Quine, I am begging you—"

I step forward again and again. And now I don't stop. My boots kick up water and ice in equal measure, the groan of the thawing river drowning out Mars's protestations.

I'm almost there—the rig five or six arm lengths in front of me—when the weight of my boot flips a shard of ice and down I go, my tailbone smacking hard, my right boot sinking into the river.

"Sylvi!" Kyn yells.

I yank my leg out and push to stand, only to find myself sur-rounded by rushing water.

"Flux. Flux!"

Kyn's still on solid ice, his movements mirroring mine as I drift downstream. He won't leave me—an uncomfortable cer-tainty that fills my chest—but he's too far away to help. The ice bumps along, the river pushing me toward the drop-off, farther and farther from the plow.

Kyn yells for Mars, waves his arms. But Mars is busy. He's saving Lenore and that's more important than anything he can do for me. My block of ice bumps another, and my thighs clench, but I'm watching the Kerce smuggler.

His dark form is still on the ice, his mouth moving. I swear I see the magic this time. Black dust soars from his lips, glistening as it stitches the ice before him. Winter bucks and squirms against his commands—it sets the air prickling—and I know: He's fighting a losing battle. That plow is going under, Winter has decided as much.

"Mars!" I yell. "I can help!"

"Then help. Give Winter her marching orders, Miss Quine, and get over here."

Panic rises in my chest as another swell of black water sloshes up and over my boots. "Tell me what to do!"

"The river is moving too quickly—"

And then the ice beneath his feet disappears. Melted in a blink. His hands fly up and his boots go under. But before I can scream, he hisses a command, and, with an indignant growl, Winter yanks him into the sky. The plow shifts again, hisses of spray rising as the bumper drops below the surface.

"He can't talk to you and Winter," Kyn yells. "Not at the same time. She—"

"Takes advantage," I say, finishing his thought. My eyes are rabid, searching, searching. Kerce magic is about more than telling Winter what to do. You have to know what needs to be done. And with Mars hovering over the plow, his attention focused solely on keeping it above the surface, I'm going to have to figure this out myself. And fast.

The river, he said.

I swivel my hips, spinning the bobbing block beneath my feet so I can see where the water emerges from the cliff face. It looks like nothing but ice jutting from the darkness, but there's water beneath it all. Rushing, pushing toward the drop-off. Beneath the surface, it's moving too fast, tugging at the plow, breaking the ice, and undoing all Mars's work.

"Sylvi," Kyn yells. "What are you thinking?"

"If we can stop the river, Mars will be able to steady the rig."

"It's the Flux, snowflake. Everything's melting."

"But we have Winter. She's ice and snow. She's everything we need."

The truth of it slams into my sternum, a punch of self-loathing. I don't want to use Winter as a tool, but if Winter doesn't stop the melting, my best friend will drown. There's nothing I won't do to keep that from happening.

And I know how to make her do it.

Mystra Dyfan taught me. There's very little about her lessons I still remember, but she hammered one Kerce word into my mind with such repetition, I'll never forget it. It was the word she shouted when I flipped the latch and climbed out the window. The word she sighed when I abandoned lessons for the foxes congregating near the coop. The word she spat when I whittled my pencil into an arrow.

"*Stiyee*," she'd say. "*Est stiyee*."

Stop. Just stop.

I can still see the exasperation on her face, disappointed that I cared nothing for her plans. Now I open my mouth, and, like

238

Mystra Dyfan did so often with me, I demand Winter give me her full attention.

"*Stiyee*," I say. "*Stiyee flux!*"

But it sounds like a question; the words flutter into the cold air. I feel Winter's confusion, her dismissal. With my eyes on the river beneath my feet, I try again, reining in the doubt, purging it from my voice. I think of the look on Mystra's face when she was absolutely done with me. With my refusal to take part in anything she had prepared. With my deep-rooted need to be free of expectations. I feel my brow crease like hers used to, and I repeat the words.

"*Est stiyee*," I shout. "*Stiyee!*"

Again and again, I repeat the command. Seconds turn into minutes, and I'm drifting farther from the rig. My heart bangs hard and erratically, my voice scratching a fire against my throat, and when I'm almost certain everyone's wrong and I've not a drop of kol in my blood, a smoky fog rises off the ice.

"It's working, snowflake!"

My block of ice steadies, suddenly stiller than it had been a moment before. I turn to Mars and his back straightens. He's so far away now, but I imagine surprise on his face and something like relief. The river beneath us is not frozen through, but it stands still. Utterly and completely. Winter's stopped the Flux just as I had asked, but a mutinous shriek across the sky and I know: She will not hold it long.

Mars lifts his gaze to mine and he nods, his mouth still moving, still working. I follow his lead, a blister rubbing on the side of my tongue. Winter sets Mars gently on the frozen surface, his steps confident on the ice as he strides to the driver's side window.

My heart sinks and the magic freezes on my tongue. There's

water inside. Even from here, I see it sloshing against the useless windows.

"Here!" Kyn calls. "Sylvi, turn around!"

But I can't wrench my attention from Mars. He kicks out at the glass with his steel-toed boots and the window shatters.

"Sylvi. Jump! Jump."

Kyn's so close now I can reach out and touch him. I'd drifted his way without realizing. He reaches across the thin expanse and grabs my collar. I jump. My boots slip as I land, but I right myself when I start to run, making my way toward Mars and Bristol's plow.

Toward Lenore.

She's there, sprawled at his feet.

My legs give out and I collapse, gracelessly, elbows and knees smacking ice.

"On your feet, Miss Quine." Mars's words are gentle, but he grabs my arm as he walks past, dragging me with him away from Lenore.

Away.

From.

Lenore.

I scream and flail and bite.

And then Kyn is there, pulling me from Mars's hold, turning my face to his. "It's not her," he says, his grip tight on my chin. "It's not Lenore."

"What?"

He steps out of my way, gives me a clear view.

"It's not her."

CHAPTER 20

WHOEVER THIS GIRL IS, SHE'S YOUNG. Younger than I am. Relief washes over me followed by guilt. Her eyes are open and vacant. She has a fresh gash on her forehead. Water mixes with blood and turns it to pink rivulets that rush toward the ice.

"But where's Lenore?" I crawl to the rig's smashed window, my arms and knees wobbly, tears freezing on my lashes.

"She was the only one inside, Miss Quine, and she was dead as soon as the plow slammed onto the ice."

I stare into the empty rig. It's slowly filling with water, but Mars's fix is holding for now. And mine too, it seems. The plow is steady. Inside, there's little to indicate any other presence in the rig—a floating satchel, soaked mittens caught on the gear shift, scraps of garbage swirling in the frigid eddies—but it's Bristol's. There isn't another plow this ugly anywhere in the Kol Mountains.

"If I had to guess," Mars says. "This rig made it safely to the camp."

I swallow back a sob. "How can you know that?"

"Her name is Rayna," Hyla says, her boots quiet as she approaches, her movements ginger. She crouches next to me and scoops up the satchel floating just inside the cab. "I met her at the rebel camp. She had a fire in her chest. Passion or desire, I couldn't tell."

Hyla unzips the satchel and peers inside. Her shoulders fall and she shakes her head. "Mars," she says. "Look."

Carefully, she lifts out the pulpy remains of what appears to be a stack of letters. The river has scrubbed the pages clean of words, but a circle of wax dangles from the mess, half the Paradyian seal just visible.

"A rebel then," I say. No one else would dare writing to the golden isle.

Mars takes the wad of paper from Hyla, attempts to separate the pages. "I don't think we could reasonably call her a rebel," he says. "But she was in camp with her brother. I assume that's how she got ahold of Bristol's rig."

I'm trembling now, my hand reaching for the roof of the plow. It's just nerves, the shock of thinking Lenore dead. "Do your rebels usually defect, Dresden?"

"No, Miss Quine. They do not. Rayna was young and she'd already developed a taste for kol. She resented what her brother had done for her."

"And what was that?" I know better than to ask for a story but I do it anyway. To cover my shaking hands, to give me a moment to collect myself.

"When her brother first approached us, he came offering information." He flourishes the dripping envelopes. "About the

Majority, about their movements, a conspiracy he'd uncovered while working at the Port of Glas. He was more than willing to share what he knew, but he had a single condition. Like so many that come to me for help, he wanted his sister freed from the Stack." He spares Rayna a glance. "I took care of it."

"You bought out her debt?"

"I did. And her brother's intelligence brought the rebels more hope than they'd had in years. It was a fair exchange."

Something about his words, about the twist of his lips.

"And if he hadn't possessed something worth trading, would you have left her to die there? In the Stack?"

"Whatever I did," he says, dropping the useless letters to the ice, "I did with the best of intentions."

"For her? Or for the rebels?"

He pulls the square of cloth from his pocket and dabs at his crusted lips. "There will always be those who choose a blissful death over a hard-fought life. I can't save them from that."

Blisters line my gums, but at least my lips have been spared. "There was no need to use Kerce magic then. She was already dead."

"You couldn't have known that," Kyn says.

"There was great need, Miss Quine. And you did well."

But Winter has other thoughts.

AFTER ALL I'VE DONE FOR YOU, FOR YOUR FRIENDS, she squalls. TO BE FORCED LOW UNDER SUCH DEMANDS. ARE YOU MY BETTER? SHALL I CALL YOU MASTER?

On and on she whines, a tempest in my head. The others observe a moment of silence after Hyla and Kyn slip Rayna beneath the ice. But my head throbs with Winter's complaints, and as we load into the Dragon one by one, I mutter Mystra Dyfan's words once again.

"*Est stiyee*," I tell Winter.

Just stop.

✳

According to the diagrams tacked up in Drypp's garage, the mines at North Bend have massive rectangular openings cut into the mountains. They're nothing like the newer mines, with their small, rounded entrances and narrow tracks that rattle workers miles into the rock. Drypp said if you look hard enough, century-old Majority markings can be found carved near the openings, though the elements have worn flat much of the distinction in the mountainside.

The elements are the reason these mines were abandoned years back. Though it wasn't the incessant hammering of storms or the swirling ocean fog that never lifts. It wasn't the disadvantages of either Ryme or Blys that rendered the working conditions impossible.

It was the monsters.

The Seacliff Road is a flat thoroughfare, cut away centuries ago by explorers commissioned by the Majority. Before they invaded in full. Before they turned Shiv Island into Layce, their newest conquest. Like the Shiv Road, it's not maintained, but the kol-flaked salt surfing the sea air keeps the ice on the road from building up. The road is rumored to be nothing more than crumbling rock, but the currents are friendliest here, and for the Abaki scaling the cliffs up from the waves below, it's their preferred way to approach the island.

Thoughts of the mines and the black ocean beyond, the wind whipping hard against the blanket tacked over Hyla's window—they're the only things keeping my eyes from falling shut. I can't count the hours I've been awake.

Dead ahead, the fog is heavy, a new layer rolling in. Tendrils of kol curl like smoke up from the tossing waves, twisting into a sky that's only ever gray. I need sleep.

I blink but it's hard to open my eyes now and the rig swerves. I overcorrect—slipping and sliding, catching the outside mirror on the rock before regaining control. My face floods with shame, but next to me Hyla snores, and behind me—his arms draped around my seat, fingers tangled in my hair—Kyn's chest rattles with sleep. He's worried about nothing in the world at this moment, least of all my driving.

It bothers me that I know his mood so absolutely. Despite Hyla's thoughts on such things, I've only known Kyn for a short time. His feelings should not be as real to me as my own, though I am glad to know my blunder's gone unnoticed.

Or not.

Mars's gaze finds mine in the rearview. He's awake and watching me drive, though he looks like he's three nails short of a coffin. His waxen skin is pasty and the kol in his eyes is fading. I can see color there beneath the black veil—blue, maybe green—and a fuzzy gray distinction where the whites should be.

"You're tired," I say.

He raises a single brow. "I'm not the only one."

I turn my gaze back to the road. "I'll sleep at North Bend.

It'll cost us a few hours, but the Seacliff Road is a different kind of dangerous and I shouldn't try it with my eyes closed. Not the first time."

"You've never been this far north?"

"Not on the Shiv Road."

"How far have you been?"

"There's a road just south of the river crossing. To the west there are a series of Majority mining camps. Nothing big like Hex Landing, but the miners need food and supplies just the same. I've run a haul out to them a few times. Beyond that, there's little reason to be out this far."

His nod is simple and quiet. He's more inviting when he's exhausted.

"I didn't realize the kol in your blood could be used up."

He leans toward the front seats, looking at his face in the mirror. With his index finger he draws a thin line beneath one eye and then the other. "It restores itself," he says, his voice ragged. "But the rate at which it does so is not at all consistent."

It's a dangerous question I'm about to ask, but I have to know. "And your body? Does it restore itself too?"

"Much like yours."

"The kol, then." I swallow, look down at the knuckles I'd bloodied punching the dash. Whole now, the busted skin new and pink. "I thought it was Winter all along. Healing me."

"She doesn't do that. I did tell you." That reprimand again, so like Mystra Dyfan. But then he softly adds, "The covenant Winter made with the queen of the Kerce—the kol keeps her bound to that. Three hundred and twenty-five Rymes ago and Kerce descendants still share a measure of it."

"And what of Mystra Dyfan's limp?" I ask. "How do you explain that?"

"It's been three centuries and the Kerce have intermarried. There were so few Kerce who survived the journey and even fewer who survived Winter. When the Majority arrived . . . I do not blame the Kerce for seeking comfort, for marrying where they loved. But, as a consequence, few have enough kol in their blood to do more than decipher Winter's whispering. Some can't even do that. And none have the power to do what needs to be done."

"To send Winter away. To banish her."

A slow nod. "You have other gifts as well, Miss Quine. Gifts the Kerce don't have."

"You should sleep," I say.

He's silent, angry. But he's tired.

"Seriously, Mars. We have, what? Four twyl blossoms left? As it is, you're the only one of us who's guaranteed a clear mind out on the cliffs."

"There are things you could do to remedy that," he says. "Things you've already begun to explore."

"The Seacliff Road isn't a place to test your theories, Mars. We won't see danger until we're near on top of it."

"Are you afraid of the kol monsters, Miss Quine?"

"Yes," I say.

He nods and meets my gaze.

"Good."

"Please, sleep."

He leans back and crosses his arms over his chest. I hit a pothole that forces my eyes back to the road, but when I check on him again a moment later, his eyes are closed. I can only hope they'll be dark as a burned wick when he opens them.

The Dragon rattles on, over miles and miles of melting highway, the black sea in the distance filling my window. Slowly, maliciously. Soon my windshield will be nothing but waves of kol.

"Sylvi," Kyn says, his breath warm on my ear. "Do you believe in truth?"

"What do you mean?"

"Right and wrong. Good and evil. Do you believe the world is as simple as all that?"

I think of Bristol and I think of Lenore. I think of Mars and I think of Drypp. I suppose I do believe in good and evil but that's not what I say.

"I don't really think about it."

"What do you think about?"

"My next haul."

"You're a bad liar."

"Sometimes I'm a good liar."

"Not today."

I sigh. "I believe that there is evil and I believe that there is good." My eyes flick to Mars's sleeping form. "I can't always say which is which." I shift, switch my grip on the wheel. "Maybe that's why I like the road, why I like traveling alone. Out here . . . survival, coin, that's all that matters. The rest is a luxury for those who don't have to worry about either."

He's yawning again, his eyes closing. "One day, you'll tell me something and it won't be a lie." He flips onto his side, his boot knocking Mars's. Mars elbows him away without opening his eyes and the two settle in, comfortable in their mutual discomfort.

It reminds me so much of Lenore, hot tears sting my eyes. I don't know what it is—if it's my need to make things right with her or the threat of telling Kyn anything honest about myself— but I know now that I was right to leave myself another way out.

"You're the last person on Layce who needs options," Lenore once told me. "You need a map and a road. You need someone to tell you where to go. Options get you into trouble."

She was wrong then and she's wrong now. Options are going to keep both of us alive. My pathetic resistance to the kol and our unplanned lack of twyl changes everything. Taking the Seacliff Road is no longer simply a dangerous endeavor. It's a deadly roll of the dice. And I know, better than anyone, how a gamble like that can turn out.

By the time I've caught sight of the mines at North Bend, the blisters on my gums are gone and I've made a decision that burns like sick in the back of my throat.

I can't stay. If I do, I'll forget why I've come. I'm not out on the road in the middle of the Flux for Kyn-the-Shiv, and I'm not here to fight Winter. I'm here for Lenore. That's it.

If I can get her back to Whistletop, everything else I've done, everything else that's happened . . . none of it will matter.

AND THERE ARE OTHER RIGS, Winter says, her voice kinder than it's been in miles.

My hands shake because she's right. The only way to do this is to leave the Dragon behind.

I COULD HELP YOU GET HER BACK.

She'd do it too. I wouldn't even need to ask; Winter looks for reasons to fight Mars. But that's an argument for later. Now, I make peace with goodbye. The first real goodbye I've ever chosen.

My eyes sting with the cruelty of it, but that's all I allow myself. I'm not big on checking your mirrors to see if the pothole you hit is still there. We have to keep moving. And from here on out, I do that alone.

We've reached North Bend, the mines yawning tall and narrow before us. I crank the wheel to the left, pulling the Dragon into the first of the two entrances. It's emptier than I expected, and I push slowly through potholes filled with slush toward the back of the cavern, the Dragon's smoke stack bumping a swinging cable strung with electric bulbs.

Dead ahead is the lift that once dropped miners deep into the island. I kill the engine mere feet from the cage doors. In the dark I can just make out the shape of a generator and what looks like a control panel for the lifts. I wonder if the generator will power the overhead lights?

My only knowledge of these mines is secondhand. Drypp passed along some of what he knew, told me it was one of the places I was sure to find stores of fuel if I was ever out this far. I got the impression he'd been out here on occasion, but he never would talk about it. Mostly Drypp's stories were old, stories of what the mines used to do, used to be. Family members who knew family members who told stories about family members whose hard-earned sweat called to the monsters out on Seacliff Road.

I don't know what I expected, really. Their ghosts to be lingering about? A list of their names on the wall? But mostly it's just a large, empty space. Taller, wider than the Shiv caves, but with that same dank, closed-off feel. I prefer the sight of wide-open snow-capped mountains, but here, inside, there's no wind beating against the trailer, no danger of ice cracking beneath the tread. And despite our proximity to the famed Seacliff monsters, I feel almost safe.

There are things that need doing and wasting time is dangerous, but I have to sleep. Even if it's just for a few hours. I flip sideways in my seat, stretching my boots out over Hyla's legs. Gently, avoiding any contact with her arm or shoulder, holding my breath and hoping I don't wake her.

A pang of regret shudders through my body and I realize the Dragon isn't the only thing I'll miss. I'll miss Hyla. I will. This brazen warrior woman from the golden kingdom, out to set right all the world's wrongs. She shifts, letting her good arm fall on my shins, her warmth a friendly sort of comfort.

She did almost crush my arm. When was that? A week ago, maybe, but it feels like a lifetime past. And all in the service of the great Mars Dresden.

With my back against the door, I can't help but catch sight of him as I close my eyes. I won't miss him, but I think I'll always be curious. About his travels and his ongoing war with Winter.

I don't let myself glance at Kyn, but it hardly matters. His face is there anyway. And his words.

"One day, you'll tell me something and it won't be a lie."

I pinch my eyes a little tighter and wonder what that would feel like.

CHAPTER 21

WINTER WAKES ME. SHE'S CLIMBED IN through our useless windows. She slaps my face with chill, but her words swirl warm and wise in my chest. **HURRY**, she says, **HURRY**.

I pull myself upright, lifting my boots carefully, needing all three of my companions to sleep for as long as possible but feeling it particularly for Hyla. Her wounds aren't healing nearly as fast as Kyn's.

I crouch in my seat and unlatch the already gaping window, easing it gently down and into the frame. I've slept at least four hours; the strength in my legs, the clarity in my thinking tells me so.

But I'm ready to be on the go now. Ready to put this portion of the journey behind me. The regret I felt just hours ago, the remorse—it all feels like a different Sylvi. The very Sylvi I plan to leave behind.

The longer I ride with Mars and Hyla, the closer I get to Kyn, the harder it is to see the girl I used to be. To remember what it was like before I took this job.

I'll become someone else if I don't leave now. Someone I'm sure to hate.

Carefully, quietly, I slip out the window. My legs are strong as they land on the dappled clay inside the tunnel. I retreat to a dark corner to relieve myself and then I set to work.

I load up my tool belt and hit the lifts, pushing my face up against the grate and peering inside. Drypp was right—four barrels of fuel sit side by side in the cage. There's a stack of smaller gas cans sitting next to the barrels, rusted and ancient. I'll need two.

I slide open the grate as quietly as I can, but it's been shut for a long time, and, as the rust shakes free, the track squeals and my heart stumbles. At this point I could explain my actions away, but if anyone wakes up, I won't have time to get done what needs doing.

I fold the gate into itself and grab two of the cans, both heavy with petrol. I tuck them against the wall of the mine and inch the door shut as quietly as I can manage.

And then I set to work: The tires are easy enough to reach— they're attached to the undercarriage. I'm plenty small. I simply squat and crab walk beneath the rig until I've reached them—two rubber tires, smaller than the ones on Mars's trailer by more than half. Slowly, carefully, I apply the socket wrench and I crank. It takes me forever, my blood races in my ears with every twist of the tool, every grating sound it makes tightening my jaw.

I'm going to get caught, they're going to wake, and this part— the tires that shouldn't be here—this is going to be impossible to explain.

At last, the second tire falls free and I roll them both out into the open and across the mine where I rest them against the rocky wall next to the gas cans. I'm dripping cold sweat, but there isn't time to worry about that. I've got to get the chassis unloaded.

The chassis will be difficult to free without making a ruckus. It's attached to the outside of the cab inside a narrow compartment Vaxton installed before the Dragon was mine. Vaxton wasn't a smuggler exactly. Not like Mars. He hauled lumber and twyl for the Majority mostly, cut trenches when they asked, but rumor has it he took coin here and there for moving small, easily stowed contraband.

To get to the compartment, I climb up onto the tank tread and slip carefully between the cab and the trailer. My blood races, warming my frozen cheeks. I can't do this without noise. The latches make it impossible; they're deep within a seam masked by the blue-and-sylver dragon scales painted onto the cab.

From my tool belt I pull a crowbar. Wedging it into the seam, I slide the bar until it connects with one of the seven latches. Fast and sharp, I engage the crowbar and with a dull click the latch pops open. It would have been louder inside the cab—Mars and Kyn have their backs pressed against this wall.

I lean against the trailer and I wait. And I listen. When I hear nothing, I slide the crowbar around, to the next latch and then the next. My gloved hands are aching with tension by the time I reach the seventh latch, and I'm certain there's a blister forming on my palm. I ignore it and slide the tool beneath the final latch. It sticks. I wiggle the bar around, switching my grip, rising on my toes so I can come at it from above. But nothing.

And that's when I see it.

There's something there—wedged in the seam. I push my face close trying to figure out what it is. And then I curse. Stupid, incompetent mechanic.

It's a wad of metal glue left behind by the idiot I hired to help me get the Dragon ready for Mars. I'll need a blowtorch to melt it away.

I drop to the ground, not nearly as quiet as I should be. I take a second to slow my breathing and lower my heart rate. I've got to climb into the cab to get the blowtorch. It's stowed beneath the seat Kyn and Mars are sleeping on.

I could kill the guy.

The sky outside the mine is pinking up, the sun pushing through a thin cloud somewhere. One more deep breath, one more tremor shaking my hands, and I climb up on the busted running board, using the door handle to pull myself upright.

"Sylvi," Kyn says, suddenly there in the window. "You scared me."

"You scared me," I say, my already primed heart taking flight. "I thought you were sleeping."

"I need to take a leak," he says.

I step off the running board and he climbs past me, his steps loping and dreamy. I wait until he's exited the mine entrance before I hop up and into the cab.

"What's going on?" Hyla asks, yawning herself awake.

"Getting to work on the rig," I say, leaning past her and grabbing for the blowtorch.

"I can come." She attempts to sit up, but I push her back in the chair. Her shoulder looks good, but she's still weak. And she needs her bandage changed. But most of all, I really don't need another set of eyes out there. "It's OK, Sessa. I'm feeling strong. I can help."

"No need," I say. "Kyn and I have things under control for now. I'll holler when we need you."

"My lady . . ."

"Mars needs to rest," I say, dropping my voice, hoping she'll do the same. "You do too, I think. You know what you can do?" I pull an ancient tackle box out from under Mars's legs, my voice quiet, my hands working hard not to jostle the box. "There's a half-inch eyebolt in here somewhere. I need one. Two would be better honestly, but I can make do with one. Can you find it for me?"

I don't wait for her to reply. I leave the tackle box on her lap and drop from the cab with the blowtorch in my hand.

"I wondered if you had one somewhere."

I turn and there's Kyn, wandering back inside the mine, looking sleep-rumpled and far more comfortable than he did just moments before.

"Had what?"

"A blowtorch. I bet the brakes are frozen solid, parked all night in the cold like this. Here," he says, "I'll do it."

He takes the blowtorch from my hands and crawls beneath the rig.

Flux.

"OK," I say. "OK, I'll work on . . . something else." The last few words fall away while my mind revs. Through the gap between the trailer and the cab, my gaze falls on the tires and the gas cans resting up against the wall. They're useless without the chassis.

Something hits my leg. "Put that somewhere, will you? I don't want to ruin another one."

It's Kyn's jacket. His spare. The one he changed into after the wolves tore his first coat to shreds. I toss it onto a cropping of rocks and something falls from the pocket.

His flint striker.

"It's actually not that bad," Kyn yells.

"Huh?" I ask, bending down to pick up the handy little tool.

"The brakes," he says. "They're not too bad. Ryme is warming faster than I expected."

"Oh. Good."

"Is it?" he calls from beneath the rig.

"No. Not really." But I have an idea now. I climb through the gap, Kyn's flint striker in my hand, my mind zeroing in on a solution.

I unzip my parka as I go and, with Lenore's sylver knife, cut away a corner of my shirt. I unscrew the lid on one of the gas cans and I dunk the square into the petrol. Dashing back to the rig, I do what I can to wipe away the petrol soaking my fingers—lighting myself on fire will definitely slow things down.

By the time I've climbed up onto the hitch, I'm holding a drenched band of fabric and Kyn's flint striker. I pull the crowbar from my belt and use it to jam the fuel-soaked cotton into the seam of the hidden compartment. When it's wedged into the gap, I strike a spark onto the tail end of it.

It blazes hot and red, but I'm worried about the lack of oxygen inside the seam. I can only hope the fire will burn long enough to warm the glue through. The flame burns for a minute or an eternity—it's hard to tell—the smell acrid, a plume of gray smoke rising into the air over my head. Stupidly, I swing at it, try to break it up, redirect it. But the smoke lifts, spreads. Stinks.

I have to hurry.

The paint job starts to crackle and peel, the menacing dragon ruined. I could try the hatch while it's still burning, but the glue needs to warm through and I might not get another try.

Finally the flame spits itself out and I crank at the seam with the crowbar. The hatch comes away with hot, sticky strings of glue attached to the flat end of the tool.

Carefully, I set the hatch and crowbar aside. I brace my back against the trailer and I lift. The chassis is heavy, and it takes a fair amount of effort to get it out of the small compartment without smacking it against the rim with every movement.

It's the hardest part of being a trucker out here. I'm smaller than the other drivers, not nearly as strong. I have to depend on other faculties to keep me in top form. But there are situations like this, where time is of the essence and all the skill in the world can't substitute for brute strength.

It takes me longer than I'd like, but finally, it's in my hands. The chassis with the small fuel tank and engine attached.

I run it back to the mine wall—aware only then that Kyn's been talking to me. Something about oiling the tank tread when he's done. I agree and dash back to the tool compartment. It takes only a second to locate the unconventional tool that stumped Kyn in High Pass. If I had time, I'd feel bad for lying to him about it.

Drypp's ice bike design is brilliant in so many ways, but my favorite aspect of its construction is that not a single tool is required to assemble the thing. Before Drypp passed, we'd take turns pressing and clicking and latching the thing into place, timing each other for nothing more than bragging rights.

I swallow back the memories and get to work. Four distinct

parts sit in front of me and I know from experience it'll take me less than three minutes to build the bike. With a little care, the tool that so confused Kyn snaps open, forming a stem and steering handles. I unfold it and attach it to the front tire—a thick rubber wheel that will grip the ice nicely. I attach this front section of the bike to the chassis. It's unwieldy to do so and I have to prop the chassis on top of the gas cans and lean it against the wall to keep it from falling over on me. Next, I snap the rear tire into place—thick enough to render the gas cans useless. The bike will stand on its own now. Only . . .

I've forgotten the saddle. I'm going to have to climb into the cab again. But I can't leave the bike out in the open. Kyn won't be much longer with the brakes and there's nothing but the twist of Hyla's neck between her and knowledge of what I've done.

I fill the gas tank with petrol and then toss the empty cans into a dark corner, my breathing heavy and uncomfortable. One hand on each handlebar, I steer the bike behind a decaying stack of crates and park it. Carefully, carefully, I open the cage doors and turn back for the bike.

"Is that petrol?" Hyla asks.

I jump, turn toward her, do everything in my power not to let my gaze drift to the bike tucked just feet from where she stands. The crates block her view, but it wouldn't take more than a shift in her stance to catch sight of the bike.

"Looks like it."

"It's a rebel stash," Mars says, suddenly behind Hyla, his strength clearly returned, his eyes dark—though the dim lighting inside the mine is not quite sufficient enough for me to know if the kol has entirely replenished itself inside his bloodstream.

"Fuel and supplies hidden all over the mountains," Mars says. "We don't need it, do we, Miss Quine?"

"We don't," I say. "The Dragon has a reserve tank if need be, but we could circle the Desolation with what's left in her primary tank now."

"Good, then," he says, his gaze expectant.

I twist my fingers into the grate and I pull, shutting the cage and leaving the ice bike so poorly hidden I'm embarrassed by my efforts.

"Put my crew to work, Miss Quine," Mars says. "Let's get your rig into shape before we lose the day."

Kyn's crawling out from beneath the rig now, blowtorch in hand.

"Miss Quine?"

I tear my eyes from Kyn. "The tank tread needs to be inspected and the windows sealed up with plastic. There are rolls of it here," I say, pointing to the opposite wall. "It's probably best if we just weld the doors shut for the stretch along the Seacliff Road. We need to keep as much kol out of the cab as we can. There's welding equipment over there—I saw it when we pulled in."

I lead them away from the cage, away from the crates and the hidden bike. I lead them away from the discarded hatch that will have to be replaced discreetly if I can't get out of here in the next minute or two.

How? How? How do I get out of here?

"Here, Sessa." Hyla places the eyebolt in my hand. "I could only find one."

My fingers close over the bolt, the smell of fuel wafting up to my nose. I smell like a tanker.

"How did you spill petrol on yourself, Miss Quine?"

"The knob on the blowtorch leaks," I say. "I'm sure Kyn's hands smell the same."

I don't meet Kyn's eyes. I don't grimace when he sniffs at his hands. I just squat and start sorting through the welding equipment—giving instructions and then standing to leave. It's a two-person job, the welding—Hyla and Kyn have it covered. I move away and Mars follows.

He needs a job, an assignment, a task. There's so much to be done to the rig, so much that could be done, so many things I could ask him to do, but my mind is with the seatless bike behind the crates, with the scorched paint on the back of the cab, with the discarded hatch that someone will surely notice before long.

"Mars," I begin, not knowing what to ask of him, "it would be helpful if you could—"

"I've a job to do that I need to undertake alone," he says, zipping his jacket closed. "I won't be long."

He's already gone, his back to me, turning into a silhouette as he strides toward the mine entrance.

I run then, to the driver's side of the Dragon, up onto the broken running board and into the cab. Both my knees in the seat, I grip the headrest with two hands and I pull. Three clicks and it's detached. Two bars protrude from the seat rest. I twist them one by one and they fall away. I leave them where they drop and climb across to the passenger side and out that door.

"What's this?" Kyn asks as I drop in front of him. He has the hatch in his hand, the hatch I'd propped against the trailer. His thumb rolls over the puckered paint hardening where it had scalded away.

"I'm taking care of that," I say, rounding him, my arm grazing his.

"Sylvi . . ." he says, his eyes wide and far too knowing. "What's in your hand? Are you—"

"Here," I say, passing him the flint striker.

And I'm running now, the headrest in my hand. As I run, my fingers fumble with the leather, stripping it away, dropping it to the ground. Another layer of leather lies beneath, seams and padding sewn into strange positions for a headrest. I flip it in my hands and find the divot.

I round the stack of crates. Kyn's not far behind, asking questions I can't quite decipher. But the panic in his chest? I feel that acutely.

I ignore it, flipping the headrest horizontally and snapping the divot onto the stem where it becomes the saddle. The ice bike's complete. It'll be a tight squeeze with Lenore and me sharing the seat, but we'll fit. This might just work.

But then Kyn's here, standing in front of me, looking like I've just kicked him in the gut.

"You're leaving," he says.

I don't owe him an explanation. I don't owe him anything. But he stretches out a hand and I remember what the kol did to me in the Cages. How it rendered me silly and careless. He saw it too. Had to watch me stroke his skin. He's a driver, the closest thing to an ally I have out here, and if anyone can understand why I won't do this, it's him.

"I can't do the Seacliff Road," I say, stepping back, out of his reach. "I can't do the kol. And I don't want to order Winter around just so I can."

"But you made a deal with Mars. He won't tell you where the camp is unless—"

"I know where the camp is, Kyn. I don't need Mars anymore." I throw my leg over the seat and wish away the ache I feel in my chest. I won't try to figure out if it's his ache or mine. There's no point. What he feels, I feel. And it's enough to have me stomping on the starter.

"Sylvi!" he calls after me.

I fly past the Dragon, past Hyla standing with a spool of solder in her hand, out into the white snow, into Winter's domain. I cross the road and drop onto the rocky slope that will take me out onto the Desolation.

It's loud, the bike's motor and the wind. But it's not loud enough. I can still hear Kyn's disappointment rattling around my insides. I rev the engine, but noise can't silence what he's doing to my heart.

I can only hope distance will do that.

CHAPTER 22

WINTER HAS TAKEN A TOLL ON THE MOUN-
tains. Especially if they were ever anything like Mystra Dyfan's stories—steep and treacherous as they
dropped off to the shores around the Pool of Begynd. This mountain trail is fraught with trees and rocks, with hardened ice and
slushy, mud-splattering puddles, but it's not nearly as treacherous
as it must have been a hundred years ago, a thousand years ago.

The bike tires are sturdy—perfect for this terrain. I split a
pair of dripping pines and the Desolation spreads vast and awe-
inspiring before me. I yank the handlebars to the left, kicking the
bike around and pulling it to a stop before cutting the engine.

I should go. I shouldn't waste time suspended here on the
shores of the Desolation—I'm not sure who will find me first,
Mars or the Shiv, but neither will let me go without some kind of
skirmish. And still I remain perched, watching.

The Desolation is like nothing I've ever seen. Ice as far as the
eye can see. I wonder how the Dragon would do on it, the tank

tread spinning and kicking as she thrusts me forward, the height of her letting me see for miles and miles. There's no perspective down here on the shore. It's nothing but blue ice and white fog hanging high overhead.

I couldn't get the Dragon down here if I wanted to. She's too big to navigate the trees and there's not even the beginnings of a road this side of the Desolation.

Behind me, the snow shifts.

I catch a half-exhaled breath and listen. And there it is again. Branches cracking, rocks shifting. It'll be the Shiv then.

Winter's whispers are hot and cold all at once.

YOUR KNIFE, she says.

The bone handle presses into my stomach, but I know that if they wished it, I'd already be lying in the snow. They've rocks and arrows and the advantage of high ground.

I've an ice bike and one sylver knife.

A knife I dare not pull.

I consider the bike for a moment, whether I should dismount. There's a sharp pain in my chest when I think of the Shiv tumbling from the cliff, the mountain closing on top of them as Kyn and I ran to safety. We did what we had to, but I've no desire to be disrespectful.

Neither am I a fool. Giving up my seat means giving up the possibility of a quick retreat. And I can't afford to do that.

More shifting, whispers. They're waiting for me to make the first move. Strategic or respectful, I can't decide. In the end, I turn toward them.

Only two have come, and they've brought a snowmobile.

A young man sits at the helm of the machine, blue rock

striping his arms. He's killed the engine, inching the skis forward with his feet. Crysel sits behind him, amber stone covering half her face, catching Winter's light and turning her into an iridescent spirit being. Her hair is plaited and her arms are wrapped loosely around the man's middle.

She wears a pair of soft leather trousers and a matching top, fur lining the seams. The sleeves almost reach her wrists. If I'd never seen her before, I'd have wondered how a child could look so sad.

"I'm sorry," I say. "Sorry about your Great Father. About the mountain skittering. I'm so sorry about everything." I let my eyes linger on her face and then his. They're so clean. Both of them. Scrubbed and clothed and silent. I can't imagine how such a thing is possible living in caves of mud and ice. But they've their secrets, the Shiv. And I suspect they've sacrificed much to keep the Desolation free of travelers.

Crysel climbs off the snowmobile and I scan her hands, looking for rocks.

"I understand the pool is sacred to you. I won't do anything to dishonor your dead. I just need to find my friend."

Crysel's hands are empty. She steps closer and withdraws something from the top of her shirt, a triangular pendant hanging from a leather cord. Shyne's necklace. She slips the cord over her head and offers it to me: a thick gold triangle, hollow, with etchings carved into the flat metal.

Paradyian.

"Shyne said you should have it," she says.

"Why?"

"Because it belonged to your mother."

She doesn't mean Mistress Quine.

"He says he's sorry it's broken." She tilts the pendant so I can see. It's clear the hollow in the center was created to hold an adornment—a gem or a curio maybe. "He says you'll never know how sorry he is that it's broken."

I'm not about to take this thing from her. It carries meaning, signifies acknowledgement of a reality I'm still not sure I believe. And it would fetch a lot of coin. This one pendant could feed them all for a year. But Crysel is impatient. She tiptoes forward and steps up onto the toe of my boot, using it to propel her high enough to drop the pendant around my neck.

The man behind her yanks the pull-rope on the snowmobile and the stench of petrol grows stronger as the engine revs to life. He glides the machine down the incline and out onto the Desolation, where he idles, waiting for the girl.

Crysel steps past me.

My mouth opens, but whatever question I mean to ask dies on my tongue. I've nothing to say, though I am sad to see her leave.

"It's not often we're allowed out on the ice," she says, her shoulder blades like wings pressing through the leather. "But today, we send the dead to await Begynd. We will not bother you, Sessa. Not today."

She leaves behind only footprints—all toes and no heel—as she steps onto the Desolation and climbs up behind the Shiv man. His thumb flicks forward and the engine thrums loud against the frozen pool. Despite the racket, the snowmobile is graceful on the ice, and it's not long before their forms are nothing but dark shapes against the white.

They ride south, back toward High Pass, and I'm heading

due east. I kick the engine to a rumble before I change my mind. Before I turn the bike around and climb back to the mines at North Bend. Before I beg Mars to explain the pendant I'm fighting to ignore.

Slowly, carefully, I drive the ice bike out onto the Desolation. Despite a slick layer of water that's formed atop the lake, the pool is solid. No cracking, no pulling. It's nothing like the river crossing at Crane Falls. I turn the bike in a slow circle, taking in the view behind me—the incline that somehow looks steeper from down here, the Shiv Road high above the tree line, the mines lost somewhere beyond it. The falls, rushing streams of white and blue—growing cascades that threaten to pull the wing free at any moment. Layce is in full Flux now and I'm tempted to stay and wait, to watch as Crane Falls breaks apart for the last time this Ryme. It certainly feels imminent.

Everything about everything feels imminent. Looming.

I complete the bike's rotation and set my face to the far shores of the Desolation. Off to my right, the snowmobile has faded from view, and before me, there's nothing but a vast spread of ice. I believe in my heart that the rebel camp is on the other side—Lenore's on the other side.

There's no knowing if the ice is solid all the way across—no knowing if I'm driving to my death or taking the fastest route to Lenore—but Winter rides my boots, wraps my fists tight around the handlebars, settles like a campfire in my chest, and I know I've done the right thing.

Confident now in the Desolation's solid nature, I give the bike more gas. The wind is frigid on my face; tears stream from the corners of my eyes and frost forms on my lashes. It's my compromised vision that keeps me from really opening up the ice bike to see what she can do. Hyla's goggles would have been useful, but I'm no thief.

It's not long before the sylver ribbon sunk deep beneath the ice begins to show itself, a glow emanating through the opaque surface, flashing on my tires, my boots. The light is not buried nearly as deeply as I thought it was. At least not initially. When I first come upon it, the ribbon seems so close that I kick my bike to a stop and climb off.

I drop into a crouch and run my hand over the ice. The light isn't quite at the surface, but it's not buried far beneath either. If it keeps spreading, keeps shallowing, it won't be long. I wonder what that means? What would happen if this strange mysterious ribbon breaks through the ice? Is it liquid? Is it light? Can it be both?

A part of me wonders what would happen if I flip the lever on the side of my boot. What would happen if I engage my crampons? Could I dig the light out?

Aside from the obvious danger, I wouldn't. Crysel promised me an unhindered trip across the ice. If I go today. And if their ancestors really are buried beneath the Desolation, I've no right to disturb them.

I leave the bike where it is and follow the gleam for several yards. It widens as I walk, a trail of light leading northeast. It's definitely deepening, the sylver fading, its source buried somewhere far below.

I'm surprised at how translucent the ice is now. Frozen lakes, streams, rivers—they're usually frosted, the ice fogged, especially when it's as thick as this is. Near the strange sylver light, though,

I see clear through the ice. Fish frozen in midflip, water shrubs paralyzed where they swayed. Bubbles captured as they rose to the surface, flecks of kol sparkling in ripples of water far beneath my toes.

And then a hand, its fingers splayed.

Dread rises in my chest and bile in my throat.

The hand is buried far enough beneath the ice that it would have been lost in darkness if not for the illumination of the sylver flow.

I brush at the thin layer of moisture atop the ice, a futile attempt to see deeper, but if there's anything attached to the hand—an arm, a body, a heart and soul—I can't see it.

A gust of wind thrusts me forward and behind me, I hear Drypp's ice bike topple over.

"We've no time for a detour, Miss Quine, but I think it's good you've come."

Mars.

His voice doesn't startle me as much as it should. I didn't expect him to simply let me leave.

"Are there others?" I ask.

"Oh yes." I hear his boots settle onto the ice—toe first and then heel. "Continue on, Miss Quine. You can't miss them."

"I don't . . . want to," I say, realizing the truth of it.

"You prefer not to know? Is that it?"

I nod, quite against my better judgment, but the sight before me has torn something from my soul. It feels naked and bare and completely wild.

"Come, Miss Quine. You're better than that."

"I don't think I am. I'm selfish," I say, trying the words aloud, letting the truth of them land like a punch to the gut. Lenore had told me so more than once. It never occurred to me that she might be right.

"Of course you are. But that's not why you won't look. You're afraid."

I *am* afraid. But of what?

"You're afraid that you're wrong about her, this spirit you've grown to love. This relationship you've built your life around is the only thing you've ever been able to rely on, and you're afraid that her kindnesses have numbed you to their cost. You're afraid that Winter is using you."

HE'S WRONG, Winter says. HE'S ALWAYS BEEN WRONG.

Mars takes another step and his shoulder settles next to mine. "You're afraid that I'm right."

MAYBE YOU'RE AFRAID OF HIM.

A sob threatens to shake me. It's like I've been thrust onto the one battlefield I've always tried to skirt. And I'm cold. So cold. I shake Winter from my arms, but she refuses to release her grasp. I roll my shoulders back, tip my chin up.

"Will you show me the others?" I ask. "Please."

He smiles, continuing forward. "I knew you were better than that."

My boots are heavy and tired as I follow. Winter rises from the Desolation, climbing my ankles, my calves, my thighs. Suffocating the muscles and joints so fiercely, I swear my knees creak with every step.

NO, she says, DON'T! YOU WON'T UNDERSTAND.

The words burn in my belly, and I wonder if the blisters there look the same as the ones on Mars's lips.

Another few steps and we're no longer following a trail of light. It's a trail of hands. All of them reaching for the surface. Hundreds of hands. I know then that the Shiv were right—this is a desecration. Mars and I are walking, however carefully, atop the frozen graves of so many.

"The Shiv," I begin, "Shyne and the others, they believe their ancestors are living souls, alive beneath the ice. Do you . . . ?"

"Do I believe their claims?" he asks, stooping, running his pale fingers along the frozen pool, tracing the outstretched palm of someone buried so near the surface, I can almost make out a face. "I do. I think it would take very little to send Winter on her way, very little to free so many."

"To send Winter away," I say, the ache of it still there, still lingering in my voice. Even as I stare at the work of her hand.

"It will cost dearly—make no mistake."

"Cost who?"

"You," he says. "And me."

I cock my head at him—surprised to hear him group the two of us so comfortably.

"It will cost us . . . everything. But these people, this island will live again." He stands, turns. "I'm prepared, Miss Quine. I only await you."

"Lenore." It's the only thing I can say. The only thing I can't sacrifice. She found me in the forest, shared her grandfather with me, her home. It's a debt I must repay. I won't leave her to Bristol.

"I understand. First things first. We must make it to the rebel camp. *All of us* must make it there." He takes my hands in his. They're cold and damp from the Desolation. Nothing at all like

Kyn's hands. "You understand? The haul must make it there or I cannot help you with Lenore. And if we need the road to get it there then we'd best not melt it away just yet. Come back with me," he says. "Please."

His voice catches on something—tears, venom, I can't tell. I stare at his scabbed lips, wonder what it'd be like to have the kol mangle mine in such a way.

"This is the first thing you've ever *asked* me to do, the first time it hasn't been an order. Why?"

He releases my hands and steps backward.

"Kyn is dying."

It's like he slapped me. "What?"

"In all fairness, he'd have died at High Pass if it wasn't for your blood—but now his life is tied to yours."

"What do you mean?"

"When you left, his veins split wide, Miss Quine. The wounds that had healed over so nicely after the Frost Whites? They're reopening."

My mind reels, and I search my feelings for any hint that Kyn's in danger. I would know that, wouldn't I? I should, but I feel nothing of him now. Only my own regret. Still, the look on Mars's face tells me he's not lying. Kyn's broken and bleeding and I'm too far away to know why.

"Winter," I say, suddenly angry. "This has to be her doing."

She's suspiciously quiet, but Mars is shaking his head. "I would blame all the world's troubles on her if I could. But this isn't on Winter. This is on you. You healed him."

"*I* healed him?"

"It was your blood, Miss Quine. It mingled with his after

the attack, healed his wounds. He's your responsibility now. You must stay close or all that your blood accomplished will be undone."

And like that, the solitude I've always known on the open road—the freedom of escape—disappears. Kyn's my responsibility. Of course he is.

A sob surprises me and I clamp a hand over my mouth.

YOU CAN'T BELIEVE HIM. Winter laughs. **I TOLD YOU, HE LIES.**

But the truth of it weighs heavy on my bones. I've felt the burden of our bond since High Pass. The threads of our emotions, Kyn's moods twisting tight across mine, knotting my gut—was it nothing more than a reminder of my duty to him? I can't decide if I'm embarrassed or relieved that I thought it was something more.

"For how long?"

Mars looks down, pulls the square of cloth from his pocket, unfolds it, folds it again. Puts it away.

"Miss Quine—"

"I can't," I say, fumbling, panicking. "I can't . . . be needed like that."

YOU WEREN'T BUILT FOR SUCH THINGS, Winter agrees. **OF COURSE YOU WEREN'T.**

"You're needed more than you think." Mars's voice is sharp, pointed. "By many hundreds and thousands more than you will admit. But just now, if you don't come, Kyn will die. I don't imagine that's a thing you want to see happen."

I stumble back, the force of his words too much. I fall, water splashing as I connect with the ice, my momentum spinning me across the Desolation, positioning my gaze on the horizon to the east. Ice topped by black, kol-drenched mountains and beyond them the Kol Sea, churning.

"The rebel camp is just on the other side of the Desolation, isn't it?" My voice is flat. I've no energy to pretend it's really a question. "Somewhere near Queen's Point. That's where your smuggling ship makes port. It has to be."

Mars goes quiet. And Winter too. I wonder if they're having a silent battle of sorts. Eventually, it's Mars who breaks the stillness.

"What will you do, Miss Quine? Tie Miss Trestman to your bike and drag her kicking and screaming back to Whistletop? The river crossing is impossible to navigate now, and that bike would never survive the Cages."

"There are other roads, safer paths. It would take us much longer, but we could find shelter to escape the Flux. Trapping cabins, dried-up mines. Drypp and his brothers survived out here for weeks without much more than I've got on me now. Lenore and I could make it. With Winter's help—"

"Entering the camp at my side is the only way you'll get Miss Trestman to listen to you. Is her life, is Kyn's worth so little that you'd forfeit both just to be rid of me? I know you care for him. I've seen—"

But I don't want to hear what Mars has seen between Kyn and me. I'm ashamed. That I mistook magic for the kind of connection Hyla spoke of. That what ties Kyn and me together is nothing more than duty.

"You swear you'll help me with Lenore? That you won't let your own personal feelings about the Majority interfere?"

"What shall I swear by, Miss Quine?"

My eyes are restless, they won't still. "What is it you worship?"

"You," he says. "Is that not obvious?"

I laugh then, but it sounds more like a sob, like rock on bone.

"I can't be what you think I am. I can't be . . . bound to another person."

"But you are. To kingdoms of them."

I run my hands over the ice, splay my fingers like the soul buried beneath me. My hand is numb now, blue almost. But still alive. I'm still alive.

"And Kyn—"

"I won't lie to you, Miss Quine. I don't understand everything about the magic you carry in your flesh. I was not born in the Pool of Begynd like you were."

I turn toward him, ready to argue.

"No, listen," he says with a curt shake of his head. "I know. I know how hard this must be. But your blood runs through Kyndel's veins and just as the Shiv depend on their proximity to Begynd, I believe Kyn's sustained healing depends on his nearness to you."

"You *believe*?"

"In so many ways, you and I are the same. But we *are* different, Miss Quine. My mother gave birth to me in our home." He smiles, a real thing, with feeling behind it, with love. "And yours . . . your mother gave birth to you in the Pool of Begynd just before she unleashed Winter on this island. She didn't know what she was doing. She didn't understand. But she let Winter in. She believed Winter's lies. And it destroyed us all."

I can't breathe. I can't.

"How can you know? H-how?" Tears rattle in my throat, catch in the corners of my eyes.

"I can't know for certain. Not until you send Winter on her way. But I believe, Miss Quine. And I've done my due diligence. I've sought out answers. I've spoken to Shyne."

My damp eyes flick to his.

"Yes, Miss Quine. I've had dealings with the Shiv before—with Shyne—but I did not offer you and Kyn up to his people in the pass. I hope you can believe me." When I don't reply, he hurries on. "This sylver river beneath our feet? Somewhere along it, the Desolation shook and a fissure formed in the ice."

"Seventeen Rymes ago."

"Shyne told you, then."

"He said a lot of things," I say, my hand finding the pendant beneath my parka.

"It wasn't far from here that he found you," Mars says.

I laugh, a mirthless, irrational outburst.

"No, Miss Quine. This part of the story is not to be disputed. There were witnesses. Shyne came to investigate the sylver flow beneath the ice and what he found was you. He thought to take you home with him, to raise you with his own children. But you opened your eyes and he saw . . ."

"The kol."

"Yes, Miss Quine. He knew then that you were Kerce and that the Shiv would not accept you. So he took you inland, to the closest Majority dwelling he could find, and he left you there. Wrapped in his own furs, on the doorstep of a woman he knew nothing about. Shyne and I have many philosophical differences, but in this I am grateful."

Abandoned then. I should be surprised, but I'm not. Not really. I've no love for Mistress Quine. But tears rush toward my lashes, hanging there like the frozen wings of Crane Falls.

"It's possible some of these interwoven truths are nothing but chance. Certainly possible you were a misbegotten child left to die in the cold. You wouldn't be the first."

I pinch my eyes shut, force the tears to fall.

"But I've watched Winter, listened to her. And she is afraid of you. Show her that she is right to be afraid."

THE ONLY THING I'M AFRAID OF, Winter purrs, her breath curling the hairs on my neck, **IS LOSING YOU.**

There's a lie there somewhere. I hear it in the tremor of her voice. And still, I can't parse out what it means. But somewhere far above us a boy is dying, and regardless of what tomorrow holds, I'm not willing to lose him.

"Tell me about Kyn," I say, my throat tight.

Mars nods, swallows, keeps his gaze on mine. "As the distance between the two of you grows, so do the wounds that had so obediently closed. He has to stay near you or the healing you've completed in him will reverse itself."

"You believe."

"Proximity matters," he says. "Presence matters. It can't all be intentions and happy thoughts. You must be there for him or he will die."

"I'm better at leaving."

"How do you know?" he says, dropping next to me, his knees wet with the Desolation. "You've not tried to stay. Perhaps you have a gift you've never unwrapped."

I can't handle the empathy in his voice, on his face. I can't handle the desperation.

"Does Kyn know?"

"He's Shiv. He suspects. Or he did before the wounds opened so fully. There is little time, Miss Quine."

He stands and extends his hand to me. I notice now how very different we are. Mars in black head to toe—his eyes darker still. Me, clad in trousers and a parka—all pale whites and soft brown leathers. His hair kol black and mine as colorless as the snow.

"Please," he says, stepping forward, his hand closer. "I want to lose Kyn as little as you want to lose Miss Trestman. He is like my brother and if it weren't for me, he wouldn't be involved in all this."

The truth of it flashes in his eyes, and then trickles down his cheek—a tear clear as the ice beneath us.

"I thought your tears would be black," I say.

"I'm just a man, Miss Quine. Warped by Winter like everything else on this island, but the kol in my eyes is no different than the kol in yours."

I try to stand, but the ice is slick and my legs aren't quite strong enough. I feel Winter swoop in, trying to push me upright, trying to help. But I refuse, collapsing again to the ice. If Mars notices, he doesn't allow it to show on his carefully arranged face.

I'M HERE, I'M HERE, Winter whispers. LET ME HELP.

I reach up and take Mars's hand instead, let him pull me to my feet.

"And the bike, Miss Quine? Shall I bring it?"

Winter's already working up a protest because Mars means to fly.

"Leave it," I say, refusing to meet his gaze. I hate losing anything of Drypp's, but it'll slow us down.

He wraps my waist with his arm and we lift into the air. It's strange, the sensations warring within me. Winter disputing his command over her and yet entirely submissive to the words dripping from his lips. Tears stream down my own face now, but they're not tears of pain or fear. I care little for Winter's discomfort in this moment. They're simply the result of the wind in my face. The force of it pushes me tight against Mars.

I can't hear the Kerce words he's whispering, but I can feel them in the rumble of his chest. They don't cease, not for a moment. Words with so much power they compel the greatest force Layce has ever known into action. It strikes me then how little he's used it—his power, his magic. More than I was initially comfortable with, sure. But as we soar over the Desolation, I can tell there's so much more stored inside. I feel it in the tremor that shakes his entire body, in the thudding of his heart against my ear, in the rattling of kol inside his lungs. He could hurt Winter—he could. I wonder what it is that keeps him from doing just that.

"There," I yell, "look."

I've no idea if my words are loud enough to be heard over the wind, but Mars doesn't slow. To the south, a flame flickers and grows on the ice. The Shiv are nothing but a thicket of shadows as they watch their dead rise into the gray sky. I can't see their faces and I can't hear their cries, but my heart breaks for their loss.

The Kerce words slow, the rumble in Mars's chest growing

faint before disappearing altogether. We're dropping from the sky. The wind that held us so carefully is now unraveling, twisting away, shedding like the thick Ryme coat of a fox when the rains replace the ice. Winter sets us down roughly and our bones rattle as we strike the ground.

"Inside, Miss Quine," Mars says, his breathing ragged. "Quickly."

He takes my elbow and we run, but he stumbles and I turn, my own hand reaching out and grabbing his.

"You all right?" I ask. But I see he's not. Kol dust is smeared across his chin, blisters cover his lips. His eyes have lightened again. Green irises are visible behind the shroud, a slick of sweat coats his face and neck.

"Go! My body will heal itself," he says. "Kyn's will not."

He stands and shoves me toward the gaping mine with a strength I would not have guessed he had left in him. A cry makes its way out the yawning entrance and I sprint toward it. The bright white of the Desolation has left my eyes handicapped. Someone's got the generator working, but the swinging yellow lights overhead are akin to darkness after where I've been, and my eyes blink and blink, trying to make sense of the shapes and sounds filling the cavern.

By the time I've zeroed in on the scene unfolding before me, Mars is there. Moving slowly, but near enough to pull me forward.

Kyn's so still. Once again there are bloodied hashmarks across his chest, open puncture wounds on his neck where the Frost White latched on. Hyla holds his hand, grease and tears streaking her face.

"It's your blood he needs," Mars says.

But my dagger is already out, already sliding across my palm. I switch hands and with blood spilling over the bone handle, I slice open my other palm as well. The fall to my knees is sharper than the pain in my hands and Mars has to pull Hyla away from Kyn's body as I inch forward.

"He's gone," I say, taking in Kyn's ravaged face, feeling the absence of his emotion inside my own rib cage. "He's already—"

"Your hands, Miss Quine."

I press my hands to Kyn's chest, our blood mingling on contact. And I feel everything, bright and wide and all encompassing. None of the sensations—the pain in my knees, the stinging bite of the slice across my hands, the ache in my back and thighs from so many hours on the road—none of it compares to what Kyn's blood shares with mine. He's in pain, the peaceful look on his face a façade. Death is fighting for him, rejoicing at the blood draining from his veins.

Strange how like Winter Death can be.

Kyn gasps and takes in a mouthful of air. And we all breathe with him. Relief.

Hyla sobs. I'm quieter, my mind churning over the emotions flooding my own veins. It's not just me sharing blood with Kyn; it's Kyn sharing his blood with me. I have no idea if it's Winter's doing or if it's the kol Mars swears races through my veins, or even if there's something of magic in Kyn's own blood, but the connection I'd been avoiding, the connection I knew was building between him and me, it's different than I thought, but stronger too. I recognize emotions as they flood me. The pain he experiences is nothing new; it's similar to the pain he experienced when the wolves attacked. The healing he feels is also familiar; it's identical to the sensations that flooded him when our bloody forms collided just after.

HE'LL EXPECT IT FOREVER NOW, Winter says. **THE HEALING. YOUR TOUCH. HE'LL CLAIM IT AS RIGHT-FULLY HIS.**

It's a terrifying thought and my hands come up and away. I lean back, suddenly afraid of what I've done, afraid of what I've started.

"Is he? Is it . . . finished?" Hyla asks.

There's too much blood to know, his and mine—mostly his.

"It's not *finished*," Mars says, something haunting in his voice. "But it's enough."

I stand and back away from the scene before me. My hands are hot and still dripping blood. But I'm relieved. I am. I don't want Kyn to die. The very idea makes me ill.

I feel it then. How much a part of me he already is. How much a part of each other our mutual wounds have made us. He needs me—my very presence—to survive. And I wonder, now, as I stumble out into the blinding white of Winter, do I need him?

What parts of me would die if Kyn were gone?

I have no answers, but Winter does—she never, ever stops talking.

Her answer tangles my boots, trips me, forces me onto my knees.

NOTHING, she says, **NOTHING YOU CAN'T LIVE WITHOUT.**

My hands turn her snow red.

CHAPTER 23

IT'S A GRIND TO GET THE DRAGON BACK INTO working order. The lookout is entirely dismantled and reassembled—a task Hyla assumes, bad shoulder and all. She'd started on the repair while I was gone, but when Kyn's wounds began to reopen, she'd abandoned everything to help him. The simplicity of her devotion shames me into silence.

Both Hyla and Mars stay well away from me until my hands heal over. The bleeding is minimal now, but my palms are tender and raw, so I wrap them in old shop rags. A couple hours later, while reattaching the hatch that had so perfectly hidden the bike's chassis, the rags become more hindrance than help, snagging on screws and hinges and generally preventing me from moving as I'd like. So, tucked between the cab and the trailer, I crouch and unravel the grease-stained scraps.

No scabs. No scars. Nothing to indicate I'd done anything spectacular at all. If I was a different kind of person, if I was Lenore, I'd linger over my hands and the baffling miracle of it all, and I'd genuinely try to decide if Mars was right about my blood or if Winter was just having a good laugh. I'd wonder how I could go all seventeen Rymes of my life and not fully realize what my body could do. But there's been quite enough thinking and not nearly enough trucking. I drop the rags to the dirt and heft the hatch back in place.

Off to my left, Kyn leans against the rocky wall. It's taken him just under two hours to right himself. The drab lighting, the blood smeared in gigantic brush strokes across his chest, his trousers black with it—it's not a pretty picture he makes. He looks half dead with his chin rolling against his chest and his hands opening and closing on his lap.

I wish I didn't know what he was feeling. I wish I could separate his angst from mine, but it's just there, in my chest, a wad so thick and clingy I have visions of spitting it against the ground and sorting through the gunk with the toe of my boot.

Instead, I keep busy, working, trying not to feel all the things Kyn's feeling and trying not to see the ancient Shiv frozen beneath the Desolation. There's even a part of me that tries to stay wedged between these two things—like if I let Kyn catch sight of the Shiv images floating through my mind, it'll increase his misery or, worse, prime him to take up Mars's cause. To insist I can send Winter away with a simple command.

I've dug out the compressor and am refilling the slow-leaking tire on Mars's trailer when Kyn pushes himself to a stand. Hyla and I both stop what we're doing and watch as he plods heavily out into the snow. I'm bundled up tightly to keep out the cold, but Kyn's wearing nothing but trousers and boots as he steps out into Winter.

Hyla meets my gaze from atop the trailer, her hands tangled in something metallic and oily. The grease drips to the ground in big, slow globs. "Should I go after him?"

"I'm not your boss, Hy."

She blinks at me and looks around. Mars disappeared a while back. Presumably to do that thing only he can do. Hyla bore up well under the instruction to stay behind, keep an eye on Kyn and make sure "that damn gun is working," but now that Kyn has wandered out of sight, it seems she can't decide which of these tasks takes precedence.

"But should I? I know what my girls would want. They would want their mother to follow, to comfort. But my husband? He would want to be left alone, to sort things out in his mind. Kyndel is somewhere in between, is he not? Young and yet a man. I do not know—"

Relief bursts through me, bright and fresh as the first snow after a muddy Blys. The relief isn't mine, I know, but I feel it vivid and open as a clean stretch of road. Kyn's fine.

"Finish the gun," I tell Hyla. "If Kyn needs us, we'll know."

Hyla nods and turns back to the lookout. "Thank you, Sessa."

I'll know if Kyn needs anything. The realization does something strange to my skin. I ignore it and flip the knob on the compressor. It hisses and spits as the motor turns, pumping air into the tire and flooding my head with enough noise that I can almost ignore the pleasure rolling like rain over the dry, craggy places in Kyn's heart.

When he returns, the lookout has been reassembled and, pending an actual test, the gun shows every likelihood of firing. I haven't let Hyla shoot the thing before now, but there's no risk of an avalanche out on the Seacliff Road. And, aside from Lenore's face, I can't think of anything that would bring me more joy than seeing an ice monster blown to pieces by a Paradyian turret gun.

Hyla and I are finishing the final welds on the doors. The welds were my idea, but I don't like it. As sparks fly and metal glows, it feels like we're constructing our own cell with fewer and fewer escape routes.

"I'm running low on clothing," Kyn says as he wanders back inside. He's dripping wet, standing there half-naked and smiling. Water races down the red rock of his shoulders, slowing as it strikes the skin of his forearms. Beads of melted snow sit like pearls on his stone cheekbone. His chest is a crosshatching of puckered pink scars, but the wounds have closed. Winter wants me to resent him, and perhaps I should, but I meet his gaze and realize there are worse boys to be shackled to.

He's the only person I've ever known to choose his emotions so completely. After all the bleeding and the dying and the slap-dizzy reality that his existence could very well be tied to my proximity, I cannot imagine another soul choosing to be happy. But I feel it, in my gut, the choice that squashes the other, more complicated emotions. They're still there, buried beneath his choice, but happy wins out. Because he's told it to.

"There's always the hatch," he says.

"Excuse me?"

"I'll kick the welds clean off before I let you die in the cab, Sylvi. And there's always the hatch."

He can feel my emotions too. *Inconvenient* is not the right word—it's something bigger and more complicated than that—but *inconvenient* is the word that swallows me whole as I stare down at his face, clean and drenched and happier than I've ever seen him.

"It's not the dying that has me worried," I say. "It's the smell."

"Not mine," he says. "I just bathed."

"Clearly."

"Melting snow has its upside. I can show you where the pool is, Hy, if you want to rinse off that grime."

Hyla arches away from Kyn's hand. "I'd rather smell," she says, collecting the welder and traipsing away.

Kyn throws me a wink and follows.

"We should take a look at the engine," I say.

"I'll be along." He doesn't turn back and I consider asking him what could be more important than the engine, but despite the grin on his face, there's something somber fighting for his attention.

When I hear the turn of the key and the rattle of metal, I understand. He's checking the load.

"I could use some help with this door," Kyn calls.

The hole in the door—the one the Rangers made with their harpoon—will have to be repaired before we get out on the Sea-cliff Road. Even without Winter's influence, the kol and salt blowing in off the sea has the capacity to damage most anything.

"Hyla has the welder," I say, walking fast in the opposite direction. Curiosity be damned, there's still value in claiming I knew nothing of the haul. Be it kol or twyl or fuzzy woolen sweaters for the rebels. I can't imagine any of it is worth all this.

"But Hyla smells," Kyn calls.

I can't fight the smile that breaks out across my face.

"I felt that," he says.

Silence as we both process the consequences of that admission.

And then, as though he's made peace with it, he softly whispers, "You smiled. I felt it."

The Sylver Dragon is buttoned up and I've scrubbed myself clean by the time Mars returns with a small burlap sack flung over his shoulder.

"Twyl," he says.

Sweat pours down his face and neck, drenches the front of his shirt. Kol lines the creases of his face and hands, his knuckles bleed, and the knees of his black trousers are caked with mud.

"You went on foot," I say.

"Yes, Miss Quine, I did. An ice bike would have been helpful, but we seem to have misplaced ours."

The loss of Drypp's bike is more painful than inconvenient, but what's done is done. "I don't imagine you'd know what to do with one if we hadn't."

Mars snorts. "Well, there is that."

"The trailer door's been fixed," Kyn says, handing the key back to Mars.

Mars drops the sack and takes the key from Kyn's hand, then slides it into the medicine bag hanging around his neck.

"Come, Hyla," he says, grabbing the woman's arm. "It's time for a bath."

"I don't mind the smell," Hyla protests.

But Mars is hauling her out into the light. "You train Paradyian warriors for battle. You can brave a cold bath."

"We need to go," I yell, though my eyes are still on the burlap sack. It's a small bag, but the hike would have been treacherous.

"He's saving the kol in his blood for the road," Kyn says.

I'm not sure what to do with the appreciation growing in my chest. Mars is the only one of us who could have done what he did. The rest of us are vulnerable to the kol blowing in wildly off the sea.

Kyn shoves at the bag with the toe of his boot. "Will this be enough?"

"If we can make it past the danger in half a day? Maybe."

"And if it takes us longer?"

I squat and tip the contents of the bag onto the cave floor.

"I don't know," I say, the meager collection disheartening. "If the monsters swarm, if the rig takes any damage, if our welds break, or the plastic sheeting on the windows tears free—" I shrug. "We'll have to draw straws or something."

"Short straw gets strapped to the hood, yeah?"

I can't help but smile. "Something like that."

CHAPTER 24

SEACLIFF ROAD IS EVERYTHING I PROMISED Kyn it would be. Shifting, wet rock on the rough-cut byway, kol flecks sparkling in gray sunlight. And wind so fierce it threatens to dislodge the newly fired welds on the door latches. Kyn leans forward as he reaches for the instrument panel, his elbow knocking mine.

I grab his wrist before he can mess with my switches, but his fingers are long and he's disengaged the heater before I can stop him. His expression is careful, his brows doing most of the talking as he tips his chin to the sight beyond the windshield.

"Best keep the kol outside, yeah?"

He's right, of course. The kol swirls on the wind, black streaks against the white sky.

I release his wrist but not before my stomach soars at the contact. I can't tell if the sensation is mine or Kyn's. Our eyes catch and there's no doubt he's thinking the same thing. He withdraws to the bench seat and I turn my attention to the road.

It's eerie up here. The mountains were to our left for much of the Shiv Road and now, there's just the wide expanse of the Kol Sea churning and churning.

It reminds me of Mystra Dyfan. Once, while escaping the promise of a test on Kerce grammar, I stole into her room, just down the hall from Lenore's and mine. I was in a cabinet there along with some interesting treasures I'd never seen before. Candlesticks and a square of lace. A stack of parchment held together with twine, each page full of charcoal sketches.

I'd never thought Whistletop anything special until I saw those sketches. The tavern and the village square, the chicken coop out back, the grumpy man at the corner shop shoveling snow, twyl growing wild through a fence I'd climbed over for years. There was a book there too, so old that the pages were yellow and brittle. The ink was faded and the cabinet dark, so I tucked it into my coat and took it out back, behind the planter boxes and the chickens, to the edge of the forest. There, on a frozen log, I read my first snippet of Kerce poetry.

The letters meant nothing to me then—reading didn't come easy for me early on. When I tried to sound the words on my tongue, they were too light, spun sugar that dissolved and left me wondering if I'd said anything at all. They sounded nothing like the whispers of Winter, so I abandoned the effort and turned my attention to the illustrations.

Meticulously drawn ships and castles with towering spires. Menacing lizards ridden bareback by dancers with watercolor wings. Flowers with simpering faces wielding swords. Trees that were also men.

But as I look out over the angst of the Kol Sea, I'm reminded of the illustration on the final page of the book. Below a poem I couldn't be bothered to read, the picture was of a bright blue ocean, curls of water topped with soft white foam. There were waves traveling one after the other, all in the same direction, like soldiers off to war. They were reaching for the shore, for the soft rolling lines of sand, but there was a tranquility to the drawing, a constancy of motion.

The Kol Sea is nothing like the ocean on that page. It bucks and fights and the white foam that crests the top of the waves spits and sloshes and, if you stare long enough—something a rig driver should never do—you see wisps of kol gather themselves together and rise into the sky.

Kyn passes a twyl blossom forward.

"We're to chew this?" Hyla asks, turning it in her hands. "I've only had the gum cut from twyl blocks."

"That stuff is boiled and full of preservatives to extend the potency of the gum. This won't last nearly as long," I say.

"The stem is useless. It's the blossom you want." Kyn uses his flint striker to burn away the petals, leaving the sticky innards in Hyla's hand and that burnt-honey smell lingering in the air. "Tuck it into your cheek," he says. "The sap will stave off the effects of the kol that's bound to slip into the cab."

Gingerly Hyla tucks the sap into her mouth. Kyn burns away two more blossoms, gum for me and gum for him. I let him drop it in my hand this time and try not to let my stomach swoop when I think about his fingers pushing the twyl into my mouth just yesterday.

"No worries, Sylvi," he says, settling back. "No worries."

"Don't chew it," I tell Hyla. She's taken to moving the twyl around her mouth. "Just keep it tucked in your cheek."

"How long is one blossom supposed to last?" she asks, adjusting her goggles to keep the hair out of her face.

"Not long," Mars says.

"And what happens if we run out?" Hyla asks.

"First things first, my friend." Mars leans forward between the seats and Kyn's fingers tangle in my hair as he pulls himself upright.

An Abaki stands in the center of the road.

CHAPTER 25

THE MONSTER'S ARMS ARE MISMATCHED. ONE is dark and muscled, so like Kyn's that I press my shoulder into his to assure myself he's still there. The other is pale and hairy with purple, puckered brands covering the bicep. Despite their differences, the Abaki's arms are close in length and breadth, whereas its legs are so poorly matched the lumbering steps are marked with a dramatic limp.

Its right leg is short and spindly—a child's leg, possibly. The left is thick and muscled and almost twice as tall. Its torso is made of nothing more than shimmering snow and flecks of kol, a self-contained storm spinning left and then right. It's what holds him together, the mixture of Winter's magic and the power of raw kol. Together they turn the Kol Sea's dead into something far more. Even without a head, this one is dangerous.

"How confident are you in those welds, Hy?"

"They'll hold, Sessa."

I press my foot to the gas. The monster senses our movement

but it's too late. It has barely enough time to stumble sideways before the rig strikes the thing, bucket first and then grill. Its body tumbles up and onto the hood. The pale arm dislodges, smacks off the windshield and lands somewhere on the road.

"There are easier ways, Miss Quine."

Of course he could order Winter to take care of this one. Of course he could attempt to negotiate with it himself—who knows, perhaps Abaki speak Kerce. But both options would deplete his power and there's no reason. Not yet.

I yank the control that raises the bucket.

"Miss Quine—"

The top lip of the bucket pins the monster's larger leg to the hood. He has little time to struggle before I slam it down, and he flies into the road. The swirling kol and magic that's holding him together stutters and vanishes. His remaining three limbs scatter, skittering on the rough rock, tumbling over the cliff.

Hyla leans forward, one hand on the dash. "Is it dead?"

"It was never alive," Mars says.

Kyn takes a swig from the canteen. "Looked alive."

"Doesn't matter. Without arms and legs, they can't hurt us." I smack Hyla on the knee. "Now you've seen a monster."

"I'm not impressed," she says. "I expected a fight."

Flashes of the past: the monster mounting Drypp, kneeling on his soft belly, pulling at his arm. The sound of bones grinding, of flesh tearing.

"This one was only acting on instinct," Kyn says. "Once an Abaki has acquired a head, they're a little more . . ."

"Intelligent?" Hyla asks.

"They're not alive," Mars insists.

But Mars didn't see the kol monster that attacked Drypp and me. He didn't see the calculation in its eyes.

"Maybe not, but they're smart. Cunning—the ones with eyes and brains."

"The intelligence belongs to Winter and Winter alone. Yes, the kol makes things more than they are, but it is just a mineral. It cannot join one limb to another. It cannot give these monsters a will. Only an intelligent being can do that."

"Up ahead," Kyn says.

What I originally assume is an opaque patch of fog turns out to be something much more.

Abaki.

It's hard to tell how many from here, hard to know which of them have two arms and two legs, hard to know which head belongs to which monster, hard to know why unintelligent, purely instinctual scavengers should be working together instead of wrestling one another to the ground to steal limbs.

"Hyla," Mars says. "The turret gun is working, yes?"

But Hyla's already moving, reaching overhead to open the hatch.

"Take this," Kyn says, handing her another stock of twyl. "You have your flint striker?"

"Yes."

"And close the hatch quickly," I say. "The kol—"

"Yes, Miss Quine. We know."

Despite the injury to her shoulder, Hyla's faster than I anticipate, opening the hatch and pulling herself onto the roof of the cab. A gust of wind blows in, stealing my breath as it strikes me in the chest. I swallow down a mouthful of twyl juice. It's already losing its flavor; its potency can't be too far behind.

"Keep her steady, Miss Quine," Mars says. He offers Hyla his arm and she pulls him up after her.

"Where's he going? There's only one gun in that turret."

"Mars doesn't need guns," Kyn says, pulling the hatch shut.

"He doesn't need to use his Kerce tongue either. We might need it later."

"I think he has doubts about the Sylver Dragon barreling over a wall of monsters."

"*He* doubts the Dragon? Or you do?"

"Not me, little ice witch. I would never."

Boots pound their way down the trailer and Mars soars into sight.

"How much strength does it sap for him to do that?" I ask.

"I'd imagine it depends on how hard Winter opposes his commands. And how stubborn the Abaki are."

Kyn and I flinch in unison as Hyla fires off a round from the turret. It strikes the ground in front of the scrum. Ice and rock explode. The flames from the round are short-lived on the damp rock but she's managed to set a headless monster's leg ablaze. It stumbles but continues forward with the others.

Mars conjures a gust of wind that shoots him high above the monsters and out of the turret gun's range. Clouds swarm about his dark form and light flashes across the sky. Lightning drops from his fist, leaving an Abaki sprawled on the road, arms and legs searching.

Hyla fires another round and another, making the rig shudder and my ears ring. But still the monsters advance.

A hand settles on my shoulder and I jump. The Dragon swerves as I strike out with my right hand. But it's only Kyn. He's climbed into the front seat and is trying to tell me something. I shake my head, attempting to clear the ringing in my ear.

"Incendiary rounds," he yells. "They're going straight through the . . ." He slams a fist into his chest.

I work my jaw, try to clear my ears, but Kyn points and I watch. A whistling bullet marks the sky with smoke as it sails into sight and through the swirling black-and-white torso of a kol monster, exploding as it strikes the ground behind it. The monster continues forward.

"She needs to aim for arms and legs. Heads," I say, though only one in every five or six monsters that climb up onto the road seems to have a head. Hyla's ammunition won't explode unless it strikes something of substance, and apparently the stormy torsos of the Abaki aren't dense enough.

But Hyla's figured it out too. Heads explode. Legs and arms follow, the magicked torsos dissolving into puffs of black and white against the churning sea beyond.

Mismatched limbs claw up and onto the road, water-logged flesh hanging from faces and elbows and knees. The ground is increasingly pockmarked, and I have to swerve to keep out of the potholes.

The rig drops and then bounces, the trailer pitching back and forth.

"Hold on, Hyla!" I yell, though the possibility of her hearing me is nil. I navigate to the right, looking for smoother driving. Kyn's leaning forward now, his face close to the windshield.

"What is it?" I yell, hoping his ears are working better than mine.

"I thought..." He's yelling too, moving his face from the patched windshield to the plastic covering the passenger-side window. "I can't get a good angle."

"There's a toggle," I yell. "For the outside mirror."

He grabs the toggle and twists the mirror into place. "Ah, flux."

"What?"

He toggles the mirror, swinging it to an angle that shows me everything I need to know. An Abaki climbs the side of the trailer. It has one leg, three arms, and a shaggy flop of hair on top of its head.

Kyn jumps to a squat, placing his feet in the seat as his hands fiddle with the latch overhead. "We have to tell Hyla," he says.

My own mirror was sheared off after the river crossing, but I keep one eye on the road and fiddle with the toggle for Kyn's, shifting the mirror so I can see Hyla high on the turret. My view is mostly obstructed so I turn my attention back to the road.

Kyn wrestles the hatch open, flinging it wide. It bounces loudly on the top of the cab and it's only then that I realize the gun's stopped firing. I glance at the mirror.

"Kyn!" I yell. "She knows! Hyla knows!"

Hyla wheels around and aims the gun, but the monster is fast, leaping the final few feet and colliding with the Paradyian warrior in the lookout. Hyla falls back onto the edge of the turret and then lifts her legs and kicks the monster in the head. The beast tumbles backward onto the trailer, kol and snow still swirling.

"Eyes on the road, Sylvi," Kyn yells, Drypp's shotgun flung across his chest. "I've got this." He climbs up through the hatch and slams it shut. But the latch doesn't catch and the door bounces hard. I reach up to grab it, but I'm too short and the door smacks the jamb with a metallic crunch.

"Fluxing Blys," I growl.

I move fast now—my eyes still on the road, foot off the gas, boot in the seat, hand reaching for the bobbing door. A pothole in the road judders the Dragon and sends the door flying skyward again and then down, thwacking my knuckles and shattering half the door jamb. I manage to wrap my throbbing fingers around the handle and pull as I drop back into the seat and press my foot to the gas. My shoulder burns and my hand tears free of the handle. The door lifts once again, flung into the air by the jostling cab.

A quick glance and I know the locking mechanism is gone, torn free when the jamb shattered. There's no way to secure the hatch now. There's rope in the outside toolbox. But even if I could get to it and tie the hatch shut, the jamb took so much damage, the door will never seal properly.

Without a stop and serious repairs, there will be no keeping kol out of the cab. I swallow down the twyl juice on my tongue— the flavor is long gone.

I chance another look in the side mirror and see that Hyla and Kyn dispatched the climbing Abaki. Hyla is manning the turret gun, her back to Kyn's as they take aim at Winter's monsters.

The Dragon's frigid now, the cab growing colder as we pound down the road. My brain wheels with one simple truth: Hyla, Kyn, and I each need another twyl blossom. And soon. I'm going to have to stop to grab the bag if one of them doesn't crawl back into the cab soon. But stopping is a terrifying proposition with so many Abaki in the road. The plastic windows suddenly seem a foolish idea. It wouldn't take much at all for the monsters to tear inside.

And then I hear her. Winter.

She's in the cab with me. Sitting on my knees, the wheel in her hands.

The image makes me laugh and the twyl pokes me in the cheek. It's dry now, like the hay Lenore spreads for her chickens.

Oh, Leni.

Tears blur my vision and I steer the Dragon into a pothole. Overhead I hear boots and hands scuffling. I hear people screaming and monsters laughing.

LET ME, Winter says. **GIVE ME THE WHEEL.**

"No," I say. "You're trying to stop us. You want us to go back."

But she bites at my fingers and I loosen my grip if only to brush the tears from my eyes. The rig stays steady with Winter at the helm. Steadier than I could keep it at any rate. My eyes blur again.

IT'S THE TWYL, Winter says. **IT'S MAKING YOU SAD.**

But I think maybe it's the kol.

THE TWYL, Winter insists.

I shouldn't trust Winter. But it makes sense. I wasn't sad until the twyl lost its flavor.

"And I'm so tired of being sad," I say. I pull the twyl from my mouth and let a gust of wind tug it up and out the hatch.

The world is a shimmer of black magic and rolling waves. I can hear them in my head, and I wonder what it would be like to feel them under my hands.

"Sylvi," Kyn says, suddenly next to me. "What are you doing?" He's anxious, I feel it in my gut, but it's a soft squishy thing. Easy to ignore.

He curses and then he's gone, scrabbling into the back as I hit another pothole and then another. But Winter's doing the driving. Not me. And the bouncing makes me laugh.

The flint striker is loud next to my ear and I try to swat it out of Kyn's hold. But he moves his hands away and lights the twyl blossom. The stench is itchy as it crawls into my nose. And then the twyl is in my mouth and it's warm and . . .

My stomach is sick.

The black glitz trimming the sky begins to fade and I twist the wheel in my hands.

"Fluxing Blys, Kyn. I'm sorry."

"No, I'm sorry," he says, a lot of shame in our shared bag of emotions. "I should have prepared all the twyl before we hit the road. It would have been easy enough to do."

My eyes are slow to clear, but I'm aware enough to pull the rig back to the center of the highway, where the thoroughfare is less damaged.

"The hatch broke," I say.

"Yeah."

The Abaki aren't swarming now. They're spread across the road. Some staring as we fly by, some giving chase, some still clawing their way up and onto the roadway.

"I've got it," I say, pointing the Dragon at the headless monster dead ahead, pushing my foot to the floor, angry to have been bested by the kol yet again, angry that Winter took advantage.

Angry that I can't puzzle out what she wants with me.

"Sylvi, don't," Kyn says. "If one of those limbs lodges under the rig, if it hits the fuel tanks or . . ."

I know what he's saying—I've hit a deer before, had to repair an air hose out on the road—but a cold slick memory slaps me across the face: Drypp's blood in my eyes, his arm hanging by tendon and sinew.

I raise the bucket and drop it down.

It slams the monster to bits and we trundle over the thing like it was never there. Thank Begynd for Paradyian ingenuity.

And then the hiss and spit of something going wrong.

I drop my eyes to the gauges.

"Sylvi, the road!"

Another Abaki. This one with a head. It stands in the middle of the highway—it has four ill-assorted limbs and the ugliest face I've ever seen, all melting skin and an eye that can't decide if it wants to be part of the face or not. My foot's to the floor and we're bearing down on him.

This is what I want. To take off a monster's head.

Hyla fires and the ground explodes in front of the Abaki, but the dust settles and it's still there.

"Kill the engine, Sylvi!"

He's right. We're overheating. Another glance at the gauges and I curse.

"You've punctured the radiator!"

"It could be a hose or a—"

"It doesn't matter what it is. If you don't stop, you'll blow up the engine."

A thin stream of smoke spits from beneath the hood and

disappears as we burn past it. I flatten my hand against the dash, feel the turmoil inside. Boiling fluids, popping and spitting, the engine getting hotter and hotter.

"Sylvi!"

I decide at the last possible minute. It's a bad call, I know it is, but I swerve, aiming to miss the Abaki. But my angle's wrong and I clip his side. He spins off and out of sight—better than under the tread, but now my problem is the Dragon. She's bucking, sliding sideways. I fight to keep her straight, fight to pull her to a stop.

"Hold on, Sylvi!" Kyn braces himself. "Hold on!"

We're barreling toward the ocean, the trailer pitching and pulling. And then with a furious sigh, the Sylver Dragon rattles to a stop.

The turret gun keeps firing and monsters fall. The sound is sharp and agonizing but I welcome it. The pain means we're alive, Kyn and I. It means we didn't plummet into the sea.

And it means Hyla's alive too.

Where Mars is, I can't say. The lightning has stopped and if ever we could use a fire bolt, it's now.

Monsters circle the rig. Stilted legs tramp toward us, arms dangling abnormally here and there. A headless Abaki captures my attention as it wanders from one side of the highway to the other. He's dragging a leg behind him, and it bumps along over the ruts in the road.

The turret gun falls silent.

"Hyla's out of rounds," I say.

"Yeah."

"You?"

"I've been out for a while."

And then *pop, pop, pop*. Hyla's handguns. Paradyian curses fly as her boots stomp down the trailer. Two Abaki fall, one with gunshots in its arms. The other takes a shot to the leg. The limb spins away and the monster collapses to his side. Still, it continues toward us, crawling, pushing, scraping. It's not alone in its effort. They're climbing onto the trailer now, onto the bucket.

Sweat breaks out along my forehead and back. My hands are hot and trembling. No, they're cold. Frigid. And I wonder where Winter is. If this is her doing. If she'll watch as her monsters pull us limb from limb.

"We're not going to die," Kyn says, reaching over and squeezing my shoulder. "You hear me, snowflake?"

"I hear you."

But I'm not so sure. There's an Abaki on the hood now; its arms are more bone than flesh. His hand is on the window, the fractured, crumbling window. It bends under the monster's weight and we're scrabbling backward, trying to get between the seats.

"Move, Sylvi!" Kyn yells. Something is in his fist.

I lurch sideways and he drives the handle of Drypp's old pick-axe at the hand as if it's some kind of saber. The handle punches a hole in the plastic but the monster grabs hold of the axe and flings it out onto the shoulder, then continues forward.

"That didn't work," I say.

"Yeah, no. No, it didn't."

There's another Abaki now. This one squats on the hood, its fingers hanging flaccid against the metal, its feet creeping forward like the blue biting spiders Drypp used to singe with his blowtorch.

The blowtorch!

It's under the bench here. If I can just—

But lightning falls onto the road—a mighty cascade of it. Everything turns gold and then white, even the shadowy places in the cab. Nothing is left in darkness. The light sears something in my eyes, whatever it is that lets me see the world. And then it's cold, so cold, and everything falls silent.

CHAPTER 26

THE ABAKI—THOSE STAGGERED ACROSS THE road and those climbing up onto it—are all frozen solid. Statues of white snow. I reach through the hole Kyn punched in the plastic and I push against the monster fixed there. Its rigid form slides to the highway, and the ice shatters like panes of glass.

I see Mars now. He's standing near the drop-off, the sea tossing behind him all the way to the horizon. Beneath his feet the ground is as churned and swollen as the waves, the wet rock busted. His eyes are green and his face is black. He sways and then crumples.

"Mars Dresden!"

It's Hyla. Her cry jolts Kyn and me into action. We climb out the hatch, kicking aside frozen Abaki as we slip and slide our way to the ground. Hyla gets there first. She turns Mars onto his back and we all gasp.

The blisters start at his mouth but they don't end there. Like creeping vines, the frostbite spreads across his face. Blue and black, decaying skin and kol, it's hard to separate one from the other.

Tears sting my eyes as I drop my gaze to the cliffs below. If Mars's lightning froze the monsters there, I can't tell. Fog clings to the rock, veiling the craggy face, but all is quiet.

"He's alive," Kyn says, his ear to Mars's chest. "He's breathing. He'll be OK, Hy. His body will heal and the kol will . . . reload or whatever it does."

"He'll be OK," Hyla sobs, shoving her goggles up onto her forehead, dirt streaking her face.

Kyn slaps Hyla on the back. "I've seen it before, yeah? He'll be OK."

"*Have* you seen it?" I ask Kyn quietly, my question for him alone.

"Yeah," he whispers. "Only, I've never seen the frostbite so—" he makes a swirling motion in front of his face.

"How long will it take?" Hyla asks. "For him to recover."

"Could be a while," Kyn says, looking to me.

"Mars said it was unpredictable," I say, remembering our conversation. "That kol replenishes itself but he never knows how long it will take."

"Let's get him inside the cab, Hy," Kyn says, stifling his own sorrow. I feel the resolve of it, his decision to lock it up and shove it away. His intention stiffens my spine. If we keep it together, Hyla will do the same. If we keep moving, the soldier will remember her duty.

"It's a good idea," I say. "Get Mars away from the cliff here, let the kol in his blood do its thing. We're going to have to figure out what's wrong with the Dragon before we can go anywhere anyway."

I stand, hoping Hyla will do the same.

Kyn slides his arms under Mars's shoulders and raises his brows at Hyla. "You got his legs, yeah?"

It's another moment before she moves, but when she does, her actions are strong and intentional. She stands, moves to Mars's feet.

I give her the best smile I can muster and turn toward the Dragon. That's why I don't see it start. I'm looking the other way—looking at the mess I've made of the rig—when a firestorm of dread consumes Kyn's emotions, burning them all away until there's only this: Hyla is going to die.

"Watch out!" Kyn cries.

I turn to see a monster bury Drypp's axe in the soft place between Hyla's shoulder blades. She howls, reaching for the monster, grabbing hold of its arm and flinging it into the road. The Abaki bumps its way over the ruined rock and disappears over the opposite side. Hyla reaches for the axe now, which is plunged deep in her back. Beneath her feet the ground trembles, the road crumbling and falling away.

"Move, Hy! Move!"

She tries to step, but the ground moves faster and she's falling.

Kyn and I are there, just feet away, when Hyla reaches out, one long arm and then two. Kyn snags her wrist and we're going to be OK. She's going to be OK.

But Hyla's not small and her momentum is too much. Her hand slips through both of Kyn's.

"No!" Kyn yells.

Hyla's fingers catch on the rock and her body collides with the cliff face. Her goggles fall from her head, tumble away toward the sea. It's a hard drop, but she's safe, clinging to the stone with trembling hands, blood drenching her back. Kyn's reaching for her, his stomach flat to the road. I'm reaching too, wishing I had longer arms. Wishing I could magic Hyla up and . . .

Could I?

Could Winter?

Of course she could.

But Hyla's got it. With great effort, she swings one hand up and grabs hold of Kyn's arm.

"I've got you. I've got you!"

"Your other arm now, Hy!" I say. "Almost there."

Hyla's golden face is white, slick with exertion, but she lets go of the rock and puts all her trust in Kyn's grip. Kyn pulls and I crawl over to help, grabbing Hyla's wrist, doing very little but not wanting to lose her. Her conviction and her warmth. Her loyalty and—

She roars.

A monster has her leg. Through the fog, I can't tell how many limbs he has, but he has a head. It's a bald wrinkled thing and it's growing closer.

"Flux," Kyn hisses. "It's climbing up."

The monster uses Hyla's body as a ladder, scaling her long legs, wrapping itself about her waist. A knobby hand reaches up and grabs the axe still wedged into her back.

Hyla roars again, but there's more agony in the sound this time. Less rage.

"Don't you dare let go, Hyla!" Kyn yells.

But she's going to. I can see the determination in her scowl.

"Don't do it, Hy!"

"I will not let this monster onto the road," she yells. "Not with Mars so weak."

My knife! I sit up, pull the knife from my belt and let it fly. It's my last one, my last weapon, and I can't remember if the bone handle says *Sylver* or *Lenore*.

The knife pierces the monster's thinning cheek. Its mouth opens, but if it screams, I can't hear the sound. With one hand it gropes, trying to free the knife. Hyla takes advantage of the Abaki's divided attention and launches a leg backward, her boot striking one of its rotted limbs. Another kick and the monster loses its grip. Its hands open and close looking for something to grab and find only air. The Abaki's limbs break free of its spinning torso and the monster plummets to the rocks below.

Hyla's stopped fighting, her hands loose. Kyn's grip is the only thing keeping her from the angry sea below. It's not until we get her up and onto the road that I realize how badly she's hurt. She's sprawled on her stomach, her breathing thin and ragged, the axe still embedded in her back. Her jacket and trousers are sodden, her boots full of blood. I reach for the axe handle, trying to understand, trying to remember how Drypp's birthday gift got out on the highway.

"Get back, Sylvi," Kyn says, pushing me away. "You can't."

"But—"

"You can't. If you're bleeding at all . . ."

I don't understand, not right away. It's the cold sick dread in Kyn's gut that gets me there. If my blood mingles with Hyla's, if it heals her . . .

The desire to run is strong. To jump headfirst into the Kol

Sea and let the monsters fight over my pieces. I can't be tethered to yet another person. I can't.

But I won't just let her die either. Not if I can save her.

"Kyn," I say, reaching for my knife. "It's OK. Let me—"

But my knives are gone. And Drypp's axe is buried in Hyla's back. I've nothing to open my hands with. It's OK. I'll pull the axe free and use that.

"I can fix it," I tell Kyn. "I can help her."

"No, you can't, Sylvi. You can't." His voice catches and he clears his throat. "She's dead." After a moment, he stands, leaving Hyla there on the ground. Just feet from Mars. The smuggler looks like death, but his chest rises and falls. Hyla's has gone utterly still.

"But you were dead. You were. And I—"

He's moving toward me now. "She wouldn't want you to."

A wet laugh lodges in my throat. "Of course she would. She's Paradyian and they're so, so . . . She has a husband! And children! She has a debt to pay. You can't take that from her. She has to live!"

Tears fall from his eyes, but his voice is steady. "She made me promise. She made Mars promise."

"What are you talking about?" I'm trying to see past him, trying to see Hyla.

But Kyn's moving me away, his hands firm on my arms. Moving me back against the Dragon.

"After the mines, Hyla saw what it cost you to do what you did. For me." Kyn's eyes are wine and rage. They're passion and loss. They're flame, the embers of a fire that could die as easily as catch. "She made us swear."

"She made you *swear*?"

"A Paradyian covenant," he says. "It's a sacred thing and I will not violate it."

I search the feelings between us, looking for weakness, for a way forward, but Kyn's decided. He won't let me touch Hyla.

I sag against the Dragon, not sobbing, but tired. I'm sick and angry and so heartbroken I could crawl into the earth, pull the mountain down around me, and sleep like the Shiv lost beneath the ice.

"Hyla was a Paradyian warrior," Kyn says, kneeling, looking me in the eye. "A soldier of the highest order. It is honorable to die in battle. It is noble to give your life fighting alongside your friends. She counted you among her friends, Sylvi. She didn't want her life to be a burden to you."

"Kyn, please."

"No, Sylvi," he says, his face more stone than I've ever seen it. "She made us swear."

CHAPTER 27

THE GROUND IS STILL PRICKLING WITH WHAT-
ever magic Mars used to freeze the Abaki. I don't know
if it would have been enough to keep the climbers off
the road, but I can feel the electricity in my feet as we work. We
haven't seen another monster since Hyla.

Kyn moves Mars into the sleeper, and, while I crawl under
the Dragon to get a better look, he wraps Hyla's body in blankets
and makes room for her in the trailer. It's not proper; she deserves
better. But a respectable send-off will have to wait until we reach
the camp.

The trailer door slides shut and the lock clicks into place—I
hear it echoing off the wet ground. When I climb out from
beneath the trailer, Mars's satchel is hanging around Kyn's neck
and he's standing bare-armed in the wind. I wish he hadn't gone
through both jackets. He doesn't feel the cold like I do, but there's
something malicious in this squall. I'm about to offer Drypp's old
spare again, but he's wrapped so fully in Hyla's loss, I realize it's

almost stifling. He doesn't need a coat. His suffering is deeper than flesh.

"It's my fault," I say. "I shouldn't have run down the Abaki."

He blinks. His lashes soft against the stone. "It's *my* fault," he says. "The axe never would have been on the road if I hadn't handed it to the monster."

Winter is doing her best to blow us into the sea. I don't have the energy to pick a fight with her just now, but it's brewing. I let her push at me, the clouds overhead bumping along, full of drink.

Blys is coming.

"You were right," I tell Kyn. "It's the radiator." I hold up the shattered remnants of a femur. "Punched a hole right through it. Our antifreeze is all over the road."

He nods, his gaze wandering away, over the sea, settling somewhere far beyond me. I watch him for a minute, watch what he does as the scene with Hyla rolls like thunder through his mind. The crumbling rock. The axe. His muscles burning. The sensations are hard and fast—they take my breath away—but his face doesn't alter.

I reach out and set a finger on the satchel resting against his sternum, trace the outline of the trailer key pressed against the leather.

"Tell me it was worth it," I say.

His eyes drop to my hand.

"Tell me that whatever it is we're hauling is worth all the carnage we're leaving behind. Tell me it's worth Hyla's life and the lives of the Shiv set ablaze out on the Desolation." My words are hard enough, so I keep my voice soft. "I may never be able to return home, and if I do, there's no guarantee it'll be with Lenore at my side. Things will never be the same for any of us. Please tell me this haul is worth it."

He blinks, long and slow. He's too full of questions to have an answer.

I drop my hand but he catches it, presses my palm to his chest. "Please. Just stand here with me."

A flash of memory—windows shattering, Mistress Quine staring.

Kyn squeezes my hand, concern replacing his stolid expression. "What is it?" he asks. "What's wrong?"

It takes me a moment, my eyes on his hand, on his stone knuckles and the etching I still don't understand. It's different, I know. This is different. But: "The last man who grabbed my hand and made me touch him was Bristol Mapes."

Kyn releases my fingers. Fast, like I've burned him.

"I would never—"

"I know." I don't tell him how I know, how I can feel his heart tremble. How it makes mine tremble too. I don't have to tell Kyn those things. He already knows. "But I'd rather choose for myself who I touch and when I touch them."

His chest constricts, his throat closes. I feel it acutely, the shame of this simple action. I'm tempted to tell him it's fine. Tempted to brush it off. But we're going to be spending a lot of time together, Kyn and I, and he may as well know this about me. I'm broken and there's very little either of us can do about it.

"I'm sorry," he says. "I won't do it again."

"Thank you."

He's searching my feelings, wondering if he should continue. There's something he wants me to know, but he's not sure.

"Whatever it is, you can say it," I tell him.

"I didn't know about Bristol. About what he did to you. I don't think Mars knows either."

I'm certain Mars doesn't know. Mistress Quine was the only one who knew, and she's long dead now.

"He may not have known what Bristol did to me, but he befriended Lenore with the sole purpose of getting me to haul his load."

"Sylvi—"

"No. He did. She's out here because of him."

Kyn's hands fly up, surrendering. "I won't argue that point. Mars isn't above deception to get what he wants. And I'm not claiming any great friendship with Lenore—I hardly know her—but she has her own mind. She'd come to her own conclusions about the Majority and the rebels long before we came to Whistletop. When Mars told her he couldn't leave for camp until he'd sorted out his business, *she* sought out Bristol. *She* asked *him* to take her to the rebels."

"She wouldn't have left Whistletop if it wasn't for Mars. He made her . . . brave."

Kyn laughs, but there's a sadness in his chest. "How can the bravest girl I've ever met think that's a bad thing?"

"Look at where it landed her!"

"You can't . . . it's more complicated than that."

I try to push the limits of this obscure connection between us, try to understand what he's not saying, but there's nothing there—nothing I didn't already know.

"It always is."

I turn my face to the mountain side of the island. The drop

to the Desolation is steep here. The rocks, sharp and deadly, are sloughing off their white wrappings, leaving rivulets of water trailing down in steady streams toward the sprawling frozen pool.

"Sylvi—" There's tension building in his chest. He has something to say. Something I don't want to hear.

"Hyla packed the solder, so if we have enough propane in the blowtorch, we can fix the radiator," I say. "But if we don't hurry, we'll lose the light."

I leave him there, staring out at the water. It's a noisy and heartbreaking sight, the Kol Sea. So many souls pulled to its depths. Ships dragged under by its monsters. Tragic swell after tragic swell crashes on the shiv-sharp rocks, but it's nothing to the waves breaking over Kyn's heart.

It's a good thing he's made of stone.

The radiator fix isn't complicated, but it's time consuming and Winter's not making things easy on us. The first rains of Blys come hard and constant.

We use the blowtorch to heat the metal on the radiator so we can fold it over the gaping hole, and then we use what little solder we have to seal up the cracks. If Hyla hadn't thought to bring the solder . . .

The ground beneath us is all standing water, our clothes heavy with rain and mud, the blowtorch struggling in the wet conditions. That's when I realize Winter's mistake. Water isn't ideal, but without antifreeze, we're going to have to get creative.

And this rain will get the Dragon up and running. It'll get us to the camp.

Maybe.

I dig a hole in the ground and line it with plastic sheeting to collect the falling rainwater and then I duck back under the rig and flash Kyn two more twyl blossoms. He uses the blowtorch to fire away the petals and I catch the hot gooey middle in my damp hands. I tuck one in my cheek and offer the other to Kyn. His hands are full, so he opens his mouth and I press one on his tongue.

"How many do we have left?" he asks.

"More than we should. If there had been three of us needing twyl . . ."

"Yeah."

When we crawl out from under the rig, the sky is black and the hole I've dug is full of rainwater. Kyn lifts the Dragon's hood and I gather the corners of the plastic, making a bag of sorts, and then heft it over to the rig. Kyn offers me his leg and I climb from his thick boot to his knee so I can hang the bag over the radiator.

"Aim true," he says, unscrewing the cap and using the hot end of the torch to work a hole in the plastic.

The water flows from the melted opening into the newly patched radiator, though there's no way for us to know if the thing is still leaking—there's simply too much water on the ground. The true test will be when we fire the engine.

"We could use some more fluid," I say, looking around, wishing I'd dug two holes. The radiator took all the liquid in the bag, but it's not full up.

"Here," Kyn says, shooing me away and climbing up on the bumper. "I got it."

His voice is staid, but there's something like mirth bubbling up in his stomach.

"What do you mean, you got it?"

But he's tugging at the laces on his trousers and I suddenly realize what he's doing. Despite the heaviness that threatens to spread both of our rib cages, I laugh. It's a good idea. And better him than me.

"Avert your eyes, little ice witch."

I turn away and leave him to it, something of lightness hanging about my shoulders.

"Aim true," I tell him. "Aim true."

CHAPTER 28

"HOW LONG DO YOU THINK WE HAVE BEFORE the Abaki try again?"

We've been on the road for almost two hours now and we haven't seen a single monster. Fog and kol swirl on the wind, pushing up against the Dragon, petting her as we squirrel away. But Winter's holding her cards close and when she plays them, we'll be hard-pressed to do much. We haven't a single functioning weapon.

"The ground back there," I say. "Whatever Mars did to it kept the Abaki away. But I can't imagine it lasting all the way to Queen's Point."

"You know where the camp is then?" he asks. "You weren't lying back at the mines."

"I've a fairly good idea," I say, blinking away the memory of his heartbreak as my bike flew past him and out into the snow. "But I've never been out here before and I've no idea what the road looks like between here and there."

Kyn stares out the window for a minute and then climbs between the seats. I watch him in the mirror, scrounging around, ducking into the sleeper. Finally he slides back into his seat and spreads the old Kerce road map on his knees. He's conflicted, likely breaking some sort of confidence. I feel the pressure of it behind my breastbone. After a moment, he exhales and his fighting loyalties quiet.

"I've only ever been to the camp once," he says, running a finger over the northeast wing of the isle, "and only by ship. This map is incomplete though. Just this side of the cliffs here, the road descends, through the mountains, all the way to sea level. The camp is there, positioned between the Desolation and the Kol Sea." Exactly where I thought it would be, but it's good to know the road itself will take us there. "Based on the instructions Mars gave Bristol, the only way to reach the camp itself is to cross the ice."

"The Desolation you mean."

He nods. "It's a short stretch, less than a mile, but I don't know if a rig as large as the Dragon has ever attempted it."

Probably not. There's not a rig quite like the Dragon on all of Layce. And still—

"The ice will hold."

"Yeah?"

"Yeah." If I'm sure of anything, it's that. Winter won't give up her hold on the isle so easily.

Based on what Kyn's just told me, the road will pitch downward soon, and we'll have a wall of mountain rock outside my window and the Desolation outside Kyn's. And then it's just a short, straight shot to the camp. A straight shot to Lenore.

"How are we on twyl?" I ask.

"We should be OK," he says, spreading the remaining twyl blossoms on his knees. There's more than enough to last us another hour.

Kyn hands me the innards of another sticky blossom and I swallow down the old, flavorless wad—not ideal, but there's nowhere to fling it. To keep the kol and the rain out, we've had to secure plastic sheeting across the hatch overhead. It was the last bit we had. We're stitched in now—we're not leaving the Dragon until we reach the rebel camp.

It's dark, our headlamps lighting the road before us, the moon overhead hidden by the clouds. Out my window, the sea is nothing but a black blur. I've stopped turning my face toward it, stopped checking the shoulder for monsters.

The driving is rough, rocks and debris churned up and thrown mercilessly into the components beneath the rig. We can't suffer another repair. The Dragon has to make it as she is, and the road is pissing me off.

Winter's doing her part too, needling me with old stories. Her past heroics, our adventures together. That scene at Mistress Quine's.

YOU'VE FORGOTTEN, she says, HOW TERRIBLE IT ALL WAS BEFORE I GOT THERE. YOU'D GO DAYS WITHOUT TALKING TO A SOUL. WEEKS WITHOUT ANYTHING TO EAT BUT WHAT YOU COULD SCAVENGE. I BROUGHT YOU TO WHISTLETOP. TO THE OLD MAN AND THE GIRL. I DID THAT AND YOU'VE FORGOTTEN.

She's a sickness in my belly now, my muscles so tight it's hard to breathe.

"Let's talk. Tell me about the Dragon. Did Drypp build her?" Kyn asks. The tension in his voice, the angst. It has me taking my eyes off the road, turning toward him.

He can't hear Winter's words in my head but he's sure to feel the strain, the conflict raging in a place no one can see. He nods at me, choosing to shut out the fear. How does he do that? How does he lock the panic away?

"He won her," I say. "In a game of dice."

He whistles. "She's quite the prize."

"Especially for a guy who didn't gamble."

"Tell me," he says. "From the beginning."

I know what he's doing. He's feigning curiosity to keep me talking, to keep me distracted. But I could use a little distraction right now, and I've never told anyone this story. Not the whole of it.

"Well," I say, turning my eyes back to the road. "Drypp knew I wanted the Dragon. I'd seen it around Whistletop, joked that one day, while it was parked in front of the tavern, I'd climb up and add my name to hers. Drypp agreed. Said it should be called the Sylver Dragon because she was restless and stinky and always covered in mud." I smile at the memory. "I was just a kid then, but I'd skive off whenever I could, watch the guys in the garage work. I wanted a rig of my own to repair and Drypp thought it would keep me out of trouble. Keep me closer to town. I had a habit of wandering off and he worried."

We hit a divot in the road, and the bucket smacks down hard, sheering rocks off the uneven surface, spewing them into the air, pummeling our sad excuse for a windshield. Kyn reaches forward and flattens out a strip of puckered sheeting.

"Who did build the Dragon?"

"Frydrick Vaxton. You know Vaxton?"

"I know his firm. I've never trucked for him."

"Well, he's dead now. Died last Ryme, but his firm had a contract with the Majority, so he had this way about him. Big head, big mouth. He'd roll into Whistletop and expect some grand welcome. He wasn't much liked in the village, but he threw around a lot of coin, so everyone smiled and served when he came. When Vaxton took up his seat at the dice tables, Drypp surprised the entire tavern by sitting down opposite him."

"Ballsy man, your Drypp."

"Not really," I say, thinking of the man who raised me. He was mostly quiet, locked away in his own thoughts half the time. But it was a kind of courage, I guess. Going toe-to-toe with Vaxton. "Drypp was *so* bad. It wasn't three hours before he was in over his head, offering up half-built rigs in the garage, the broken tractor out back. Free drinks for a year. I think he genuinely expected the dice to understand he was the better man. But they have a nasty streak, the dice, and that night, Drypp was on the losing end of it."

"So, how'd he end up with the Dragon?"

"Magic," I say, the truth bitter on my tongue. "It came down to a single roll of the die. Vaxton had put up the Dragon—just to see what Drypp would do, I think. And of course, he took the bait. There was a genuine risk he'd have to sell off the tavern or the garage to cover what he'd bet. I was sick with worry. Sitting there, trying to figure out how to tell Lenore we'd be living on the street. But there was no stopping now. Drypp had made the bet, he had to throw 'em down."

"And he won?" Kyn says.

HE HAD SOME HELP, DIDN'T HE?

"It was the first thing I ever asked of Winter," I admit, my voice quiet.

"She tilted the die?"

"I've seen it in my head a thousand times. The die catching on its side, a winning roll if it fell left, a losing roll if it fell right. Winter hot in my stomach, her whispers cold on my skin. WATCH, she said, WATCH." I shift in my seat, a favorite memory fading into something soiled. "A thin gust of air trickled through the open window and . . ."

". . . it fell left."

"One tilt of the die and the Dragon was mine."

Kyn whistles. "How old were you?"

"Too young to drive. Fourteen Rymes, maybe. I had to put blocks on the pedals so I could reach them, but I was a hard worker and it wasn't long before I started trucking around Whistletop. The locals don't care how old you are—they just care that their wares get hauled. Drypp didn't mind as long I stayed close to town. After a season of that, he sort of unclenched. He was getting older, moving slower. He was only opening the garage a couple days a week. My income helped keep us afloat and I didn't mind handing it over. I had the open road and no one telling me what to do. No one gaping at the kol in my eyes and assuming I'd take up their cause. No one trying to convince me to join their rebellion."

"No one but Winter."

He's not mean when he says it. He's just following the story. Just going where I'm leading. And he's right. Winter's been in control a lot longer than I realized.

The road pitches forward, the incline moderate, nothing like the Cages, but we're descending now. The Kol Sea out my window is replaced by flinty stone rising up as we drop lower and lower. The danger should be behind us now—the kol and the monsters—but she won't shut up, Winter. She's tipping her hand, trying to scare me into turning around, promising me safe passage if I do.

YOU'RE TOO LATE, she croons. YOU WON'T FIND THE GIRL YOU'RE LOOKING FOR WHEN YOU REACH THE END OF THIS ROAD. AHEAD THERE'S ONLY TREACHERY AND LOSS. GIVE UP THIS MADNESS AND I'LL BRING BACK RYME, A GIFT FOR YOU. SOLID ROADS AND ANOTHER SEASON OF TRUCKING, OF PUTTING COIN IN YOUR POCKET. THAT'S REALLY WHAT YOU WANT, ISN'T IT?

"She's not going to let us reach the camp," Kyn says, his jaw clenched. Whatever gut feeling I have, he's getting enough of it to be wound tight.

"Not without a fight."

And then they rise up before us, an army of Abaki. They're not crawling or lumbering. They're just there, standing. Waiting. Winter's guard barring the way.

TURN AROUND, she barks. THERE'S NOTHING FOR YOU HERE.

"She's not messing around," Kyn says.

I won't turn back. But I can't exactly plow over the monsters. Not again. We can't risk more damage to the rig, can't risk Abaki leaping onto the hood, clawing their way inside.

"It's going to have to be me, isn't it? I'm the only weapon we have left."

Kyn smiles. My eyes are on the road, but I feel it in my gut. I hope it makes its way to his face too. If there's anything that can rival Winter's beauty, it's Kyn's smile.

"You're going to have to take the wheel," I say.

"Thought you'd never ask."

I use my heel to release the seat and I kick it back. Kyn slides behind me, careful to avoid my hands when he puts his on the wheel.

"What does it mean?" I ask, grazing the etching on his index finger. "It's a Shiv symbol, isn't it?"

"It's the sign of Begynd."

"I thought you weren't devout?" I say, climbing onto the bench seat, pressing my hand against the thick plastic secured over the hatch.

"I'm not. Or, I wasn't. I just liked the look of it."

"Maybe pretend you're devout now," I say. "A little prayer couldn't hurt."

"Yeah, no. No, it couldn't."

I scrounge around beneath the bench seat, searching for something sharp and finding only pliers.

"Here," Mars says, startling me, pulling the pliers from my hand and replacing them with a utility blade. He's propped in the doorway of the sleeper, holding the velvet drape for support. He looks bad, but the blisters have faded, replaced by soft pink skin. The kol in his eyes has yet to return.

It's strong, the wave of emotion that strikes me. So strong it nearly knocks me over.

"I'm glad you're alive," I say.

ARE YOU? Winter whispers. SHALL I TELL YOU HIS GREAT— EST LIE?

I ignore her and lean closer to Mars so I can hear him over the noise.

"I'm not much for fairy stories," he's saying. "I prefer the old histories, but did your tutor ever tell you the one about the goblin thief who lost his wings to an ogre?"

Winter laughs. A low, deep growl and I think maybe Mars is still asleep, dream talking like Lenore did as a child. But he dips his head and starts again. "Brandle the Winged Thief. My mother used to tell it to me. Poor Brandle lost his wings in a fight with an ogre, and in order to collect the treasure he'd buried across the great sea, he had to—"

"Build a bridge," I say, remembering the firelight on Mystra Dyfan's face, the glee on Lenore's.

"*Liatha ee frenth*," he says, lifting his eyes to the windshield, to the Abaki growing large. "Make me a bridge."

"*Liatha ee frenth*," I repeat, the words clumsy on my tongue.

"She'll listen, Miss Quine. She has to."

I WILL NOT BE COMPELLED, Winter snaps.

"She *has* to," Mars repeats, his jaw set.

My fist tightens around the utility blade and I hold his gaze, waiting for the unbelief, waiting for the indecision. Waiting for the need to run to swallow me whole. But, in this moment, with Mars's green eyes holding mine, all I feel is ready.

YOU'RE NOT WHO YOU THINK YOU ARE, Winter says. YOU'RE NOTHING WITHOUT ME.

But there's only one way to find out.

I stand and drag the blade around the edges of the plastic covering the hatch. The wind pulls it up, flapping loudly against it. One last cut and it flies away.

Kyn squeezes my boot. "She took Hyla," he calls over the wind. "She set her wolves on us. You can do this!"

But Kyn hasn't even scratched the surface. If Shyne's right, and Mars too—if the stories they're telling are true—then Winter took my mother, Maree Vale, queen of the Kerce. She took almost an entire generation of the Shiv and she buried them beneath her rage. If the stories are true, she's lied to me, kept me close all these years so I wouldn't send her away, so she wouldn't have to pay for her crimes.

If the stories are true—

I put one foot on the arm of the driver's seat and one foot on the arm of the passenger's seat and I step up, rising like a lightning rod into the storm. Winter's squalling now, rain pummeling my face, forcing its way into my mouth.

FOOL, she says. **I BROKE YOUR MOTHER. I CAN BREAK YOU.**

The bald violence of the admission staggers me, steals my breath. But there's a tremor in her voice. Mars is right. Winter's scared.

"Maybe," I say. "But first you're going to build me a bridge." Feeling reckless, I whisper into the wind, "*Liatha ee frenth.*" The words on my tongue are loose and clumsy. My inflection is wrong, but Winter understands. I feel her buck at the command, attempt to refuse it.

But out in front of the Dragon a road is forming atop the broken rock. An ice road, one that lifts when the road drops.

"Faster, Sylvi," Kyn yells. "Faster!"

He's right. Winter's obeying but she's doing it in her own time.

I fling my arms wide like I've seen Mars do, and I scream into the storm, "*Liatha ee frenth!*"

It's fast. Her power is breathtaking as she takes the falling rain and freezes it into a road that takes the Dragon up and over the army of Abaki. The monsters don't look around as we rise above them, they don't move at all. Winter's too busy to give them marching orders.

She's building us a bridge, screaming all the while.

It soars up and over the rout of dead limbs and swirling magic. I keep talking, the Kerce words easier now to voice, easier now to remember. I could have her descend, drop the Dragon gently onto the Desolation, but I decide there's no reason.

My words keep Winter building high into the sky, Kyn's string of curse words turning to triumphant whoops as firelight and shadows flicker into view far below. It's the rebel camp.

"You're doing it, Sylvi! You're doing it!"

I lower my voice and whisper the bridge lower, keeping the incline gentle so the Dragon's bucket doesn't sheer off the charmed ice. When at last the ice road meets the ground, the rig rattles onto cobbled stones, rain-splattered and roughly placed, but solid beneath the Dragon's tank tread.

We did it.

We made it to the rebel camp.

And for the first time since she blew the windows out of Mistress Quine's cabin, Winter's got very little to say.

CHAPTER 29

I COLLAPSE INTO THE CAB. INTO A CRUMPLED heap between the seats. I'm sobbing. I can feel the tug in Kyn's chest, the same victorious exhaustion. When I open my eyes, he's there, arms draped over the wheel, his face turned to mine.

"How in fluxing Blys did we get here?" he asks.

I slide my hand across the dash. "In the belly of a Dragon, of course."

"Is that why it smells?" Mars asks.

My shoulders shake, and then Kyn's. "It does smell." We're laughing, all of us. Like children trapped inside too long. Mars takes a look around the cab, then reaches up and runs a finger over the ledge of the open hatch.

"And Hyla?" he asks.

Kyn shakes his head.

"I'm sorry," I say.

A simple nod. And then, "Miss Quine." With some effort,

he pulls the crusted square of cloth from his pocket. He offers it to me, and then thinks better of it. "I suppose it's time for a new one."

Kyn nods at the mirror. "Your lips, Sylvi."

But I can feel them, the blisters. I tilt the mirror anyway, taking in the damage. It's nothing to what Mars suffered when he froze the Abaki and electrified the road, but Winter's taken a bite out of me. My mouth is peeling, blue blisters lining my bottom lip and cutting in at the corners, kol dust smeared down my chin. But it's the sight of my eyes that holds me captive.

The kol dust has multiplied. It's stayed confined to the whites, but the flecks have more than doubled. They're more black than white now, my sylver irises shining brightly.

"The kol won't be such a problem for you now, Miss Quine."

"Neither will Winter," Kyn says. "You should have seen her, Mars."

"I saw," he says, his grin careful. "The bridge was magnificently constructed, Miss Quine. Brandle would be proud, but let's tread carefully where Winter's concerned."

"You can't be serious," I say.

"Deadly." He shifts, trying to get comfortable. "There are things that must be done and you've forced her hand with conviction for the first time. She won't be happy about it. Like you said, she'll obey, but she'll do everything in her power to fight you."

It's not the response I expected from Mars, but he's like Winter in that way. Predictable in his unpredictability.

"Look," Kyn says.

I turn toward the patched window. The rain has slowed, falling in big heavy drops that play like a drum against the Dragon's hood.

The camp is smaller than I expected. And closer to the sea. I can hear waves crashing against the rocks even now, but the mountains between here and there dull the sound, keep the wind from carrying kol directly into the settlement. Ten or fifteen simple dwellings have been constructed on either side of the road. Stone walls and roofs with chimneys that jut up into the sky.

Past the structures, farther down the lane, there's a square with a larger building at its head—a gathering hall, maybe—and a few small rigs parked against it. There's a large fire pit there, turning those gathered around it into growing shadows.

But no, they're running toward us. Toward the Dragon. Kyn turns off the headlamps and kills the engine. We can see them now, men and women and even a few children rush toward the rig, their hoods flipped up against the rain.

One man stands head and shoulders above the others. His hood has fallen away and his arms are raised high over his head. His brown hair is windblown and long, longer than the men wear it here on Layce. His beard, on the other hand, is cropped short, shorter than I'm used to seeing.

"They are here!" he cries, his voice booming. "They have come!"

"Flux," Kyn says. "I was hoping we'd beat him here."

"Another Paradyian?" I ask.

"Commodore Dakk Reyclan," Mars says, his voice quiet. "Hyla's husband."

"Her husband?" I ask, the man's smile turning me heartsick. "He's here? On Layce?"

"I'll talk to him," Kyn says.

"*I'll* talk to him," Mars corrects.

"I was there," Kyn says. "It should be me."

"We've a history, friend. And Dakk will not be easily consoled. Best leave it to me."

Dakk's pushing forward, craning his head, trying to see into the cab. I didn't think I'd have much reason to be grateful for the mangled windows, but I am. In this moment, I'm glad he can't see inside. Every step he takes toward us tears great wide chunks from my heart. I can't imagine having to tell him what happened out on the Seacliff Road.

And then I see her.

Lenore.

She's pushing through the crowd, ducking beneath elbows and weaving to the front. She tips her hood back and her auburn braids spill out onto her shoulders. She rises on her toes, trying to see. And I remember why I'm here.

I scrabble out the hatch, half falling, half climbing down the side of the Dragon, until my boots splash onto the cobbles.

"Leni!" I call, "Lenore!"

The crowd continues to gather, pushing closer and closer to the Dragon. It's a different kind of noise than I've heard in days. It's people. And excitement. It's celebration. Every one of them wants to touch the Dragon. Whatever she's carrying has them overjoyed. But I've never cared less about a haul. Lenore is here. She's here!

I'm standing before her now, but her gaze is set beyond me. She's looking at the bridge of ice climbing up and into the mountains.

"That's . . . amazing," she says, her brown eyes wide. "Your doing or Mars's?"

I hadn't considered what others would think of the magicked road. There wasn't time for that kind of deliberation and, even now, even to Lenore, I'm not sure what to say. Her gaze drops to my face and her mouth falls open.

"It was you," she says, pulling a handkerchief from her pocket. "I've had ideas for years now, about you and Winter, about your Kerce blood. But that's something right out of one of Mystra Dyfan's fairy books. Mars said you were special, but . . . I didn't think you'd come, Sylvi. I told them all you'd never do it."

I take the handkerchief from her and press it to my lips. "You've been wrong before," I say. "Remember the excavator?"

"You were eight! And you sunk it in a pond."

"Still drove it."

"I cannot believe you're here." She puts her hands on her hips and laughs. "You should have heard what I said about you, Sylver Quine. I told Mars you were a selfish brat who cared more about steel and Paradyian tank tread than you ever did about the people of Shiv Island."

"She's omitting the expletives," Mars confirms, suddenly at my side. "Nice to see you again, Miss Trestman. I'm glad you made it here safely."

"And you," she tells him, beaming. "I can't believe you got her here."

"In all fairness, it was Miss Quine who got *us* here. Take her inside, will you? There's something I can't put off, but I'll be along soon. We've much to discuss." He turns and presses back into the crowd.

"Come on," Lenore says, tugging my sleeve, turning toward the square. I glance back briefly, looking for Kyn—something is wedged between his ribs, tight, uncomfortable, and it pinches at mine—but before I can find him, my eyes catch on the large Paradyian man knocking on the door of the Dragon.

Dakk, they said his name was. He's two short minutes from misery and the knowledge squeezes my already shaken insides. I duck my head and jog to catch up with Lenore, who's still talking.

"I told Mars you'd gladly turn over whatever coin the Rangers required so you could truck where you pleased. That you wouldn't blink in the face of abusive Majority taxes, but you'd never sacrifice your own comfort, even to do the right thing for Shiv Island." She stops in front of the large fire pit and stares into the flames. "I guess I owe you an apology."

"No," I say, twisting the handkerchief in my hands, trying to shut out Kyn's discomfort. "I owe *you* an apology."

"Yes," she says, spinning to face me, her braids flying. "You do. You were awful!"

I was terrible, but she throws her arms around me anyway and suddenly I'm crying, my face pressed into her sweater, my body shaking.

Lenore's OK. She's OK.

"You hungry?" she asks.

"Starving."

"Come on inside then," she says. "We've had an interesting few days around here, but there's plenty of food."

I follow Lenore into what I had assumed was a gathering hall and find it's being used for several different purposes. There's no electric lighting, but a wide hearth sits in the center of the room blazing brightly. Around it sit a dozen wooden tables and benches, not so different from those in Drypp's tavern. In one corner, they've set up a row of camp beds and, in another, crates of supplies are stacked floor to ceiling.

Just in front of the fire, two golden-haired children sprawl on their stomachs. I don't recognize the game between them—something with wooden pegs and marbles—but the children? They're Hyla's. I've never laid eyes on them before, but there's no doubt in my mind. They're miniature versions of their mother. Two tiny lionesses, manes of soft curls falling about their shoulders.

"Leni," one of them says, "where has everyone gone?"

"Outside, silly! There's been a surprise."

"A surprise!" the girl says, leaping up, grabbing her sister's hand. "I bet I know what it is! Can you guess, Katsy?" They're wearing matching sweater dresses and scarves, leather boots that aren't quite right for this weather. When they stand, I can see they're likely a couple years apart. The older girl tugs her sister toward the door.

I want to stop them, want to reach out and offer them something, but I'm paralyzed by all that Hyla's death means for these two. They scamper past us, pushing the door open, their musical voices jabbering on in Paradyian.

"Leni," I say, "we can't let them—"

And then a wail shakes the night. It's the soul-wrenching cry of a man who has lost an arm or a leg. A heart. It's one whole person torn in two.

"We can't let them go out there. Not now."

But they're already out the door. I follow, slow and unsure. I don't know these girls. I have no right. Lenore rushes past me.

"Katsy, Kree," she calls. "Wait, wait."

The girls stop and Lenore catches them just at the fire pit. In the distance, the cries are terrible, clear and unabashed. The crowd has gone silent.

"Is that Father?" the older girl asks, her startled face tipping up to mine.

"Take them somewhere," I say. "Somewhere they can't—"

But I look around the small camp and realize there's no safe place out of earshot, no way to outrun what's happened to their mother, to shut out the cries of their father. Inside my own chest, Kyn's heart breaks.

"Come, girls," Lenore says. "Back inside. I could use your help with the cakes."

The girls protest, but they're no match for Lenore. I know from experience. She shuffles them back through the door, and though my boots are heavy, I don't linger outside. There's only agony out here.

When the door closes behind me, I'm alone, but voices and pots clang somewhere nearby. There are several doorways off this gathering hall, I realize, and though I'm tired, I take to walking around the room, poking my head into darkened doorways, doing what I can to shut out the sound of suffering. Dakk's cries have turned to sobs now, but they're far from quiet.

I stick my head into the kitchen where Lenore's just whisked the children. It's a crowded space, small and steaming. The girls stand on crates and receive instructions from Lenore and a wispy-haired gentleman wearing an apron.

Next to the kitchen, there's a room full of boots and shovels and coats—it smells unremarkably like feet and I don't stay long. On the adjoining wall, another room holds two miniature camp beds, the blankets on top woven with glittering ribbons. Above the beds, there's a wall full of colorful drawings affixed to the timber with twyl chewing gum—I imagine this is where Hyla's girls have been sleeping. My heart trips and I back out slowly.

There's just one more room to explore. It's on the opposite wall, in a corner not quite touched by the warmth of the fire.

It has a cell in it.

The cell is dark and fusty, the lone high window covered with a scrap of metal. A thin wax taper mounted just inside the door gives the room its only light. It's not much, but I can see well enough.

Bristol Mapes is sprawled on the floor, asleep.

When Lenore enters, she's quiet, respectful. "He said a lot of things about you," she says. "Out on the Seacliff Road. Things I didn't believe at first."

I swallow.

"There was so much kol on the air and every gust of wind made him jump. It was a nightmare there for a stretch. If we hadn't had so much twyl . . ."

"Did he treat you well?" I ask, my voice catching. "You seem well."

"You don't need to worry about me, Sylvi. The same roughnecks who brought their rigs to you for repairs hauled their beer guts into the tavern night after night. I know what they're capable of. I can handle myself."

"I know. You just . . ." I swallow down all the tension I've carried for miles and miles. "You left your knife."

"Hyla gave me this," she says, pulling a golden handgun from her waistband, holding it to the light. Not nearly as big as the ones Hyla carried, not nearly as ornate, but it's Paradyian. There's no doubt in my mind.

"You have any idea what to do with that?" I ask, my lips pulling despite everything. She's still Leni and I'm still Sylvi and I can't remember ever seeing her hold a gun.

"I've been practicing," she says. "I was hoping to show Hyla." She slides the gun away and wraps her hands around the bars. "What happened to her, Sylvi? She was so . . . strong."

"The Seacliff Road happened," I say. "It was a nightmare for us too."

"Abaki?" she asks, pressing her forehead to the bars.

I nod.

For a long minute we stare at Bristol, the candlelight like another presence. Watching, waiting. I'm sure we're both thinking about Drypp. About what the first Abaki did to our lives.

"They have to post a guard here," Lenore says. "I haven't had my turn yet and the Abaki aren't as plentiful on this side of the point, but I think I'd like to shoot a monster with Hyla's gun."

"She'd like that," I say. But my smile is uncomfortable. I don't want to think of Lenore anywhere near one of Winter's monsters. Not after what they did to Drypp. Not after what they did to the strongest woman I've ever met.

"Why's Bristol locked up?" I ask. He and Lenore haven't been in camp long—four days maybe—but it doesn't take long for someone like Bristol to wreak havoc. The idea of him being close to Hyla's girls for any length of time sets a panic stirring in my chest.

"Here," she says, pulling a board from a hook on the wall and handing it to me. Affixed to the board is a wrinkled sheet of paper and a charcoal pencil hanging from a bit of twine. "The charges against him."

"'*Perpetual and public drunkenness,*'" I read, squinting in the low light, "and '*Actions detrimental to the rebellion.*'"

"Eventually there'll be a trial. I think they were waiting on Mars."

"What did he do, Leni?"

She sighs. "He left the keys in his plow, to start with."

"Rayna," I say.

"You saw her on the road?" She turns toward me. "I figured she never made it past the monsters."

I think of Bristol's rig when it slammed onto the river crossing. How beat up it already was.

"I'm sure she saw her share of monsters, but she made it as far as the Serpentine. The plow went under there. Her too," I say. She doesn't need to hear the worst of it. "Did you know her?"

"I saw her in camp is all. Just that first day. But Bristol started drinking as soon as we arrived and I didn't think to check for his keys."

"At least he wasn't drinking on the road."

"I searched the rig before we left. Dumped the bottles I found."

I snort. "Did you?"

"He wasn't happy, but I know Bristol well enough to know his drinking habits. Privilege of a tavern wench."

"Mars said Rayna didn't like it out here."

"I couldn't say. But she took something when she left. Something the rebellion worked very hard to get their hands on. They think she meant to barter with it, to trade it to the Majority for her job back. When they wouldn't send someone after his rig, Bristol set the twyl house on fire."

"The twyl house?"

"The rebels have been hoarding twyl chewing gum. They'll need a lot of it for what they have planned and Bristol nearly ruined everything. He's an animal when he drinks."

I swallow back the memories, the bars between Bristol and I a small comfort. The door opens in the main room and voices fill the silence.

"Do you think they'll really try him for these crimes?" I ask, my finger tracing the charges. "Do the rebels care much for justice?"

She places a soft hand on my shoulder. "That's all they care about, Syl."

She leaves me there alone, her voice bouncing back, promising a hot meal. My stomach growls, but I watch Bristol snore for another long moment and then I pull the charcoal pencil from the board. With Hyla's girls shimmering gold in my mind, I take a deep breath and add my own charge just below the others.

I've only Winter as witness to Bristol's crimes against me and I don't imagine judge or jury would welcome her in their courtroom. But if anyone will hold Bristol accountable for what he did all those years ago, maybe it'll be the rebels.

And maybe I'll get to see it.

CHAPTER 30

SEATED AROUND A TABLE IN THE GATHERING hall is a somber group. Mars and Kyn are there, and Lenore. They're joined by three others I haven't met: an elderly woman and two men—one of whom is decidedly Kerce. His left eye is marked with a flake of kol. Bowls of stew and a heaping tray of crusty rolls steam into the air.

Mars introduces everyone, but I'm tired and the names don't stick.

Kyn slides down so I can sit, handing me a mug of something hot. Boiled chocolate, smells like.

"How is Hyla's husband?" I ask.

"Devastated," Kyn says. "It was awful, Sylvi. But you, yeah, you know."

"I'm so sorry."

"Dakk will mourn her," Mars says. "There is no doubt. But he's strong. He'll pull through. He's telling the girls now."

I swallow down my tears. "They're so young."

"No one forced Hyla's hand, Miss Quine. You can be sure of that. She chose her service to Paradyia and she chose this particular battle with her family in mind. Everything she did, she did for them."

"But why are they here?" I can't fathom why they've come. This Paradyian family could have stayed on their own island and been happy and safe. Why take up the rebel cause?

"Hyla and Dakk were our greatest allies in Paradyia," the elderly woman says, "but with the letters gone, I fear we are adrift."

"We are not adrift," Mars says.

"Rayna's letters?" I ask. "The ones in her satchel?"

"We'd been told there was a stack of letters," Mars explains, "correspondence between someone in the Paradyian high court and a Majority councilman in Glas. It was Rayna's brother who told us they existed. The letters gave every indication that Paradyia had a traitor. A highly ranked official who was trading state secrets to the Majority for stores of kol. Hyla and Dakk had long been friends of mine and have intimate connections to the king. I approached them on my last visit to Paradyia and they agreed to take these letters to the court once we had acquired them. In exchange for proof of treason against one of his own, we hoped the king would offer his services to us."

"What services did you expect the king of Paradyia to offer you?" I ask.

"Soldiers," Lenore says, very matter-of-fact. "To make war on the Majority."

A wave of revelation washes over me. It's so simple. He practically told me.

"Your army," I say, remembering the conversation Mars and I had while trucking the Cages.

"Indeed."

"It was brilliant plan," Lenore says, "and I'm sorry to see it wasted, but Mars is right, we're not adrift. Sylvi's here now. Though I don't understand why you hauled a trailer out here so close to the Flux. Surely it slowed you down."

"What do you mean?" I ask, sipping the chocolate.

"Sylvi," Kyn says, his stomach twisting. "Can I talk to you for a sec?"

"No, I'm talking to Lenore," I say, setting the chocolate aside. It's too hot against my blistered lips. "What do you mean you don't understand? You're the one who asked me to take this job."

"Miss Quine," Mars says, pushing his plate away, standing. "I think it's time you allowed me to tell you that story."

"What job?" Lenore asks, her brow furrowing. "There was no job. I asked you to help the rebels. And you refused. But you're here now, so you must have changed your mind."

My mind flails, fights to pin down the details of our original conversation. The conversation where she said Mars needed me. That I was the only one who could—

I'm on my feet now, kicking my way off the bench, flying toward the door.

"Sylvi," Kyn says. "Wait!"

Mars pushes away from the table, reaching out an arm. "Miss Quine."

But I dodge it and slam outside. The fire pit hisses and spits as rain continues to fall. Winter's building up to something. I can feel it.

"Miss Quine, please."

"Sylvi," Kyn says jogging to my side. "Why don't we take a walk, yeah? Over here. We can talk about . . . there are some things we should explain. Mars really. Mars should explain."

Kyn steps in front of me, cutting off my path to the Dragon. His hands are in his pockets. He's shoved them there so he doesn't reach out for me, shoved them there so he doesn't pull me into his chest. He's ashamed of something. Afraid of what I'll do when I find out.

I blink up at him, our shared emotions punching me in the gut, turning my arms and legs weak. I reach for him and he does the same, stepping forward, pulling a hand from the pocket of his coat.

"Snowflake," he says.

But Mars's medicine bag is around his neck. I snatch it and push my way past him and the Dragon both, my boots hard on the rough road as I make my way to the back of the trailer. I tear the leather bag open. Phials of twyl liniment and kol spill out onto the ground. But the key is in my hand now. I jam it into the lock and turn.

Somewhere behind me Lenore's saying, "You let her pull this trailer all the way from Whistletop? What were you thinking?"

"Miss Quine—"

"Sylvi, please," Kyn says. "Let me explain."

But I'm not letting anyone do anything. I jump onto the bumper and grab the handle on the roll-up door. Kyn reaches out and I offer him a single glance that has him tucking his hands

back into his pockets. I yank the metal handle and the door trundles up and away.

And then I drop to the ground, collapsing on the cobbles.

The only thing in Mars's trailer is a whispered I TOLD YOU SO.

She did too. Winter told me Mars was a liar. She told me not
to trust him.

"There never was a haul," I say, my body so heavy I could sink
through the stone. "No kol or twyl or Paradyian weapons. Nothing to help the rebel cause."

"That's not true, Miss Quine." Mars is on his knees now, his
black eyes glossy, his blistered lips trembling. "You were the haul.
You're the weapon we all need."

CHAPTER 31

THE DESOLATION IS A SHORT WALK FROM camp, but it feels like another world altogether. There's a wooden fence here, marking the edge of the frozen pool. The rebels' attempt at respect, I suppose. I've been leaning against it for hours now, watching as night turns to day. Feeling Winter's glee at my disappointment, ignoring her as best I can.

Rain is coming again, its perfume thick and heavy, when a small rig pulls up to the fence and parks.

Kyn's driving but he's not alone. Mars and Dakk climb out of the rig, followed by Lenore. Dakk lifts her like a child and sets her on the hardpack. She has her braids pinned up now—it's how she wears her hair when she's plucking chickens. Makes me wonder who she plans to butcher this morning.

The four of them crunch toward me, Kyn's angst growing with every step. It's been increasing steadily over the past few hours, his emotions so apologetic I can't make myself yell at him.

He tried to tell me. After the Shiv caves, he did. I was the one who turned him away.

It's Mars anyway, Mars who orchestrated all of this.

"We need to talk, Miss Quine."

I turn toward him and lean my hip against the fence, my arms crossed. "For someone who's always wanting to tell me things, you lie an awful lot."

"I let you believe what you needed to believe. That's not the same thing."

"You know how much more dangerous that road was because of the trailer?"

"I do, Miss Quine. I was there."

I want them to leave, all of them, but there are things I need to know. If it wasn't the Dragon Mars wanted, I'm at a loss. I have no idea why I'm out here. All night I've been stewing, and although I understand Mars's personal desire to have Winter sent away, I don't see how it helps the rebels at all.

"Sylver Quine," Dakk says, stepping closer, bowing his head, filing the sharp corners off my anger. "Kyndel has told me of your exploits. How you did everything you could to save my wife. I am grateful. My children are grateful. The king and queen shall hear of your valor." Tears sparkle in his eyes, collect in his soft brown beard.

I could have done more. That's what I think. I could have ordered Winter to call off her Abaki before that monster buried an axe in Hyla's back. I could have opened my veins and shared my blood. She'd be here now if I'd been brave enough.

No, I didn't do everything in my power to keep her alive. Hyla would have though. She would have done anything for her friends.

"She was so brave," I say, fighting to keep my composure.

"I know that, Sessa," he says, the tears flowing freely down his face. "I do. She braved the Kol Sea and the devil spirit of Winter just to meet you. To bring you to Paradyia. It was her greatest wish to present you to her king."

"Paradyia?" I glance to Mars and then to Kyn. Mars's face stays remarkably blank. At least Kyn has enough integrity to look uncomfortable.

"You will come?" Dakk asks. "You will help us?"

"I don't . . . what?"

"Aren't you going to help?" Lenore snaps. She's on edge. The set of her teeth, the narrow slit of her eyes. All nerves and ready arguments. I have no idea what I've done to deserve her fury.

"Stop, stop," Kyn says. "Dakk, Lenore, you two need to let Mars explain. Sylvi has no idea what you're asking of her. No idea what you want. That's not why she made the trip."

"Why *did* you make the trip?" Lenore asks. "Because I'm wracking my brain, and if you didn't come to help the rebels—"

"I came for you!" I say, pushing away from the fence. "To take you home. So life could go back to the way it was—"

"The way it was before I grew a conscience? Or did you simply want life to go back to the way it was before I left and you suddenly had to take care of the tavern and the garage all by yourself?"

"Drypp left them to us, Leni! And that's not an easy thing to do under Majority law. Two women in the Kol Mountains with the ability to fend for ourselves? Drypp worked hard to make that happen, did everything he could to stay on good terms with them so we wouldn't lose our livelihood. We have a responsibility to him—"

"Don't talk to me about my responsibilities to my own grand-father," she says, turning away.

"What does *that* mean?"

She whips her head around. "He could have stayed with me like I asked. Stayed and helped me with the replanting, but you wanted to go fishing. You took him with you that day and I needed him at home. And when you brought him back, he was bloodied and half-dead."

Her accusations crack a fissure between us. She blames me for what happened with the Abaki.

"That's not fair," I say, wishing she'd take it back, needing her to. The weight of Drypp's death is too much for me to carry.

"Fair! Who was it that nursed him day and night? Not you. You were out the road, running from what you'd done."

She's never said any of this before. I didn't know. How was I to know we were already broken?

"I was out on the road," I say, refusing to fold under her words, "making the coin that kept us afloat!"

Her head is shaking now. "I thought you'd learned to put the needs of others first, but you haven't. You'll always be my sister, Sylvi, but you're still the same selfish girl you've always been."

"You don't know what you're talking about," Kyn says, step-ping between Lenore and me. There's something righteous in his anger. Something offended and indignant. He's going to tell her what I did for him, going to use it to make her see. I feel the words on his tongue and I'd rather he didn't. It's an intimate thing. Pri-vate. I don't want our connection used as a weapon.

"*I'm* selfish?" I yell, pushing past Kyn, fighting to drown out his words. "I came here for you!"

"So your life wouldn't have to change. So *you* wouldn't have to change. Well, guess what? I'm not going back to Whistletop. I made promises to the people here and I'm not running out on them. You can stay and help or you can run again. But either way, life will never be the same for you." She glances at my lips. "If you don't know that already, you haven't been paying attention."

"Miss Quine," Mars says. "Let's walk. I think some space would do us all good."

He takes my elbow, but I fight my way out of his grip, flick my cheek at Lenore, and climb over the fence and out onto the Desolation.

"One of these days you're going to run out of road," she calls.

Mars follows behind me, his boots splashing through last night's rainwater. There's a swoop in my stomach, so I turn back and see Kyn, his arms bare, his hands in his pockets, his eyes on mine.

I'm sorry, he mouths. But he doesn't need to. My ribs are taut with his apology, my spine as rigid as his.

I nod and turn away again, falling into step with Mars.

"How far can I go?" I ask. "I don't want Kyn to suffer."

"It's a good question," Mars says. "A question I don't have the answer to. Though, after you'd fled the mines at North Bend, it was nearly half an hour before Kyn's wounds started reopening."

"So, we're fine. We have miles."

"It would seem."

We walk in silence for a while, the ebb in my stomach fading as Kyn falls farther and farther behind. My anger at Lenore, the injustice of her disappointment settles like a heavy pack on my shoulders.

"Would you like an explanation?" Mars asks.

"Yes," I say, burrowing into my coat. "And quickly. Winter has another storm brewing."

"Where would you like me to start?"

"When did you know about me? About my . . ." I wave a hand.

"Not until Miss Trestman," he says. "I knew the Desolation had split, of course, years before, knew the Desolation Shiv had their theories, knew Shyne harbored the strangest of the ideas, but I didn't put the pieces together until Miss Trestman told me what she suspected about you."

"Which was?"

"That it was your presence that kept Drypp alive all those months."

My gaze snaps to his. "You knew about the Abaki attack?"

"I did. Miss Trestman said her grandfather was almost dead when you got him home, but he recovered—miraculously even. She said that whenever you went on a run, Drypp's wounds would fester and open up again. It wasn't until you took a job that kept you away for longer that he finally passed into death."

By the time I'd returned from a run to the northwestern wing, Drypp's body had been burned and his ashes spread. It's the way things are on Layce. To move on quickly.

There is no yesterday . . .

"Lenore never said."

"She was using it to bargain with, I think. She regrets the deception."

I choke. "I've known Lenore a lot longer than you have, and she doesn't regret a thing right now. Trust me."

One side of his mouth lifts. "Be that as it may, she had no coin to secure my services on behalf of her father. She thought she could use the information about you to barter with."

"You freed her father from the Stack?"

"Not yet," he says. "But I will."

All these things I didn't know about Lenore; I let the pride of thinking sharing a home was the same as sharing a life. They tried to tell me, Kyn and Mars. Hyla. They all tried to tell me that Lenore had made up her own mind about the Majority. It's maddening, the realization that two girls, raised so closely, seeing the same wrongs, walking the same paths, can come to entirely different understandings about the injustices around them. One chooses to fight and the other to flee. How does that happen?

"But why do you need *me*? Why the deception? I'm not so hardheaded that I wouldn't have listened. You didn't have to lie—"

"Would you have listened, Miss Quine? Would you have believed that you were the lost child of the Kerce queen? That a few words from your mouth would be enough to send Winter from Shiv Island?"

Winter rumbles and rain drops from the sky. I've no hood. Not since the Cages.

"I don't know," I say. "I would have listened, but Winter has always been my everything. My friend. My freedom. My source of income." I don't say my savior. I don't want to think about Bristol Mapes anymore.

"Exactly," Mars says. "When Miss Trestman told me how you felt about your Kerce tutor, I realized you needed to see Winter's nature before you would understand. The mountainfolk on Shiv Island hold Winter in such high regard, and you especially. It would take more than a magic display by a Kerce smuggler to convince you. You needed the Shiv Road, Miss Quine. Otherwise, you would not have believed."

I don't think he's wrong. But I can't believe that makes him right.

"So that's your story? You let me believe you needed my rig to get me here? So I could what? Travel to Paradyia? It makes no sense."

"The medallion," Mars says, with a little nod. "The one around your neck. It belonged to your mother, Maree Vale."

"The markings are Paradyian."

"Because she was Paradyian, born and raised. The sister of the Paradyian king. Her marriage to the Kerce king was political in nature, but it was a happy one. They had children. Two princes."

"Shyne only mentioned one."

"There were two," he says. "I have it on good authority. When the Majority invaded, the king loaded his wife and children onto the royal ship along with the queen's retinue and they set sail for the safety of Paradyia. They were to ask the king to send help, but they never made it there. The ship ran afoul of the Kol Sea. Like much of the party, the eldest prince, heir to the Kerce throne, was lost. His mind addled by kol, his body thrown over the side of the ship and dragged beneath the waves by Winter's monsters."

Mars breathes deep, his eyes wandering away. To a ship maybe. And a boy long forgotten.

"No one talks about him," I say. "The crown prince. He's not mentioned in the stories."

"No," Mars says, his voice quiet, his brow furrowed. "He's not. And he should be remembered. He would have been an excellent king."

I don't ask him how he knows, how he could possibly know anything about a boy who died centuries ago. "His brother survived though."

"Only just. The young prince washed ashore with his mother and the remaining members of the royal party. Not far from here actually." He looks toward the shore, toward the low mountains separating the camp from the sea. "The Shiv found them—saved them, to be sure—brought them to the waters of Begynd and nursed them back to health. And though their dissimilar languages presented difficulty, they lived in peace for a short time."

"But the queen was curious," I say, remembering the cautionary angle to this tale.

"She was. She wanted to understand Begynd. Her Paradyian upbringing had taught her to probe and to seek, but the Shiv were different. They did not question the ways of Begynd. He cut them from stone, breathed life into their bodies, and he cared for them. How his magic worked was not a thing they sought to understand.

"Despite warnings from the Shiv, the queen took her people west. She was heavy with child at that point and thought to establish her kingdom on the other side of the Kol Mountains."

"But she never made it."

"No," he says, averting his eyes, chewing at his lip, "by the time the party had reached High Pass, they were sick and failing. The farther they wandered from Begynd's Pool, the higher they climbed, the more rapidly they were undone. The queen was close to her time and she was angry. At the Shiv. At their creator.

And Winter took advantage. Seeing the opportunity to blot out Begynd and secure the companionship she had long desired, she whispered promises to the Kerce queen, whispers that drove the queen further and further into madness. By the time Winter laid out her bargain, the queen could think of little but the destruction of the Shiv who had banished her people from their pool."

Mars licks his lips, adjusts the cuffs on his jacket.

"Winter's proposal was simple: If Maree Vale, queen of the Kerce, would carry a phial of Winter's magic down to Begynd, if she would ensure it reached the fount deep below, Winter promised that the Shiv would suffer for their crimes against her. She promised to swear allegiance to the Kerce, to bow as a subject to the rule of Maree Vale and her children.

"But though Maree was frail, she knew better than to leave the fate of her kingdom to the word of a winter spirit. She demanded they strike a proper covenant—a Paradyian tradition that Maree knew well. Winter had faith in her own strength and agreed to the queen's demands. She would do anything to end the reign of Begynd."

"A covenant?" I ask, the word drying my mouth, the idea worse. "Like Hyla made with you and Kyn?"

"Yes, Miss Quine. Though ours wasn't nearly so formal. Paradyian tradition demands that a covenant be witnessed by two others. The queen offered her remaining son as witness, but Winter had only the kol. It wasn't quite proper, but the queen knew her time was short and she knew that her unborn child's best chance at survival lay in the great pool, not in the clutches of Winter."

"So they agreed," I say.

Mars nods. "Winter mixed her magic with kol and encapsulated it in the curio on the queen's medallion."

His eyes drop to the heavy triangle resting against my sternum. He reaches out and lifts it, runs his thumb over the etchings.

"She was so sick," Mars says, his voice thawing, warming. "Thin, even, for a woman so close to her time. When she knelt to say goodbye . . ." He shakes his head, his eyes wet.

"To her son?"

He swallows, forces a smile. "Yes, to her son. When she said goodbye, she used the ancient Kerce gesture employed when choosing a successor. She grazed her cheek softly with her knuckles, opening her palm to him, giving the boy all that she had left to give: her throne, and her duty to the Kerce." His hand raises and he mimics the gesture I've seen used so crudely, used myself even, throwing it at Lenore just moments before. "She knew she was going to die, you see? She knew how little strength she had left."

It sets my hands shaking. "And the boy?"

"He knew. When the young prince returned the gesture, he understood what it meant. He didn't expect all that came after, but as his mother turned and started down the mountainside, he knew it was the last he'd see of her."

Mars takes a great, shuddering breath and I find myself doing the same.

"I'm sorry," I say.

He dips his head, doesn't ask me what I'm sorry for.

"Winter accompanied the queen as far as she could. When the heat of Begynd would allow her to go no farther, the queen proceeded alone. She'd only just made it to the shores of Begynd when she went into labor."

"With me," I say.

"Yes. With you."

He waits. Maybe he expects me to argue, I don't know. But I tuck my hands deep in my pockets and wait for him to continue. When he does, his voice is steady and sure. Practiced, even.

"It took me many years to gather accounts about what happened next, and even then, there are variations. What I know is this: After the queen gave birth in the great pool, she slept one night in a Shiv dwelling, a Shiv woman in attendance despite the rift between the two peoples. When the nurse woke, the queen was gone and the child was crying. She gathered the young princess in her arms and set off looking for the mother. But it was too late. The worshipers on the shore pointed to the waters, to the queen swimming out toward the fount. They tried to stop her, the Shiv, but she was powered by a magic incalculable and untold. With a strength that was not her own, she dove low, plunging the medallion into Begynd's fount."

"And Winter took the island."

A dip of his chin. "The Pool of Begynd froze solid and Winter stretched her legs once again."

I lift my eyes to the Seacliff Road beyond Mars's shoulder, remember what the Desolation looked like from up there. It's strange to look back at the road that caused such misery when you're safely past it, hard to appreciate just how painful it was to travel.

"And still, I don't know why you worked so hard to get me here. To a rebel camp on the far side of Layce."

"The Paradyian queen is dying," he says.

"And?"

"And the king and I have struck our own bargain. A bargain only a few of the rebels know anything about. We were already in the process of securing Rayna's release so we could get our hands on the letters when Miss Trestman contacted me through Mystra Dyfan."

"You know Mystra Dyfan?"

"There are very few Kerce left, Miss Quine, and I'm not nearly as young as I look. I likely know them all. The king of Paradyia is a collector of history. He had heard the Shiv accounts of their powerful creator, he'd read every book detailing the Kerce persecution, and he has long believed that it's only in the Pool of Begynd that his beloved can find healing."

And now I understand.

"So instead of offering up the treasonous letters, you offer me. I send Winter away and the fount of Begynd flows freely."

"The Paradyian queen bathes in the pool," he continues, "and is healed. In return, her king sends an army to snuff out the Majority."

"And like that, the people of Layce are free of both Winter and their overlords."

"Yes," he says. "Just so."

"But how will they feed themselves? How will they earn a living? Winter is their livelihood. It's all they know. Their homes will become a battlefield. Paradyian war machines driving their roads and soldiers tearing through their villages. Through Whistletop."

"They're suffering, Miss Quine. The people on Shiv Island need this war. They need someone fighting for them."

The ice beneath my feet pitches—no, it's me. I pitch sideways and Mars catches my elbow.

"Miss Trestman is right, you know. There's no going back to the way things were before the Shiv Road. There is only this."

He spreads his arms wide. Rain falls, splashing on the Desolation, but not a single drop touches his coat. I realize I'm drier than I should be as well.

"As long as you live, Winter can be sent from Shiv Island. She never loved you. She never wanted good things for you. She kept you safe and numb so you couldn't feel the knife she slid between your ribs."

His words are cruel and exacting but, for the first time, I don't see Mars as a threat. I don't see him as a force of nature. I see him as a little boy who wants nothing more than to avenge his mother's death. And in some ways that's more dangerous.

"I'll meet the Paradyian king," I say.

His arms drop and his face brightens. "Miss Quine—"

I hold up a hand. "But I won't make any promises about Winter. Maree Vale doomed generations because of a personal vendetta. She was sick, I know, but she was careless. We have to do better." The determination in my voice surprises me.

"I've thought on our dilemma for a very long time, Miss Quine."

"Three hundred and twenty-five white winters," I say, remembering Shyne's story. "You've aged well, brother."

His eyes flash and I know I'm right. The young prince who witnessed Winter's covenant and the princess born in the Pool of Begynd. We are quite a pair.

"I aged until adulthood and then no more," he says with a shrug. "As witness to the covenant, I too am trapped by Winter's curse. Not in the depths of the Desolation, no. But frozen in time nonetheless."

"This," I tease. "This, you could have told me."

"No, Miss Quine," he says, his imperious tone returned. "You cannot believe the truth about yourself until you've killed the lie. Like Winter and Begynd, the two cannot coexist."

"Winter's not dead."

He tips his face to the cracking sky. "No, she's not. But she's been reminded of her place. It's not something you do once. It's something you must do every time you hear her voice. She must be told who you are and who she most certainly is not."

I turn his words over in my mind, unsure what to make of them. It's a miserable way to fight. The same thing again and again.

"They must've grown tired of waiting," Mars says, his gaze on the shore.

Kyn and Lenore trudge toward us, rain smudging their forms, their heads bowed low against the onslaught. The sky is split wide now, Winter releasing a downpour guaranteed to melt all but her deepest frosts.

Like Mars, I don't feel a drop of it.

She wouldn't dare. Not now.

Now that all her secrets are laid bare.

CHAPTER 32

THERE'S NO GUILT SWIMMING IN KYN'S GUT when he and Lenore reach us. He's chosen pride instead, the grin on his face carving a dimple into his cheek and a divot from my heart. Rain washes over his black curls and stone shoulders, his bare arms crossed and steaming in the cold. He did the one thing I hoped he'd never do and, despite my own apprehension, I realize he had every right. It's his story as well.

"He told you," I say, turning my attention to Lenore. I'm not used to feeling shy of her, but I do. It feels like she caught us kissing.

"He did," she gulps. She's using her hands to shield her face from the deluge, but the rain is relentless, forcing its way into her nose and mouth.

"*Liatha ee frenth,*" I whisper, and, with a hiss, ice arches over us, the rain molding itself into a bridge as it falls. It's not nearly as grand as last night's display, but it's sufficient.

"Well made," Mars says, craning his neck. "Though, perhaps it's time to expand your Kerce vocabulary, Miss Quine."

"Good luck with that," Lenore says.

I pull my jacket off, dry for the most part, and slip it over her shoulders. She drags the sleeve across her face.

"I'm sorry, Sylvi," she says. "I didn't know—"

"I didn't do it for Kyn," I say, avoiding his stare. "I did it for myself."

"I don't understand."

"I couldn't stand the thought of losing someone else who . . . who mattered. Not when it was in my power to stop it. So, see? Regardless of what Kyn told you, I'm still that same selfish girl who climbed out windows and hotwired tractors."

"Snowflake—"

"The road might have changed my mind about some things, Leni, but it hasn't turned me into a martyr. I saved Kyn because I wanted to. Because I couldn't imagine losing him."

I turn to face Kyn now, my chest so full of his emotions I don't understand how it could possibly be this light.

"Even before the mines, there was something, I don't know, something I would have fought hard to keep hold of." I do my best to ignore the smirk on Mars's face. "I'm glad you're alive—you can't imagine how glad—but I did it for myself. Because I was afraid of what I'd lose if you were gone."

"What the hell happened in those Shiv caves?" Mars asks.

Kyn shoves him sideways and steps closer. "It's OK for it to be both, Sylvi. Flux, I'm elated you get something out of this. If you didn't, you might . . ." His eyes trail away, over the ice.

"I might leave?"

He turns his face to mine and smiles. "And then where would I be?"

"I shouldn't have acted like this was all your fault," Lenore says. "I abandoned the tavern because I couldn't stand watching the rebellion from afar. Once Mystra was gone, and then Drypp, and you out on the road, the tavern was nothing to me. Just an obligation. But I didn't think what my leaving would do for you and the garage. And for that I owe you an apology."

I swallow down the anguish of it all, because the truth is: "It's done. By now, the Rangers have taken possession of both. Soon they'll hand everything over to the Majority."

"I'm sorry, Sylvi. I really am."

"It's not your fault," I say, thinking of Crysel and the snow-mobile, of Jymy Leff. "The Majority knows what I am now, and they think they can use me for their purposes. I just wish I'd seen value in the rebellion when you did. You tried to tell me."

She smiles, but it's sad and small. "You had another voice to contend with. But do you see it now, Sylvi? That the Majority is an enemy worth fighting?"

"I suppose that's all I see. But how that happens . . ."

Lenore throws her arms around my neck and squeezes. "*You* are how that happens. Didn't Mars tell you?"

Winter growls and the bridge shudders overhead. I pull away from Lenore, ready to fight, but it's just bluster.

"Fear not, Miss Quine," Mars says, offering his arm to Lenore. "If Winter's planning to destroy you—and I would expect nothing less—she'll wait until she has something to barter with. Just as she did with Maree Vale."

Mars leads Lenore out into the storm. Kyn and I follow, and

with a word that leaves a blister on my tongue and kol dust in the corner of my mouth, every drop of falling rain freezes in place.

"Ah!" Mars says, pulling up, flicking a raindrop from the sky. "And what if we did . . . this."

I don't see his mouth form the words, but overhead a gust of wind shifts the clouds, and, there, the sun! Shimmering down on the Desolation. The raindrops catch its light, a million prisms reflecting Sola's radiance. I can't help but think of Hyla.

"Is there no good that can come from suffering?" she'd asked.

I wish I had an answer, but the question doesn't infuriate me as it used to, and I suppose that's something.

Mars and Lenore march on, flicking raindrops from the sky as they go, sending splashes of color skittering across the ice.

"May I?" Kyn asks, reaching out, his eyes on my hand. My heart fires and then his, and suddenly they're off, racing each other for some undetermined prize.

It's everything that's ever terrified me. I'm utterly exposed with Kyn, and retreat isn't possible. My darkest memories, my worst mistakes—all of it is his to examine at will. To doubt and sort through if he chose. To live with. And still he stands here with me. He asks to hold my hand.

I slip my fingers into his, twisting them, locking us together as tightly as I'm able.

"I'm sorry I lied to you about the haul," he says.

"Your gut's been apologizing for hours. It's OK."

"It's *not* OK."

"No," I say, meeting his gaze. "But I'm guessing it's the only time you'll get away with lying to me, so I'll let it slide."

"That's terrifying. But thank you. You might have chosen to

save me at the mines, but you had no idea what it would cost to drag me away from the wolves at High Pass. There's a lot of this that's unfair."

I lift a lazy shoulder. "If I'm going to have anyone tearing up my insides, I'm glad it's you. You're kinder than Winter."

He steps closer, his gaze moving over my face. "She's still in there, I think. I can feel her sneaking around."

I can feel her too. For so long, I was worried she'd leave me, and now . . .

"But I'm not alone with her anymore," I say. "You're in there too."

"Will you ever send her away?"

"From the island or from my heart?"

"Either?" he says. "Both?"

"I don't know if I can do that without destroying myself," I say, letting my gaze wander his face, take in the warmth of his eyes, the glimmer of stone across his cheekbone. His lips. "And that would destroy you."

His eyes go wide. "I hadn't thought of that. For Begynd's sake, we've got to keep you safe!"

A smile hooks my lips, tugs. "Sounds a little selfish."

"I'd just like to be consulted whenever you decide to do something dangerous. That's all I'm saying."

"Like take on Winter?"

"Nah, you've got her all figured out," he says, quietly, stepping closer. "I just need a heads-up on the really hazardous stuff."

My heart stutter steps at his nearness. "I think I can do that."

"Thank you, little ice witch," he says, pressing his forehead to mine. "I mean it."

The wind picks up and raindrops bump into one another, ringing out across the expanse. We listen for a minute, watch the rainbows dance.

"We'll figure it out," Kyn says, leftover raindrops glistening on his lashes. "We'll learn everything we can about Maree Vale and Winter. About Begynd. Everything there is to know about how the kol works. We'll talk to the Shiv and the Paradyians." He squeezes my hand. "We won't make the same mistakes they did, yeah?"

The same mistakes . . .

"I guess Shyne was right," I say, turning it over in my mind. "Yesterday does matter." The thought is a dangerous one, the words mutinous on my tongue. "Understanding what happened, it's how we're going to save tomorrow."

Kyn smiles and I have to remind myself I'm not the kind of person who melts at a thing like that.

"What?" I ask.

"Nothing. I just . . . I think you're right, snowflake. I fought it for a long time too—understanding the history of my people— but I think it's the only way forward."

I've been wrong for so long, it's strange to hear I might have gotten something right. "Yeah?"

"Yeah," he says, the pride in his chest expanding, filling mine. He bumps my chin with a stone knuckle. "Welcome to the rebellion."

Acknowledgments

Novel writing and rig driving may not seem like similar vocations, but I've found they do have a few things in common. Both are solitary endeavors requiring long hours in a chair and far too much time in your own head. To the driver and the author, the unraveling road can feel endless and fraught with difficulty. But these obstacles are part of the adventure and, like Sylvi, I didn't get here alone.

Along the way, many have climbed up into the cab, reminded me to keep my eyes on the road, and kept me company when I needed it most. I'd like to thank them.

To Matt, for supporting my need to tell stories and for never asking why. For drawing and redrawing the Sylver Dragon as I saw it in my head. For answering all my weapon-related questions, and for catching my mistakes when I thought I knew what I was doing. Thank you for loving me and for being my partner in all things.

To Justus, I'll never forget your enthusiasm for this story and its world. For your willingness to brainstorm with me and for being proud of your mom, thank you. It means more than you'll ever know.

To Jazlyn, for being the best snuggler and officemate a mom ever had. Your imagination inspires me. Thank you for demanding I tell you stories. I hope you like this one.

To Mom and Dad, for your unwavering support and for being curious about this strange job of mine.

To my grandparents, for pushing my books on anyone who'll listen. I have you to thank for a generation of readers.

To Jill Williamson, Stephanie Morrill, and Jenny Lundquist, for your friendship and for reading early versions of this story and continuing to cheer me on.

To Stephanie Garber for Thursdays, and to Kristin Dwyer for believing that this was *the book*. To Adrienne Young, Stephanie Brubaker, Alexis Bass, Jessica Taylor, Joanna Rowland, Jennieke Cohen, Kim Culbertson, and Rose Cooper. Your companionship has made all the difference.

To my Soul Sisters: Natali Corrington, Lacey Jordan, Julia Bolognesi, Sharon VandenBos, Elisa Calhoun, Allison Calhoun, Amanda Calhoun, Ashley Eastlund, Frances Houston, Sharon Wilkinson, and Stephanie Luke. My dedication about covered it, but I'm so glad we get to live life together.

To Wade Webster, for sharing your expertise of the road and big rigs. Finding you a willing conspirator and all-around fount of knowledge was a fun surprise. I'll take the blame for every error and thank you for all the details I managed to get right.

To my agent, Holly Root. What a journey this has been! Thank you for guiding me safely back to the shelf and for believing that we'd get here. To Taylor Haggerty and the rest of the crew at Root Literary, thank you for working so hard on my behalf and for cheering when this book sold. I'm so glad you're all on my team.

To Maggie Lehrman, for seeing something in my book worth pursuing. Thank you for that faith.

To Ruben Ireland, for pulling Sylvi from my mind and rendering her so perfectly. I think there's magic in your blood.

To Marie Oishi, Hana Anouk Nakamura, Jenn Jimenez, Nicole Schaefer, Brooke Shearouse, Jenny Choy, Patricia McNamara O'Neill, and everyone at Amulet Books, for creating a beautiful package and treating this story with the utmost care. It's been an honor.

To Shasta Clinch, for your kind precision and heroic catches. Your touch on this story was illuminating, and I'm grateful.

To my editor, Emily Daluga, who made this book better in every way. Your clever editorial eye is gold, and it's such a privilege to work with you. Thank you for falling in love with Sylvi.

And finally, to my Lord and Savior, Jesus Christ. The One in whom I have believed. Thank you for gifting me a spark of your infinite creativity, and for teaching me to walk on water. Five years ago, when the idea for this story arrived, I had no idea how necessary sea legs would be. But you knew and you taught me to keep my eyes up. It has been the one discipline that kept me from going under. Thank you for every hard lesson and every glimpse of grace. I am eternally grateful.